BETWEEN TWO TRIBES

FOREST B. DUNNING

Hardcover ISBN: 978-1-63490-660-9
Paperback ISBN: 978-1-63490-659-3

Published by BookLocker.com, Inc., Bradenton, Florida, U.S.A.

Printed on acid-free paper.

This is a work of historical fiction, based on actual persons and events. The author has taken creative liberty with many details to enhance the reader's experience.

BookLocker.com, Inc.
2016

Second Edition

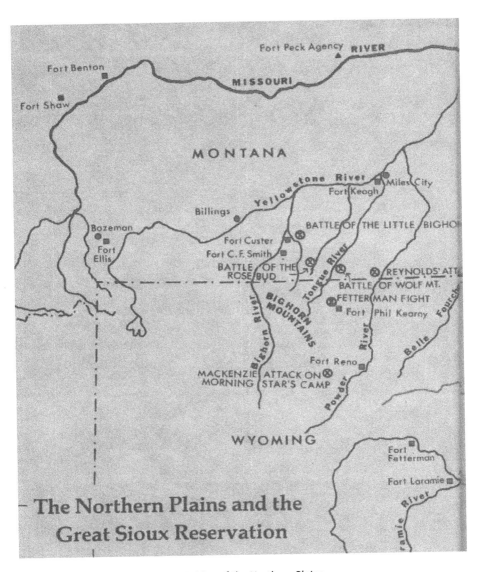

Figure 1. Map of the Northern Plains

ACKNOWLEDGEMENTS

No book, even those which are "self-published" are the product of a single person. Authors stand on the shoulders of previous authors, editors, historians, researchers, family members, friends, photographers, and publishing staffs. So it is with this book. I could not possibly have completed this book without the help and support of a large number of others who gave me support and encouragement.

First in line for acknowledgment is my long suffering wife, Susie who has put up with my frustrations with computers, bureaucracies, the internet, poor memory, and a myriad of tantrums and unquotable language for the past year. Without her unwavering support and computer assistance I would be in the looney bin and this book would not be even close to a publishing date.

Coming in a very close second is my son Shane Dunning. His computer skills have made molehills of my mountains of computer ignorance. Without his constant help in surmounting glitch after glitch most of which were self-imposed, this book could simply not exist. In addition, his ability to surf the internet and find information that few people even knew existed has been a wonderful resource. He was able to find old newspaper accounts, collections from obscure and long dead historians and ethnographers, as well as edit the book for both content and form. His help has been invaluable.

This book contains information from a variety of sources, from the Smithsonian National Archives, Range Riders Museum, Montana Historical Society, to Native American oral history and early newspapers. Also included are the memories of local families to include photographs and hand written accounts. My thanks go out to the very helpful staff from the Smithsonian and Montana Historical Society. Also especially helpful were Neil

Thex and Gerry Robinson that generously shared their family histories and lore.

The folks at BookLocker, especially Angela Hoy, have been of invaluable help in the publication process.

Finally, this book absolutely could not have been possible without the previous work of Margot Liberty, Helena Huntington Smith, John-Stands-In-Timber, Thomas B. Marquis, Ellen Cotton, and photographers L.A. Huffman and Christian Barthelmess who preserved the history of the Cheyenne Tribe, and the early pioneers of the Tongue River and Rosebud Valleys.

TABLE OF CONTENTS

Prologue

My purpose in writing "Between Two Tribes" as a historical novel was two-fold.

First, I wanted to tell the history of southeastern Montana in the late 1880's and early 1890's as the early white settlers came into the Rosebud and Tongue River Valleys. This would include major associated tributaries like Hanging Woman Creek, Otter Creek, Muddy Creek, and Lame Deer Creek. Central to that time period was the saga of the Northern Cheyenne Tribe, from its trials and tribulations following the Custer Fight, forced removal to Oklahoma, and their epic fighting return to the Tongue and Rosebud valleys. Their subsequent settlement on a new reservation with white neighbors led to a clash of cultures as both "tribes" learned to live with each other.

Second, I wanted to tell that story in an entertaining and interesting way. One of the difficulties in writing a "historical" novel is the inherent conflict between writing an entertaining story and closely adhering to the historical record. Often events which are historically significant happen over a course of years and may not even deemed important at the time of their occurrence. So it is with this novel. It is first a novel which endeavors to tell an entertaining story, while coincidently informing the reader of Cheyenne and white history and cultural practices which led to conflict.

The story as told uses real names of early settlers and Indians and the events depicted are generally true but are enhanced by imagined conversations and actions. In addition, some of the events are not necessarily in the historical order in which they occurred which may offend some historical purists. Obviously, no one has recorded the thoughts and conversations from well over one hundred years ago. But, they can be imagined in the historical context of the times. For cursory readers, hopefully they will be entertained and come away with a better appreciation for prevailing cultural pressures of the time. To those who desire a more in depth and accurate depiction of the early reservation period, the Montana Historical Society is the best resource. However, a comprehensive history of southeastern Montana and the Cheyenne Reservation period from 1880 to 1900 has not yet been written. I may make an attempt at that endeavor in a future book.

Victors write the history books so the Cheyenne historical record is relatively thin during the early reservation years. George Bird Grinnell at the end of "The Fighting Cheyennes" provides some insight. Thomas Marquis in his valiant attempt to record the stories of the last Cheyennes from the Custer Fight inadvertently provides a window into early reservation life. John Stands-in-Timber and Margot Liberty give invaluable perspectives in "Cheyenne Memories" and their associated works. Orlan J. Svingen has done yeoman's work in his examination Indian Department documents during the early reservation period. White history of the area is more robust with a number articles and papers written by local residents. However, the record here is primarily family centric and tends to present a sanitized version to put their families in the best light. Events like the exploits of Stuart's Stranglers were simply not discussed or recorded in detail at the time. Even Granville Stuart who gives the most credible "Stranglers" account withholds vital information on the scope of the operation and the identity of the targets. Newspapers record discovery of various "John Doe Rustlers" found hanging from trees or gate posts. No names of the hangmen are revealed and the only record is the oral history which may not be reliable.

This story is told through the eyes of Willis Rowland, a mixed blood Cheyenne Agency interpreter, who lives on the Cheyenne Reservation and has a foot in both the Cheyenne Tribe and the "White Tribe" of settlers, ranchers, townsmen, military, and lawmen of the day. I have endeavored to use his persona to frame the stark cultural differences between these "tribes" and at the same time illustrate how leaders of good will on both sides were able to bridge the most dangerous situations. Interwoven among all the cultural conflict is a mystery involving a white outlaw band moving stolen horses, white rustlers butchering local rancher's cattle for sale to sawmill and railroad interests, and Indian Department policies of forced assimilation and bureaucratic incompetence resulting in Cheyenne starvation. All of these forces plus a series of illegal Cheyenne killings of white settler's cattle near the Reservation led to the murder of white settlers during two separate incidents during the summer and fall of 1890. The identification of the murderers by Willis Rowland and their subsequent unique punishment brings resolution to the mystery.

Willis Rowland, Cheyenne name Long Forehead, was a real person who served as a part time interpreter at the Cheyenne Agency during early reservation period. He was a primary interpreter on the Northern Cheyenne Reservation for nearly 30 years. His exploits as the First Sergeant of the Cheyenne Scouts are fully documented in Grinnell's Fighting Cheyennes. He is also liberally quoted in "Cheyenne Memories" by John Stands-in-Timber and "The Cheyennes of Montana" by Marquis. Rowland served as the Chairman of the Tribal Council and raised a family on Rosebud Creek near Busby, Montana. At least twice during his career he was selected to join a delegation to Washington as a representative of the Cheyenne Tribe. However, in this book his activities as an undercover stock detective/deputy sheriff in the pursuit of white and Indian outlaws operating in the area in and around the reservation are fictitious as are all the specific conversations between parties.

I was raised on and around the Cheyenne Reservation and thereby hopefully gained some local perspective. During the research for this book, I was surprised to learn that some of the Cheyennes I met in my youth had become quite prominent in the tribe. Donald Hollowbreast, when I knew him, was a large deaf man who "tromped" wool for my stepfather, Wilson Moreland when we lived at the mouth of Hanging Woman Creek. He was an artist who painted on weathered cattle hip bones and skulls because he could not afford canvas. In addition to cash, my mother gave him a set of paint brushes and paints when we paid him for his service. Don went on to publish a weekly newspaper called the Birney Arrow and wrote several articles in addition to his artistic talents. Willis Medicine Bull peeled the pine slabs that graced the outside of our porch. On the next page is a picture from the family archives of a picture of Willis with draw knife in hand and a big grin on his face. He once took me down to a willow patch and carved me a whistle out of a piece of willow branch. At the time I did not know that he was a member of the Contrary Society and would be designated as a future Sweet Medicine Chief of the Cheyenne Tribe. Both men had the reputation of being "good Indians" and hard workers by the white community which didn't necessarily have the same regard for other tribal members.

The ranchers depicted in the book surrounding the Reservation are the real families that settled there. Their personalities are recorded as their children and friends remembered them. To the best of my ability, I have recorded the "tenor of the times" together with the respective interests and biases of both Indians and whites. Central to the book is the clash of cultures in which white settlers, Indians, half breeds, soldiers, and civilians are trying to make a living in the best way they can, given their respective circumstances. In many ways the area's unique weather and geography drove the actions of both white and red actors in their respective pursuits.

My greatest hope in writing this book is to try and accurately relate what an incredibly turbulent time that particular period was, and how well the players were able to negotiate the potential pitfalls. I hope that my intimate association with the founders and their descendants permits a perspective not available to other authors who were not raised in the area. That there was no "Wounded Knee" or "Johnson County War" was a tribute to the men and women of both Cheyenne and white settlers of that time. It could have all turned out very badly. The book is written to entertain and educate at the same time.

I give you "Between Two Tribes".

Figure 2. Willis Medicine Bull circa 1955 at Wilson Moreland Ranch, Birney MT. Photo Courtesy of Forest Dunning Family.

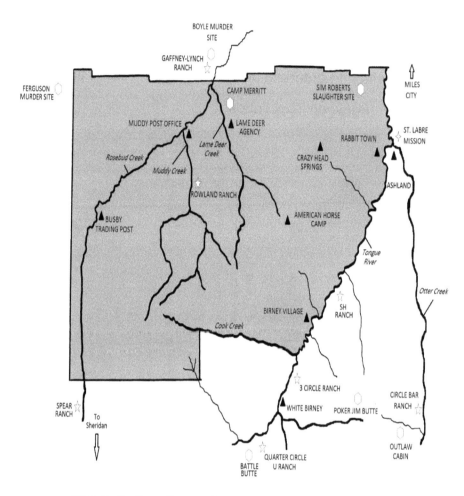

Figure 3. Northern Cheyenne Reservation (Gray) and surrounding area

Chapter 1. The Mormon Horse

The horse carefully picked his way down a faint deer trial that ran parallel to a draw near the head of Muddy Creek, Montana. It was early spring and the ground was still cold and muddy with patches of snow in the timber and on the shady side of the high bluffs that bordered the valley that encompassed the creek. The horse moved slowly, planting his left front foot firmly on the ground before moving his hind feet forward. For the next step he put minimal weight on the right front foot before hopping ahead. Reaching the bottom of the draw, he stopped between a big sand rock and some pine trees where the sun had melted the snow revealing some of last year's grass and some fresh green shoots. He grazed hungrily and rested before moving on toward the creek.

Muddy Creek in the spring of 1890 was on the newly created Northern Cheyenne Reservation in southeastern Montana. It was a meandering stream set in a valley between high buttes that flowed north into Rosebud Creek and thence on to the Yellowstone River. Home to some of the best grasslands in North America, it had been cherished by the buffalo and the people who hunted them. However, when the buffalo were nearly exterminated by 1885, they were rapidly replaced by cattlemen and thousands of head of cattle to eat the nutritious grass. The grass and timber on the Cheyenne and Crow Reservations were the subjects of especially envious attention by white pioneers moving into the area.

The horse, tired of eating snow, moved toward the creek seeking a drink of running water. Intersecting an old buffalo trail which paralleled creek, he turned on to the trail where the travelling was easier and soon came to a place that crossed the creek. Stopping in the running water, he drank his fill and let the injured foot soak awhile before continuing downstream on the old buffalo trail. Picking up the scent of other horses, he increased his pace despite his injury. After another couple of miles the horse rounded a bend in the creek and sighted a group of cabins, a teepee, log barn, and set of corrals. Letting out an anxious nicker, he was excited to hear an answering call from several horses in the corral. Travelling at a three legged trot he rapidly closed the distance to the corral. After exchanging a greeting of snorts and foot stomping, the exhausted horse leaned against the corral and dozed off. A faint pink glow in the eastern sky heralded the approaching day break.

Willis (Willie) Rowland awoke to the sound of the excited horses and barking dogs. Throwing off his buffalo robe, he reached for his pants, rough shirt, and pulled on a pair of high topped boots. Grabbing his jacket and lever actioned rifle, he opened the flap on the canvas teepee he shared with his five brothers and noted the rapidly dawning morning. Stopping momentarily, he listened for more horse activity which might indicate they were being harassed by wolves or a mountain lion. Hearing none, he proceeded to the corral to discover the cause of the disturbance. He was immediately joined by two of the family dogs which he commanded to stay behind him. Standing at the corral was a big sorrel horse, covered with mud, head down and obviously worn out. Noting the white saddle marks high on the horse's withers, Willie knew that this horse was broke to ride. He went back to the barn picked up a halter and half a pail of oats, and returned to the tired animal. The horse allowed himself to be haltered and greedily tied into the oats while Willie continued the examination.

Willie found an exceptionally well formed animal, of good temperament, with a missing right front horseshoe and a badly split hoof. Willie thought the horse was salvageable but would be lame for weeks and looked for a brand which would indicate ownership. The brand was located on the left hip and was a Box D Eight, a brand with which Willie was not familiar. However, he noted that the upper right portion of the Box and parts of the Eight were fresh marks, indicating that the brand

2

had been changed from the original. The original brand was clearly an L D S which was widely known to be a Mormon Church brand for Latter Day Saints. Given the way the horse was branded, Willie suspected the horse was stolen. Leading the horse to a box stall in the log barn, Willie locked him away from the other horses, pitched him some hay and proceeded to the kitchen to make some coffee and assess the situation.

Willis Rowland was a 27 year old man with a Scottish/American father and a Southern Cheyenne mother. That made him a "mixed blood" or as was known at the time, a "half breed". In Willie's case, he received the best genes from both "tribes", gaining the sharp intelligence and stubborn grit of his father's Scottish heritage with the Cheyenne athleticism and sense of humor from his mother. His father was a retired U.S. Army Cheyenne/English interpreter and the first white man to settle in the area which had become the Northern Cheyenne Reservation. In fact, Willie and his brother James had also served as Army interpreters on various occasions.

Willie, despite the normal prejudices of the times, was on equally good terms with both whites and Indians. Since he had been educated with the Army officer children at the various Army forts where his father interpreted, Willie had received a level of schooling far beyond that of the average white settler. However, beginning at about age twelve, he had also been instructed in Cheyenne warrior ways by a maternal uncle, given the Cheyenne name of Long Forehead, and was later inducted into the Crazy Dog warrior society. Furthermore, he was not intimidated by perceived rank or station in life having dealt with Army officers and Cheyenne chiefs during his many years of interpreting.

Mixed bloods such as Willis Rowland were common during the late 1880's/1890's. Early white travelers to the western United States were almost exclusively male and the only women available to them were the Native American women. In the course of life many of these early white men "married" Indian women who bore children of mixed blood or "half breeds". Some of these unions were permanent, but most were transitory and the white men moved on after a time to return to white settlements and a white wife. The mixed blood children generally remained with the tribe of the Indian mother to be raised as Indians but were not fully accepted by either the Red tribe or the White tribe. A fortunate few like Willis Rowland were raised in a permanent relationship between a white man and a red woman and learned to successfully tread the narrow bridge between the two tribes.

With eight brothers and two sisters, Willie was ready to move on with his own life. He had his eye on a nice piece of ground on Rosebud Creek about eleven miles north of the Rosebud Battlefield (Crook versus Sioux and Cheyennes, June 1876, the week before the Custer fight) and wanted to file a homestead claim. However, his small salary as a part time interpreter and the few cows of his own that he ran with the family was not sufficient to make the move to his own place. Despite his education and native intelligence he was not generally as welcome in the White Tribe as he was in the Cheyenne Tribe because of the white biases against anyone showing nonwhite blood.

Interestingly, the common general bias against nonwhites was in conflict with the white western custom accepting people as individuals regardless of their race or prior station in life. Black, Spanish, Oriental, Indian, or mixed bloods were often accepted as full members by their white brethren after they had proved their worth to their fellow workers. There are countless stories of black and brown cowboys being harassed by individual whites only to have the harasser confronted by the whole crew. The same cowboy who cussed Indians as no better than dogs, would commonly intervene on behalf of an Indian girl being accosted by a white man. Often the same man who would advocate dissolution of the Indian's Reservation would also treat the individual with full respect and invite him to eat at his table. Thus the issue of white bias was much more nuanced than is generally reported.

Willie/Long Forehead had been courting a girl named Bear Woman, the daughter of Elk River, a traditional Cheyenne warrior. That relationship was gaining strength and Willie was anxious to start his own family. Willie let his mind wander and smiled to himself as he remembered when he first met Bear Woman and her mother. Cheyenne mothers looked on suitors with great distain and Willis was no exception, especially since he wasn't pureblood Cheyenne. After Willis began to show interest in Bear Woman and she returned the attention, her mother had berated Willie in a sharp voice. "Who are you to come around this girl? What have you ever done in battle? How many times have you touched the enemy?" The mother, knowing that the Cheyennes had not been at war for nearly ten years, expected Willie to withdraw, hanging his head, like most of the other young men had done. It was a common problem for young Cheyenne men at this time to prove their worth, because there were very few who had the opportunity to count coup (touch or strike an enemy with a hand or weapon) like the Cheyennes of old. She was very surprised when Long Forehead softly replied that he had counted two coups to his credit. He then told her to ask Howling Wolf, a respected Cheyenne Scout, if this were not true and walked away.

The coups to which Willie Rowland/Long Forehead referred, were counted in August 1880 near the present town of Glendive, Montana. Willis Rowland, and three Cheyenne Scouts, Howling Wolf, Shell, and Big Footed Bull were scouting with a patrol of eight U.S. soldiers searching for Sioux hostiles who had killed a stagecoach driver four days before. The body of the stage driver had been found by another party of soldiers and two Sioux scouts, but the Sioux said they could not find the trail of the hostiles. Rowland, sensing that maybe the Sioux scouts were lying about losing the trail of their fellow Sioux, suggested to the sergeant leading the patrol that the Cheyenne Scouts go to the spot the driver's body was found and take a closer look. Sure enough, Howling Wolf picked up the trail and Shell discovered where the hostile Sioux had left the stage road. They determined that they were following a party of four men and a small band of loose horses. After some hard riding, the Cheyenne Scouts spotted two Sioux men butchering a buffalo, and suspected the other two were camped nearby. The scouts followed the two Sioux back to their camp and then brought up the Army patrol. Just as the patrol arrived the four hostile Sioux broke camp and started moving out. The scouts and the patrol engaged the group at about 300 yards and knocked one Sioux out of the saddle breaking his leg and stampeding their band of horses. Rowland and the Scouts rushed forward on their horses toward the downed man. Shell and Rowland stopped to kill the wounded Sioux and count coup, while Howling Wolf and Big Footed Bull went after the loose horses. With the soldiers in tow, they all galloped after the remaining Sioux. Rounding a hill, scouts and soldiers ran into the hostile Sioux, and with them all firing they killed one man and wounded another. The wounded Sioux rode a short way off and fell off his horse. Again, Shell and Rowland killed the wounded Sioux and counted coup. Howling Wolf and Big Footed Bull scalped the three dead Sioux. The fourth Sioux got away because the Scouts and soldier's horses were played out while the remaining Sioux's horse was fresh. Packs found on the recovered horses contained mail from the stagecoach. The Scouts were allowed to keep the recovered horses and returned to Fort Keogh for a scalp dance. That was how Long Forehead/Willis Rowland earned his two coups at the tender age of seventeen and was inducted into the "Dog Soldiers" of the Crazy Dog military society.

The "Crazy Dogs" got their name by taking a vow of suicide in defense of their villages. They would drive a stake in the ground with a rawhide rope attached to it and the other end tied around their waists. The rope could not be untied until either the enemy was defeated or the warrior was killed. They also frequently acted as the camp policemen to insure discipline in behalf of the chiefs. Of the three Northern Cheyenne military societies, the Swift Foxes, Elk Horn Scrapers, and Crazy Dogs, the Crazy Dogs were the most prestigious.

Willie's attention returned to what to do about the injured horse with the changed brand. Normally, Willie would have sought the advice of his father and/or Agent Upshaw, the Indian Agent for the Northern Cheyenne tribe. However, both men had gone to Miles City, Montana for the fifth annual Montana Stock Growers meeting and would not return for a few days. Willie knew he needed to report the horse to someone, but the sheriff of Custer County Montana was 75 miles away, also in Miles City. In the end he decided to keep the horse in the barn and out of sight until his father returned.

Figure 4. Willis Rowland circa 1913. Photo courtesy of the Smithsonian Institute

Chapter 2. Spring 1890 - The Storm Clouds Gather

Sheriff Tom Irvine was not looking forward to the next week. The Spring Meeting of the Montana Stock Growers Association would start on the following Monday and trouble was in the air. All winter there had been reports of horse stealing and illegal cattle butchering from all over Custer County, Montana. Now with the arrival of prominent ranchers from the recently constituted state, Sheriff Irvine could feel the pressure coming his way. As the only legally constituted law enforcement officer in the county, it was his responsibility to find and apprehend the horse and cattle thieves committing depredations within his territory. With the rapid arrival of spring, he wouldn't be able to use the vagaries of a treacherous Montana winter as an excuse for inaction.

The Custer County Sheriff's Office was housed in a big red brick building on the Main Street of Miles City just down the street from the MacQueen House, the newly built grand hotel which would serve as the meeting place for the Stock Grower's Association. The Office included a jail with six individual cells and a large "drunk tank" together with a room in the front of the building which held a "Deputy Dog" desk for reception, a boarded off cubby hole for the Sheriff's desk, a long plank table, and a dozen or so chairs. A potbellied wood stove, gun cabinet with an assorted collection of rifles and shotguns, and a large map of Montana Territory with Custer County outlined in red, completed the office accouterments.

Figure 5. Sheriff Tom Irvine in his later years. Photo Courtesy of the Montana Historical Society

Affectionately known as "The Red House", it had served as a temporary residence at one time or another for probably half the population of Miles City.

Miles City was named for General Nelson Miles, the U.S. Army commander who had established Fort Keogh, the first permanent military buildings at the junction of the Tongue and Yellowstone Rivers. That group of buildings which was built on the west side of Tongue River in 1877 was designated Fort Keogh for Captain Miles Keogh, who was killed on June 25, 1876 at the Battle of the Little Big Horn. Miles City was born as an adjunct to the Fort, housing civilian contractors providing lumber, hay, grain, meat, and other services to Fort Keogh. It also was an important landing point for steam ships which plied an active trade along the Yellowstone and Missouri Rivers. As the civilian population grew General Miles soon directed that the civilians move to the east side of Tongue River to provide some separation between his troops and the rowdy collection of buffalo hunters, cowboys, whiskey sellers, brothels, "friendly" Indians, and other flotsam of the frontier. Thus "Miles' City" was born.

Figure 6. Col. Nelson A. Miles. Photo Courtesy of the Montana Historical Society

In the long decade between Fort Keogh's founding and the spring of 1890, Miles City had grown to become an important town. The country that had originally been settled by "cow outfits" and a few "horse outfits", now had homesteaders, large ranchers, small ranchers, sawmill men, wolvers, railroaders, surveyors, telegraph builders, saloon men, merchants, butchers, bull whackers, miners, cattle and horse thieves, prostitutes and lowest of all, the "government men" of the U.S. Land Office. This mob of humanity was turned loose on several hundred thousand acres of "free" government land with all parties trying to garner their piece of the American Dream. To add to the confusion was also the presence of two Indian tribes – the Northern Cheyenne and the Crow Tribes and their jailers/protectors, the soldiers of the U.S. Army at Fort Keogh and Fort Custer. This was the volatile mixture in which Sheriff Irvine was now tasked to provide law and order.

Sheriff Tom noted that X. Beidler, (U.S. Marshall and former Virginia City vigilante) Granville Stuart (President, Montana Stock Growers and former Virginia City vigilante) both were already in town together with four Montana Stock Growers "stock detectives" headed by Billy Smith. In an effort to "get ahead" of the situation, Sheriff Tom decided to try and arrange a meeting between himself and the two old vigilantes. Knowing that everyone eventually ended up at the bar in the MacQueen House, Sheriff Tom ambled up the street and bellied up to the bar. He was in luck. Standing at the bar was Teddy Blue Abbot, Granville Stuart's soon to be son-in-law. Teddy was a long time cowboy who had made the cattle drives from Texas to Montana several times. Prior to his engagement, Teddy was widely known as a fun loving, hard drinking, skirt chasing, but very competent stockman.

"Hi, Teddy" Sheriff Tom said.

Teddy replied: "Damn, Sheriff Tom. I just got here. I ain't had time to do anything you'd want me for."

"Aw hell, Teddy. Since you got engaged to Mary Stuart you haven't been worth a damn to a guy in my profession." Tom grinned.

"Yeah, I know," drawled Teddy. "I just don't know how you stay in business without all the fines I used to pay."

Figure 7. Teddy Blue Abbott. Photo Courtesy of the Montana Historical Society

"Say, Teddy". Do you think I could get a word with Daddy Stuart on the Q.T.?" Tom asked.

Teddy's eyes narrowed. "Law business?"

Tom replied: "Of a sort. We got all these cattlemen coming in for the Association Meeting. I know there's been a lot of butchering of stolen beef and horse stealing going on. Everybody's going to be on my ass to do something about It, but with only four deputies and a county the size of the State of Pennsylvania, I'm going to need some help. I was wondering if I could make some medicine with Daddy and Marshall "X" to figure out a plan for the summer. Maybe use Billy Smith and his crew. Make them special deputies or something."

Figure 8. The MacQueen House. Photo Courtesy of the Montana Historical Society

"What about the Injuns?" Teddy commented. "Ain't they killin' cattle too?"

Sheriff Tom agreed. "They're a big issue. Especially close to the reservation. One big problem though is the Army. A lot of the butchering is being done by Cheyennes and Crows, and while I am the only law officer in the county with authority, the Army ain't going to be too happy about white guys who work for me or the Association going on to the reservation to drag some buck down to the Red House where he might get hung. Them Indians is hungry, 'cause the dumb assed government ain't sent 'em all the beef they been promised. The Army don't want anybody to stir 'em up to the point where a bunch of ranchers, soldiers, and Indians end up dead just because a Cheyenne buck was trying to feed his kids."

"Both Cheyennes and Crows? Teddy asked.

"Well, yeah." Tom said. "Most of the Crow Reservation is out of the county, but they still got problems over there. That reservation is a lot bigger and the Crows got a better deal than the Cheyennes 'cause they were friends of the white man. I don't have a cattle butchering problem with the Crows. The two reservations border each other, so there ain't no white man cattle on the Cheyenne side for the Crows to kill. Besides, they lease out their land to the whites for grazing and kill some of those cattle.

"I'd bet they steal some horses, though." Teddy suggested.

"Damn right." Tom agreed. "That's their culture. They steal horses from the white man, the Cheyennes, and even make an occasional raid up on the Blackfoot Reservation. Money don't mean much to an Indian, they measure wealth with horses, though that's changing. What about the meeting?"

"Stuart is tied up all afternoon with the Northern Pacific Railroad guys. Since the railroad built a stockyard, we are shipping thousands of cattle to the east right here from Miles City. They got some new kind of cattle car they want to show him. It's supposed to be easier on cattle so they weigh more when they get to Omaha or Chicago. But they also want the cattlemen to pay an extra 25 cents a head for the shipping. I'll see him tonight. I'm sure he will want to talk to you. I think he is also supposed to have supper with Marshall "X" so maybe I can kill two birds with one stone. They go back a long ways to '65 when they cleaned up the Sheriff Plummer gang in Virginia City. You better be on your best behavior, Tom. Them two is hell on crooked sheriffs." Teddy teased.

"That was a hard time." Tom added. "Didn't that Vigilance Committee hang 65 men including the Sheriff?

Teddy grinned. "Something like that. Daddy Stuart don't talk about it much, but he can be hell on wheels when he gets goin'. Even though I'm about to be a member of the family, I can't get much out of him. He did tell me one story about "X" Beidler though. They was hanging a guy name of "Clubfoot George" for killing an express driver in Virginia City when the guy broke down and begged for his life. He was crying that he was already a cripple, was now a Christian, had a good mother, and promised to leave the country if the Committee would just let him go. "X" was trying to put the noose around his neck but he wouldn't hold still, all the while crying pitifully. Finally, "X" got the rope on and they kicked the box out from under him and finished the hanging. One of the spectators came up to "X" and asked him if he didn't have any feelings for that man? Daddy Stuart told me "X" growled to the man: "Damn right I felt for him. I felt for his left ear!" Those guys were tough old bastards, they had to be, and still are."

Tom laughed. "Yeah, but the country was sure better for it. O.K. It's Friday now and the Meeting begins on Monday so let's try for tomorrow. Once all the members get here he will be so tied up with politics we won't get nothing done. Say hello to Mary for me. Since you don't drink no more, have a ginger ale on me."

Tom and Teddy Blue shook hands and they parted company. As Sheriff Irvine left the MacQueen House he was thinking, "I hope this thing works out, I damn sure want those guys on my side."

Figure 7. Granville Stuart. Photo Courtesy of the Montana Historical Society

Granville Stuart was in many ways the father of the State of Montana. He was one of the very first pioneers arriving in Montana Territory in 1857. A member of the party which discovered Alder Gulch, the richest placer gold strike ever found in Montana, he made a small fortune on the strike. Out of Alder Gulch grew the town of Virginia City, one of the toughest mining districts in the west. Stuart took his gold stake and invested in a mercantile store, a freighting business, and prospered mightily providing services to the miners. When a band of outlaws called "the Innocents" began robbing and murdering miners, freight wagons, and stagecoaches, Granville Stuart organized a Vigilance Committee to clean up the area. With a small group of men during the years of 1865 and 1866, the Committee either shot or hanged over 65 known outlaws and banished many more. Among the outlaws hung was the duly elected Sheriff Plumber of Virginia City, who was also the leader of the "Innocents". Stuart then went to Oregon and bought a herd of cattle which he drove to Montana and started a ranch to provide beef to the miners. He was one of the first stockmen to recognize the potential of Montana's vast grasslands for the beef business. He married a Shoshone Indian woman and raised three mixed blood daughters who were by all accounts beautiful, well educated, and very respectable. He had a very large ranch which was well stocked with good cattle, a school, a store and about a dozen cowboys. Later, he became active in the Montana Territorial Legislature and was a founding member of the Montana Stock Growers Association.

Early Saturday morning Teddy Blue Abbott dropped by the "Red House" with a message from Granville Stewart to meet him and "X" Beidler at the Fort Keogh's Commandant's Office at 01:00 P.M. Cheyenne Indian Agent R.L. Upshaw, Bill Rowland (formerly General Miles' interpreter for the Cheyenne surrender), and CPT E.W. Casey (Commander – Cheyenne Scouts) would also be in attendance. The cover story for the meeting was a courtesy call by the President of the Montana Stock Growers on Col. Peter Swaine, Commandant. Stuart requested that Sheriff Irvine find an excuse to visit the Fort before lunch and Col Swaine would invite him to stay and eat. Everyone would "accidently" be in the same place at the same time. The utmost secrecy about the contents of the meeting was required.

Sheriff Irvine was excited that Granville Stuart had moved so quickly but he knew that Stuart was a capable and decisive operator. He was also surprised that Col. Swaine would be so receptive to such a request. The addition of the Indian Agent and a retired U.S. Army interpreter married to a Cheyenne woman offered unique insight into reservation conditions. He wondered why CPT Casey had been included in such a high level meeting. The military response showed a high level of concern.

The first thing he did was check his jail to see if any soldiers had been picked up by his deputies the night before. Sure enough, one Corporal Jim Smith had been found passed out behind the Keg Saloon and had been "invited" to share one of the bunks in the drunk tank for his "health and safety." Sheriff Tom told "Deputy Dog" Jack Johnson that he would return Corporal Smith to Fort Keogh about 11:00 later that morning. He then went over to the Court House to borrow the Mayor's surrey for the trip to Fort Keogh. Following a forty five minute tirade from the mayor on the subject of not embarrassing the city by the arrest of any important Stock Growers, he located the surrey in the Custer County Barn and hitching it up he drove the rig to his office.

Waiting for Sheriff Irvine when he returned was one of the first "prominent ranchers" to come in from the country in the person of Captain Calvin C. Howes (former ship's captain) from the Circle Bar Ranch in the Otter Creek country, a tributary to Tongue River. Captain Howes had been one of the earliest settlers in Custer County, coming to Miles City in April 1880 and establishing a ranch on Tongue River about 55 miles south of Miles City. Later, in 1884 he went into a partnership with George Miles (Gen. Miles' nephew) and Judge J.W. Strevell, established the Circle Bar Ranch on Otter Creek, and built one of the largest cattle herds in the Territory

"Howdy, Cap'n, good to see you again." Sheriff Tom said, extending his hand. "What can I do for you?"

The old ship captain firmly shook the Sheriff's hand and replied with a strong Boston accent:

"Good to see you, Tom. I just thought I would drop by and impart a little information you might be interested in."

The Sheriff said: "Let's go into my office where we can have some privacy and you can tell me about it."

After sitting Captain Howes down, the Sheriff brought two cups of coffee and said: "Shoot".

Captain Howes started: "Well Tom, you know that there have been a lot of "hard cases" roaming the country, and a substantial number of cattle and horses have come up missing. Nobody wants to question a man too closely, and generally we mind our own business unless we know something for sure. There is a cabin clear up Cow Creek next to a spring and four or five men are living there. They claim to be hunting wolves for the Stock Grower's bounty, but they have a corral built into a bunch of cedar trees, where it's difficult to see. I'm trying to get an Otter Post Office established and sent my son Levi up there with a petition to get their signatures. He rode up there and a guy came out of the cabin to meet him. Levi was carrying the petition inside his coat and when he reached in to get it, the guy drew a pistol and jumped behind an open flour barrel. Flour went everywhere. Levi threw his hands up and rapidly explained what he wanted. After seeing that Levi was unarmed, the man calmed down and he eventually signed the petition but never invited him into the cabin. Levi said there were cattle in the corral, but he was in no position to go over and check brands. We kind of asked around to see if anyone knew them and one of our cowboys said he saw one of them going into a butcher shop over in Suggs, WY last fall. As you probably know that is the toughest town in WY and only about 40 miles from Otter Creek as the crow flies. They are building a railroad into there and need lots of meat for the grading crews. I don't know if they are thieves for sure, but they sure act like it.

Sheriff Tom asked: "What was the name he signed on the petition?"

"Jack Smith was the name he signed. For whatever that's worth." Captain Howes snorted.

"Anything else?" said Tom.

"Well, my neighbor, Charlie Thex, tracked one of his missing horses to Suggs and just out of town saw a washout filled with "green" hides with the brands cut out." Howes offered.

"Suggs is out of my jurisdiction." Tom grinned.

"Yes, but Cow Creek isn't!" Captain Howes said firmly in his best "Captain" tone.

"O.K., Captain Howes, I'll take it under advisement and try and get a man on it. Thanks for filling me in. Can you show me on the big map out in the office about where the cabin is?" said the Sheriff rising from his chair.

Captain Howes stood up and the two men walked to the map where Howes made a pencil mark locating the cabin. The two men shook hands and Howes left for the MacQueen house. The Sheriff returned to his desk to contemplate the way his morning had begun.

About 10:30 Sheriff Irvine told Deputy Johnson to get CPL Smith cleaned up and prepare him for return to the Fort. He unwrapped the reins of the mayor's driving horse and the surrey, and backed up the two man buggy and turned it around. Since the horse was acting up, the Sheriff took off at a smart trot to "take the edge off" in preparation for the trip to Fort Keogh. At the eastern edge of town he turned around and headed back the office. There he found a forlorn CPL Smith awaiting his ride to the Fort. He pulled up to the Red House and motioned CPL Smith to climb aboard with the greeting: "How are you feeling this morning, Corporal?"

"Not so good, Sheriff Irvine." Corporal Smith replied meekly.

"My boys said they found you pretty boogered up. What the hell were you drinking?"

"I don't know, Sheriff Irvine. When I asked the bartender to mix me something special for my birthday, he said he would fix me right up. The next thing I knew I was on my way to the outhouse, but I don't remember gettin' there. Now I've missed morning formation and when I get to the Fort there will be hell to pay." CPL Smith held his head in his hands.

Sheriff Tom chuckled. "Don't take it so hard, Corporal. It's a fine spring morning and you are going home in the Mayor of Miles City's buggy with the second highest official in town as your driver. You can tell your buddies you must be something special in this town."

Corporal Smith forced a weak smile. "Bet you First Sergeant Ferris won't be impressed."

As they crossed the bridge over Tongue River, Sheriff Tom said seriously: "Tell your friends not to try and come back over this bridge alone after dark. There's been a group of tramps that waylay travelers here, rob them and beat the hell out of them. I'll tell the Adjutant that we picked you up for your health and safety last night and I couldn't get you back early enough for morning formation. Maybe they will go easy on you. A man does have a right to a drink on his birthday."

Smith brightened up. "Gosh, Sheriff that would be really good of you."

Tom grinned. "Well, I got my instructions from the mayor this morning. He said don't arrest any prominent citizens just because they were having a little fun and bringing business to town. I don't think he meant you specifically, but he is a patriotic man and if it wasn't for the Fort, Miles City wouldn't be here. You didn't get in a fight, shoot out any lights, or try and ride your horse up the stairs of Meg's parlor house like some people. That makes you a prominent citizen in my book."

By the time they reached the Headquarters Building, Corporal Smith was feeling much better. Sheriff Irvine and Smith dismounted the buggy and walked into the Post Adjutant's Office to report CPL Smith's return to the Post. After explaining to the Adjutant the circumstances of CPL Smith's "failure to repair" (not being at the appointed place at the appropriate time) Sheriff completed his delivery and turned to go. He was stopped by the sudden appearance of Colonel Swaine, the Commandant, who inquired as to what brought the Sheriff to Fort Keogh. After a brief explanation, Col. Swaine thanked the Sheriff for looking out for his troops and invited the Sheriff to lunch in his personal quarters. The Colonel directed his Sergeant Major to have the Sheriff's buggy brought to his quarters. With that the Colonel and Sheriff departed for lunch. The stage was set for one of the most important meetings in Montana history.

Figure 8. FT Keogh Officer's Quarters. Photo Courtesy of the Montana Historical Society

Chapter 3. A Plan is Born

After a nice lunch Col. Swaine invited Sheriff Irvine into his sitting room.

"I expect that Stuart and Beidler will be here shortly. I told the Sergeant Major to redirect them from my office to these quarters. There will be less loose talk that a meeting is taking place."

A soft knock at the back door brought Col. Swaine to his feet. "That will be Upshaw and Rowland. They had lunch at the Post Canteen and I had CPT Casey bring them over here under the guise of Cheyenne Scout business."

The three men were ushered into the room by Col. Swaine and a round of introductions and handshaking followed. No sooner had the introductions been completed when Granville Stuart and Marshall X. Beidler arrived under the able charge of the Post Sergeant Major. A new round of introductions ensued followed by Col. Swaine inviting all to take a seat at the Col.'s expansive dining room table. A round of coffee cups appeared and Captain Casey and the Sergeant Major helped Col. Swaine fill the cups. When all were seated and served, Col. Swaine began:

"Granville sent me a message that Sheriff Irvine here wanted to have a meeting with him to discuss some of the cattle butchering and horse stealing going on in the country. Since it is well known that a lot of the butchering is being done by Cheyenne Indians and the ranchers are talking about reprisals, Granville thought maybe the Army might have an interest in that, which we surely do."

Col. Swaine nodded to Granville Stuart. "Your thoughts, Granville?"

Stuart, ever the diplomat: "I think we owe a debt to Sheriff Irvine for giving voice to a concern that we all share concerning this issue. We have a bunch of angry Stock Growers on their way to town and they will be demanding that something be done to cut down the theft of their property. A lot of those guys want to form a Vigilance Committee and go out and start hanging white cattle thieves and shooting Indians. "X" and I have some experience with that sort of thing and I think we should try and avoid that if possible. Unless it is handled very carefully, innocent people will die and we will have a three sided range war, ranchers and cowboys against Indians and rustlers, small ranchers and rustlers versus large ranchers, Army fighting Indians to keep them on the reservation and Army fighting ranchers and cowboys to protect the Indians. I can foresee a hell of a wreck. Is that how you see it, Sheriff?"

Sheriff Irvine nodded his agreement. "I think you got it pretty close to right, Mr. Stuart. As it stands right now with the law being what it is, my office with me and four deputies and "X" as the U.S. Marshall are the only legally appointed law enforcement officials in Custer County. Our authority is unclear on the Cheyenne and Crow Reservations as well as here in the Fort and its surrounding military property."

Col. Swaine quickly weighed in. "It's not unclear on this military reservation. I have the authority, not the civil authorities."

"Not entirely," Sheriff Tom argued. "You have authority over the military by courts martial, you have authority over Indians if they are your prisoners, and you have arrest authority of civilians on the military reservation. However, you can't court martial civilians on or off the military and Indian reservations. Civilians and non-prisoner-of-war Indians must be turned over to local authorities to be tried in a civilian court."

Agent Upshaw stepped in with a comment. "On the reservation we have our own tribal courts and judges. Do you think you can come on the reservation and arrest a Cheyenne and haul him off to Miles City?"

"Not that I want to," sighed Sheriff Tom. "But what if we catch a Cheyenne killing a beef off the reservation? What if a Cheyenne kills a white man off the reservation and then goes back on the reservation. Who has the authority to apprehend him? That's what I mean by the law being unclear."

Col. Swaine banged his fist on the table. "Gentlemen, let's get this straight. The people at this table are as close to all the legal authority that there is in this part of the world. I propose that we handle this in the following manner:

> Indian on Indian crime on the reservation will be handled by the Indian Police and Tribal Courts.

> Indian on White crime off the reservation will be handled by the Sheriff and the civilian courts. If an Indian commits an offense off the reservation but escapes back to the reservation, the Indian Police will apprehend and then turn the offender over to the Army. The Army will help transport Indians from the Agency to the Sheriff's office. I don't want there to be any incidents of white deputies shooting Indians "trying to escape". We will use Captain Casey's Cheyenne Scouts to make these transfers.

> White on White crime on or off a military or Indian reservation will be handled by the Sheriff and the civilian courts unless it involves a soldier on the military reservation."

"What do you think, gentlemen?" the Colonel concluded.

Sheriff Irvine responded immediately. "I think that's really helpful. It sure solves a lot of problems for me because I don't have worry about the Indian problem on the reservation. Using the Army to transport Indian prisoners frees my deputies up for chasing criminals rather than administrative duties. But, how are we going to handle White on Indian crime on the reservation? Whites aren't going be tried in Indian courts are they? Hell's bells, since the reservation hasn't been surveyed, nobody even knows exactly where the reservation is!"

Agent Upshaw jumped in. "God, no! The Indian Police will do the arrest and turn the suspect over to the Army for delivery to you, just like an Indian. Is that O.K. with you Colonel?"

Colonel Swaine thought about it for a moment. "I guess we could do that."

Col. Swaine continued: "You know maybe we should just station a troop (cavalry troop-about 30 mounted soldiers) or two at the Lame Deer Agency for the summer. That way we would have escorts there to transfer prisoners and at the same time we could run some patrols along the edge of the reservation. It might discourage some white men with trouble on their mind from aggravating the Indians or if a rancher had a complaint he could voice it to us. Bill Rowland what is your take on the situation?"

Rowland thought a minute before answering. "Well the Cheyennes aren't going to like having soldier boys on their doorstep, especially if they think they are trying to catch Indians butchering the white man's cattle. Them Cheyennes are on pretty short rations and their families are hungry all the time. There's almost no wild game left on the reservation because it's all been hunted out. They been getting by this winter because they have been able to salvage some dead cattle that either froze or went through the ice on the river. Indians will eat meat a white man wouldn't touch. Most of the time they go to the rancher and tell him what they want and usually the rancher will give them his deads. The trouble comes when they don't ask and the rancher finds them butchering something and jumps to the conclusion that the Indians killed it. That makes for a pretty touchy situation. The other thing that happens is that when white man's cattle stray on to the reservation, the Indian figures the cow is eating his grass so he's entitled to some of the meat. It starts out like that and then the Indians start hazing anything that's close over the line. Upshaw, why don't you tell us why the Indians are so hungry all the time? I was talking to American Horse yesterday and told me that they get beef every two weeks but it only lasts for one. "

Agent Upshaw shuffled uncomfortably. "The problem started small and has got worse every year. As you know after Custer was killed in '76 the Northern Cheyennes scattered into small bands all over this part of Montana and Wyoming. Then when they started surrendering in '77, they were all split up. Two Moons with about 300 members came here to Fort Keogh where they were allowed to stay and the Army fed them as prisoners of war. About 600 under Dull Knife and Little Wolf surrendered to the troops from Fort Robinson in Nebraska and were taken there where they were held and fed as prisoners of war. Another 100 or so closely related to the Sioux were captured with them and ended up on the Pine Ridge Agency in South Dakota where they got their rations from the Indian Department. There were maybe another 200 in really small groups who didn't surrender but floated around and weren't fed by anybody. Then the Army and the Indian Department made a really stupid decision. They sent the prisoners at Fort Robinson to Indian Territory in Oklahoma to be with the Southern Cheyennes at the Darlington Agency. The Indian Department hadn't budgeted the Darlington Agency for the additional 600-700 mouths to feed so the agent down there was short of rations, especially meat. Then the agent tried to make them farmers and also cut the meat ration for the Southern bands to help feed the new arrivals. That caused dissention between the two tribes, so no one was happy. Also they weren't used to the climate and about 150 got sick and died. So anyway, in '78 Little Wolf and Dull Knife took about 400 of their people and broke out of Darlington Agency and started home. They fought their way all the way back north to Nebraska where the bands split. Little Wolf and his band made their way to Montana where they were convinced to surrender to Col. Miles here at Fort Keogh. That made them prisoners again and so he joined Two Moons group where they were fed by the Army. Dull Knife's band tried to make it to the Pine Ridge Agency to join that group under Little Chief but were captured by the Army and taken to Fort Robinson. Initially, they were well treated but were told that they had to go back to Oklahoma and wouldn't be allowed to proceed to Pine Ridge Agency, because that Agency had no rations for them. When they refused the Commander at Fort Robinson locked them up and wouldn't feed them until they agreed. They tried to break out of the Fort but most of them were either killed by the soldiers or froze to death. Some were recaptured and sent back to Darlington. Dull Knife and his immediate family made it to the Pine Ridge Agency. Eventually, some families at Darlington and Pine Ridge made their way individually to Fort Keogh and joined Little Wolf and Two Moons where they were fed by the Fort. There got to be so many Indians here that Miles sent Two Moon's band to Lame Deer and Muddy Creeks where there was still game, and Little Wolf to Tongue River between Hanging Woman and Otter Creek. He still provided some cattle on the Army's dime and he made it work until he got the Northern Cheyenne Reservation established and turned over to the Indian Department. The Indian Department had a hell of a time getting Congress to give them a large enough appropriation to feed everyone because there was no record of how many Cheyennes were where. The ones that had left Darlington and Pine Ridge were still on their rolls and those agents didn't know which ones were there and which were here. It was a mess that is still not fixed. We are still trying to get an accurate census but each Indian has two or three different names depending on what age and which family member you are talking to. In a nutshell, the problem is that we have a lot more Indians on the reservation than the Indian Department and Congress knows about, and they aren't going to give us the money to feed everybody adequately until we can prove how many we have."

"So the white ranchers have to donate their cattle to feed Indians because of government mismanagement?" Stuart asked in a sarcastic tone.

Upshaw answered wearily. "It's not good, I know. But in the meantime we still have starving women and kids and desperate bucks to deal with. The big ranchers are not paying for all that government grass that their thousands of cows are eating. The Stock Growers pay out many hundreds of dollars in bounties for predator control, why not pay something to keep the Indians from eating your cattle?"

"Because, I don't think you want us to put a bounty on Indians." Stuart smiled. "If we pay to kill a wolf, the wolf is dead and can't kill another cow, that's not the case with a Cheyenne. Although, a lot of my members would like the idea of including Cheyennes on the predator list."

"Hold on." Colonel Swaine interjected. "I don't like where this conversation is going. Let's focus on some practical actions we can take to make it better for both the whites and the Indians. Stuart, your members are losing a lot more cattle to white rustlers than the few eaten by Indians."

Stuart grinned. "O.K. Colonel, I was just jabbing the government man. By the way, I don't have anything against Indians. Remember, I married one and my three daughters are half-bloods. But what you are saying about white rustlers is sure true. As a matter of fact, "X" and I were just talking about that subject last night. He has information about some big organized gangs operating all over the mountain west. "X", why don't you share what you found out with all of us?"

Figure 9. John "X" Beidler. Photo Courtesy of the Montana Historical Society

The tough little vigilante leaned forward. "Ever since I got appointed a U.S. Marshall, I have been diggin' into this rustling business pretty hard. Up to the Canadian border to talk with the Mounties (Royal Canadian Mounted Police), down to Colorado, New Mexico, and Arizona, I have talked to lawmen all over the west. Two major gangs are operating in our area. They mostly focus on horse stealing but cattle sure enter into it. One is Teton Jackson's outfit working out of Jackson Hole. The other is the Wild Bunch down in Wyoming in the Big Horn Mountains. The Jackson Hole crowd focuses mostly on horses and it is a slick operation. They send men west down into the Utah Mormon settlements and north into central and western Montana to each steal five or ten head a week. After collecting the horses in Jackson Hole they take about a hundred at a time and move them down the Outlaw Trail and trade them to another gang stealing horses in New Mexico, Arizona, and Northern Mexico. They just swap horses. Then they peddle the southwest horses up here to the very communities they stole the original horses from."

"What about the Wild Bunch?" asked Sheriff Tom. "They seem closer to our area."

"They are," agreed Beidler. "But they work together sometimes. Kid Curry and his Wild Bunch have the contacts in Canada and they are doing the same thing with Canadian outlaws that Teton Jackson is doing in the south. That is when they are not robbing banks and trains. But they are as much into cattle as horses. Cattle are slower to move and it takes a lot more of them than horses to make the same money. Those guys team up with a legitimate rancher and bring him unbranded calves or yearlings. Then they also get the rancher a brand that can be "worked over" for a neighboring big outfit's cattle."

Upshaw interrupted. "I don't understand the term "worked over".

"It means changing someone else's brand into your own. Take the brand the Bar V Bar (‒\/‒ for example, that can be changed to the T X T simply by adding an upright under the two bars and an upside down V to the existing V turns it into a TXT", explained the marshal. "That trick is happening more and more as there gets to be more homesteaders in the country with just a few cattle. The key to that working for the rustlers is to have a place out of the way where they can stash stock while waiting for the brands to heal up. That Hole-in-the Wall country down by Buffalo, WY is perfect for that. Then the rancher makes a drive to the railroad, sells the cattle, and spits the proceeds with the rustlers," "X" continued. "Right here in your area the thieves are a little different. Here there is a big local demand for beef. You have two or three sawmills working up Tongue River making lumber for all the new homesteaders, this Fort, new telegraph lines, Miles City, and the Northern Pacific Railroad crews. Those sawmill crews run 200+ men each that have to be fed. Then the Northern Pacific is still building west and they have to feed their grading crews. There is a new railroad pushing west out of Gillette, WY on its way to meet up with the Northern Pacific. Those crews have to be fed. I hear that the Wild Bunch has that business pretty well tied up with the butchers in a tough new town called Suggs City. Then of course we have all the Cheyenne and Crow Indians on their reservations that the Indian Department has to feed. Those cattle are trailed in and the Indians do the butchering. A whole lot of the beef from this area is not going to Omaha by train, it is eaten right here."

"But don't the butcher's know where the cattle come from?" Sheriff Irvine inquired.

"Maybe. But if they ask too many questions their local supply dries up and so the price goes higher. Most of those butchers are working on fixed price contracts to supply the crews." "X" explained. "They contract with a guy to supply them with maybe 20 carcasses a week. The carcasses come already dressed with the hides off so the butcher doesn't know whose cattle they are and doesn't care. Sometimes you will find a pile of hides, but usually the brands are cut out so you can't tell who the cattle originally belonged to."

"I just got a report this morning of a pile of hides like that over at Suggs City from an Otter Creek rancher," Sheriff Irvine offered. "But what can we do about all this thievery with the people we have is what I want to know?"

Colonel Swaine said thoughtfully: "Let's break this problem up into parts. I already outlined some of what we could do with the Cheyenne butchering, whites misbehaving on the reservation, and patrolling the reservation boundaries. What more can be done to solve this in the big picture?"

Granville stood up and stretched. "I know I will be under a lot of pressure to recommend something about the white rustlers. My membership wants to organize a Vigilance Committee and hang some folks. We've been there and done that haven't we "X"?"

"Yep," replied "X". "But I'm not so sure it would work now like it did in '65. We didn't have honest sheriffs, U.S. Marshals, a new State Legislature, and Federal Judges like we do now. While it's really hard to cover the country with as few lawmen as we got, there ain't two or three citizens a day gettin' killed like there was then. I thought we done a good a job in Virginia City, but there were a couple of those hangings that I wasn't particularly proud of."

Sitting back down Granville continued. "That is for sure. However, a couple of our "high powered" members, relatively new to the country, are accusing me about being weak on the subject. They are from North Dakota and like to do things in a big way. One is a guy named Theodore Roosevelt and the other is a Frenchman with a title, "The Marquis de Mores" I think he is called. Both have some money, run good sized outfits, and have been hit pretty hard by the rustlers. I know they are going to bring up the subject from the floor, but I'm going to try and knock that kind of talk down. It's just too easy for that kind of activity to get out of hand."

"I'm really glad to hear you say that Granville," exclaimed Col. Swaine. "We need to do this in the right way if we possibly can!"

Sheriff Irvine chimed in. "I agree, but in most cases my deputies and I are out manned and outgunned when it comes to taking on a major gang. Those outlaws are mostly experts with a gun and a rope and they can ride anything that has hair. Most of them are game sons 'o' bitches. I need to be able to call on somebody for help! Can you do that Colonel?"

Colonel Swaine hastened to reply. "Absolutely not! The Army can't operate that way unless the President declares Martial Law. And I doubt that he will do that just for a law enforcement matter."

Sheriff Irvine turned to Granville Stuart. "What about Billy Smith and your Association stock detectives? They are all tough guys and have a reputation as man hunters. The joke is that they work for the Montana Stock Grower's Assassination."

Stuart smiled slyly. "Now Tom, you know that those boys are just brand inspectors, bean counters, and broke down cowboys. They wouldn't hurt a fly. However, if you were willing to give them deputy status, I'm sure that the Association wouldn't mind helping you out. Under your strict supervision, of course."

Sheriff Tom felt that Stuart was "pulling his leg". "I guess I sure wouldn't mind having Billy Smith with me if we were trying to take on a big outfit. We could even find a place for a bean counter or two." Tom replied dryly.

Stuart turned serious. "Let's get together after the big meeting. I intend to try and shoot down this Vigilante talk during the public meeting. "But, since I am also the Chairman of the Executive Committee, maybe we could run an operation or two with you and your deputies. We've got eyes and ears that you don't have because our members throughout the white community can feed us specific information about names and locations of bad guys. I do have a big concern about the Cheyenne Reservation and those problems. "X" and I have heard that there may be some collusion between white gangs and bad Indians. Most of that involves horses not cattle, where they hide stolen horses on the reservation and pay the Indians in whiskey. Because our information gatherers can't search the Reservation, we have a big information gap there. Upshaw and Rowland, do you have any ideas about that?"

Col Swaine weighed in. "Captain Casey, can the Cheyenne Scouts gather that kind of information?"

"Boy, I don't know," mused Casey. "I don't see how we could keep it quiet. Once the word got out that we were asking, it would be all over the villages in less than a day."

Shaking his head, Bill Rowland supported Casey. "Colonel. That is not a good idea. This has to be kept completely secret. When you are dealing with Cheyennes, loyalty to family, military society, and tribe comes before white man law. Hell, you don't know that certain members of the Cheyenne Scouts or their families aren't involved. I know that some of them have been in on the cattle butchering."

Agent Upshaw turned to Stuart, "I may have an idea, but I will need some help from your Association and Bill Rowland to pull it off. And it must be kept absolutely quiet."

Stuart quickly replied, "I'll listen."

Upshaw started. "As I see it we have an information problem with hungry Indians killing white man cattle, bad Indians working with bad white guys to steal and hide horses on the reservation, and maybe Indians butchering cattle and trading the carcasses to white men for whiskey. To find out good information we need someone who has a good reason to travel on and off the reservation, is familiar with both Cheyennes and whites, and is honest and reliable enough to provide useful information to me, Sheriff Irvine and the Association, or the Army."

"Where in hell are we going to get someone like that? Sheriff Irvine inquired.

"I'll get to that in a minute," Upshaw continued. "I asked Mr. Stuart a few minutes ago, why his organization would pay thousands of dollars to kill wolves to preserve his member's cattle, but wouldn't donate a few cattle to keep Indians fed. While I appreciate his answer, it doesn't solve the problem. Suppose Mr. Stuart could divert part of that "predator fund" into some money that I could use to purchase cattle from ranchers neighboring the reservation to supplement what I get from the Indian Department. That would require someone to go around the perimeter of the reservation getting bids on small groups of cattle from the local ranchers. He would be welcome at the ranches because it would be a way to sell cattle without the time and expense of making a drive to the railroad. He would be very welcome on the reservation because he would be bringing food for starving people. In the course of his travels a lot of information useful to the Association, Sheriff Irvine, and the Indian Police could be accumulated."

"That is an intriguing idea, Stuart said enthusiastically. "But, that takes a really special person. Who have you got in mind?"

"We will need Bill Rowland to help us out on that." Agent Upshaw looked at Rowland. "What about one of your sons,

Bill? I was thinking of either Willis or Bill Jr. Willis serves as a part time interpreter for me and Bill Jr. is a member of the Indian Police. All of you live and are known and respected on the reservation."

"God, Upshaw. You are really putting me and my family on the spot," Rowland protested. "That could get somebody killed if it wasn't handled just right."

"On the other hand it could be a huge help for both the Indians and the neighboring ranchers," argued Upshaw. "If we don't get this solved, there may be lots people killed on both sides."

"I can't commit my kids. They are grown men and need to make up their own minds. Of the two, Willis would be the best choice. He has the kind of personality that everybody likes, served with the Cheyenne Scouts when just a seventeen year old kid, and has the maturity to keep his mouth shut." Rowland finished. "But I don't know that he wants to be a spy."

"We don't need to know now, Bill," commented Stuart. "If we are going to do this, a lot of groundwork needs to get done first. But, if Willis is willing that would be a big help."

"I could make him a deputy and put him on my payroll," offered Sheriff Irvine.

"And for every rustler we take down, that ought to be worth at least equal to fifty wolves from the Association Predator Fund," added Stuart.

"Alright! Alright! I'll see if he wants to do it," Rowland said in an annoyed tone. "If he does I'll send him down here to talk to Irvine and Col. Swaine. But, I don't like putting my family in harm's way!"

"It would sure be for the greater good of this new country if we could get these problems under control," remarked Col.

Swaine. "Gentlemen, I think we have made substantial progress in working out some potential solutions. What have we learned? We all agree that there is a serious problem with cattle rustling and horse stealing in this area. Both whites and Indians are probably involved. Since some of rustlers operate in large gangs, the county law enforcement needs assistance with information gathering and operational reinforcement when targeting these gangs. They also have little practical authority on the Crow and Cheyenne reservations. If this cattle butchering and horse stealing isn't stopped the situation could lead to a war between angry settlers and hungry Indians. That could cause hundreds of casualties among both sides. As the party responsible for protecting both Indians and settlers, the Army has a vested interest in making sure such a war doesn't take place. The Army will commit to full cooperation with the civilian authorities when it comes to law enforcement involving Indian crimes or crimes on the reservation. We can't however use federal troops to fight white gangs off the reservation. Between the resources of the Stock Growers Association and the Sheriff and his folks, I think there are sufficient forces to meet the white gang problem without the Army. Let's wind up this meeting and go our separate ways and put these ideas into practice. Perhaps we can meet again during the August Stock Growers Meeting to work out any unresolved issues."

The meeting broke up and Sheriff Irvine secured the mayor's horse and buggy and returned them to the County Barn. His head was spinning with what he had learned today and the possibilities it promised. He was most pleased with the Indian piece of the puzzle. The willingness of the Army to transport prisoners, back up the Indian Police, patrol the reservation boundary, and provide information was huge. If Agent Upshaw and Bill Rowland could convince Willis Rowland to become a deputy, he could foresee some major advances in cutting down the criminal activity in that part of the county. Most problematic for the Sheriff was the conversation between Granville Stuart and himself. Was Stuart really going to let him supervise the MSG stock detectives during operations? Would detainees be brought in to Miles City for trial, or hanged on the spot? What did the Sheriff himself think about vigilante activity in his county? How should he react to operations by MSG stock detectives he had not supervised? Sheriff Irvine was torn between wanting to do everything "by the book" and knowing that if he did the problem would not be solved. He decided to wait until his meeting with Stuart after the MSG Spring Meeting before wrestling with the issue.

Chapter 4. Man of Two Tribes - April 1876 to April 1880

William Rowland was the first white man to settle into the Tongue River/Upper Rosebud area. He had run away from home as a teenager and joined the Southern Cheyenne tribe in Indian Territory. He eventually married a Southern Cheyenne woman and started a ranch in Nebraska on the Plum River (Platte). There he got into a terrible fight with three of her brothers, Hard Robe, Lone Bear, and Little Fish and shot one of them. During the fight Rowland was hit in the head with a hatchet and knocked unconscious and left for dead. His wife's brothers burned down his ranch and took his wife back to a Cheyenne village. Sometime later he regained consciousness and made his way to a neighboring ranch and a subsequently to a doctor. The doctor treated his head injury, but the hair grew in white over the scar. Later, he would joke with the Cheyennes that he was a rich man because his head had been filled with silver. With his ranch gone, he joined the U.S. Army at Fort Laramie as a Cheyenne language interpreter. He found his wife in a Cheyenne village near that Fort and they were reunited. From that point on Rowland was a key player in the Army/Northern Cheyenne saga that would play out to their final surrender.

The interpreter was the highest paid civilian person on an Army Post, normally second only to the Post Commander. They had the same status as officer's children and were allowed to attend the same post schools. Therefore their children were some of the best educated people on the frontier. Bill Rowland made sure his children took full advantage of those opportunities. Interpreters had a unique insight into the U.S. Army strategy from their daily contact with the highest ranking military officers. As the essential go-between between the leaders of opposing military forces, interpreters had to know the language and customs of both sides to convey accurately the **intent** of both

Indians and whites. They also needed to be a good judge of white and red character to serve as a trusted intermediary. As such they acquired a broad and deep understanding of Army/Indian Department policy and its effect on their Indian subjects.

Bill Rowland was involved in nearly every significant engagement with the Cheyenne tribe after the Custer Fight. He was in charge of scouts with Gen. Ranald S. Mackenzie when Dull Knife's village was captured in November of 1876 on the North Fork of Powder River. Following that fight he went back to Ft. Keogh to advise Col. Nelson Miles. In late December of 1876, he brought Col. Miles the information that a large band of Sioux and Cheyenne were camped on Tongue River in the vicinity of the mouth of Hanging Woman Creek, Miles and Rowland immediately started south with a troop column in early January, 1877. They then fought the Battle of the Butte, sometimes called the Battle of Wolf Mountain on January 7, 1877 near present day Birney, MT. Between these two battles the Cheyennes lost most of their horses, food, and lodges.

The Cheyennes were worn out and starving. After a miserable winter on Powder River, the Dull Knife and Little Wolf bands surrendered at Fort Robinson, Nebraska in April 1877. They were treated well while the Army tried to decide what to do with them. In the meantime, there remained at least half of the tribe still considered hostile. During the Battle of the Butte, Miles had captured four Cheyenne women which he took with him when he withdrew back to Fort Keogh. Using Rowland (Long Knife) and Broughier (Big Leggings) as interpreters, Gen. Miles sent Sweet Woman, one of the captives out to meet with Two Moons' band and convince them to surrender. After prolonged negotiations, Two Moons brought in his band and surrendered to Miles at Fort Keogh in late April 1877.

Rowland was then sent to Fort Robinson to help move those Cheyennes to Indian Territory in Oklahoma. At Fort Robinson, the Dull Knife and Little Wolf bands were joined by a few families from Little Chief's band who were not intermarried with the Sioux. When these bands heard that Two Moons was being allowed to stay at Fort Keogh, they refused to go south. After tense negotiations Rowland was told to tell the Cheyennes to try the Darlington Agency for a year. If they still didn't like it there they could come back to the Pine Ridge Agency in South Dakota or maybe go to join Two Moons. Given this promise, Rowland accompanied this group of 600 to 700 Cheyennes south to the Darlington Agency in Oklahoma. Darlington Agency was the Agency for the Southern Cheyennes, and while the Northern Cheyennes spoke the same language and shared many customs and relations with the Southerners, they had actually functioned as separate tribes for over fifty years. Following safe delivery of this large band, Rowland returned to Fort Keogh.

During Rowland's absence, Col. Miles troops were called out to fight Chief Joseph and Miles asked Two Moons' warriors if they would like to join the Army as scouts and fight the Nez Pierce. They fought well and Miles would later use their service as a reason to form a new Northern Cheyenne Reservation. This success led to the more or less permanent formation of the Cheyenne Scouts. The Scouts would see service for about the next twenty years and were disbanded in 1896.

The move of the Northern Cheyennes to the Darlington Agency was a disaster. In the first month in the new southern climate, 150 of them came down with fever and ague. The sickness continued to the point that by the spring of 1878 almost one third of the Northern Cheyennes were dead. Little Wolf went to the Agent and told him that he was going to take his people home. When the agent refused to allow them to go, they waited for about another month and then left the Agency. The rest of the summer they marched north fighting soldiers, cowboys, and settlers, finally crossing the Platte River in October where the bands split. They had fought and marched for nearly 700 miles.

Little Wolf proceeded north and hid out in the Nebraska Sand Hills until spring and then headed for Powder River. On the Little Missouri he was met by Lieutenant Clark and some of the Cheyenne Scouts. After some negotiations, Little Wolf agreed to accompany Clark to Fort Keogh. There Miles welcomed Little Wolf and accepted his surrender in April 1879. Miles then promptly enlisted all the young men as Cheyenne Scouts to pursue a few small bands of hostile Sioux who were still active in the area. As Scouts employed by the Army, Miles could pay the young men $20 per month and rations, which would allow them to feed their families, and avoid the tender mercies of the Indian Department. Bill Rowland expertly handled the negotiations with Little Wolf and arranged for his seventeen year old son, Willis Rowland (Long Forehead) to serve as the First Sergeant/Interpreter for the Cheyenne Scouts.

Figure 12. Little Wolf and Dull Knife, Courtesy of the Smithsonian Institute

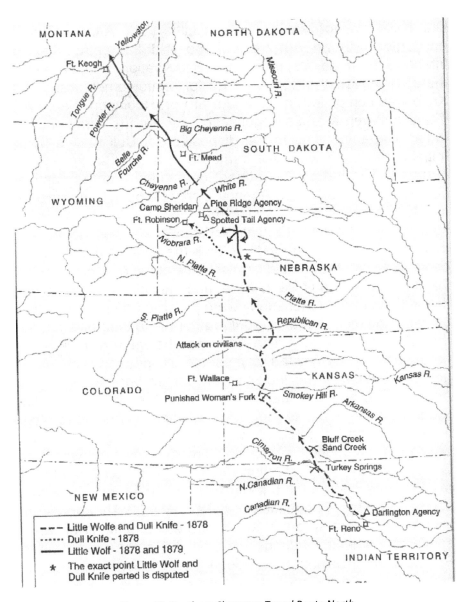

Figure 10. Northern Cheyenne Travel Route North

Dull Knife did not fare as well as Little Wolf. After a chance encounter with an Army patrol, he told the patrol that he intended to head for the Sioux Reservation and surrender there. However, the troops called for reinforcements and Dull Knife was compelled to surrender at Fort Robinson, Nebraska. There followed a tense negotiation between the Army and the Indian Department as to the disposition of Dull Knife's band. Initially, the band was well treated and housed in an unused barracks. The Indian Department demanded that the captives be returned to Darlington Agency, partly for budgetary reasons. In addition, some of the young men had murdered and raped settlers near Oberlin, Kansas and that state was demanding their return for trial. The Indians took the position that they had been told that they could come home after a year in Indian Territory if they didn't like it there, and they didn't. Furthermore, they didn't get the rations they were promised and so many had got sick and died that they would rather die in their own country than in Indian Territory. The Army was between a "rock and a hard place." They wanted to preserve the peace which wasn't going to happen if the Indians were forced back to Darlington Agency. The Indian Department would not let them go to Pine Ridge Agency, because they said they had no rations for them there. The standoff continued while the Commandant awaited a decision from higher authority. Communication between the Cheyennes and the Army was very poor. The Fort did not have a Cheyenne interpreter but did have a Sioux interpreter and some of the Cheyennes spoke Sioux. Therefore the translations went through two interpreters, neither of which spoke the other's language well. At the same time, William Rowland was visiting Pine Ridge Reservation with his son James Rowland to find out for Col. Miles which Sioux bands may be missing from that reservation. When he found out that Dull Knife was being held at Fort Robinson and the interpreter problem, he sent his son James to the Fort to interpret between Dull Knife and the Commandant, Captain Wessels. However, by the time he arrived, Captain Wessels had already received orders from higher headquarters that the decision had been made that the Cheyennes would be sent south to Darlington Agency. Furthermore, some of the warriors must be sent to Kansas to stand trial for murder and rape. It then fell to James Rowland to inform the Cheyennes of the decision. To say that the Indians reacted badly would be an understatement.

They absolutely refused to go south. Captain Wessells then ordered the Indians to be locked in the barracks and given no food, water, or fuel. Despite James Rowland's repeated objections, the Army continued the starvation policy. Finally, the Indians tried a breakout during a bitter winter night which was in effect, a mass suicide attempt. Initially, the breakout was surprisingly effective. Most of the Cheyennes made it out of the Fort and scattered to the surrounding hills only to be hunted down and shot or frozen to death. Some were recaptured and a few including Dull Knife made their way to the Pine Ridge Agency. There William Rowland reported the details of the slaughter to the Agent and arranged for Dull Knife and about 58 survivors to stay at Pine Ridge. Of the approximately 150 Cheyennes captured with Dull Knife, 64 were killed, 20 sent south to Kansas for trial, and the above 58 were allowed to stay with the Sioux. A few more were missing and presumed dead. Following the creation of the Tongue River Reservation, most of the survivors made their way to their final home on Rosebud Creek.

The year after the Dull Knife breakout, William Rowland retired from his duties as the Fort Keogh interpreter and established a ranch on Muddy Creek, a tributary to Rosebud Creek, on what a few years later would become the Cheyenne Reservation. His son Willis, continued as the First Sergeant of the Cheyenne Scouts for another two years. Bill Rowland continued to be actively involved in promoting good relations between Cheyennes and their white neighbors for a number of years. His son Willis eventually served the tribe as Tribal Chairman.

Figure 11. (Left to Right) White Bull, Bill Rowland, and O.D. Wheeler. Photo Courtesy of the Montana Historical Society

Chapter 5. Man of Two Tribes – The Son April 1890

While the "powers that be" at Fort Keogh were debating the future of Montana in general and Custer County in particular, Willis (Willie) Rowland was minding his own business on the family ranch on Muddy Creek, Montana. Today he was on a big "circle" looking for Rowland cattle following the end of a long Montana winter. He needed to get a rough count of how many had survived and what kind of shape they were in. While the winter had not been especially harsh, the location of the Rowland ranch was not the best positioned for winter grazing.

The ranch was in a beautiful grass filled valley surrounded by high pine covered hills with red shale outcrops. Muddy Creek was a slow moving meandering watercourse fed by springs along most of its length. The ranch received a generous amount of moisture due to its higher altitude and favorable geographical location. However, the same factors which made it a premier "grass" ranch for most of the year, were not helpful during winter. Because the creek flowed mostly north and west, the high hills to the east and south meant that the valley was one of the last areas to see snow leave in the spring. Even by mid-April, deep snow drifts still lay in the tree covered areas and only the few east and south facing slopes were dry.

The cattle were mostly located near the creek and on the lower slopes where the snow had melted and exposed the previous season's still nutritious dry grass. Spots of green had begun to appear where the sun shone the longest and the cattle were hungrily devouring the green shoots wherever they appeared. Cows were thin, but for the most part in relatively good condition but they were too few in number. In another month the country would support ten times the number of cattle the family owned. While his dad had made a good living as an Army interpreter and now drew a pension for his many years of service, the large family meant that money was still tight. The family was too large for this cow herd to support.

Willie finished his "circle" and rode on into the corral and unsaddled his good bay horse. After rubbing the horse down with a saddle blanket, he pitched the horse some of the precious hay that they had cut the previous summer. Taking the tally book from his pocket, Willy counted up the "picket fences" (entries were marked in the tally book with an upright for each cow up to four with a slash for the fifth through the previous four) and was pleased to note that only three of the 144 cows were missing. There were a couple of draws that he hadn't checked so it was possible he could have a full count. Figuring that his dad would be happy with that, he closed up the tally book and headed for the house.

Home was five log cabins hooked together with a teepee pitched outside. The cabins were made of pine logs about 12 inches thick and each cabin was fifteen to thirty feet long with only one window. Logs were chinked with a combination of yellow clay and cow manure. The roofs were boards covered with tar paper followed by another layer of boards. The boards were topped with red shale up to about four inches deep. As the shale eroded, tufts of grass and an occasional prickly pear cactus had begun grow out of the shale.

One cabin served as the kitchen/dining room and had a Majestic wood cook stove, barrels holding flour and sugar, open shelves with canned goods, and a plank topped table about 15 feet long, with benches on the sides and wood chairs on the end. Of the five cabins only the kitchen had a wood floor, which Mother Rowland kept scrupulously clean.

Another cabin attached to the kitchen functioned as the living room. It had a generous sized fireplace flanked by large boxes for firewood with hinged tops covered by buffalo hide robes. The boxes served the dual functions of storing wood and seating places for the living room. Several rifles rested on nails driven into the logs. The mantle of the fireplace held a prehistoric buffalo skull nearly twice the size of a modern buffalo. It was painted with the Morning Star embalm of the Cheyenne Tribe. A Scottish claymore hung above the buffalo skull with the blade pointing down. Bill Rowland used to joke that he had hung the claymore over the buffalo skull to remind his wife of who was in charge. Nonetheless, visitors noted the sharp skinning knife Mother Rowland kept in the wide belt around her waist and often remarked how soft spoken Daddy Rowland was when he addressed her.

Of the three smaller remaining cabins, two were sleeping rooms and one was a store room. Mama and Daddy Rowland occupied one of the sleeping rooms and the two girls the other one. Zachary and James Rowland were grown men and had families of their own and had already moved out. That left Willie and the five younger boys to sleep in the teepee which was another reason he was anxious to move out.

The next day Willie went looking for the three head of cows he had missed on his first tally. First he rode up Muddy Creek to the teepee of Little Wolf, the Cheyenne "Sweet Medicine" Chief who had led the tribe on the fight north from Oklahoma. Little Wolf was Rowland's nearest neighbor and a good friend of the Rowland family. He now had very little contact with most Cheyennes since his self-imposed banishment in 1880. It happened this way: Little Wolf had two wives, the younger of the two had been the subject of flirtatious attention from another Cheyenne man named Starving Elk. The two men had argued during the return from Oklahoma, and Little Wolf had warned the man to leave his wife alone. One night in a drunken jealous rage he shot and killed Starving Elk in the Sutler's Store at Fort Keogh. Cheyenne law dictated that any Cheyenne who killed another Cheyenne was subject to banishment from the tribe. Upon recovering from his drunken state, Little Wolf who was then living on Tongue River, banished himself from contact with other Cheyennes. Before he left he told people that he could not remain as a Chief and was leaving for Muddy Creek with his wives. If the Army or the other Old Man Chiefs wanted anything more of him he would be on the Muddy. After some discussion the Army decided to let the Cheyennes settle the issue among themselves. From that time forward, Little Wolf's best friends were the Rowland Family and the Walt Alderson family who settled on the head of Muddy Creek following their devolution of their partnership with John Zook from their ranch on Tongue River.

Figure 12. Little Wolf in Old Age. Photo Courtesy of the National Archives, Smithsonian Institute

Approaching Little Wolf's teepee, Willie called out a greeting in Cheyenne. Little Wolf's older wife appeared and asked what he wanted. When he asked for Little Wolf, she grunted, returned to the teepee, and Little Wolf stepped out with a big smile on his face, obviously glad to have some male company.

"How are you, Long Forehead?" Little Wolf asked using Willie's Cheyenne name.

"Very well, Father," replied Long Forehead using the term of respect duly accorded to an older Cheyenne man.

Since no polite conservation with a Cheyenne should come directly to the point, Long Forehead asked how the rations drawn a week before were holding out, informed Little Wolf that his father had gone to Miles City and was expected back tonight, talked about the warming days, and finally asked obliquely if his wives had seen any Rowland cows while gathering wood. Little Wolf reported that his younger wife had seen two cows in the draw south of the teepee, but he didn't know if they belonged to Long Knife (Bill Rowland) or Walt Alderson. Long Forehead said he would ride up and see and thanked the old chief.

As Willie rode south (up the creek) he thought of how sad it was that Little Wolf should come to such poor circumstances after all that he had given to the Cheyenne tribe. He soon located the two missing cows and started them down Muddy Creek toward home.

Willie wondered what news his father had picked up at Fort Keogh and Miles City and hoped his dad was bringing a couple of cans of peaches and some fresh raisins. After a long winter, he was craving fruit. Every time he thought about raisins, he chuckled, remembering his old Cheyenne Scout friend, White Bull. He had liked raisins so much that when the Cheyennes were encouraged to farm, he had planted raisins and was very disappointed when they didn't come up.

Dropping the cows at the house, Willie continued down the Creek for another four miles to the Muddy Post Office and Trading Post operated by the Sy Young family. The Post Office was a 2x4 shack with shelves made into cubby holes. From the inside looking out without the letters in each hole, the whole place looked more like a chicken house than a post office. The customer side was a brass panel with various size small doors which provided access to an individual box. To check his box required Willie to insert a brass key with the #2 stamped on it into the door, open it, and check the Rowland's box which was #2. It should have been #1 because William Rowland was the first settler, but Sy Young had appropriated that box for the very good reason that he was the Postmaster. Since there was no mail in the Rowland slot, he proceeded on to the Trading Post where he was greeted by Sy Young, the proprietor.

"Howdy, Willie. How are things up the creek?"

Willie extended his hand and replied, "Good Sy, I'm sure tired of winter though. But, I'm not sure which I like less, snow or mud. Got news of anything going on?"

"Well, I'm hearing that there's been a lot of cattle butchering going on. And I heard that the Crows are raising hell about losing a bunch of horses." Sy commented.

Willie's head jerked up sharply, "Did the Cheyennes take'em? We don't need trouble like that over here."

Sy thought a minute. "You know, I heard it two ways. The first was that it was white men who stole 'em and the second was that it was the Cheyennes. The Crows said that they tracked them across Rotten Grass and Lodge Grass creeks and up Grey Blanket to the Cheyenne Reservation line and then over the Rosebud divide."

"Wait a minute," Willie objected. "That's pretty far south to be Cheyennes, it's barely on the reservation and white men are pretty thick on Upper Tongue River. I don't think Cheyennes would go that way."

"Yeah, I know," said Sy. "That's why some people thought it could be white men. It looked like maybe they were headed for Deadwood or Spearfish. They need lots of horses over there and buyers ain't too particular about checking brands."

"Well, I'll tell my brother Bill Jr. about it. He's on the Cheyenne Police Force. Agent Upshaw would be really upset if it was Cheyennes or even if it wasn't them and the Crows blamed them for the stealing. The Crows and Cheyennes don't get along very well anyway and an incident like this doesn't help. Dad and Upshaw should be home from Miles City tonight. I probably need to go to Lame Deer tomorrow and see Upshaw and talk to him about it. Other than that, I'll mind my own business. Anything else," Willie asked?

"Bob Ferguson was in today to get his mail. He was complaining about his cattle tally being short about a dozen head. Hadn't found any deads, just cattle missing. He figured that Dull Knife's band that just got in last fall from Pine Ridge had probably ate 'em. I think he's probably right."

Willie shook his head angrily, "I wouldn't be surprised. Those folks are pretty hungry over there. A ration of forty head of cattle every two weeks just ain't enough for the whole reservation. Upshaw has asked for more money from the Indian Department but they say Congress hasn't authorized it. If something doesn't change this whole reservation is going to blow up."

"Yeah, more and more Indians are coming to this reservation from other places but they only have the amount of rations for the original bunch," Sy observed. "Hell, some of them are even killing their horses for food and you know how the Cheyennes hate that."

"When it dries up and it gets a lot harder to follow a trail, I would bet that the butchering picks up," predicted Willie gloomily. "By the way, have you seen any drunk Cheyennes come in here? Upshaw wants me to keep an eye out for that stuff. There is starting to be a lot of whiskey selling going on, especially around Rabbit Town. He is really hot to keep it off the reservation."

"No, I haven't seen much of that here, but it's a pretty long ride from Rabbit Town and Ashland to here. I would guess by the time they get to my store they are pretty well sobered up. You can sure tell by looking at the squaws though, if they've got black eyes and are all beat to shit, their man has probably been into the whiskey." Sy shook his head in disgust. "They ought to hang a white man who sells whiskey to Indians, they can't handle that stuff."

Willie answered, "I sure agree with that. Have you heard where they are getting the whiskey?"

"Not that I would want to name," Sy replied. "They got a couple of bars over at Ashland, I guess anybody could buy whiskey there and resell it to the Cheyennes."

"Well, if you see that kind of shit happening over here, let me know, maybe I can get the Crazy Dogs to deal with it. That's the best way. If that doesn't work then I guess we can try the Indian Police."

With that, Willie said goodbye started the ride home. As he rode, he pondered his conversation with Sy Young. As a young man looking forward to getting married and maybe starting a family, he was concerned about the neighborhood and how it seemed to be deteriorating. Most of the Cheyennes were good people, just trying to live their lives in a rapidly changing time. However, like any large group, they had their own bad actors. Most of these were just criminals and would be outlaws in any society – red or white. The ones that Willie worried about were the young men who were trapped between the old ways and new realities.

In traditional Cheyenne culture, men had two main functions – protecting the people from harm and providing food for their families. To Cheyennes food meant meat and meat required hunting. With the buffalo gone and most of the wild game on the reservation hunted out, traditional young Cheyenne men had no way to perform this basic function within the confines of the reservation. Also, as a defeated people, the protection function of the warrior was no longer an option. As such, young Cheyenne men were, in effect, emasculated. They had no game to hunt and no enemies to fight. There was no way to "prove" themselves to their family, future wives, band, or tribe in the traditional ways. Further, wealth and stature in the Cheyenne tribe were still measured in coups and horses rather than white man's cattle or money. Willie well understood the "young man problem", because he was living it and he was much better prepared than the average Cheyenne to deal with the white man's world.

The pressure on young men to provide meat for their families was intense. They were allowed to hunt on the reservation without restriction with the result that there was little game left. But many of the reservation borders were not fenced or even known in 1890. Except for the eastern border marked by Tongue River, the lines were invisible to both whites and Indians. It was common practice for white settlers and even some Indians to exercise a "squatter's right" (occupy a piece of land prior to formal survey), and then exercise their homestead rights when the survey crews made it to their area. As game became scarce, Indian hunters pushed the limits of the reservation and beyond.

Horses provided another source of temptation for the young men. Cheyenne culture encouraged the accumulation of horses through warfare – stealing from the enemy. They historically stole horses from the Crows, Blackfeet, Pawnee, and Ute tribes and of course later the whites. Even after reservations were formed there continued to be occasional horse raiding parties between the tribes. White settlers were an obvious and easy target for enterprising traditional young men seeking wealth and status. Because horses were equally valued by both Indians and whites, they could also serve as a common currency between the races.

The final temptation in this volatile mix was the proliferation of whiskey sellers on the periphery of the reservation. Indian introduction to alcohol by whites had started long before the reservations were formed. It was well known by both Indian and white leadership that many Indians had an outsized negative reaction to alcohol compared to whites. The cause was probably genetic because whites had developed some resistance to alcohol effects over hundreds of years while Indians had none. Nonetheless, many Cheyennes developed a taste for whiskey which caused havoc with anyone coming in contact with them when drinking. Under the influence they would beat up family members, make unreasonable trades of horses, highly prized possessions, and even wives and daughters to attain a modest amount of liquor. For these reasons, whiskey and other alcohol were prohibited in most Cheyenne camps by the chiefs and absolutely outlawed on the reservation by the Indian Department Agents.

When Willie was about a mile from home, he spotted the remaining missing cow which filled out his tally. She was a big old roan longhorn cow with one horn missing and Willie had mixed feelings about finding her. He was glad to find there were no "deads" for the winter, but if they were going to lose one, he had hoped it would be her. She had the reputation of being an old "rip" that was always willing to charge a rider, throw her tail up and lead the other cows to the tall timber, or otherwise make life miserable for any cowboy who had the misfortune of trying to deal with her. When she saw Willie, she turned toward him with a snort and shook her head at him. Willie grinned and took down his rope from the saddle, and approached her at a high trot, swinging the rope. He figured she would head for the timber to lose him so he positioned his horse between her and the nearest group of trees. Fortunately, she wheeled and started up the creek at a high lope, moving toward more cows about a half a mile away which was where he wanted her to go. When she reached the other cows, Willie stopped his pursuit and moved away perpendicular to her direction of travel. He then made a wide circle away from the group of cows to let her calm down and let her herd instinct kick in. She stayed with the herd and dropped her head to graze. He then headed to the corral and home.

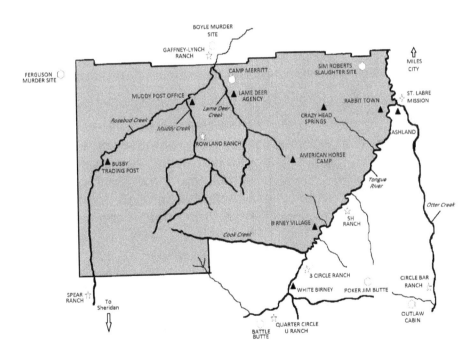

Figure 13. Northern Cheyenne Reservation and Adjacent Area

Chapter 6. The Stock Growers Meeting

Granville Stuart gaveled the sixth Spring Meeting of the Montana Stock Growers Association to order on Monday morning at 09:00 in the MacQueen House ball room. The Pledge of Allegiance was recited, an opening prayer was said, and a full house was seated as the meeting began. The minutes of the previous meeting were read and approved. The Treasurer's report was read. Several questions were raised about the amount of money paid for predator control, the future of the program, and associated issues. Stuart ruled that these questions were out of order at this time but promised to allow the questions to be raised under old business after the agenda was approved. The Treasurer completed his report and the report was approved.

Figure 14. Granville Stuart. Photo Courtesy of the Montana Historical Society

Stuart then moved on to the President's report. He noted that the main purpose of the Spring Meeting was to organize and schedule the Montana Stock Growers' approved roundups. He reported that the Roundup Committee had developed a preliminary plan which would be published that afternoon. The Roundup Committee would hear objections and suggestions that evening and the final schedule would be approved by the General Membership the next day. Northern Pacific Railroad had requested some time to address the membership on the subject of a new and much improved railroad cattle car. Stewart had seen the car and thought it had possibilities and recommended Northern Pacific be added to the agenda. The car would be parked in Miles City for the next three days for perusal by the membership. He also reported that the Brand Inspection Committee had developed a list of rules for the distribution of brands. These had been submitted to the new State Legislature and were adopted without exception.

As Stuart attempted to move on to new business, Member Theodore Roosevelt from Medora, North Dakota rose from his seat and was recognized.

Figure 15. Theodore Roosevelt. Public Domain

He began, "Fellow stockman, I rise to bring before this historic gathering a motion to approve the following resolution:

"Be it resolved, that the Montana Stock Growers, having suffered severe and outrageous depredations against our property, raise a force of honest stockmen and remove the thieves and outlaws from our midst by force of arms."

Figure 16. Marquis De Mores. Photo Courtesy of the Montana Historical Society

The motion was immediately seconded by the Marquis de Mores, also from Medora, North Dakota. The motion was met by thunderous applause and pandemonium reigned for over five minutes.

Stuart waited until the initial impact died down and then gaveled the meeting back to order. He recognized Judge Stevell, the Federal Judge for the State of Montana. Judge Strevell opposed the motion, arguing that such action could put the newly formed State of Montana in a bad light. He urged that respect for civil law and order be maintained and that

Montana demonstrate that the State could govern itself without resorting to extralegal means. Other members countered with the demand that something must be done to control the thieves and save the cattle industry. Col. Swaine rose to point out the Army would oppose any such action by the Association which had the effect of endangering the peace between settlers and Indians.

Finally Stuart struck the gavel sharply and addressed the assembly, "Fellow Stock Growers, I fully understand and sympathize with those of you who want to take direct action to eliminate the scourge of thievery and banditry which has afflicted our industry. The Montana Stock Growers should vigorously defend any Member who uses force in the defense of home and herd. Distances between ranch and town are vast and the numbers of civil law enforcement are pitifully few. As you all know, I participated in a successful vigilance operation over twenty years ago to clean up the gold fields from the murderers and road agents which afflicted us. However, that was then, this is now. We now have a State Legislature, Federal Judge, U.S. Marshall, and elected sheriffs in all counties. Late last year Montana attained statehood. That means a Governor, State Legislature, State Courts, and a state wide police force.

These outlaw bands are well organized, well mounted, and well-armed. In addition they have a network of small ranchers, homesteaders, and tradesmen who sometimes provide support for them. These are mostly family men trying to support their wives and children. If an operation was to shoot or hang some of these family men or God forbid, injure a member of their families, this organization would lose public support and the whole operation could devolve into a big cattlemen versus small cattlemen confrontation. Remember, we all operate on public lands and in the United States, vote counts rule. There will always be more small operators than large ones.

I urge caution and patience. Give our new state a chance to get organized. It is not an all or nothing game. Table this motion until next year. We can support and supplement our local law enforcement officers with our stock detectives. I give you my word. If these depredations are not substantially reduced by next summer, I will support a direct action operation and will lead that effort myself."

With that speech, the question was called and the motion was defeated, but by a bare majority vote. Stuart had prevailed but it was obvious that cattlemen were still upset. The meeting proceeded with the publishing of the roundup schedule, some discussion of the predator bounties, and the Northern Pacific rail car and freight charge issues. That night a number of parties were held, whiskey consumed, vast sums of money passed over the poker tables, and a grand time was had by all. The next day Stuart gaveled the meeting to a close and the stockman scattered to do their required shopping before heading home.

Chapter 7. Room 26

The next morning Sheriff Tom Irvine received a visit from Teddy Blue Abbott, Granville Stuart's soon to be son-in-law. Stuart requested his presence at a meeting in Room 26 of the MacQueen House at 01:00 that afternoon. Tom arrived promptly and was ushered into the room and amazed to find also present the following characters:

Granville Stuart – President, Montana Stock Growers.

J.W. Strevell – Federal Judge, State of Montana

"X" Beidler – U.S. Marshall, State of Montana.

Col. Peter Swaine – Commandant, Fort Keogh.

R.L. Upshaw – Indian Agent, Northern Cheyenne Reservation.

William Rowland – Retired Cheyenne/English Army Interpreter.

"Billy" Smith – Chief Stock Detective, Montana Stock Growers Association.

"Teddy Blue" Abbot – Granville Stuart's Son-in-Law.

Granville Stuart's visage was grim as he addressed the group.

"Gentlemen, you were all present at the meeting two days ago when a proposal to form a Montana Stock Growers Association Vigilance Committee to deal with the rampant thievery problem was defeated. I publicly opposed that motion, not because I didn't think the direct action was necessary, but because of who proposed it. Such an action has to be very tightly controlled, known only to a very few people, and conducted by serious highly competent men. While I respect the men who proposed the action, they are amateurs and adventurers in these endeavors. To announce to the all the outlaws and thieves in the country that such a committee will be formed

64

precludes any element of surprise which is necessary for success. However, you saw the tenor of the meeting. There was a clear majority for a Vigilance Committee, and only by the barest of margins was it defeated. We could easily lose control and several undisciplined vigilance mobs form. You heard me vow to lead a Montana Stock Growers effort next year if things didn't improve. I need the people in this room to help me avoid that course of action."

Judge Strevell spoke up. "What are you asking us to do, Granville?"

Stuart continued. "Gentlemen, the people in this room constitute as much of the duly elected or appointed law enforcement authority as can be found in this new state. I propose that we form a small group, not more than twenty men, to target and eliminate the worst of the worst outlaws by direct action!"

"No!" exclaimed Strevell. "Have you lost your mind? What exactly do you mean by direct action? What about the rule of law? Who would select the targets?"

"X" Beidler answered, "You would, Judge."

Stuart continued. "Hear me out. Direct action means that we shoot or hang every targeted man on the spot. Only the worst of the worst will be killed. A Jury consisting of a Federal Judge, a U.S. Marshall, and the elected Sheriff of the local county must unanimously pass judgment for selection. The Judge runs the Jury and sets the rules of evidence. But, we don't have to have lengthy trials, missing or compromised witnesses, and the jurisdictional issues of a formal legal process. Once a selection is made, we will follow the criminal to the gates of hell, Montana, Wyoming, Dakotas, or Canada. That is the plan, are you in or out? I need your answer, gentlemen."

"Your plan is intriguing, Granville," Judge Strevell opined hesitantly. "However, I have concerns about plan execution. Good on the ground judgment will be required to separate the worst outlaws from small fry or wholly innocent men who happen to be in the wrong place. Who will lead this execution squad?"

"I will," calmly replied Stuart.

The room was stunned. Judge Strevell was the first to recover. "Are you sure, Granville? At age 60 you are no spring chicken any more. It means a whole summer or more of hard riding and fighting in the worst of weather over the whole State of Montana!"

"I'll try and squeeze out one more summer," Stuart said dryly. "Besides, I wouldn't delegate something this important to anybody else. Having done this before, I know the pitfalls, the kind of men we need, the nature of our opponents, the geography, and most of all the people in this State. We will clean up this new State and make it a fit place to raise our children and grandchildren! What is your pleasure, gentlemen? Are you in or out?"

A vote was taken, Stuart's proposal gained unanimous approval, and the history of Montana was forever changed.

Following the vote, the meeting got down to the specifics of how to organize and execute the plan.

First the Selection Committee was appointed. Judge Strevell was elected Chairman, "X" Beidler, and Sheriff Tom Irvine chosen as members. Strevell was tasked with setting the rules of evidence, Beidler with proposing outlaws for inclusion on "the list", and Irvine the job of compiling and organizing the targeting information. Once on the list each target was assigned a maximum punishment. The options were warning, warning with a severe rope beating, banishment, and death by shooting or hanging.

Stuart was Chairman of the Operations Committee. He would select a group of hard riding, experienced, veteran man hunters to deal with the selectees on "the list". Assisting in this effort would be Billy Smith of the Montana Stock Growers stock detectives and Teddy Blue Abbott, Stuart's son-in-law. Billy was known as an extremely tough and experienced gunfighter who never backed down from a fight. He would ramrod the fighting element. Teddy Blue would act as Stuart's outside man, delivering confidential MSG messages to arrange for fresh horses, lodging, food, and guides along the man hunters' route. A password, the number 26 (Stuart's room number) was selected to recognize and verify those doing the Operation Committee business. It was to be used in a sentence like "I just rode 26 miles to get here," or "I passed 26 head of elk on the road" to identify a messenger.

Sheriff Tom Irvine would serve as a clearinghouse for information. An Information Committee composed of "X" Beidler and his fellow sheriffs and deputies would share information in their respective counties. However, the other sheriffs and deputies would not be appraised of the existence of the Vigilance Committee. Irvine would make a card file on each potential "selectee" noting most recent sightings, description, and known associates, to accumulate evidence for the Selection Committee and location information for the Operations Committee. He would also coordinate and fund the activities of undercover agents and informants used by the Committees.

Col. Swaine provided access to the U.S. Army Telegraph system. This was very helpful since Ft. Keogh telegraph operators could send telegrams to various Army Forts in the region including Ft. McGinnis which was next to Stuart's ranch on the Musselshell. In addition, when the Operations force was in the field, it could send and receive messages from the nearest military telegraph. A courier system was set up between Ft. Keogh and the Custer County Sheriff's Office to insure that Irvine rapidly received information. In addition, a daily courier system between Ft. Keogh and the Lame Deer Agency was established, manned by the Cheyenne Scouts.

Activities on the Cheyenne Reservation would be coordinated by Agent Upshaw and Bill Rowland. Bill Rowland would ask his son Willis to serve as an undercover deputy of Custer County and the Cheyenne Police so he would have authority both on and off the Cheyenne Reservation. Upon acceptance the existence of the Vigilance Committee would be disclosed to him.

With the operational details worked out, the meeting broke up. All members swore an oath not to divulge the details of the meeting for a period of twenty years.

Chapter 8. The Proposal

Bill Rowland arrived home on Muddy Creek in the evening two days after the Room 26 meeting. He was welcomed home by barking dogs and excited kids after his tiring trip. Arriving at the house he backed the wagon up to the door of the store house and with the help of the whole family rapidly unloaded his prized cargo. Finishing the unloading task, he moved the wagon to an open faced shed, unhitched the team, and threw the lines to the older children who took the horses to the barn where they removed the harness and fed the hungry team.

Arrival home after a trip to the "big city" was always an exciting time for homebound children and the rest of the family. There were gifts to be distributed, news and current events to be discussed, and a supper together as a family to be eaten. Muddy Creek in 1890 could be a lonely and boring place. Visitors and news from outside the immediate family was a rare and welcome treat to be savored. Following supper the family moved to the living room where Daddy Rowland distributed the gifts and sweets to excited children and related his story of his trip to Miles City. He recounted the happenings at the Montana Stock Grower's meeting, parts of the visit to Ft. Keogh, and his discussions with Agent Upshaw. Conspicuously absent from the discussion was the meeting at Col. Swaine's office, the meeting in Room 26, and the related discussions with Agent Upshaw.

The next morning following breakfast, Willie and Daddy Rowland went on a ride to check the cow herd and decide when to move them to summer pasture. Before leaving Willie showed his dad the big sorrel horse in the box stall with the changed brand. Bill agreed that the horse was probably stolen and examined the horse's damaged hoof. He suggested that Willie bring the blacksmith from Lame Deer home to put a corrective horseshoe on the foot to keep the crack from widening. In the meantime they dressed the hoof with iodine and pine tar and decided to keep him in the box stall where his movements would be restricted.

On the ride to look at the pasture and cow situation, Willie showed his dad the tally book, related his conversation with Sy Young about the stolen horse herd and Bob Ferguson's comments about missing cattle. Daddy Rowland then briefed Willie about his secret meetings at Ft. Keogh and the MacQueen House. Willie was astonished to hear his name mentioned in such august company.

"I'm not telling you what to do, Willie," Daddy Rowland finished. "It's a dangerous job and I told the group that I would ask you to take a look at it. It would probably pay pretty good and maybe give you and Bear Woman a start in life if you want to go that way."

"How is this any more dangerous than chasing Sioux with the Cheyenne Scouts?" Willie asked.

"Well, for one thing you would be mostly by yourself. You wouldn't have Howling Wolf, Shell, Big Footed Bull, and the U.S. Army backing you up. If the wrong Indian or white man figured out who you were working for, you could be ambushed and come up missing and no one would find you."

"How much do you think it would pay," Willie inquired.

"That's the wrong question, Willie," Daddy shot back. "The reason to do it is to help feed the Cheyenne People and clean up the neighborhood for your nephews, nieces, and your future kids. However, Sheriff Irvine said he could make you a deputy sheriff, Upshaw figured he could make you a full time interpreter with cattle buying responsibilities, and Stuart mentioned a reward from the Stock Growers."

Willie was suddenly embarrassed. "Sorry, Dad. I guess I just got ahead of myself. I got to dreaming of my own place. But, why me, couldn't Jimmy or Bill Jr. do it?"

"Well, Jim is married and has a family so it's too dangerous for him. Bill Jr. is already known to be on the Cheyenne police force so bad Cheyennes would suspect him if he started asking the wrong questions. Besides, you get along better with whites than he does and also have the better contacts with the Army. What do you think, Willie?" Bill asked.

Willie was quiet for a few moments. "Dad, I think I'd like to take the job. The People are hungry so it would be good for them. If we don't get a handle on the cattle butchering problem, this Reservation could blow sky high. And if we could stop some of the whiskey trading and horse stealing by white men, it would be a good thing for everyone. What do you think I should ask for?"

Daddy Rowland thought a bit. "The first thing is to make sure everyone is in the tent. You need to talk to Agent Upshaw, Sheriff Irvine, and Granville Stuart. Make sure you can get the money for cattle from the Montana Stock Growers, real authority in the form of a badge from Custer County, and Agent Upshaw's financial and administrative support on the Reservation. Might also stop by the Fort and see Col. Swaine and firm up the Army's help. Let them know that you want to help but would also like to come out of this with something for yourself. I'm proud of you son!" Daddy Rowland slapped his son on the back and they continued their ride.

Chapter 9. Proposal Accepted

Willie arose early in the morning following the conversation with his father, went to the kitchen, and made himself breakfast prior to the ride to Lame Deer to meet with Agent Upshaw. The day was overcast with heavy clouds promising rain or snow. Willie untied the yellow slicker from the back of his saddle and put it on before saddling his bay horse. By the time his horse was saddled a cold mixture of rain and snow was already pelting the ground. He swung into the saddle with the stray thought in his head that a yellow slicker sure made an easy rifle target. Shaking the thought off Willie started the seven mile ride to Lame Deer Agency at a high trot.

As he rode along Willie began to think about how to go about actually doing the job of an undercover agent on and off the reservation. The key seemed to lie with the purchase of cattle from local ranchers and the delivery of those cattle to hungry Cheyennes. How could he maximize the value of the limited resources he expected to get from the Montana Stock Growers Association? Willie honed in on the contracts which supplied the Cheyennes with their biweekly beef rations.

The Indian Department contracted the beef rations for both the Cheyenne and Crow Reservations from politically connected sources. Those sources built in a large profit for themselves over and above what the same amount of cattle would cost in a local sale. Even assuming that the Congress appropriated enough money for Indian rations, this corruption at the national level reduced the amount that was actually available at the local level. Another problem was just the general issue of dealing with a government contract – the specifications. Local agents had little flexibility to adjust the specifications to maximize the amount and kind of beef purchased. Where the local agent was corrupt, there were sometimes attempts to deliver low quality cattle below specifications. However, these attempts were usually met by objections from local Army commanders which had a vested interest in keeping Indians happy. The Army could do little about the shortfall resulting from corrupt national contracts.

The Cheyennes were fortunate in one respect – they had an honest Indian agent in R.L. Upshaw. A former Confederate Army officer, his father had served as an Indian Agent for a tribe back east so he was somewhat familiar with the problems Indians faced. Although not by nature a genial person, he was scrupulously honest. That being said he was not at all enamored with Cheyenne culture and considered most of the Cheyennes a dirty, shiftless, and obstinate lot. Like most of his fellow agents his idea of progress was to try and move his Cheyenne flock to give up the old ways and assimilate with the white culture. He often complained about the pace of assimilation and disparaged the Cheyenne religious practices which he felt retarded progress. However, he did note in his reports to his superiors that in most matters the Cheyennes were very honest and the Cheyenne women were exceptionally chaste.

The 40 head of cattle the Tribe received every two weeks met the specifications required by the contract. Those specifications required young cattle between one and two years old, meeting specific weight and health benchmarks, delivered to the Muddy Corrals slaughter site on the first and 15th day of the month. Upshaw insured that contract cattle he received met the specifications, but there were not enough of them to feed the Reservation population.

Willie figured that if he had complete flexibility with the Montana Stock Grower's money, he could feed substantially more people by buying cattle which wouldn't meet the government specifications, but would still be a very welcome addition to the Cheyenne diet. Ranchers always had some cattle which were of little value to them due to age, infertility, or medical issues. There was usually no local market for these "out" cattle and the expense to move them to a market was higher than the value they would bring. Most ranchers would willingly sell these cattle for a low price if someone else would move them. Since Willie could move them himself or get some Cheyenne help to bring them to the Reservation, he was about the only local buyer. That provided a lot of leverage.

To mix freely with both Cheyennes and whites, Willie had to present an image that was not threatening to either side. The cattle buyer cover could go a long way towards that end since it benefited both sides. However, he also knew that everyone enjoyed news and a good story or joke. Therefore he decided to develop a list of stories or jokes which he could use as he made his cattle buying rounds. This would enhance his cover and make him doubly welcome to parties on and off the Reservation.

About two hours into his ride, Willie topped the high hill above the Lame Deer Agency and looked down on the Lame Deer Village. Lame Deer Creek ran south to north before emptying into Rosebud Creek and was named for the Sioux Chief Lame Deer who was killed there in a battle with Col. Nelson Miles in 1877. The Agency Office was located at the north end of village, about where Alderson Gulch runs into Lame Deer Creek. The Agency buildings consisted of an office building, house for Agent Upshaw and his wife, a blacksmith shop, a warehouse building for ration storage, a butchering area, a flour mill under construction, and further north was Camp Merritt, the occasional home of two troops of cavalry (about 60 men) from Fort Custer detailed to Fort Keogh. (Note: Fort Keogh was an infantry post and Fort Custer was a cavalry post. When Fort Keogh needed fast moving mounted soldiers, they "borrowed" cavalry units from Fort Custer but they were under the command of Fort Keogh).

Figure 17. Early Lame Deer Agency. Courtesy of the Montana Historical Society

Ironically, the Agency's buildings had been built almost exactly on the location of the Walt and Nan Alderson house which had been burned to the ground in the spring of 1884 by the very Cheyennes now served by the Agency. The Alderson couple had moved on to a "squatter's ranch" on that location in April 1883 where Mrs. Alderson was the very first white woman in that part of southeast Montana. They built a very fine four room house in preparation for the birth of their first child which was due in March 1884. By all accounts they were on good terms with the Cheyennes, often feeding them in their home. When Mr. and Mrs. Alderson left their house to go to Miles City for the birth of the baby, the house was occupied by a few of their cowboys. An old Cheyenne named Black Wolf came by the house and asked for lunch. He was served and took his plate to a log pile, finished his lunch, and took a nap in the spring sun.

He was wearing a big black hat with a tall crown that appeared to be a perfect target. One of the cowboys named Hal Talifarro bet another cowboy that he could shoot the hat off the old Indian's head without touching him. However, the shot went low and nicked the old man who was convinced that Talifarro had meant to kill him and staggered off to raise a war party. The cowboys fled to Sy Young's Trading Post to get help but upon their return, the Cheyennes had fired the house, shot the dog, cut up the saddles, and burned the hay stacks. All this happened on the exact day that the Alderson's first child was born. The Alderson's decided not to return to Lame Deer and established a new ranch across Tongue River from the mouth of Hanging Woman Creek. A couple of years later, the Zook/Alderson Partnership dissolved, and the Aldersons moved again, this time to the head of Muddy Creek where they became good friends to the Rowland Family and Little Wolf.

Willie rode down to the Agency Office where he was welcomed enthusiastically by Agent Upshaw. "Come in, Willie. It is really good to see you, again. Please come to my office and sit down."

They went into Upshaw's office, sat down at a small table, and Upshaw started the conversation. "Did your dad talk to you about what went on in Miles City with Col. Swaine, Sheriff Irvine, and Granville Stuart?"

"Yes, he told me something about it. I guess you guys want me to be an undercover deputy sheriff on and off the reservation to try and shut down illegal cattle butchering and horse stealing. Is that right?" Willie asked.

"That is partly right, but there is a lot more to it," Upshaw replied. "The real issue is how we can keep the peace between angry settlers and hungry Indians when there is horse stealing and cattle butchering inflaming the settlers. A lot of the butchering and horse theft is done by white men, but Indians are doing their share too. Whites are anxious to blame the Indians, sometimes because of prejudice, but also because they would like the government to reduce the size of the reservation or eliminate it. They see the reservation as a bonanza of grass and timber that they could put to better use and thereby benefit. The Yellowstone Journal runs editorials weekly advocating elimination of both the Cheyenne and Crow reservations. When the Cheyennes kill settler's cattle to feed their families, it supports their positon. Then when you introduce whiskey into the mix things get really volatile."

Willie scratched his head. "Any chance of getting a cattle ration increase in the near future?"

Upshaw looked grim. "Not this year. As you know we are still trying to get an accurate census. We just don't know how many people are on the reservation and what their names are. You have been part of helping with that problem. People leave to go visiting relatives on the Sioux and Arapaho reservations and others are coming here for visits, so no census is ever accurate or complete. I have to get an accurate list before the Indian Department can get the budget request into Congress for the ration appropriation. We are always behind. That's why I pressed Stuart to provide some cattle from the Montana Stock Growers to help feed people until the rations caught up with the census."

"Are you sure that he will provide the cattle? Willie asked intently.

"Yes! If Stuart says he will do something he will do it. I don't doubt that, I just don't know how much money he is willing to allocate to the project, and I don't know how much beef we can get with the money. Have you got any ideas on how that should work, Willie?"

"Well, I was thinking about that on the ride over here. If you will give me free rein to make the best deal I can with the local ranchers, I think we can do a lot of good. There are lots of "out" cattle that can be bought pretty cheap, particularly if we don't have to deal with rigid government specifications, answered Willie.

"What are "out" cattle?" Upshaw asked.

"They are cattle that could not normally be sold to a Government or eastern buyer. Dry, old or lame cows, broke dick bulls, orphan calves, or other cattle that are not worth the time and effort to drive them to a rail road siding. These cattle can feed lots of Cheyennes if the price is right. They don't have to be number one quality," Willie finished.

"Oh, I see. Since this is not U.S. Government money, we don't have to meet their specs. Any other ideas?" Upshaw inquired.

"Absolutely," Willie replied thoughtfully. "If we don't have to bring the cattle all the way to Lame Deer for slaughter, it would help. Right now Cheyennes come from all over the reservation every two weeks to draw their rations. The cattle are killed at the Muddy Corral under government supervision and the carcasses brought to Lame Deer for distribution with the rest of the rations. If I can buy cattle on Otter Creek and take them across Tongue River to Rabbit Town, let the Rabbit Town Cheyennes kill and butcher them, the cattle don't lose as much weight and the Cheyennes don't have to make a trip to Lame Deer. It is better for everybody. Besides, if I present the cattle as a gift from local ranchers to local Cheyennes, that will create an obligation under Cheyenne culture to look out for the ranchers who made the gift. They will protect those ranchers from white rustlers or other Cheyennes."

Upshaw was stunned. "You have really thought this out! But how do we know that the cattle will be shared fairly and not go just one family?"

"We use the military societies to do the slaughter and distribution," Willie suggested. "Most of the villages are dominated by one military society. For example, the Swift Foxes may strongest in the Birney area, Elk Horns in Rabbit Town, and Crazy Dogs in Lame Deer. The Chiefs usually designate one of the military societies to act as camp policemen and they are honor bound to distribute fairly. We let the Chiefs know that this is what we want and they will insure that it happens. It enhances the prestige of the Chief and the military society to be selected to help feed the people. If they don't do it right, another society will be given the honor."

"Is there anything else?"

"I think that it is important that we don't say anything about this to the Chiefs until we absolutely know that we can do it. Don't promise more than we can do. On ration day call all the Chiefs together and tell them that the white cattlemen will be making some gifts of cattle to the Cheyenne people," Willie concluded.

"Willie, have you made up your mind to do this? And if you do what support from me do you need?" Upshaw asked pointedly.

"Well, Agent Upshaw," Willie began. "I would like to have some sort of official status, maybe an undercover appointment to the Cheyenne Police. What can you do?"

"I've been thinking about this for over a week." Upshaw said. "It's hard and dangerous work that you are uniquely qualified to do. And it is one of the most important jobs I have ever given anyone. Here is what I think the Agency can do. We can make you a full time interpreter and an undercover member of the Cheyenne Police. That gives you arrest authority if you need it on the Reservation. Your pay will be $100.00 per month for a term of one year. That contract can be renewed. We will also pay some expenses when you travel off the Reservation on official business. I would not object if Sheriff Irvine also pays you as a Custer County deputy. Is there anything else you need?"

Willie was impressed. One hundred dollars a month was the equivalent of a ranch managers pay at a time when top hands were only making $30.00. He had been making $3.00 per day as a part time interpreter and averaging about $18.00 per month. If he could get additional pay as a Custer County deputy, he would be able to save enough to over time to file on a homestead claim.

"I think you have answered my questions," Willie replied. "Now I need to get a deal with Sheriff Irvine and Granville Stuart. I'm really looking forward to working on this. It's a lot more interesting than chasing cows. Oh. By the way, I may already have sort of a lead. A stray sorrel horse with a split hoof and a "worked over" brand showed up at our place on Muddy about a week ago. It sure looks like it was one of a group of stolen horses that was left behind when it couldn't keep up. I'll give a full description to Sheriff Irvine so he can run down the old brand and the new brand. Maybe we can come up with something."

Saying goodbye to Upshaw, Willie started home to get a fresh horse, and prepare for a trip to Miles City.

Chapter 10. Deputy Rowland

About 10:30 A.M. Sheriff Tom Irvine was visited by a courier from Fort Keogh with a note inviting him to come to the Commandant's Office at about 01:00 P.M. today. He wondered what Col. Swaine had on his mind that required a meeting so urgently. Hoping that there was no trouble brewing on the Cheyenne Reservation, Sheriff Tom began tying up loose ends prior to the meeting. He secured his horse from the County Barn, tied it outside the Red House, and quickly walked down to the MacQueen House for a quick lunch. After lunch he returned to his office, held a brief conference with "the Deputy Dog" Jack Johnson on the release of two prisoners from the night before, and mounted his horse for the short ride to Fort Keogh.

Arriving at the Fort shortly before the appointed time, Sheriff Irvine tied his horse to the hitching rail outside the Post Headquarters building and entered. He was immediately greeted by the Adjutant who ushered him into Col. Swain's office. Col. Swaine arose from behind his desk, and strode toward the two with hand extended.

"Hi Tom, very good to see you again," boomed Col. Swaine. "I have someone I want you to meet. Sheriff Irvine please meet Willis Rowland."

Willie quickly rose from the chair in which he was sitting, turned to Sheriff Irvine, and extended his hand.

"Hi, Tom. I haven't seen you since I left the Cheyenne Scouts."

Sheriff Tom's eyes lit up in recognition. "Willie, you are a sight for sore eyes! I hope your dad convinced you to work with us."

At that point the Colonel waved the Adjutant out of the room and gestured to his two guests to take the seats in front of his desk. Col. Swaine started the conversation.

"Tom, Willie and I have been discussing his potential role in the operation that we discussed with Upshaw and Stuart a few days ago. He and Upshaw have come to an agreement for his job on the reservation. However, before he commits to anything further, he would like to hear from both of us as to how we see his role, what support we can offer, and how long this operation would take. Is that about it, Willie?"

"Pretty much," Willie replied. "I told dad that I would take a hard look at what you want to do. I'm interested for a number of reasons but the main one is that I'd like to make sure there is peace on the reservation. I live there, the family lives there, and I would like to make a home and raise my own family there. But, the mood on the reservation is ugly. The Cheyennes are hungry and scared. They have to go off the reservation to hunt for meat because the reservation is out of game and the cattle ration is too small. When they leave the reservation, it may be for wild game or it may be for beef, it depends on what they find first and how much risk there is to get it. If they are discovered butchering beef, they will kill the person or persons who find them. That's why this deal depends on the Montana Stock Growers providing the money or the cattle to feed the Cheyennes until Upshaw can get a good census finished and the ration level increased. If Stuart can do that, I'll work my ass off to make sure the Cheyennes and the neighboring settlers don't go to war if there is an incident."

"Have you heard anything about white men and stolen horses on the reservation?" asked Irvine.

"I heard that there was a bunch of horses moved across the Crow Reservation to the Upper Rosebud and nobody seemed to know whether it was Indian or white men who were moving them. They were pretty far south to be Cheyennes so I thought it was probably white men heading toward Deadwood or Hole-In-The-Wall country. Then we found a lame horse with an altered brand on Muddy Creek about a week and a half ago so now I'm not so sure that they aren't on the Cheyenne."

"That's bad," interjected Swaine. "What makes you think it wasn't Cheyennes just raiding the Crows or the Blackfeet?"

"Because of the altered brand," replied Willie. "Cheyennes don't know enough about white man brands to do the alteration. "I'm certain that a white man did that. What I don't know is if the horses are still on the reservation or not."

"Back to the business at hand," Col. Swaine resumed. "What help do you need from the Army side of this operation?"

Willie thought for a minute. "The big thing is the courier service between Lame Deer and Fort Keogh. While I need them to get messages to Irvine, I don't want my name associated too closely with the Cheyenne Scouts carrying the messages. Some of the new Scouts are from the Dull Knife's band which has only been back on the Reservation since last fall. There are rumors that some of them have been involved in the cattle killings and I don't trust them. I'll give information to Upshaw for transmission to you and when you need to get a message to me, send it through Upshaw. Are you going to station a couple of cavalry troops at Lame Deer?"

"Yes. We will reoccupy Camp Merritt for the summer, maybe longer. If you get wind of some reason they need to patrol a certain area, have Upshaw send me a message and I'll authorize it," Col. Swaine concluded.

Sheriff Irvine spoke up. "Colonel, I think Willie and I need to have a long conversation about becoming a deputy of Custer County, but we don't need to waste your time with that. I know we are trying to keep all this as quiet as possible, so I suggest that Willie go to the MacQueen House and check in. I'll get "X" and come to his room this evening about 08:00, brief him up on where the operation is so far, and your telegraph guy can contact Fort McGinnis and let Stuart know that Willie may be coming in the couple of days."

The meeting broke up with Willie leaving first followed five minutes later by Sheriff Irvine. Willie went to the Post Canteen to shoot the breeze with a couple of old friends from his Cheyenne Scout days to allow Irvine time to leave the Fort well before he made his way to the Miles City Livery to put up his horse. Then he went to the McQueen House, checked in and found his room. With a couple of hours to kill, he decided to take the nickel tour of Miles City.

Willie returned to the MacQueen House after supper and awaited the meeting with Sheriff Irvine and Marshall "X" Beidler in his hotel room. Precisely at 08:00 the two lawmen arrived and the meeting began. After introductions, Sheriff Irvine got right down to business.

"Willie, do you think that you want a deputy sheriff's job with Custer, County? Before we disclose any more information to you, we need to know."

"Before I answer that question, I need you to answer a couple of my questions first. Are you offering me the job? If so, how long could I expect to keep it? What are the terms?"

Sheriff Irvine replied, "That's easy, the answer to the first question is a "yes". We need you with us. The answer to the second question is that officially the contract would run for a year, and could be extended beyond that. The positon pays $75.00 per month plus expenses. Expenses include $5.00 per month if you use your own horse, travel expense when on official business, and so on. For example, the county will pick up your hotel room, meals while you are in Miles City, a horse from the livery stable for your trip to see Stuart, those kinds of things."

"What about insurance?" Willie inquired.

"We usually only provide insurance to married men. Are you married?" asked Irvine.

"No, but I'm thinking about it," said Willie.

"Well, if you tie the knot let me know and we will address it. How does that sound?"

Willie thought for a moment. "O.K. That sounds good to me. I'll take the job."

Irvine smiled broadly, "Welcome aboard, Deputy Rowland. I'll get all the paperwork ready. I assume you are going to see Stuart right away so I will have all the paperwork ready for your signature when you get back. "X", why don't you bring our new deputy up to speed on Stuart's operation?"

"X" Beidler launched into essentially the same briefing he had given at the Room 26 meeting. He outlined the activities of the two major interstate gangs, Teton Jackson's horse thieves operating out of Jackson Hole and running horses south to Old Mexico, New Mexico, and Arizona; and Kid Curry's Wild Bunch which was involved in all kinds of lawless activity including train and bank robbery, cattle rustling, and horse theft on a grand scale. The Wild Bunch ran their operations out of the Hole-in-the-Wall country in the Big Horn Mountains with a satellite operation in Landusky, Montana and north into Canada. Then there were the local operations which primarily involved butchering illegal beef and selling meat to sawmill, rail road, and telegraph building crews. There was occasional cooperation between the interstate operators and the locals. Usually this involved locals providing the interstate operators fresh horses, safe houses, and way stations for stolen horses or cattle at a liberal fee. "X" followed with a satchel full of "wanted" posters of prominent outlaws that were known to be operating or travelling through the local area. He gave Willie a brief description of each criminal's specialties, descriptions, unique marks, and known associates. It was also pointed out by him that sheriffs and deputies were fully authorized to share in rewards offered for some of the more serious offenders.

This caused Willie to pose a question to Sheriff Irvine. "Sheriff Tom, say I identify an outlaw with a reward, do I have to take him down myself to get the reward?" What if I get information that he is in Ashland or Birney and lead you and "X" to him, but you make the arrest, who gets the reward?"

Tom replied, "We usually do a split in that situation. The informer gets twenty five per cent if he doesn't participate in the arrest, fifty per cent if he does. The rest is distributed equally among the rest of the arresting party. In most cases it is too dangerous for one guy to try and make an arrest by himself so we don't encourage that."

"You can't collect a reward if you are dead," noted "X".

"Gotcha," exclaimed Willie. "That makes complete sense to me."

Discussion then turned to the upcoming meeting with Granville Stuart. "X" needed to tie up some loose ends on an upcoming operation on the Missouri with Stuart and offered to take Willie with him to Stuart's ranch. Willie asked if the county would pay for a horse for the trip, since his horse couldn't make it that far, so Irvine advanced Willie $20 for trip expense money. Willie and "X" agreed to meet on the outskirts of Forsyth and go on together from there. Willie took the same oath that the other participants in Stuart's Room 26 meeting, not to talk about Stuart's plan for a period of twenty years.

Chapter 11. Stuart Speaks

Willie left Miles City before daybreak on a horse rented from the Ringer & Johnson Livery stable. It was forty miles to Forsyth but he made good time, arriving just before 10:00. He met "X" Beidler on the road to Junction City, and the two continued up the Yellowstone to the mouth of the Big Horn River. Using the ferry at Terry's Crossing, they crossed the Yellowstone to the north shore and then stopped at Junction City for a late lunch.

Junction City was a tough little town comprised primarily of saloons, brothels, and a few legitimate businesses. It was on the downhill slide and shortly would cease to exist. It owed its origin to the steamboat trade which was rapidly being supplanted by the new railroads. Junction City was the upstream terminus for steamboats on the Yellowstone River. Upstream of the mouth of the Big Horn River, the Yellowstone became too shallow to accommodate the big flatboats that had brought people and freight into that part of Montana Territory. Now it was on the wrong side of the river because the railroad had been built on the south side so it could service Fort Keogh at Miles City and Fort Custer near the Crow Agency. Furthermore the rapidly growing frontier town of Billings was becoming the commercial center for southeastern Montana. One function which Junction City could still perform was as the jumping off point for travel overland north to the Musselshell and on to the Missouri River. It was known as a favorite rest stop for outlaws travelling the Outlaw Trail north to Landusky, MT and Canada, and south to Hole-in-the-Wall. The trail continued on to Jackson Hole in Wyoming, and Brown's Hole in Colorado, and Robber's Roost in Utah. "X" liked to visit Junction City because he had a couple of paid informants who could bring him up to speed on recent outlaw travel up and down the Outlaw Trail.

The stay in Junction City was very brief. Willie and "X" ate a quick lunch and Beidler disappeared for a few minutes to talk to his contacts. Then they were back on the trail north at a high trot over the divide to the Musselshell which they reached just at dusk. Following the Musselshell they rode into the small town of Mosby about 10:00 that night, put up their horses, ate a late supper and found a bed at a "road ranch" which doubled as a saloon, hotel, and eating house. Both were tired after a ride of nearly a hundred miles.

The next morning the two ate a leisurely breakfast before cutting west across country to Box Elder Creek. They had pushed their horses pretty hard the day before so they took their time before turning up Ford's Creek to Fort Maginnis which was adjacent to Stuart's DHS ranch. "X" stopped at the Fort long enough to check for any telegraph messages for himself or Stuart before proceeding on to the ranch. Stuart's ranch was located on Ford's Creek, near where two cold water springs gushed pure icy water into the creek. The ranch buildings consisted of two large residences occupied by the Stuart family and the Reece Anderson family, a schoolhouse, a log stable, blacksmith shop, and bunkhouse with room for about ten to a dozen cowboys. The ranch buildings were about nine years old and formed a large open square with the bunkhouse, stable, and blacksmith shop making part of the corrals such that the whole set up was a small fort. At the time Stuart built the ranch, the Blackfeet Indians were still raiding, and defense was paramount in its construction.

Willie and "X" went straight to the Stuart house where they were met by an enthusiastic Granville Stuart.

"Come in. Come in," he boomed. "I've made that ride a bunch of times and you made good time. We didn't expect you for a couple of more hours."

"X" and Willie dismounted stiffly and shook hands with Stuart. "I am really glad to meet you, Mr. Stuart," Willie began.

Stuart immediately interrupted, "Call me Granville. We are all friends. Come with me and I will show you where to put up your horses."

Figure 18. Granville Stuart in his younger years. Photo Courtesy of the Montana Historical Society

Granville led the way to the log stable where the horses were unsaddled, rubbed down, and given a generous helping of oats and hay. As they walked toward the house, Stuart questioned Beidler, "What's the latest news?"

"X" replied, "Outlaws heard about the resolution to raise a vigilante force at the Stock Growers meeting being defeated. They are becoming even more and more bold. I talked to a couple of contacts in Junction City and they told me that the Wild Bunch has plans to increase their operations to and from Canada. "Harvey "Kid Curry" Logan has moved to Landusky to handle the cross border stuff with Canada. Henry Lonabaugh and Bob Smith are still collecting horses in Hole-in-the-Wall, and "Big Nose George" Parrott and Bill Carey are in charge of moving stock back and forth between Landusky and Hole-in-the-Wall. They are looking forward to a profitable summer."

"We will see what we can do to change that," Stuart said grimly. "Willie, how are things on and around the reservation?"

Willie answered quickly, "Not good, Granville. The Cheyennes are hungry and butchering off the reservation has increased.

They really don't have any choice. There isn't anything left to eat except dogs and horses on the reservation. We expect that now that the snow has mostly gone off the butchering will increase. Upshaw is really concerned that whiskey selling has increased and we worry about what the Cheyennes are doing to get the whiskey."

As they approached the house Granville said, "Let's continue this conversation after supper. I'm sure you guys are hungry so I'll see if the ladies can make supper a little earlier than usual."

"X" and Willie were invited into the house where they met the rest of the Stuart family and were given a room to share. After washing up and taking a short rest they went down stairs where Mrs. Stuart and the older girls had nearly finished preparing supper. Granville ushered them into the dining room where they joined Teddy Blue Abbot at the expansive dining room table. Following a bounteous supper the men retired to the living room.

Figure 19. Granville Stuart's First Wife. Courtesy of the Montana Historical Society

Granville Stuart started the conversation. "I'd like to welcome Willie to the group we hope will rescue Montana from the grips of the outlaws and thieves. His addition fills a big hole in the dragnet we are about to undertake. Let me sum up where we have come in the two short weeks since our initial meeting in Room 26 of the MacQueen House. We have set up the Information Committee headed by Sheriff Tom Irvine. That Committee is gathering information from all over the Territory and feeding it to Tom. "X" is meeting with Sheriffs from other counties to enlist their help in this effort. On the surface this is just normal law enforcement coordination. The other sheriffs do not know of the existence of this Vigilance Committee because we have to keep our members to the absolute minimum necessary for the operation. The Selection Committee chaired by Judge Strevell has already selected a number of targets for the operation. Most of these are well known outlaws with wanted posters in existence. Billy Smith and I are nearly finished in recruiting the fourteen or fifteen men which will make up the Operations Committee. What we need now is for the Information Committee to find exact locations where the targets can be found. Then we will need local guides to bring us to those locations and also help sort out the targets and their close associates from the small fry or innocent bystanders. The way I propose to do this is to contact Montana Stock Growers that I know personally to be men of good reputation to provide these guides. Probably only one or two guides will be used for each major Yellowstone tributary. When the operation starts we will go from drainage to drainage until we have covered the bulk of Eastern Montana. Teddy Blue will be my "telegraph man" who carries messages in front of the Operations force and arranges for guides, fresh horses, food, rest points and fresh information. We will start here on the Musselshell and Upper Missouri River down to Wolf Point and then go south to Billings and start on the Yellowstone. From Billings, I have engaged Northern Pacific Railroad to provide us an engine, passenger car, and two stock cars for horses. We will move from Billings east on the NP stopping at each major drainage where we have targets, unload, do our business, reload, and proceed to the next drainage. When we get to Glendive, we will disembark the railroad and work the Little Missouri to Medora and then to Fort Union, up the Missouri and back to the Musselshell. I expect the whole operation to take no longer than sixty days."

Willie was flabbergasted with the size and scope of Stuart's vision. It encompassed nearly half of the State of Montana and parts of Wyoming and North Dakota. However, as impressed as Willie was, he had to pin Stuart down on his small part of the big picture. "Granville, how do you see my part in this plan? Where does the Cheyenne Reservation fit into this?"

Granville glanced at "X" Beidler before replying. "I think you heard "X" talk about the big organized gangs running horses from Wyoming to Canada and south to Mexico. That is a big part of the picture but not the biggest part. The biggest part that is hurting the Stock Growers and endangering the peace between the Indian tribes and white settlers is cattle rustling and butchering. You have these issues with the Cheyennes and maybe the Crows. But it is bigger than that. We have the same trouble up here with the Blackfeet, Crees, and even Metis crossing the border from Canada. Your job is to try and reduce tension between whites and Cheyennes by helping feed some people, identifying white outlaws operating on and next to the reservation, and bad Indians who are committing crimes on and off the reservation. On reservation crime by Indians will continue to be dealt with by Upshaw and the Chiefs. I don't see our Committee ever going on the Reservation unless it was to take on a white gang and I think that could be handled by the Indian Police and the Army. We need you to feed us information on white outlaws who may be using the reservation as a safe haven, solving Indian crime off the reservation, and finding white rustlers who are selling beef locally, maybe with Indian help. Does that sound alright to you?"

"Yes, for the most part," replied Willie. "You mentioned helping feed people. What are the Montana Stock Growers prepared to do to help out?"

Stuart grinned, "I'm glad you asked that Willie. I can't leave the contribution open ended because my term as President of the MSG ends in a year and I can't bind my successor. However, when I was talking to Upshaw he was telling me that by next year he could have a new Cheyenne census done which should mean a larger meat ration. I thought that maybe a contribution of $250 per month out of the predator fund for a year would be about $3,000 total. How many Cheyennes could you feed on that?"

Willie made quick calculation in his head and came up with about 25 head per month at $10.00 per head. "Wow! That could be a pretty good number, if I could have free rein on the purchasing. Right now the Cheyennes are getting 40 head every two weeks to feed over 1,100 people. But that is for prime young cattle on a government contract at about $45 per head. If I can buy the most meat for the least money by buying "out" cattle from neighboring ranches, I'll bet I can get another 25 to 30 head per month. Those ranchers always have cattle they can't sell back east and they won't have driving costs or freight if they sell to me. Old cows, broke dick bulls, dry cows, and orphan calves can feed a lot of Cheyennes. It would clean up the rancher's herds and create a lot of good will. If I make a big deal about how the local ranchers are making a present to the local Cheyennes, it will create an obligation for the Cheyennes to return the favor. They will be more likely to tell me about what they know about white men stealing cattle and even protect those ranchers from other Cheyennes."

"I like how you are thinking, Willie," Stuart beamed. "Hell, that $3,000 might more than pay for itself. I'll commit to $250.00 per month for a year and a free rein. Anything else you need?"

"Well yes," said Willie. "As a member of the State Legislature, can you pass a law outlawing the sale of alcohol to Indians off the reservations? It is getting to be bigger and bigger problem every year. I would like a letter of introduction to MSG members. If a breed like me shows up with no introduction I will just get run off. Also is there any bonus from the MSG for busting up any of the local gangs doing the butchering? I'd like to come out of this with a few cows of my own so I can start a family."

"Willie, I will make you a promise. The liquor law is easy, I can't believe we haven't passed one already. So is the introduction letter, I'll make one up for you tonight. And, if within a year you deliver a local gang of rustlers to the law enforcement authorities or the Committee, I will personally get you twenty young cows and a bull. How's that?"

"More than fair, Mr. Stuart," Willie replied.

"Call me Granville," Stuart grinned.

The next morning after a good breakfast, Willie began the return to Miles City. Before leaving DHS, Stuart gave Willie a check for $250.00 drawn on the Stockman's Bank of Miles City and a fresh horse. He also gave Willie a note to the livery stable saying that he would return the rented horse at the first opportunity. The livery stable operator could use the DHS horse in the meantime. Willie said good bye to Stuart and Beidler and kicked his horse into a travelling trot toward the Yellowstone. By nightfall Willie was between Junction City and Forsyth. It was a warm night so Willie made camp, hobbled and picketed his horse, rolled out his slicker to lie on, pulled the saddle blankets over his shoulders and promptly went to sleep.

The sun found Willie in the saddle again and about 08:00 reached Forsyth where he ate breakfast and then moved on to Miles City where he arrived about noon. He exchanged horses with the livery stable and gave the liveryman Stuart's note. Saddling his own horse he rode over to the Stockman's Bank and cashed the MSG $250.00 check and then stopped by the "Red House" to officially report the horse recovered on Muddy Creek. Deputy Johnson took the report and notified Sheriff Tom who invited Willie to lunch at the MacQueen House.

At lunch the Sheriff asked Willie, "How did it go with Stuart?"

"Great," replied Willie. "He really is a straight shooter. We made a good deal for feeding the Cheyennes and I learned a lot more of the big picture plans. He is quite the mover and shaker, isn't he?"

"Yeah," Sheriff Tom said. "You know I guided him all over Tongue River, Rosebud, and both the Little and Big Horn Rivers back in '80 when he was looking for a place to locate his ranch. He finally settled at Ford's Creek on the Musselshell, but I got to know him pretty well on that trip. He is a good operator and one of the fairest men I have ever met."

The Sheriff continued. "Granville is one of the few cattlemen to allow his cowboys to have their own cows. Most owners don't want their cowboys to homestead and build up their own herds because they are afraid they will brand their ranch's mavericks with their own brands. Stuart's idea is that a man with his own cows is more likely to respect private property than one who doesn't. I don't know who is right, but heard of a guy who used to work for him built up a good herd of milk cows on his own place. He was making a decent living selling milk and butter to the Army at Ft. McGinnis when the winter of '86/'87 hit. He asked Stuart if he could buy some hay to keep his cows alive at the same time that Stuart's cows were dying by the thousands. Stuart sold him the hay. Do you want to bet that if someone steals some of Stuart's cattle, he won't be the first man to help Stuart get them back? Stuart's cowboys will go the ends of the earth for him unlike most of the big Wyoming owners who are at war with their own former help."

Willie responded. "That is quite a story, but I can believe it after meeting him. Do you think that is why the Wyoming big outfits can't break up the Hole-in-Wall Gang? Are they are protected by all the small ranchers who resent the big outfits?"

"Absolutely," added Irvine. "Those big outfits tried to make it a crime for a cowboy to save up and start his own ranch. By passing a law that only members of the WY Stock Growers Association could sell cattle in that state, they pissed off damn near everybody in Johnson County. Now the WY Stock Growers can't get a conviction in Johnson County for damn near anything. A lot of those settlers were soldiers from Fort McKinney who mustered out in Buffalo and homesteaded small farms and ranches. They didn't like being told what they could and couldn't do, especially by big cattlemen--many of which were foreigners from England and Scotland. There were more settlers than big owners so they have the votes. The biggest trouble is that the outlaws in Hole-in-the-Wall have helped the little guys against the big owners so outlaws get protection regardless of what they do outside Johnson County. And some of those outlaws are really bad people."

"So that is what Stuart was trying to prevent here, when he wanted the Vigilante Resolution defeated?" Willie asked.

"I think so. Stuart knows that this area has a lot of small cattlemen, so he didn't want to create an "us versus them" situation. We have enough trouble with the reservations near us. What are your plans now that you have Stuart's blessing?"

Willie thought for a minute. "I think I will hit the road for Ashland. That's where a lot of the Cheyenne trouble seems to be. It's not that much further from home and I would like to poke around there and see what I can see. We need to try and develop some good contacts there who can feed us good info. They have a couple of big lumber operations there that require a lot of beef and the saloons are going full blast. Beef, saloons, and outlaws all seem to go together. I'll check in with Captain Howes while I'm there and see if I can buy some Cheyenne beef from him on a future trip."

"Do you need anything more from me?" Irvine asked.

"Have you heard anything more from "X"?

"He is up at Fort Benton poking around." Sheriff Irvine said. "I did hear a funny story about him from Col. Swaine's wife though. The first time she met him was on the Northern Pacific train on the way to Miles City. They were discussing the new train service and she asked him if he was married. He told her, "Well, yes." Mrs. Swaine then asked. "Is she an Indian lady?" When "X" replied that she was, Mrs. Swaine asked him if she was in Miles City? "X" told her, "No, I sent her out to roam." Mrs. Swaine said, "Rome, Italy?" To which "X" commented, "No mam, southeast Montana with her own people."

Both men laughed at the white joke. It was a good story, but Willie wasn't so sure what Long Forehead thought about it. The fact that "X" had dumped his Indian wife was not a positive in Long Forehead's world. However, he quickly decided that Sheriff Irvine didn't mean any disrespect to Indians, and the fact that he felt comfortable enough with Willie to tell him the joke indicted a level of trust.

"Can you think of anything else I can do for you," Sheriff Tom asked.

"I don't think so," Willie replied. "I set up a bank account at Stockman's Bank. You can deposit my check there. I've got my badge, my travelling money, my horse, and my orders, now I just need to do the job. Thanks for all your help. I'll be in touch by courier through Col. Swaine."

Sheriff Irvine picked up the lunch check. They said good-bye and Willie was on the road again.

Chapter 12. Ashland, Rabbit Town, and St. Labre

The Tongue River road paralleled the west bank of Tongue River mostly staying a couple hundred yards from the river. Near the river a proliferation of cottonwoods, plum thickets, chokecherry trees, and wild rose bushes made travel difficult so the trail stayed out of the river bends. Willie spotted the first Cheyenne teepee about three miles below Ashland. Cheyennes liked to camp in these bends where wood and water were close to the teepees. As he rode closer to the point where Otter Creek joined Tongue River, the number of teepees increased. He rode up on a little knoll and gazed out upon the Rabbit Town/Ashland Community. To his front was the Cheyenne village of Rabbit Town, to the east right across the river was the St. Labre Mission, and further southeast also on the east side of the river was the white man town of Ashland.

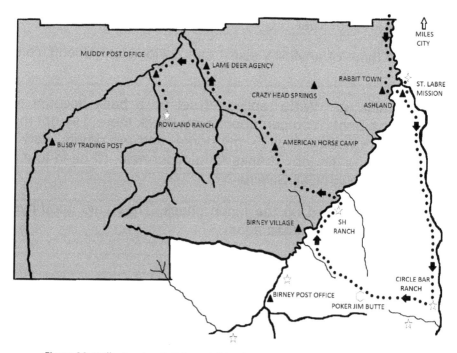

Figure 20. Willis Rowland's Trip to Ashland, St Labre Mission & Circle Bar Ranch

Rabbit Town was mostly inhabited by Little Chief's Band of Cheyennes, recent arrivals from the Sioux Pine Ridge Reservation. Most had married into the Sioux Tribe at the time of surrender and had been allowed to stay with their Sioux relatives rather than going south to the Darlington Agency with Little Wolf and Dull Knife. However, after the Northern Cheyenne Reservation was established, the survivors of the Dull Knife band which had been "parked" at Pine Ridge were permitted to move to the Montana reservation. Little Chief's band was considered Sioux by the Indian Department and were refused when they requested to join their fellow Cheyennes. Then trouble broke out between the Little Chief band and the Sioux. The Cheyenne Scouts from Ft. Keogh helped capture several small bands of renegade Sioux which caused resentment against the Cheyennes at Pine Ridge. After some of Little Chief's people were attacked and their lodges burned, they were allowed to move to the Cheyenne Reservation and settled in Rabbit Town.

As Willie rode through the village he noted that these people were even poorer than the Cheyennes at the other villages. The women and children showed more signs of malnutrition, the horses were thin, and many of the lodges were in need of repair. He considered calling on Little Chief but decided against it. His dad had often told him that Little Chief (a Sioux) was a dour and stubborn man inclined toward avarice. Since he wasn't prepared to offer him anything, Willie opted to wait until later to disclose the MSG feeding program. However, Willie decided that Rabbit Town would be the first village to benefit from the program.

Crossing Tongue River Willie entered the booming town of Ashland. Ashland was named for Ashland, Ohio by a lumber boss who had grown up there. It was formed after the creation of the Northern Cheyenne Reservation in 1884 when lumber camps were forced off the new reservation by the Army. Prior to formation of the reservation, there were several lumber camps primarily cutting timber for railroad ties to build the Northern Pacific Railroad. While there were camps on both sides of Tongue River, two of the largest camps were located on Tie and Logging Creeks within the boundary of the new reservation. These two large camps moved to the confluence of Otter Creek and Tongue River and established one large camp named Ashland. The logging operations then moved their crews to the east side of Tongue River and cut the area that would subsequently become the Custer National Forest.

On his way into Ashland, Willie noted huge ricks holding thousands of railroad ties piled up on the banks of the river awaiting the spring floods which would start in a couple of weeks. When the spring rise came the ties would be dumped into Tongue River and floated to Miles City where they would be recovered before reaching the Yellowstone. Inland from the ricks were the big sawmills where the ties were shaped and some of the larger logs cut into lumber, most of it for regional consumption. Piles of slash (throw away wood pieces) and slabs littered the landscape and the pungent scent of raw wood and wet sawdust filled the air. Past the mills, Willie entered the town of Ashland. Awaiting him was a wide single street lined with tents, log cabins, and a few frame buildings. There was a large general store on the south side of the street, a Chinese laundry, a Post Office and as he continued to the east a livery stable. As he reached the end of the street where a bend in Otter Creek came close to the road which proceeded on up the creek, he came upon a big ice house, slaughter house and butcher shop. Turning his horse back up the street, Willie observed the north side of the street. Again a proliferation tents, tent houses, shacks and frame buildings met his eye. The center of commerce was the two saloons about forty yards apart. The first was the Club Buffet and the other the Ashland Bar. Between the two was Olga's Eatery, run by a friendly middle aged Norwegian woman named Olga Salversen. Here Willie stopped for a much needed meal.

"What's good today?" asked Willie.

"Is all goot," Olga replied while pouring him a steaming cup of coffee. "Da special is beef stew. You want?"

"Sounds good to me," Willie said. "Anything going on around here?"

Olga dug deep with a long handled dipper into a huge pot and filled a generous bowl full of meat, potatoes, and carrots, which she placed in front of him. "Vell, the lumber guys figger to start floating ties next week, dat will be exciting."

Willie took a big spoonful of steaming succulent stew. "This is really good stew. Where do you get your meat?"

"Da butcher, down at da end of da street," she said. "Dat guy get some of him beef from Cap'n Howes. He got dem good short horn cows, not "piece of crap" longhorns. He save best for me and I pay him goot!"

Willie laughed. "You sure know your meat. Have you got anything for dessert?"

"You betcha!" Olga said. "How you like punkin' pie?"

"You betcha! Willie teased as she handed him a huge piece of pie.

Further conversation revealed that Olga was married to a sawmill foreman named Avon and had come from the "old country" five years earlier. They had relatives up river where there was a large Norwegian community. Her brother was a stone mason and was busy going around the country erecting stone buildings out of the plentiful sandstone in the area. He was currently doing a big job for John B. Kendrick of the OW ranch at the head of Hanging Woman Creek. Willie asked if she had heard of any news of horses being stolen or cattle being killed by the Cheyennes. She said there were rumors but no one knew anything for certain. She also reported that the biggest trouble she had was Cheyennes rummaging through her garbage trying to find something to eat. Willie left a nice tip and bid her goodbye.

Figure 21: Nuns at Early St. Labre Mission. Photo Courtesy of the Montana Historical Society

From Ashland, Willie rode his horse north to the St. Labre Mission. The Rowlands, Catholics in the Scottish tradition, were not especially devout or regular churchgoers. However, they had been baptized into the Church and attended services occasionally. Therefore Willie was familiar with the teachings of the faith and a supporter of the Catholic school ran by the Ursuline Order of Catholic nuns. Agent Upshaw also assisted the St. Labre outreach to the Cheyenne Tribe with an education contract from the Agency. Willie knew he could expect a welcome reception from the resident priest and the nuns.

The St. Labre mission had been established to minister to the Cheyenne Indians in 1884 with the founding of the Reservation. While the Cheyennes were exposed to Catholics as early as Father DeSmet in the early 1800's, there was no regular contact with the tribe until 1883 when George Yoakim, a convert to the faith and recently discharged soldier from Ft. Keogh, contacted Father P. Barcelo, the priest in Helena about a mission to the Cheyennes. Father Barcelo and George Yoakim spent several months with the Cheyennes and Father Barcelo appealed to the Rt. Reverend J.B. Brondell for a permanent mission to the area. Rev. J. Eyler and Mother Amadeus and three Ursuline Sisters arrived at a log cabin and farm at the junction of Otter Creek and Tongue River in April, 1884 to start the new Mission. By the spring of 1890, the Mission had grown to include a sanctuary, Indian boarding school for fifty children, a store house, stable, and housing for several nuns and Father A. van der Velden. Father van der Velden and Deacon George Yoakim both served the St. Labre Mission for nearly twenty years following its establishment. George Yoakim was nearly lynched by a group of drunken cowboys in 1884 when they objected to his support for the creation of the Cheyenne Reservation. He spoke the Cheyenne language and served as an interpreter as well as a missionary. Willie thought both men could be good contacts for both his food distribution efforts as well as his law enforcement mission.

Willie called on Father van der Velden in his office. He explained to him the Montana Stock Growers feeding plan to supplement the Cheyenne diet. This was accepted by the priest as a gift from God, since the Church was always looking for a way to benefit their starving potential flock. He immediately called in George Yoakim and told him the "Good News". There followed a long discussion as to the most effective methods to use this resource. Willie also brought up the need to keep the Cheyennes away from whiskey, a proposition that was met with most hearty approval from the two churchmen. He disclosed to them that he was an undercover deputy, showed them his badge, and asked for their help in identifying whiskey sellers, outlaws, and bad Cheyennes. He also asked them to help him gain acceptance into the Rabbit Town society, and offered to let the Church help direct the beef allocation to the most needy, including some beef for the Church's Cheyenne School. This proposal was also met with quick and enthusiastic acceptance. Yoakim suggested that parents of children who allowed their children to attend school be given a larger ration. That would bring them into closer contact with the Church and thus provide more information. Willie reluctantly agreed to try this for a limited time, pointing out that the Cheyennes most opposed to the white man's religion were the least likely to provide useful information to the Church. If he could pursue other alternatives through the Chiefs, military societies, or other avenues he might get better information. The churchmen saw the wisdom of this approach and agreed not to allow the student's parents to become dependent upon the near term ration increase. Willie was invited to eat supper and stay the night which he accepted gratefully.

That night Willie mapped out his travel plan for the next two days. He decided to go up Otter Creek to the Circle Bar and visit Captain Howes to arrange for his first cattle purchase. Then he would ride up Cow Creek and try and get a look at the outlaw cabin which Captain Howes had described to Sheriff Irvine. From there he would go west over the Otter/Tongue River divide to Poker Jim Butte and down Poker Jim Creek to the SH Ranch for the night. The following day he would cross Tongue River, go up Tie Creek to the divide, visit American Horse, and then go down the East Fork of Lame Deer Creek to the Agency. There he would report in to Agent Upshaw and hopefully get home to Muddy by dark. It was an ambitious plan.

Willie left St. Labre Mission shortly after daylight and went back to Olga's Eatery for breakfast before starting his ride up Otter to the Circle Bar Ranch. The trail east out of Ashland was thousands of years old, serving as a primary migration route for buffalo moving away from Tongue River to the grassy high divides between the Tongue River and Powder River drainages. It was replete with historic battles between Cheyenne and Crows and later Cheyenne/Sioux war parties versus white trappers, Army scouts, and settlers. The trail was also the favored route for Sioux and Cheyenne to move in an east/west direction when travelling between the Northern Cheyenne and Pine Ridge Reservations after both tribes surrendered.

Figure 22. Circle Bar Ranch. Photo Courtesy of the Montana Historical Society

About two hours later the Circle Bar came into view. It was situated at the junction of Taylor Creek and Otter Creek. A main house, bunkhouse, barn and other outbuildings graced a bench on the north side of Otter Creek. Immediately to the east of the ranch buildings stood a small conical hill with a stone fort on top. Two or three men armed with .50 cal. Sharps rifles could command the area for a mile or more around the hill. It was here that Captain Calvin Howes and family had established his ranch in 1884. In partnership with George Miles (Gen. Nelson

Miles' nephew) and Judge Strevell they ran thousands of cattle between Otter Creek and the South Dakota line. Furthermore, they were among the most progressive cattlemen in the area, breeding the ubiquitous longhorn cows brought up from Texas with English Shorthorn bulls from Oregon and the eastern states. The resulting "cross" made superior beef compared to straight longhorns.

As Willie rode into the ranch he was greeted by Ed McGhee, the Circle Bar foreman, who asked his business. Willie introduced himself and stated that he needed to speak to the boss about buying some cattle and had a letter of introduction from Granville Stuart. That immediately erased the suspicion the foreman may have had about a strange "half breed" showing up on the ranch. He was escorted to the main house where he was introduced to Captain Howes and his family. Willie presented the letter of introduction from Granville Stuart at which time Captain Howes quickly invited him into his house. Asking his wife to prepare a couple of cups of coffee, Captain Howes eagerly hustled Willie into a small study.

"What is on Granville's mind?" Captain Howes asked.

"This is confidential, Mr. Howes, Willie began. Noting Howes' nod he continued, "Mr. Stuart is preparing for an operation which may involve your ranch. Subject to your approval of course, he would like you to provide information on the movements of outlaws and thieves operating in the Otter Creek area. In addition, he would like you to provide a good fighting man who knows the area thoroughly to act as a guide should we locate a target in your area."

At that point Willie produced his badge and continued. "While I am an appointed deputy of Custer County, my role is as an undercover operator with responsibility for the Cheyenne Reservation and area associated with it. You may know my father, Bill Rowland. As part of my cover the Stock Growers are funding the purchase of a few cattle per month to help feed the Cheyennes until the Agency can get their rations increased. We are seeking the maximum meat for the lowest price, so "out" cattle are preferred if the price is right. The idea is to reduce the incentive for Cheyennes to go off the Reservation by providing additional beef, while I gather information for Sheriff Irvine and Stuart's operations. I will be contacting most of ranches bordering the Reservation to buy cattle. However, only a few MSG members will be told of my undercover role of information collection and transmission for Sheriff Irvine."

"How can we communicate?" Howes asked.

"The password is the number 26. If someone comes to you with a request from Stuart or Irvine to provide horses, shelter, or information, he will use that number in a sentence. Teddy Blue Abbott will be probably be the guy making arrangements for operations and he will use the number. When you need to contact me, send a letter to Agent Upshaw disguised as cattle bid/offer. Upshaw has fully knowledge of Stuart's plan. If you have highly confidential information that needs to be acted upon right away send a rider to deliver the letter. I can have the Cheyenne Scouts get it to Fort Keogh and on to Irvine in eight hours. If you want me to come and talk to you personally, say that you have 26 head for sale and I'll be here."

"You have my full support. It sounds like Stuart is making things happen," Howes declared. "What else can I do to help?"

"You can find me some cattle to bring to Rabbit Town. I need at least seven or eight head probably next week. I'll pick them up and drive them myself. Also figure out who your guide is going to be and tell him the password. When I get back to pick up the cattle, I'd like to have your guide take me up Cow Creek and look over that outlaw camp." Willie finished.

The cattle buyer cover worked amazing well. First it was true, tangible, and made perfect sense to ranchers, foreman, and cowboys. They immediately saw the benefit to their ranch, the Indians, and a perfectly logical reason for Willie to be riding around in their area. Captain Howes called Ed McGhee into the house and over a cup of coffee talked about the feeding program. Willie described the kinds of cattle he wanted to buy and they worked out the details. Ed said he could easily get ten or twelve head together in a couple of days and have them in the corral for Willie's choice.

Concluding business, Willie accepted Mrs. Howes' offer to stay for lunch and then mounted his horse and began the trip over the Otter/Tongue River divide. He rode up Otter Creek to Cow Creek where he turned west up the creek. Again, the trail was marked by an old buffalo trail now used by cattle. The country was timbered with a combination of Ponderosa Pine, junipers, and cedar trees with a series of grassy parks. The bottom of Cow Creek was filled with plum and chokecherry thickets all of which were in bloom. The scent from their flowers made a sweet perfume that wafted up from the creek and mixed with the pungent scent of pine and cedar trees. There were occasional bogs in the creek where springs broke to the surface creating a small circle of cattails and an occasional ash or cottonwood tree. About four miles up the creek where the main trail swung north away from the creek bed, Willie noted a side trail going south back toward the creek. Fresh horse tracks turned into the side trail from the main trail. Willie suspected that the trail led to the outlaw cabin described by Captain Howes. Resisting the urge to look for the cabin, Willie bypassed the side trail, but carefully studied the turn off, imagining how it would look at night, in preparation for a possible visit by Stuart's operation.

Another two miles brought the trail to the top of the divide where the country opened up into big grassy parks. The area was dominated by Poker Jim Butte, a large bluff whose sides were mostly grass but with a liberal scattering of single Ponderosa Pine trees and small clumps of cedar. The top of the butte was ringed with a thin layer of sandstone with a grassy park on top. Willie rode to the top of the butte where he was rewarded with a panoramic view of the whole country. To the southeast lay the Hanging Woman Creek drainage, to the south the Tongue River Valley up to the Big Horn Mountains, west and north across Tongue River lay the Cheyenne Reservation, and to the east was the Otter Creek drainage and the top of the Powder River/Tongue River Divide. At his immediate front and slightly north was the ten miles of rough country through the Tongue River breaks that he needed to traverse to the SH Ranch on Tongue River. Selecting Poker Jim Creek as the shortest route down to Tongue River, Willie rode about a mile north before turning west into the broken cedar draws and sand rock cliffs that characterized the creek.

The ride from Poker Jim Butte to the SH took about three slow hours as he negotiated sand rocks, cedar trees, and sage choked draws before finally reaching the valley floor. After watering his horse in Tongue River, he made good time to the SH Ranch.

The SH on Tongue River was a division of a much larger British company with interests in Idaho, Nevada, and a big cattle operation on Powder River in Wyoming and Montana. Originally the Tongue River operation was a "horse outfit" for the larger company, drawn to the area by the large wild hay meadows at the mouth of O'Dell Creek. In 1884 Joseph Scott moved 5,000 head of steers into the area and trimmed down the horse operation. The winter of 1886/1887 decimated the large company, although the Tongue River division survived better than their other cattle operations. Joseph Scott sold most of the horses and replaced them with cattle after the bad losses of 86/87. The larger company struggled financially for several years with Joseph Scott still managing the Tongue River division. Eventually the Tongue River division was sold to the Brown Cattle Company.

Willie rode into the SH where he was conducted to Joseph Scott for an interview. After presenting his letter of introduction to Mr. Scott, he was reluctantly invited to supper and offered a bed in the barn for the night. The British class system was on full display and if Willie had not been so tired from the long ride he would have crossed the river and spent the night in a Cheyenne teepee. While Mr. Scott was favorably disposed toward the Montana Stock Growers feeding plan, he let Willie know that so small an operation was probably not worth his time. Given his shabby treatment Willie did not share his status as an undercover Custer County deputy or mention any of Stuart's pending operations. He also resolved not to purchase any cattle from the SH.

Willie left the SH early the next morning and crossed Tongue River and was back on to the Reservation. This part of the Reservation was Indian Birney (as distinguished from White Birney, eight miles upriver) where Little Wolf's Band had settled after the return from Oklahoma. The Cheyennes were really two closely related tribes, the Suhtai and the *Tsis Tsis Tas*, and the Birney Community was mostly Suhtai. Both tribes had intermarried to such a degree that in actual blood there was very little difference but they still retained some vocabulary and minor cultural differences within the tribe. Willie recalled trying to explain the differences between the tribes to Agent Upshaw when he first became Agent. Upshaw couldn't get the two names pronounced correctly, stumbling time after time. Finally in frustration Willie said, "Look Upshaw, just remember them as the 'Shoot Highs' and the 'Tits-n-Shits', that's close enough." The main difference between the tribes was the location of the two main religious symbols, the Sacred Hat and the Sacred Arrows. The Sacred Hat was Suhtai and the Sacred Arrows were Tsis Tsis Tas. The Sacred Hat was almost always at Birney, but the Sacred Arrows were moved around various

Figure 23. American Horse at Teepee. Photo Courtesy Montana Historical Society

villages, sometimes residing with the Southern Cheyennes. However, both tribes recognized and revered the two symbols. Another difference was that in the Birney Village the strongest warrior society was the Swift Foxes, while in Lame Deer and Muddy the Crazy Dogs held sway. It would be important to recognize the differences when it came to food distribution.

By midmorning Willie was nearly to the head of Tie Creek near the Lame Deer/Birney Divide. He was anxious to get the latest Reservation news since his departure nearly a week ago. Completing the climb to the top of the divide, it was just a short ride to American Horse's Camp. American Horse was a minor chief and good friend of Bill Rowland. He was also one of those people who seemed to know everything that was going on in the tribe. The camp was a large teepee and a partially built new log cabin. Willie rode his horse to the nearby spring for a welcome drink of water. He was greeted by barking dogs rushing out from the vicinity of the cabin. Goa, American Horse's daughter yelled at the dogs to come back and she was joined by American Horse himself. American Horse waved him over and recognizing Willie his face broke into a wide smile.

"Hello, Long Forehead. Welcome to my camp. Come in for some coffee. What are you doing on this side of the Reservation?" he asked in Cheyenne.

"Working for Upshaw." Long Forehead replied. "I'm trying to get all the Cheyenne names into his big book. He has to show all names to get the Great Father to send more cattle for Cheyennes on ration day."

"That would be real good," American Horse observed. "Right now nobody gets enough. Last week we got meat on ration day, today it is almost gone. No good. Children are hungry."

Goa ducked inside the teepee and brought out two cups of coffee which she handed one to her father and the other to Long Forehead. "We don't have much coffee either, but more than meat."

"I know. I know," said Long Forehead disgustedly. "Upshaw can't get enough cattle to feed everybody. I really worry about the old folks, widows, and kids getting enough to eat, since they can't hunt. In the old days the military societies used to take care of those people but now I don't know. American Horse, have you heard anything about that?"

"I think the military societies are trying to help," American Horse replied. "I heard that the Elk Horn Scrapers got permission from Agent Upshaw to go hunting on the Great Father's land that is not on the Reservation last winter. They got a few deer over by Otter Creek and distributed some to the old people and widows."

"That's good." Long Forehead observed. "As long as they don't kill some white man's cattle and get in a fight. Have you seen any groups of white men with loose horses or Cheyennes driving shod horses?"

"I saw some tracks over by that timber," American Horse pointed with his chin toward to the west about a mile away. "Horses had shoes on. Maybe seven or eight sleeps ago. Going toward Rabbit Town. Why do you ask?"

"I heard from Trader Young that somebody stole some horses and brought them onto the Crow Reservation. Crows tracked them from Rotten Grass up Grey Blanket Creek but stopped at the Cheyenne boundary. Then a lame horse with a strange brand came to our camp on Muddy," Willie explained. "Upshaw doesn't want Crows blaming Cheyennes for what some white men did. He told me to ask around."

"I don't know. Maybe white men, maybe Crow, maybe Cheyenne." American Horse suggested.'

"Well, keep a good look out. I got to go report to Upshaw. I hope to get home before dark. Thanks for the coffee." Willie rose and shook hands with American Horse, mounted his horse and moved on to the Birney/Lame Deer trail.

Willie trotted into Lame Deer and went straight to Upshaw's office. Fortunately he found the Agent at his desk.

"Willie, I'm really glad to see you back," exclaimed Upshaw rising from his desk. "Come in and tell me about your travels."

Willie shook hands with Upshaw and turned and closed the door. Both men sat down and Willie began.

"I've been all over hell and back. I went to Miles City and met with Swaine and Irvine at the Fort. Swaine was really helpful in that he will set up a courier service using the Cheyenne Scouts to quickly get messages to Fort Keogh and on to Sheriff Irvine. Irvine made me a deputy of Custer County and gave me a salary and a badge. He and Marshall Beidler briefed me up on the outlaw situation and showed me a whole lot of wanted posters with pictures and descriptions of outlaws operating in this area. Then Beidler and I rode all the way up the Musselshell to Mosby and spent the night. The next day we rode on to Stuart's Ranch and Fort MacGinnis. Beidler picked up some information when we went through Junction City and some more at the Fort MacGinnis telegraph station. We had a good meeting with Stuart. Beidler brought him up to date on the latest outlaw movements and I got introduced and questioned him about the Cheyenne feeding program. He committed to a sum of $250 per month and gave us free rein to buy "out" cattle and distribute them as we see fit. The money is limited to the year that he is head of the Executive Committee, but he would support further contributions if the program worked. I brought up the sale of whiskey to Indians and he said that he would introduce a bill to outlaw the practice. Finally, he asked that I get bills of sale from the ranchers I buy cattle from and that you do the accounting and send the sales slips to him each month. We spent the night there and the next day "X" went on north and I turned back for Miles City. I made it as far a spot between Junction City and Forsyth where I slept out for the night and rode on to Miles City the next morning. Sheriff Irvine and I met for lunch where I gave him a progress report, cashed the first $250 check from the Montana Stock Growers, and then headed for Ashland right after lunch. Then I spent the night at the St. Labre Mission and secured their support to help gather information in exchange for some input on how Rabbit Town beef was distributed. Yesterday morning I rode to the Circle Bar and had a conversation with Captain Howes about the feeding program and secured his help with Stuart's operations. From there I rode over the divide and spent the night at the SH. Then I cut over to Tie Creek to the top of the divide where I talked with American Horse about some strange horse movements and then came on to Lame Deer. I figure I have ridden over 500 miles in the last six days. Any questions before I head for home? I'm about used up."

"Not now," said Upshaw. "Rest up for a day and come back and we will plan out how to propose the MSG feeding plan to the 44 chiefs and work on the census project."

They shook hands and Willie wearily swung back into the saddle for the final seven miles to Muddy.

Chapter 13. The Chiefs

Two days later Willie was back in Agent Upshaw's office discussing the Montana Stock Growers (MSG) feeding plan and the census problem. The MSG program presented an opportunity use one program to enhance the other. Without an accurate count of who was actually on the Reservation, the appropriate amount of rations could not be requested. Congress rightly demanded that the Indian Department provide them with accurate figures so they could appropriate the correct amount of tax dollars. The Indian Department in turn demanded that their Agents provide them with the numbers backed up by actual names and locations. Agent Upshaw was on the hook to provide that information for the Northern Cheyenne Reservation.

Gathering information intelligible to the white bureaucrats from the various reservations was an extremely difficult task. This was doubly so on the Cheyenne Reservation because of the wide dispersion of the tribe among various other tribes before the creation of their own reservation. At the 1884 initial reserve only the Two Moons and Little Wolf bands were actually on the reservation and they comprised only about one half of the tribe. The remaining bands were on the Southern Cheyenne, Pine Ridge Sioux, and Arapaho reservations. Many were married into those tribes, so deciding to which reservation a family belonged was problematic. Most were enrolled on the first reservation where they were sent after their individual surrender. Once on the rolls of one reservation it was very difficult to transfer the enrollment to another. Adding to the confusion was the propensity of family members to travel between reservations visiting relatives without notifying the respective Agencies. When the "visiting" relatives stayed from a few days to a few months or even took up permanent residence, the difference between the rations allocated annually to the Northern Cheyenne Agency varied sharply from the numbers showing up on ration day.

Another issue was the confusion of what constituted a "band". To the white authorities a band was the group of Cheyennes under a definable chief such as the Little Wolf Band, Dull Knife Band, or Little Chief Band. However, in Cheyenne culture there were ten distinct bands each with four "chiefs" elected for ten years. They in turn elected four "old man chiefs" which made the "Council of 44 Chiefs" who could set policy and direction for the whole tribe. The Council of 44 was becoming less important in tribal administration since the formation of the reservation and the importance of the Agency to the tribe. Distribution of rations, Cheyenne Police Force, and appointment of tribal judges all served to weaken the power of the chiefs. Nonetheless they still held sway in social and religious areas so their blessing was always helpful when trying to introduce something new like the census and the MSG feeding program. Willie acting in the role of Long Forehead, intended to make maximum use of the Council of 44 to gain acceptance of the very traditional members of the tribe where information was the most difficult to obtain.

Previous attempts at an accurate census had failed miserably. Upshaw had attempted to record each Cheyenne's family name in previous years. However, because Cheyenne names changed over their lives from children to adulthood there was no consistency. In his youth a Cheyenne may have the name Running Boy which changed in later life to Yellow Mule. In addition, under Cheyenne culture all uncles were called father, aunt's called mother, and cousins were brothers and sisters. Wives did not have the name of their husbands and children's names bore no resemblance to either father or mother. When asked by a census taker the name of his father, a child would answer with the names of his father, all his father's brothers, and all his mother's brothers. Given the complexity of the

Cheyenne language, unless the question was posed in exactly the right way, the answer could be completely wrong.

Willie suggested that each Cheyenne be given a "white man name" which included a first name and an English translation of his adult Cheyenne name. Wives and children took an English first name and the same last name as the adult father. Thus on the rolls of the agency the roll would look as follows:

Spotted Mule would become James Spotted Mule – Father

Sweet Woman would become Sara Spotted Mule – Wife of James Spotted Mule

Running Boy would become Tom Spotted Mule – Son of James and Sara Spotted Mule

Sits By the Water would become Mary Spotted Mule – Daughter of James and Sara Spotted Mule

Using such a system would provide a unique name on the rolls which could be translated into the English and thence on to the Indian Department. Upshaw could then set up a training course for interpreters/census takers on exactly how the forms were to be constructed and filled out. Then Willie and Upshaw addressed how to organize the census takers. First the four "old man chiefs" would be invited to the Agent's office and told of the plan and how it would be used to get the promised level of rations. Then one of the four chiefs from each of the ten historic bands would be selected by the "old man chiefs" to insure that all members of his band were counted and recorded. It would be emphasized that it was a high honor to be selected for this heavy responsibility. A "gift" of one horse would be given to each of the "old man chiefs." The selected "band chief" would also get a horse to supervise the census but subsequently would become his own. Each individual who was appropriately recorded would get a silver quarter. It was important to characterize the horses and quarters as gifts from the Great Father and not payment for services rendered. If the gifts were presented in this fashion, it would be in line with Cheyenne culture and reinforce the authority of the chiefs.

It was planned that on ration day, the Council of 44 would be called together after the approval of the "old man chiefs" and the census plan would be presented to the Council for their consideration. Upshaw would give a big speech which Willie would interpret that explained the census taking and its importance. If the approval of the "old man chiefs" was already in hand, the Council of 44 could be expected to bless the program. As a final announcement of "good news" Willie would inform the Council of 44 of the gift of cattle by neighboring ranchers to the Cheyennes to help feed the People for about one year. It was hoped that all of these plans would come to fruition in time to protect the Cheyennes and the neighboring settlers from the pressures of hungry stomachs, Indian and white criminals, vast cultural differences, and bureaucratic inaction.

With the ration distribution coming in four days it was important to bring the "Old Man Chiefs" together for approval before all the Cheyennes were gathered. Therefore Upshaw dispatched Willie to Rabbit Town and Birney to notify Little Chief and Grasshopper to come a day early. Two Moons was already in Lame Deer so Upshaw sent Bill Rowland, Jr. to the Busby Trading Post to tell White Bull, the successor to Dull Knife.

Figure 24. White Bull (Ice). Photo Courtesy of the Montana Historical Society

Figure 25. Two Moons. Photo Courtesy of the Montana Historical Society

Figure 26. Little Chief. Photo Courtesy of the Montana Historical Society

Three days later the first part of the plan came together. Grasshopper from Birney District arrived first, followed by White Bull from the Rosebud District, and Two Moons for the Lame Deer District. Little Chief from the Rabbit Town was predictably late, showing disrespect to the Agent and the other chiefs. Two Moons, the best English speaker, summed it up best during the wait. "Goddam Sioux son-of-bitch. Him heap pain in ass!" Finally Little Chief arrived with no apology to fill out the group of "Old Man Chiefs."

Upshaw opted to overlook the insult in view of the larger issues and began the long explanation of the need for an accurate census to get more rations. Willie carefully interpreted the reasons for supporting the census and outlined the need for a "white man name" for each individual Cheyenne. Little Chief objected to the renaming, complaining that it would make the process too complicated. Willie replied that if they didn't change the names the People would continue to receive inadequate rations. Little Chief was adamant that he would not support the name change idea. Willie then explained the use of the separate band chiefs to supervise the census and the gift of a horse to each "Old Man Chief" and each "band chief" to help make the census a success. Upon learning of his impending gift, Little Chief dropped his objection to the program.

Willie then explained the Montana Stock Grower's "gift" of cattle to the Cheyennes and how it was related to the success of the census program. The news of imminent increase in the meat ration met with instant approval from all the chiefs and the tone of the meeting improved dramatically. Even Little Chief nodded his approval when Willie suggested that the strongest military society in each district direct the distribution. Willie then requested that each "Old Man Chief" select a "band chief" to supervise census activities of his band in the Meeting of the Forty Four Chiefs the following day. The chiefs assented to the proposals and Upshaw thanked them for their cooperation and they adjourned outside where each chief was awarded his "gift" horse. Willie insured that Little Chief received the worst of the four horses presented.

The following day excitement filled the air. It was a beautiful May spring day, green grass was growing rapidly, it was warm but not hot, plum and chokecherry trees were in full bloom and the cottonwood trees were beginning to flower and leaf out. Rumors of increased rations were circulating and people were looking forward to the afternoon feast that Upshaw had directed coincident with the meeting of the 44 Chiefs. A big open tent had been set up to accommodate the meeting. Four fat steers were turning on spits over a bed of coals, people were greeting relatives and old friends, wives and daughters were making fry bread, and the "old man chiefs" were circulating among their bands seeking out band chiefs to give them a preview of the meeting to come. Children were playing the hoop game under the supervision of old men and also participating in foot races. Horse racing by the young men had attracted an active betting crowd. The public tone was festive and upbeat which was exactly what Upshaw intended.

Willie and Agent Upshaw were actively checking on the preparation and distribution of rations. The actual meeting was scheduled to begin at 04:00 P.M. that afternoon. Upshaw wanted all rations fully distributed before the meeting began. The Cheyenne Police had been detailed to slaughter the 40 head of cattle at the Muddy Corral the day before and were bringing the carcasses by wagon to Lame Deer. There they would be weighed, cut up, and distributed according to the specifications prescribed by the Indian Department. Each Cheyenne would be given seven tenths of a pound per day or about ten pounds for 15 days. However, no allowance for bones was made so actual consumable meat came closer to one half pound per day. It was somewhat instructive that the meat ration for U.S. Army troops was one and two tenths pounds per day and bones were not included. This explained why the Cheyennes were hungry all the time.

At about 03:30 a herald or "camp crier" was sent through the crowds summoning the 44 Chiefs to the big tent for the formal "Meeting of the 44 Chiefs". The four "Old Man Chiefs" were seated in the front facing the remaining forty chiefs. Upshaw began the meeting with a speech which Willie carefully and specifically translated into Cheyenne. He described how the Indian Department counted Indians and why the count was wrong. Because the count was wrong the Indian Department wouldn't give Upshaw the rations needed to feed all the Indians. That is why the Cheyennes were hungry. He explained that to get the right count he needed to show the Great Father a paper that had the name of each Cheyenne written on it. Because Cheyenne names were always changing and getting all mixed up he wanted to give each Cheyenne a "white man name" to put on the paper. This is the name they needed to use when drawing rations and for Agency business. Otherwise they could use whatever name they wanted. Long Forehead emphasized that they needed every single Cheyenne to be recorded regardless of age. Each person counted would be given a silver quarter and an ink stamp on their hand. That way there would be no double counting. The "Old Man Chief" was responsible for getting all Cheyennes in his district registered. The ten bands would select one of their four chiefs to act as the "Census Chief" to make sure everyone was counted. The "Census Chief" from each of the ten bands would be reported to the Old Man Chief of the District. The Great Father was making a gift of one silver dollar to each of the 44 Chiefs that attended this meeting. In addition, each of the Census Chiefs would receive a horse to use in the census collection. Once the census was completed to Upshaw's satisfaction, the "Census Chief" would be given the horse as a gift from the Great Father.

Then Agent Upshaw announced the Montana Stock Grower's Feeding Program. He began by saying that he was concerned that continued cattle butchering of white man's cattle by Indians would cause violent reprisals from the affected stockman. He reported that he had attended a "big council" of white cattlemen where some of the cattlemen had wanted to attack any Indians off the reservation. This suggestion was opposed by the "big chiefs" of the Montana Stock Growers Association and the Army at Fort Keogh. He said he had addressed the council and reported that the Cheyennes were hungry because the Indian Department did not have a good count of how many Indians were on the reservation. He also revealed that the Cheyennes were getting blamed for lots of missing cattle and horses that had been stolen by bad white men. Many of the stockmen that bordered the reservation were very sorry that their Cheyenne brothers had been badly treated and wanted to know if they could do anything to help. The Montana Stock Growers had decided to help the Cheyennes to get some more beef until the "new count" had been made and the Indian Department meat ration could be increased. They would make "gifts" of some cattle to their neighboring Cheyenne brothers for about a year. Willie announced that he would be Upshaw's representative to the ranchers and that he would gather the cattle and drive them to the reservation. He asked that Cheyennes note the brands on the cattle and protect that rancher's cattle from harm from other Cheyennes or bad white men. He concluded with the announcement that these cattle would be delivered to the military society selected by the "Old Man Chief" of the district. They would conduct the slaughter and distribution of the meat within the district rather than travelling to Lame Deer. Lastly he emphasized that normal ration days would continue and these cattle would be a supplement to the existing meat ration. He thanked the Council for their attention and asked their approval for the census program and the MSG supplemental meat program.

The announcements were met by much enthusiasm among the Council members. It was some of the first positive news they had received in a long time. They were impressed that Agent Upshaw was consulting them as opposed to just making an announcement that they must comply with. At that point Long Forehead and Agent Upshaw exited the tent and let the Council continue its deliberation, confident that the Old Man Chiefs would direct the council members toward a positive conclusion.

At about 08:00 that night Long Forehead and Agent Upshaw were summoned to the Council tent where they were met by the Old Man Chiefs. The Chiefs said that the Council had approved the two programs but that they had several questions about specifics. Every one of the four band chiefs in each band wanted to be the "Census Chief" so they could get the horse. The "Old Man Chief's" decided that each band would select its "Census Chief." If there was a tie the "Old Man Chief" of the district would select among the finalists. They also wanted to know if Long Forehead was going to take into account the population differences between districts. He assured them that he would, but noted that some people in remote parts of the reservation couldn't always come to Lame Deer on ration day, especially during the winter. If these people's ration was being shorted he might give them some extra out of the supplemental. Also the bands doing the best job on the census might get a little preference. This generally resolved the objections of the Council and both proposals were approved.

Chapter 14. Bob Ferguson Goes Missing

Two days following the euphoria of the successful Chief's meeting bad news shook the Agency. Rancher Bob Ferguson who owned a ranch with his brother and sister-in-law was reported missing. The ranch was right at the eastern edge of the reservation on the Rosebud. This was the same Bob Ferguson who had reported that he was missing a dozen cows and suspected butchering by Dull Knife's band. He also reported missing some horses and he was out searching for them when he failed to return on the evening of May 6. His brother went out looking for him for the next two days without success. Then, with neighbors they combed the high hills, timbered draws, brushy hills, and high divides of the ranch but found nothing. They moved their search onto the eastern part of the reservation to a distance of about five miles. Finding no sign of the man or his horse they suspected foul play and contacted the Agency to conduct a reservation wide search. The Cheyenne Police with Willie and his brother Bill Jr. led a search along the western Cheyenne boundary with the Crow Reservation. They found some of the horses that Ferguson had been looking for nearly twenty miles west of the ranch. Willie noted that none of the horses found were geldings, only mares with young foals and one stallion. Discussion with Bob Ferguson's brother revealed that seven geldings were missing. A pattern of horse stealing activity was beginning to emerge. However during another two days of searching nothing new was found.

Meantime the Yellowstone Journal in Miles City saw the disappearance as another opportunity to rail against the presence of the Cheyenne Reservation and speculated that Cheyennes were responsible.

Willie returned to Lame Deer and had Upshaw send a message to Col. Swaine requesting the use of the Cheyenne Scouts to widen the search. Three days later Captain Casey and his platoon of scouts arrived to support the Cheyenne Police. They set up a headquarters at the newly formed Busby Trading Post and developed a formal search pattern with the use of a gridded map. At this point Captain Casey took charge of the search and Willie was released for his first cattle buying trip.

Figure 27. Early Busby Trading Post. Courtesy of the Montana State Historical Society.

Chapter 15. First Cattle Buying Trip

Willie began his cattle buying trip with a ride to Rabbit Town. As he rode along he planned out how would be the best way to get the most out of his first trip. While Willie had reservations about dealing with Little Chief, he recognized that he had to meet with him if he was to help the people of Rabbit Town. One mitigating factor was that there were several other highly respected chiefs and military leaders with which he could also deal. Little Hawk was the head of the Elk Horn Scrapers military society and also a chief. Since the Elk Horns were the most prominent military society in Rabbit Town, it would probably be them who would do the distribution. Therefore he decided to visit Little Chief and Little Hawk and ask them to make preparations for receiving and distribution of the cattle he expected to buy from Captain Howes. He also needed to visit St. Labre Mission and prepare them for receipt of their part of the distribution.

Arriving at Rabbit Town about midmorning Willie rode straight for Little Chief's Lodge and called a greeting. Twin Woman, Little Chief's wife appeared and asked what he wanted. Willie replied that he had come to speak to Little Chief on behalf of Agent Upshaw. In view of Little Chief's arrogance at the Chiefs' Council, Willie did not accord Little Chief the same courtesy he had shown Little Wolf a few weeks before. He dismounted his horse and approached the lodge before Little Chief came to the entrance thereby showing Agent Upshaw's authority. Little Chief came, opened the lodge flap, and welcomed Long Forehead into his lodge. He was unusually amiable and invited Long Forehead to be seated and asked Twin Woman to bring coffee. Explaining the purpose of his trip, Long Forehead asked that Little Hawk come and join the conversation about how the cattle delivery was to be handled. Little Chief sent a child to invite Little Hawk to join them which he did a few minutes later. Long Forehead told them that he would bring the cattle from Captain Howes the following day probably when the sun was high in the sky. When the cattle arrived, he would require help getting the cattle across Tongue River because the water was so high. Long Forehead asked Little Chief if the Elkhorn Scrapers were going to be the society to distribute to the Ashland District since they were the largest society. While it was obvious who should perform the duty, he wanted Little Chief on record as approving the selection. Little Chief confirmed the choice and Little Hawk said he would gather his soldiers and asked Long Forehead if there was anything special they had to do. Long Forehead replied that the cattle should be killed in public where the tribe could see the "white man gifts". Furthermore the Elks should cut out the brands and show them to the people so they could recognize who was an especially "good" white man rancher and ask the people to protect his cattle from other Cheyennes and bad white men. It was understood that the meat was to be equitably distributed. Both chiefs agreed that this was the best "Cheyenne" way to do the program.

Willie swam his horse across the swollen Tongue River and stopped for a late lunch at Olga's Eatery. He noticed that most of the rail road ties were gone from the ricks along the river.

Olga gave Willie a warm welcoming smile, "How you do, Willie? What you do back in this country?"

"Hi, Olga," Willie replied. "Couldn't stay away from your punkin' pie. I got a new job as a cattle buyer for the Reservation. Your beef stew was so good last time, I am going up to the Circle Bar and get some of Captain Howes' beef to feed the Cheyennes."

"Bad idea, Willie. Them Injuns get taste of that good beef, they won't eat ration beef." Olga teased, "Probably make butcherin' problem more bad."

Willie laughed, "Gosh, I hope not. I'm not buying good cattle. Just old cows and bulls. Some cripples and stuff like that. I'll leave the good stuff for you! What's your special today?"

"Roast Beef, mashed potatoes, carrots and peas. All coffee you want." Olga said. "Apple pie for desert."

"Wow, bring it on," declared Willie. He then asked, "Where is Avon? I saw most of the ties are gone."

"Him down at Miles City, ketchin' ties," Olga replied. "Only a couple guys know how to do that tie ketchin'. Avon learned that in the old country."

Willie exclaimed, "I'd really like to see that. Do they really walk on the ties as they float down the river?"

"Yep, Avon been doin' that since he was 12 years old. They pay big bonus for all ties they get out of water at Miles City."

Olga served Willie a big helping of the daily special followed by a huge piece of apple pie. After finishing his meal, he said good bye to Olga and headed for the St. Labre mission to have them prepare for the arrival of cattle the next day. There he met with Father van der Velden who asked that he deliver cattle designated for the Mission to the slaughter/butcher shop in Ashland. Willie was happy to agree to the arrangement because in addition to accommodating the Mission, it gave him a good opportunity to meet the butcher and find out how the local beef were handled. Returning from the Mission he stopped at Ron's Meat Market to make the arrangements.

Tying his horse to the hitching rail at the front of the shop, Willie entered the shop where he met the butcher Ron Smith. Ron was a big burly man with a bloody apron and an accommodating attitude. After introductions, Willie began to question the butcher on the specific procedures to get an animal butchered at his facility.

"I will be bringing about a dozen head tomorrow about noon. Two head go to the Mission and I need to drop them here to be slaughtered and the rest I will take on to the reservation. Can I use your corral to sort the two off?" Willie asked.

"No problem," Ron Smith replied. "It will only take a couple of minutes to do the sort. We only kill once a week, on Wednesday's. Then they hang for two weeks before they are cut up. We sort of run a feed lot to hold them until the Wednesday kill date."

"How do you keep the carcasses from spoiling during the hanging period?" Willie inquired.

"Come on and I'll show you." Ron said.

Ron led the way toward the back of shop and into a room with several hanging carcass. Willie noticed that the room was decidedly cooler than the outside. He recognized the scent of wet sawdust which hung heavy in the air.

"We have lots of sawdust from the saw mills and put up ice in the winter time," Ron explained. "The ice is cut into blocks from Tongue River and hauled to a big ice house next door and covered with sawdust. The sawdust provides insulation and keeps the ice from melting. We built this room so we could bring in fresh ice blocks every day and use them to keep the meat cool. The room is surrounded by sawdust so the blocks take a long time to melt. It keeps the meat cool and fresh."

"You guys really put a lot of thought and work into this project." Willie said admiringly. "Where do you get your beef?"

"From all over. There are lots of cattle in this country. Mostly local sources," Ron replied evasively.

"Do all cattle come to you live? Or can I deliver to you a carcass and have you cut it up for me. It must be a chore to get rid of all the guts and hides you generate here." Willie opined.

"I prefer to buy the cattle live and kill them myself," Ron said. "We will process a carcass for a local rancher but they usually do it themselves. I don't buy any carcasses for resale to my customers. A man could get into trouble doing that."

"So you don't sell any beef to the sawmill crews?" Willie asked.

"Nope, not usually. Once in a while if they are running short. They mostly buy carcass beef from local contractors and use their own butchers and cooks to cut it up." Ron replied grimly.

"Where do those local contractors get their carcass beef?" Willie asked sharply.

"They buy from local ranchers, I suppose. There is a guy from the lower Rosebud that supplies most of the contracts. They say he kills his own beef and delivers the carcasses with the hides off directly to the mills." Ron replied carefully.

"You don't think he is legit?" Willie pressed.

"I didn't say that," Ron hastened to reply. "I don't know nothing to say he isn't. But I heard he is pretty good with a gun."

"Well I have to buy some cattle for Lame Deer and Muddy. I just don't want to get into a jam with cattlemen close to the reservation by buying cattle I shouldn't. Would you tell me who he is?" Willie asked.

"I'd rather not. Probably said too much already." Ron said guardedly.

"O.K. I understand that. I don't want to get you into a jam either. What paperwork do you need on these Circle Bar cattle I'll be bringing you tomorrow?" Willie concluded.

"Well, I guess that I would like to see a bill of sale signed by Captain Howes to the Cheyenne Agency. Then you could give me a bill of sale from the Cheyenne Agency to the Mission consigned to Ron's Butcher Shop for slaughter. That should cover me." Ron acted relieved that the conversation had turned in a different direction.

"I can do that. I'll see you tomorrow about noon. It's been really good to meet you." Willie shook hands with Ron and swung up on his horse and moved out on the Otter Creek trail.

The ride to the Circle Bar took about two hours. He arrived to find Ed McGhee and Charlie Thex doctoring a saddle horse in the corral. The horse had been attacked by a mountain lion and had several deep scratches on his rump. To doctor the horse Ed McGhee led the horse into a corner with a gate on one side. Then Charlie Thex swung the gate toward the fence trapping the injured horse between the gate and the side of the corral. He then tied a soft rope between the gate and corral so the horse could not back out. Then they treated the deep scratches with iodine and kerosene. The horse bucked and screamed in pain as the iodine penetrated the scratches, but it was necessary treatment. The horse could not be ridden for a couple of weeks but could be expected to make a full recovery.

Willie dismounted just as the two men turned the horse loose. Noticing Willie the two men turned toward the main gate and Willie.

"Howdy, Willie!" Good to see you back in the country. Have you met our neighbor, Charlie Thex?" greeted Ed.

"No, I haven't had the pleasure," replied Willie extending his hand.

"Good to meet you too. Are you the Indian cattle buyer the Cap'n told me about?" asked Charlie as he pumped Willie's hand.

"Yep. That would be me. You got any cattle picked out for me, Ed? Willie inquired as he turned to Ed McGhee for the mandatory handshake.

"I got eighteen in the horse pasture. Will that be enough to get you started?"

"That ought to be plenty. Can I take a look at them?" Willie asked.

Ed motioned toward a gate, "Ride through that gate, the horse pasture is only about forty acres. They will be down by the crick. Take a good look and I will meet you up at the Captain's house. Meantime I will tell him you are here. He told me he sure wants to talk to you when you got here. I think he wants to talk to Charlie at the same time."

Willie rode through the gate which Ed closed behind him. Down by some boxelder trees near the creek Willie noted a small group of cattle. There were two old bulls, one cancer eyed cow, seven dry cows, two cows with knocked down hips, and six orphan calves from the year before. All of the cattle seemed to be in pretty good flesh. Willie rounded up the group and moved them a few yards to make sure nothing was too lame to make the trip to the reservation. Since all were acceptable he turned back toward the house.

Ed met him at the gate which he opened. "Willie, the old man wants you to stay for supper. You can't get that little bunch back to Ashland this evening, and I have an extra bed in the bunkhouse, so you may as well spend the night. Let's put your horse up and your bedroll in the bunkhouse. Then we will go up to the big house."

About 05:00 P.M. Ed and Willie made their way up to the "big house" for dinner with Captain Howes. Willie noted that Charlie Thex was also in attendance. After greeting them warmly, Captain Howes ushered them into his "study" while supper was being prepared. He asked Ed to bring some wood in for the ladies while he talked to Charlie and Willie. Ed was somewhat confused by being cut out of the group, but nonetheless proceeded out to the wood pile.

Captain Howes started the conversation. "Willie, how did you like the cattle that Ed picked out? Were they acceptable?"

"Yes, they are about what I expected. If we can afford them, that is. How do you have them priced?" asked Willie.

"I want to be fair to the Stock Growers and fair to the ranch and my partners", Howes began. "It seems to me that the seven dry cows and the two bulls ought to be worth at least a quarter of the price of a good steer. The cancer eyed cow and the two cows with the bad hips are not worth much. The small yearlings if left out for the rest of the summer would put on some good flesh but still would be cut backs next fall. I'll price the cull cows and the yearlings at $5.00 per head and the dry cows at $10.00. The big bulls should be worth $12.50. Let's see, that makes about $140.00 for eighteen head. How's that?"

"Sounds fair to me Captain Howes. The only problem I have is that it spends me down too far on my budget. This is the first month we are doing this and I need to make a good impression on the whole reservation. These 18 would work for Ashland and Birney but that is only about a third of the Cheyennes that need fed. The rest are in Lame Deer, Muddy, and Busby. I'll tell you what, I will take this 18 head for $125.00. Next month, I'll buy some more we can make up the $15.00 difference on those cattle. I'll just over pay next month." Willie offered.

"I guess that would be all right," Howes accepted. "It's only thirty days and we already have them gathered. Those three cows are pretty much worthless anyway."

"Good. Please write me two bills of sale. One for two head and one for 16 head. Two head are going to the Mission and I need to get a separate bill of sale for the butcher in Ashland. He is pretty cautious," Willie reported while digging out his wallet. He counted out $125.00 and laid it on the table.

"Glad to hear it," Howes snorted as he wrote out the bills of sale. "I wish the saw mills would be as cautious."

"By the way, who is the contractor that supplies the two sawmills in Ashland? Ron Smith told me he did very little business with them." Willie asked.

"Damned if I know, have you heard anything Charlie?" Captain Howes turned to Charlie Thex after handing the bills of sale to Willie.

Charlie growled, "Rumor has it that it is a guy from the Lower Rosebud named Sim Roberts. His brand is the $B which just happens to fit nicely over several neighboring brands. He used to work up around Big Timber where he was accused of being a horse thief. He shot and killed the only witness, supposedly in self-defense. Then he and the dead man's brother exchanged shots after the court dismissed the case for lack of evidence. Roberts thought it best to move to the Rosebud. I hear he is a good cowman, but too quick to use his gun."

"Do you know if the sawmills buy their beef live by head or by the carcass?" Willie asked Charlie.

"Almost entirely carcass," Charlie replied. "They bring the carcasses in by wagon with the hides already off. I don't think there is a hide to be seen when they cross the river."

"Do they come on the reservation when they are delivering by wagon?" Willie mused out loud.

"Well, maybe for a little way," Charlie said. "If they kill the cattle at his ranch on the Rosebud, then they would come over the divide between Rosebud and Tongue River. The main wagon trail is on the west side of Tongue River all the way up from Garland. They would be on the reservation for four or five miles until they crossed the Tongue River ford between Rabbit Town and Ashland."

The Howes ladies called supper so the confab broke up as the men moved to the dining room table. Supper conversation centered on the prospects for the new state of Montana and the Montana State Legislature. Willie reported that Granville Stuart would file a bill outlawing the sale of liquor to Indians both on and off their reservations. Levi Howes asked Willie about the "Ghost Dance Craze" that was sweeping the Sioux and Blackfoot Reservations. He reported that last week when he was staying at a cow camp across the river from the Birney Village that the "tom toms" and singing were going all night. He was wondering if the "Craze" had spread to the Cheyennes. Willie replied that not much was happening on the Cheyenne as far as he knew. There was an old medicine man named Porcupine who sometimes visited the Birney Village that had taken up the new religion but had not made many converts. Willie said he would check it out when he delivered some of the cattle to the Village.

When supper was over Captain Howes asked Charlie Thex and Willie to stay a little longer for some more business discussion. Again they retired to the Captain's study.

Captain Howes again started the conversation. "Willie, you asked me to select a good man to serve as a guide and fighter if Stuart's operations came to this area. I have asked Charlie here if he would serve in that capacity and he has accepted. Charlie has come up the trail from Texas at least twice, hunted buffalo all over this country, fought Indians and even trailed an outlaw or two. He also served about six months with the Texas Rangers. I have complete confidence in his honesty and ability to keep his mouth shut.

Willie turned to Charlie. "Welcome aboard as Captain Howes would say. Has Captain Howes briefed you on Stuart's plans for cleaning up the cattle and horse thieves in Eastern Montana?"

"We went over what you told me last week. Has there been anything new since then?" Captain Howes asked.

"A couple of new developments," Willie said grimly. "Bob Ferguson from the Upper Rosebud has been missing for about a week and a half. He went looking for some of his horses and didn't come back. We did a search and found some of the horses, all mares and colts, seven geldings were missing. He also reported missing about a dozen of his cows earlier this spring, probably butchered by Dull Knife's Band. The Cheyenne Scouts are doing a grid search but nothing has been found yet. I think he's dead. Then I got word that a bunch of shod horses came down the divide between Tongue River and the head of Lame Deer Creek, heading towards Ashland. I don't think it is Cheyennes unless they are working with some white guys. Most Cheyenne ponies are not shod and so the horses were either stolen white man horses or a bunch of white men. Neither case is positive. Stuart will probably make his move in June but he may not make it this far until early July. How about the guys on Cow Creek, anything new on them?"

Charlie spoke up. "They are keeping a low profile. I heard that it may be some of Doc Middleton's boys from Nebraska. We can't pin anything on them from around here, but they are definitely on the dodge. So far they are leaving us alone. Do you want me to slip up there and take a look?"

"Might be a good idea," Willie said. "Those kinds of guys can't help themselves when it comes to stealing. They won't bother you until it is time to pull up stakes and leave. Then they will pull a big raid and be out of the country. If we can get a good description of them, maybe we can find them on Sheriff Irvine's wanted posters. If they are already on Stuart's target list, he can take care of them when he comes this way."

Willie continued, "I think I passed that place when I was here last week. There is a fork where the main trail kind of swings north and right after you go past two big pine trees there is a trail that comes in from the southeast. I didn't see the cabin but there were fresh tracks that turned in that way headed for the creek. Is that the way to the cabin?"

"Yep," replied Charlie. "The cabin is about 150 yards down in the brush by the creek. You can't see it from the main trail. It used to be an old trapper's cabin who tried to keep it out of the way from traveling Indians. These guys took it over and fixed it up some."

"Good. That's where I thought it was." Willie stated. "You might keep an eye on them. If they hear something about Stuart's activities up north, they may pull up stakes and move on. When they leave they will steal anything not nailed down."

Business done, Willie said goodbye to Captain Howes, thanked the Howes women for the delicious supper, and walked to the bunkhouse. Charlie Thex mounted his horse for the short ride to his ranch. As Willie entered the bunkhouse he found Ed McGhee intently braiding a hackamore.

"Get your business done?" Ed probed.

"Yep, all bought and paid for." Willie replied. "I'll start early and get most of the trailing done before it gets too hot."

"Where are you takin' them?" Ed probed again.

"Two are going to Ron's Meat Market in Ashland for the St. Labre Mission School. He will do the slaughtering and butchering for those two. That's quite a cooling operation where he hangs them," Willie commented. "Then I will take the other sixteen across the river to Rabbit Town and give about ten to the Elks Warrior Society for slaughter and distribution and then take the other six up river to the Birney Village. I expect to get the Swift Foxes up there to slaughter and distribute those cattle. There are probably twice as many Cheyennes in Rabbit Town as there are in Birney Village."

"Don't you worry that those warrior societies will just take all the beef for their families and cut the other Cheyennes out?" questioned Ed.

"Nope, I don't worry about it at all." Willie explained. "The warrior societies in the old days served as camp policemen. If they are given a task by an "old man chief", it will happen. They are honor bound to distribute fairly. If any one of them tried to steal extra meat the other members would kill his pony and beat the hell out of him with quirts."

"Really," said Ed in a surprised tone. "I had no idea they were that organized. I just thought that they were a bunch of thieving bastards."

"Most white people don't know a hell of a lot about Cheyennes," Willie declared. "My mother is a Southern Cheyenne and my father is one hundred per cent Scotch American and was the chief interpreter for General Miles. I was raised and educated by the white man in the forts we lived in, but my mother's uncle taught me the warrior ways. I've had a foot in both camps all my life. There is good and bad in both tribes but you have to know how to operate in white and red cultures. The hell of it is that a half breed is never fully accepted by either whites or Indians. I get by better than most because I've been educated in both cultures." You can talk to me as an educated white man and we understand each other. If I talk to a Cheyenne, it will be as warrior of the Crazy Dog Society and we will also understand and accept each other."

"I'll be damned. This is the first time I ever talked to anybody who really knew anything about Indians." Ed declared. Then with burning curiosity he asked, "What do Charlie Thex and Granville Stuart have to do with the Circle Bar and the reservation?"

Willie fell back on the cover story. "Well, I thought we talked about that when I was here last time. Stock growers are raising hell about all the cattle they are losing to Indian butchering. The butchering is happening because the government is not buying enough beef to feed all the Cheyennes on the reservation. The game is all hunted out and the Indians can't feed their families. To make up the difference Agent Upshaw started giving some Cheyennes permission to hunt game off the reservation on public land. When they couldn't find game, they started killing beef. Then Upshaw wouldn't let them off the reservation, but some went anyway. A few Stock Growers wanted to form a Vigilance Committee and kill any Indian found off the reservation. To lower the temperature, Stuart decided to fund a few cows from neighboring ranches to feed the Cheyennes until we could do a new count of the population on the reservation. So as you know, I was hired to go around buying these cows. But one of the things that I found out was that there were a lot more cattle being killed by white men than by Indians – mostly to feed white men. We didn't want to buy any cattle from a suspicious source so I asked Captain Howes the name of the contractor who supplied the saw mills in Ashland. He didn't know so he asked Charlie Thex who knew a lot about it. Most people don't want to say anything because it might cause them some trouble. Trouble doesn't seem to bother Charlie too much."

Ed broke out laughing, "That is for sure. Charlie is one tough son-of-a-bitch and he ain't afraid of much. What have you heard about Charlie?"

"Not much, Captain Howes said he had come up the trail from Texas a couple of times and spent some time as a buffalo hunter." Willie offered.

"Let me tell you a little bit about Charlie," Ed began. "He came up the trail from Texas the first time when he was just sixteen. At that time he was going by the name of Sheely Scott. That was about 1877, the year after the Custer Fight. He and a friend stayed to hunt buffalo and rode into this Otter Creek Country and up and down Tongue River. They sold their hides and stopped at a saloon in Stoneville, Montana (now Alzada) and got into a poker game. His friend caught a gambler cheating and the gambler shot and killed him. Charlie then shot and killed the gambler. Because the gambler had a lot of friends in the area, Charlie made tracks for Texas. He hung around Texas and served about six months with the Texas Rangers. Then he and a friend went down to a "darky hang out" and got into a fight in which they got the hell beat out of them. Charlie and his friend got their guns and returned to the "hang out" where they shot up the place, killing some of the "darkies". Because that area of Texas was still governed under Reconstruction, Charlie headed back north where he joined a herd on the way to Montana and changed his name from Sheely Scott to Charles (the X). They turned the cattle loose at Telegraph Point, WY which is about where Suggs, WY is today. Charlie remembered the Otter Creek Country from his first trip and made it over here and bought a homestead from Johnny Edwards. He had a horse stolen about two years ago and took off after the thief. He returned with the horse and nothing more being said. Then earlier this year a small time cattle thief named Archie Carnes stole about a hundred head of cattle from Charlie and a couple of neighbors. Charlie and two other guys caught up with him on Powder River with the cattle and Charlie captured him at gunpoint. They tied him up and talked about what to do with him. Charlie voted by tying a hangman's knot into his saddle rope and suggesting that they get on with it. The other two chickened out and told Charlie that they really didn't want to hang the man. After some more tense discussion Charlie agreed to tie him to a cottonwood tree and whip him half to death with a rope. Then they shot his horse, left him afoot and drove their cattle back to Otter Creek. He is a good friend and a real bad enemy. We are really glad to have him around."

"That is quite a story," Willie agreed. "I'll damn well make sure to keep him on my side."

At that point Willie said good night to Ed and climbed into his bed roll for the night. It had been a long but productive day.

Figure 28. Early Circle Bar Ranch with small Fort on top. Photo Courtesy of the Montana Historical Society.

Chapter 16. The Hand Game

Willie left the Circle Bar about daylight with his eighteen head of cattle and hit the trail to Ashland. The cattle moved out pretty well considering the drag of the two crippled cows and about four hours later drove the little herd into the corral at Ron's Meat market. Ron met him at the gate and they sorted off two dry cows for the Mission donation. Willie showed Ron the Howes' bill of sale consigning the cows to the Cheyenne Agency and then made a bill of sale which transferred two head from the Cheyenne Agency to Ron's Meat Market for the account of St. Labre Mission.

Following the transaction Willie gave himself a treat by visiting Olga's Eatery for a late breakfast. Completing his breakfast he rode the short distance to the St. Labre Mission to visit Father van der Velden and inform him of the donation cattle delivered to Ron's Meat Market. The sun was high in the sky when Willie rode to the ford across Tongue River and signaled the Elks to come across and help move the sixteen head across the river. Little Hawk sent four young men on good horses across the river which was in full flood. All made the crossing in good order and Willie led the four back to Ron's Meat Market's corral where they gathered the little herd and moved out for Rabbit Town.

Approaching the river, Willie directed one Elk rider into the water on the up river side and one on the down river side. Following their placement, he and the two remaining riders rapidly pushed the cattle into the river. The frightened herd piled into the swollen river with tails raised and eyes rolling in fear. All was going well until the cattle reached about the middle of the river and a floating tree hit the swimming group causing four head to turn down river and back toward the Ashland side. Willie shouted to the front two riders to finish moving the leading twelve head to the far shore and he and the other Elk riders would deal with the remaining four. As the four cows with

Willie and the remaining Elk riders were swept downstream in the middle of the river, one of the crippled cows was in serious trouble. Willie yelled to the two trailing Elks to stay with them and roped the crippled cow around the neck and urged his horse toward the west bank. As his horse gained bottom, he was able to pull the exhausted cow to the bank.

The two Elks and the three remaining cows were swept around a bend still in the middle of the river. Meantime the two Elk warriors with their twelve head had finished the crossing and were moving their cattle in good order. Seeing the wreck in progress, Little Hawk directed four Elk riders to gallop down river and help get the three head out of the river. He and another Elk came to Willie's aid with the crippled cow. She was nearly dead when they arrived so with Willie's horse dragging the cow and the two Cheyennes pushing they got the cow out of the river. Because the cow was still struggling, Little Hawk promptly cut her throat and removed the rope. He then put the rope on her two hind feet and motioned Willie to drag her toward Rabbit Town.

Shortly whoops and yells were heard from down river and the six Elk warriors and the three remaining cows appeared. The whole muddy mess of tired cattle and wet warriors arrived in the middle of Rabbit Town to cheering squaws, war whoops from old men, chattering children and laughing warriors taunting each other. The whole village was in a festive mood as they looked forward to full stomachs and much conversation about the day's excitement.

Little Chief called for quiet, the old man chief gathered himself, and launched into a magnificent speech in which he heaped praise upon Agent Upshaw, Long Forehead (Willie), and the ranchers who had donated the cattle. He recalled the greatness of the Cheyenne past and spoke at length on the valor and honor brought to the Cheyenne people by their warrior societies. Finally he thanked the Elkhorn Scrapers for their help and told the people that the Elks would make sure that the meat was distributed fairly. While Willie thought the speech was a little much, he had to admit that Little Chief looked every inch a chief and could certainly deliver a good talk.

Long Forehead signaled that he wanted to speak and Little Chief promptly recognized him. He began in the Cheyenne tongue:

"My fellow Cheyennes, I bring greetings from the Great Father in Washington, Agent Upshaw, the Big Chief of the White Man Ranchers, and our neighboring ranchers. Our neighbors have heard that the Cheyennes have fallen on hard times and wish to make a gift of some of these cattle to help feed the Cheyenne People. Today I bring the first gift, perhaps later there will be more gifts. Yesterday, I visited the Circle Bar Ranch, Captain Howes is the chief of this ranch and he gave me these cattle to help feed the Cheyennes. Not all of these cattle are for the Cheyennes at Rabbit Town, a few of them must go to the Birney Village where there are also hungry people. Remember that Captain Howes is a special friend to the Cheyenne People and keep his cattle safe from Cheyenne and White Men who would kill or steal his cattle. The Elk Horn Scrapers will kill these cattle and divide the meat among you. They will show you the marks on the hides which show that they belonged to Captain Howes before he made his gift to you. By those marks you will know his cattle. Now I call on Little Hawk, leader of the Elk Horn Scrapers to explain to you how he will kill these cattle and distribute their flesh. I will go and pick six head to go to the Birney Village. That will give Rabbit Town ten head and Birney Village six. I must start now to get there before dark."

Willie quickly selected six head that could be expected to rapidly make the twelve mile trip to Birney Village. He took three dry cows, the cancer eyed cow, and the two largest yearlings for the trip. He left the big bulls because they had been fighting all the way from the Circle Bar and were likely to try and brush up when it got hot in the afternoon. Willie asked Little Chief to send a messenger to Grasshopper in Birney Village announcing his coming and requesting the help of the Swift Fox Society when he arrived. Little Chief selected a fourteen year old boy named Young Mule to be the messenger. The boy hopped on a scrub paint pony and galloped away.

Willie followed with his tiny herd at a much slower pace. One of the dry cows he had selected had also been the lead cow of the larger bunch. She was a big rangy cow who liked to step out and travel and was a natural leader. Since the little group moved at about two and a half miles an hour, Willie estimated that he should arrive at the Birney Village in the early evening.

Late in the afternoon, Long Forehead was joined by a group of Swift Foxes under the leadership of Tall Bull. Tall Bull was a good friend of Long Forehead because they had both served in the Cheyenne Scouts when Willie was its First Sergeant. After Long Forehead had left the Scouts, Tall Bull's natural leadership ability had led him to rise to the rank of Sergeant. When he left the Scouts, he was immediately elected to be one of the 44 chiefs and the head of the Birney Swift Fox military society. As they rode along Long Forehead and Tall Bull discussed old times and Willie disclosed that the Scouts were busy looking for the missing white man, Bob Ferguson. He told Tall Bull that he thought the white man was dead, probably killed by white horse thieves or some of Dull Knife's young men doing some butchering. Tall Bull immediately recognized the danger to the Cheyenne people from the event and hoped the man had been killed by other white men. Willie reminded him that the white men would still blame the Cheyennes if it happened on the Reservation. Long Forehead asked Tall Bull if any of the Swift Foxes had organized hunting parties off the Reservation. Tall Bull said that he had received permission from Upshaw to hunt deer up Hanging Woman but only got a couple of miles above Lee Creek before some cowboys from the OW Ranch told them to leave that country. They didn't want trouble so they came back to Birney Village.

As they rode south toward the Birney Village, they passed a number of teepees and small cabins along the river. Tall Bull sent a rider to each of these families inviting them to come to the Birney Village to receive their share of the cattle distribution.

About dusk they arrived at the Birney Village which was a cluster of teepees and small cabins on a greasewood flat next to the river. In the center of the Village was an open circular area bounded by open sided shelters with roofs made of leafy branches of willow and cottonwood trees. The shelters provided shade and some minimal protection from rain. A few crude tables and benches were also present and some cooking fires were being tended just outside the leafy arbors.

The six head of cattle were driven to the edge of the circle where each was assigned to a Fox warrior for slaughter. Porcupine, the medicine man, offered a prayer blessing the flesh of the cattle and apologizing to the spirits of the cattle that they had to die so the Cheyennes may live. Warriors were instructed to make a clean shot away from the crowd of women, children, and old men. Any warrior who had to make more than one shot was met with taunting and derision. The cattle were quickly dispatched and the squaws made quick work of dressing and skinning. The carcasses were cut into quarters and hung on the edge of the shelters to cool. Hearts and livers were carefully saved into kettles and also hung on the edge of the shelters. The hides were heavily salted and rolled pending further processing. Later the hides would be washed, brains and ashes rubbed into the fleshy side, and then staked out on the ground with the raw side up for tanning.

After the butchering was complete the social activity began. Grasshopper gave a speech similar to Little Chief thanking the

Great Father, Agent Upshaw, and the ranchers who had made these gifts. Long Forehead spoke briefly thanking the Swift Foxes for their help in moving the cattle and reiterating that the division should be done fairly in the old Cheyenne way. Then Young Bird of the Contrary Society suggested that there should NOT be a hand game played between the Contraries and the Swift Foxes.

The Contrary Society were the clowns of the Cheyennes. When in character they did everything backwards. A Contrary would walk into his teepee backwards and ride his horse with his face toward the horse's tail. The Contrary Society's suggestion that a hand game NOT be played really meant that a hand game SHOULD be played. This was met with joyous approval from the audience.

The Cheyenne Hand Game was a betting game featuring four small bones two of which were red and the other two black. When it was announced that the game would feature the Contraries versus the Swift Foxes, that announcement did not mean that only members of the two societies could participate in the game. It meant that the Contraries and Swift Foxes would organize the two sides necessary to have a game but all could participate. The first part of the game consisted of choosing sides and collecting bets. A solid dark blanket was laid between two fires and the bets placed on the blanket about six inches apart from highest bet to lowest. About an hour of negotiations was necessary to match the bets to insure equality. Some were easy. If a Swift Fox player bet a quarter and a Contrary player bet a quarter they had a match and the two quarters were placed on the blanket opposite each other. However, most of the bettors did not have money and wanted to bet things. This required that the game administrators match up the relative value of the "things" the players wanted to bet. For example, a small sack of tobacco might be placed opposite a deck of playing cards. If an item like a bridle was too large to be placed on the blanket, then a place holding item like a stone would be added to represent the bridle. The bridle might be opposed by a cooking pot which was represented by a similar sized stone. Intense interest and long discussion about the relative value of "things" was conducted by both sides to insure the relative values were "fair." At the end of the hour all of the negotiations had been completed and an assortment of quarters, nickels, pennies, and place holding items were on the blanket.

Long Forehead's attention was drawn to one of the items on the blanket, a small gleaming brass key with the number 24 embossed on it. He immediately recognized the key as a post office key similar to the one he had used when he had last checked the Rowland mailbox. Why would anyone bet a post office key which would open his mail box? Long Forehead immediately thought of the missing Bob Ferguson and wondered what his post office box number was. Of course the key could have been lost by a post office patron and found by a Cheyenne attracted by the bright brass color. Nonetheless he resolved to identify the bettor during the subsequent game activity.

The game began with a coin flip to decide which team would start the game. The Swift Foxes won and received the bones. Two of their members were selected as bone handlers and were each given a red bone and a black bone. A designated "guesser" was selected by the Contraries. The "guesser" squatted about four feet in front of the two bone handlers who began by extending their hands palms up showing a red bone and a black bone in each hand. Three drummers who doubled as singers began a song. The bone handlers then began a "dance" in which they jerked their bodies this way and that, moving the bones between hands, putting hands behind their back, trying to confuse the "guesser" as to which hands the bones were held. When the song stopped both handlers extended their closed hands and the "guesser" was invited to select a hand from each bone holder. The hands were opened and the results tallied. On the first round selection of two black bones meant the Contraries lost and the Swift Fox team won a point. Each team had eight willow sticks so a stick was moved from the Contrary pile to the Swift Fox pile and the Foxes retained the bones. The drums began again and the process was repeated. This time the "guesser" selected a red bone and a black bone which was considered a "tie" so the process was repeated. On the third iteration the guesser selected two red bones. This caused the Swift Foxes to provide a "guesser" and the Contraries two bone handlers. The process continued until one side or the other had all sixteen sticks which concluded the game and the bets were settled. At the end of this game the Swift Foxes had sixteen sticks and were declared the winners.

The bets were settled by the winner and loser coming to the blanket and the loser handing to the winner his bet. Thus everyone who had won or lost what items and to whom was disclosed to all participants. Long Forehead watched closely as the settled bettors approached the key. He was very surprised when Young Mule, the messenger Little Crow had sent to Birney Village came forward to accept a small beaded pouch which had been opposite the brass key which he retained. Willie resolved to check the key number with Sy Young and see if it was related to Bob Ferguson. If so he would have his first good lead on what may have happened to him.

Long Forehead spent the night with Tall Bull and left early the next morning for Lame Deer and Muddy. Tall Bull told him that the Porcupine had added several converts to the Ghost Dance religion and that many of the Birney Cheyennes were interested in it. When asked a direct question if he knew anything about cattle butchering off the Reservation, Tall Bull admitted that he knew it was going on but did not know who was involved. When pressed, he reported that last winter some of the widows and old people had found sacks of fresh beef tied to their lodge poles during the night. He opined that he really didn't care to find out where the beef came from or who brought it. In so doing he expressed the prevailing attitude on the Reservation.

The people needed additional beef for their very survival. If some young men went off the Reservation and killed some white man's cows and brought the meat back to feed poor people, so be it. They just hoped they wouldn't get caught and bring trouble to the tribe.

At Lame Deer he reported his activities to Agent Upshaw, gave him the bills of sale from Captain Howes, and told him about the Ghost Dancers, and his suspicions on Young Mule. Upshaw told him that the Scouts had found nothing new on the reservation and were expanding their search west toward the Crow Reservation. He suggested that Willie proceed immediately to Muddy and ask Sy Young about the key. From there he could go to the Rosebud and buy some cattle for the Dull Knife band at Busby and check with the Scouts and Cheyenne Police on the Ferguson search.

A couple of hours ride brought Willie to the Muddy Post Office where he met with Sy Young. Sy confirmed that Bob Ferguson's post office box was indeed Number 24 and Young Mule's key did match. As Willie rode home to his dad's place, he pondered on how to proceed with the new information. He doubted that a fourteen year old boy had been directly involved in a white man's murder at the far end of the reservation from his home, especially if white horse thieves were involved. The odds were that one of the participants had given the key to Young Mule as a gift or payment for some small service. And the odds that the giver was a Cheyenne were very strong since a white man would have recognized the danger in keeping a murdered man's post office key in his possession.

Arriving home, Willie's mother fixed him a late lunch and then he joined his dad to discuss what he had discovered. Bill Rowland agreed with Willie's conclusions that Bob Ferguson had probably been killed by Cheyennes from the Dull Knife band. However, the key suggested that at least one Rabbit Town Cheyenne had been involved. That pointed to young men out on a hunting trip and Bob Ferguson seeing something he shouldn't have seen. Since the area between the head of Rosebud Creek and Busby had been pretty well searched, that suggested that the body should be found north and west of Busby where the Scouts and Police were searching now.

Chapter 17. The Ferguson Affair

Leaving early the following morning, Willie saddled a fresh horse from the corral and rode to Busby to find his brother Bill Jr. and Captain Casey. He found Captain Casey in a tent adjacent to the newly built trading post but Bill Jr. was out with the searchers. Willie disclosed the disturbing results of his post office key information and his father's suspicion that Ferguson's killers were probably members of the Dull Knife band with some help from at least one Rabbit Town Cheyenne.

Captain Casey reported. "We haven't found anything on the Reservation in spite of the grid search. Some of my Scouts are complaining that they think we are wasting their time."

"How many of your Scouts are from the Dull Knife Band and how long they had been with the Scouts?" Willie asked.

Casey replied, "I had four recent recruits from the Dull Knife band but they have only been with the Scouts for about a month."

Then Willie asked an important question. "Who were the ones doing the complaining? Was it the new recruits?"

When Casey said yes, Willie's suspicions were immediately aroused. Why would any Cheyenne complain about paid duty next to his family and band unless he had something to hide? The Scouts fit the profile of adventurous young unmarried men which would normally be expected to be the hunters and warriors for the tribe. There had also been rumors that some of the Scouts were involved in cattle butchering. Willie decided that maybe some members of the Scouts were not looking very hard for Bob Ferguson.

"Captain Casey, I think there is a strong possibility that some of your Scouts are or have been, guilty of cattle butchering. That doesn't mean they were involved in Ferguson's disappearance but may know something about it. It is really hard to keep that kind of thing completely quiet. Let's look at the grid search map and you point out where your Scouts were when they began complaining."

When Casey identified the area in the northwest corner of the reservation near the Crow reservation line, Willie made a suggestion. "What do you think about the idea of searching that area again? If we combine the Cheyenne Police with the Scouts for joint patrols and search that area again I can accompany one patrol and my brother Bill Jr. the other. We can listen carefully to the Cheyenne conversation between the Scouts and maybe pick up something."

Casey immediately agreed and wanted to lead the patrol himself. Willie selected Casey's patrol which held the four new recruits and just tagged along listening. When Casey led the patrol in a bee line for that area of the Reservation, Willie noticed that the new recruits became increasingly uncomfortable. Reaching the center of the area, Casey detailed each squad in a different direction and Willie accompanied the squad with the recruits. They seemed to be upset that the patrol accompanied by Bill Jr. was going toward the Crow line. This caused Willie to leave the patrol and go to his brother with a warning. A couple of miles west Bill Jr. noticed two buzzards circling to the north of their position. Turning toward the north and spreading the squad the Cheyenne Police soon found a dead horse and saddle which fit the description of Bob Ferguson's mount. A messenger was sent to Captain Casey and the other squads to assemble at that point.

Captain Casey rode up to the dead horse and surveyed the scene. The location was just off the Cheyenne Reservation and probably on the Crow Reservation. He sent a squad in each of the three directions out to a half mile and had them return and report. They soon found a cow's head and gut pile but no body of Bob Ferguson. During this search Willie had held back near the four recruits which seemed very nervous. As they circled the area Willie heard one recruit tell another to try and keep others away from the dry wash at the bottom of the hill. With that information in hand he immediately rode to the dry wash. He found no body but did note that there were finger marks on the edge of the wash where it looked like soil had been caved off down into the bottom. He called his brother Bill to his side and quietly explained what he had seen. The two dismounted and began to kick the loose dirt and sand at the bottom of the wash with the tows of their boots. After a few minutes, Bill hit something hard which proved to be the heel of Bob Ferguson's boot. Minutes later the entire body was recovered. Ferguson had been shot through the body in two places and his horse killed. His guns, money, and key ring were missing. The shots indicated that at least two shooters were involved.

Captain Casey immediately placed the four recruits under arrest. Their names were Black Medicine, Powder on the Face, Little Eyes, and White Buffalo. They denied any connection with the shooting. However, a search of Little Eyes and Powder on the Face's lodges revealed Bob Ferguson's pistol and a set of his keys. They were taken to Miles City four days later and housed in the Sheriff Irvine's jail.

Willie did not want his cover compromised so he told Captain Casey to give his brother Bill Jr. credit for overhearing the conversations of the recruits and discovering the Ferguson body. He didn't even ride back with the search party, opting instead to notify the Ferguson family of the discovery. He rode directly to the Ferguson Ranch where he made the notification and told the family that the body was being taken to Miles City where the Fort Keogh Post Surgeon would do an autopsy and then release the remains to the family.

From the Ferguson ranch Willie rode to the Spear Ranch where he presented his credentials to Willis Spear and asked to purchase some "out" cattle on behalf of the Montana Stock

Growers. He also imparted the news of the discovery of Bob Ferguson's body and the arrest of the Dull Knife Cheyennes. This was probably bad timing on Willie's part because Spear told him "I'll be damned if I will give any of my cattle to feed those murdering bastards." That probably summed up the attitude of most of the Upper Rosebud ranchers given the circumstances.

Unsuccessful with the Spear purchase, Willie decided that he would go home by way of the Walt Alderson Ranch which was only a few miles through the hills. He considered that given the fact that the Dull Knife band had already eaten about twelve of the Ferguson cattle over the winter, he would wait until their brother was buried and then use the Montana Stock Growers money to reimburse the Ferguson Family for the those cattle. He stopped briefly at Walt and Nan Alderson's to give them the news about Ferguson and then rode home for a well-deserved night's sleep.

Chapter 18. The Birney Trip

Agent Upshaw was not a happy man. The Ferguson Incident as it was now called had created great consternation both on and off the Cheyenne Reservation. Ranchers on the Upper Rosebud were highly upset with the murder and were talking reprisals. Upshaw had sent a message to Col. Swaine at Fort Keogh asking for patrols along the southeast reservation border to discourage vigilante action against the Dull Knife Band. Indians were afraid of communal punishment for what a few young men had done. Now complaints were coming from the white neighbors near Birney District about Ghost Dancing and the Rabbit Town District from increased Sioux and Cheyenne travel back and forth between the Pine Ridge Agency and the Northern Cheyennes. In addition, changes to the Indian Department leadership probably meant the Agent Upshaw would probably be replaced. Upshaw was in a funk when Willie came through the door.

"It's about time you showed up," Upshaw growled. "This whole reservation is afire with rumors and problems and they all want me to do something about it."

"Well hells bells, Upshaw!" Willie reacted. "What the hell do you want me to do? We found Ferguson, arrested some of those responsible, distributed cattle in Rabbit Town and Birney, set up networks on Otter Creek, and today I am going to visit the Gaffney Ranch and try and buy some cattle for Muddy and Lame Deer."

"I know! I know!" exclaimed Upshaw. "I'm not mad at you. You've been fine. I'm just frustrated that in spite of all our efforts things are still going to shit. I just don't know where to start first."

"It's springtime," Willie replied. "Sap always rises in the spring. People get more active, bulls want to breed cows, birds are building their nests, outlaws are stealing horses, ranchers are branding calves, shit is happening. That's the way it is! Deal with it."

"O.K.! O.K.! Let's sit down and figure out where we should go from here. Do you have any good ideas?

The two men moved into Upshaw's office and sat down.

"I think you need to help me to decide where and what you want me to work on," Willie began. "It's near the end of the month and Stuart should be sending us a new $250 check for June. Should I go to Miles City and pick that up? It's important to the feeding program. On the other hand I think I need to get back to Rabbit Town and find out who Young Mule has been hanging around with. I also need to go back to Otter Creek and see if Charlie Thex has found anything about the outlaws on Cow Creek. Tall Bull tells me that Porcupine has been successful in converting a lot of the Suhtai to the Ghost Dance Religion. I should be there checking that out to see if that could get as violent as it is with the Sioux. A swing through the Birney ranches with news of the feeding program should also be done. I can't be everywhere."

Upshaw leaned back in his chair and thoughtfully looked at the ceiling. "I don't think it is necessary for you to go to Miles City. I can send a message to Granville by way of the Army telegraph to have the check sent to Sheriff Irvine who could cash it and send us the cash by Army courier. I could go see Gaffney myself and do the Lame Deer/Muddy cattle buy since it is only five or six miles down the road. I think the Ghost Dance thing is the most important long term threat to peace in the area. But, if we had another incident like Ferguson anywhere that would take precedence. What do you think about that?"

Willie also examined the ceiling. "That would sure free me up some. I could take the MSG money I have left and make a circle through the Birney area ranchers. It would take a day or two for them to gather the cattle. That way I could spend a couple of days in Birney Village finding out how far this Ghost Dance Craze has spread. By that time I could go back to the ranchers and pick up a few cattle, drop them at Birney Village, and take the rest on to Rabbit Town. That would put me in position to go see Captain Howes and get an update on the Cow Creek situation."

"And maybe find some information about Young Mule's associates," added Upshaw. "That sounds like a good plan to me. Let's do it!"

"I'll start for the Birney country tomorrow morning. As long as you're sending banking messages to Irvine, ask him to send me twenty dollars of my pay and deposit the rest in my bank account," Willie requested as he walked out the door.

Riding back to Muddy Creek Willie was deep in thought. If he left home and rode up the east fork of Muddy Creek to the divide and turned almost due east, he could hit the head of Bull Creek which ran into Tongue River just about two miles above the Quarter Circle U Ranch owned by George Brewster. He decided he would attempt to get cattle from two ranches on this trip, Quarter Circle U and the Three Circle. Both were located on Tongue River, members of the Montana Stock Growers, and adjacent to the Cheyenne Reservation. Given his treatment by the SH, they would receive none of his business.

Arriving home on Muddy Creek, he checked on the sorrel horse which was doing well, but would require at least another four weeks before anyone could ride him. The family had named the horse Red Mormon and he had become a family favorite. Willie aired out his bedroll and checked the interior for lice. Glad to find none, he prepared a sack of jerky, crackers, coffee, and sneaked a couple of cans of peaches for a treat. Most of the meals would be provided by the ranches he visited as it was the custom to feed visitors well. However, it never hurt to be prepared and the Cheyennes he visited were always short of coffee.

After supper Willie and his dad moved to the living room. He wanted to get his dad's take on the Ghost Dance religion which seemed to be picking up steam across the west.

"Dad, Upshaw wants me to go over to Birney Village in the morning and check out this Ghost Dance stuff. What do you know about it?"

"I heard some about it when I was at the Stock Growers meeting," Daddy Rowland began. "I talked to Agent Armstrong from the Crow Reservation, who has had some trouble with it. It started with a Paiute Indian in Nevada name Wovoka who had a vision of a new religion. The religion is kind of a strange mix of Christianity and Indian ideas but it is for all Indians, not just Paiutes. It claims that all Indians who have died still live in a big village in heaven. Living Indians could bring all these ancestors back to life on earth and see a return of the buffalo if they prayed and danced a certain way. Then the living and the dead would be reunited and could push out the white man. Part of the religion was the idea of wearing a special "Ghost Shirt" with the sun painted on one side and the moon on the other. If properly blessed the shirts could turn bullets. A lot of Indians all over the west were interested and some traveled to Nevada to meet the "Messiah" and learn how to become a priest in this new religion. One was a Sioux named Short Bull who brought it back to the Pine Ridge Reservation. Another was a Crow named "Wrapped-Up-His-Tail" on the Crow Rez. Remember last summer when that bunch of Crows came over here to try and get the Cheyennes to join them?"

"Yeah," replied Willie. "That didn't go over all that good with the Cheyennes, at least the ones in Lame Deer. We sent them packing."

"That's right, and it was a good thing they did," continued Daddy Rowland, "Wrapped-Up-His-Tail found a short sword and had a vision in which he swung the sword and all the trees in front of him fell down. He took that to mean that he could do the same thing to soldiers. Then he got about twenty followers to go shoot up to Armstrong's office at the Crow Agency thinking they were invincible. Armstrong called out the Army from Fort Custer and the two sides squared off. Then Wrapped-Up-His-Tail made a bravery ride in front of the soldiers swinging his sword. The Army fired from long range and mostly missed but one bullet hit the "medicine man" in the heel. He ran away and his group seeing that the "Ghost Shirts" didn't work broke up and scattered. A Crow policeman named Fire Bear followed Wrapped-Up-His-Tail and shot him in the back of the head."

"So did that end the Ghost Dance Craze in Crow country?" asked Willie.

"Pretty much. But it has got to be real strong among Sioux on the Pine Ridge. I heard from American Horse that Porcupine from Busby went over to Pine Ridge and that Short Bull made him a priest in the new religion," Daddy Rowland concluded.

"Really!" commented Willie. "I met Porcupine last week when I was bringing the Howes' cattle to Birney. He gave a prayer to the cattle spirits before they killed them. But I didn't think it had anything to do with the Ghost Dance stuff."

"Probably didn't," Daddy replied. "Porcupine was a Cheyenne medicine man before he became a Ghost Dance priest. But those priests mix up Ghost Dance beliefs with the old religion of whatever tribe they are preaching to. He could do an old Cheyenne prayer and still be a Ghost Dancer."

"So have you heard what those Ghost Dance Ceremonies are like?" inquired Willie.

"I heard that they fast and take sweat bathes for several days, sometimes chewing peyote. Then they get into a big circle and hold hands dancing the circle one way and then back until people fall down and pass out. When they fall down the remaining dancers cover the person with a buffalo robe while that person has a vision of their dead relatives who come and talk to them. When the last dancer falls the dance is over. I don't know much more about it," Bill Rowland finished.

"That follows pretty close to what I heard too. Tall Bull was telling me about it. He thinks it's a bunch of shit but I guess a lot of the Suhtai older folks are buying into it."

"I guess you could go over there and pretend to join, go through the ceremonies, and find out what it is all about," suggested Daddy Rowland. "If it's just singing and dancing then I say leave them alone. If they are talking about an attack on the neighboring white men then you will have to do something about it."

Thanks Dad. I'll see how it all plays out," said Willie as he arose to go to bed."

The next morning found Willie on his trip toward Birney. He travelled south about three miles up Muddy Creek before turning up the left fork toward the Tongue River divide. Hitting the divide, Willie turned southeast down the divide until he reached the north fork of Bull Creek where he turned back east. From there he made good time since it was all downhill and on a good trail to Tongue River. Almost immediately upon reaching the valley floor, Willie found himself directly across the river from Battle Butte or Pyramid Butte where Gen. Miles and Willie's father had defeated a Sioux/Cheyenne force in early January 1877. While sometimes considered a minor engagement by historians, the Battle of Wolf Mountain or Battle of the Butte, was significant in that it put Cheyennes in a weakened condition and caused the Two Moons band to surrender three months later.

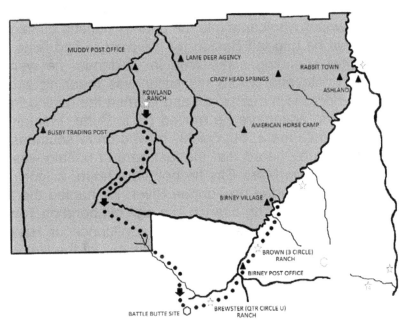

Figure 29. Birney Trip

He decided to cross the river and ride through the old battlefield since it was on his way to George Brewster's Quarter Circle U ranch. Riding up to the battlefield from the south, Willie noted the tall conical hill still bathed in red and yellow hues, despite the green grass and grey sagebrush that covered most of the area. The Tongue River road/trail took him along a small sandstone cliff that ran for about a half a mile as he rode north. Climbing up a small rise just to the east of the Butte he noted the old rifle pits the Sioux/Cheyenne warriors had dug in an attempt to hold off General Miles. He figured somewhere near his location was where the Cheyenne warrior Big Crow was killed making a bravery run. Tying his horse to a stunted cedar tree Willie climbed the Butte where a rifle pit was dug into the very top and noted the old shell casings which littered the area. Returning to his horse, Willie continued his short trek to the Quarter Circle U.

The Quarter Circle U Ranch was established in 1882 by George Brewster who came into the country hunting buffalo. As a young man he had left Boston for the west to find fame and fortune. After spending some time in California, he went to Virginia City, Nevada where his sister was teaching school. There he worked in a quartz mill and learned the mining trade. Requiring more adventure he moved on to Butte, Montana to work in the mines there, but quickly moved on to southeastern Montana where he heard that the last herd of buffalo was still roaming. Arriving in Miles City he bought a team, wagon, and saddlehorse and started up Tongue River. He hunted the area for a while before locating a ranch in a nice big bend on Tongue River about three miles south of the confluence of Hanging Woman Creek and Tongue River. He was one of the first white men on that section of the river. Because surveyors were in short supply, he took a "squatters right" on 160 acres until the surveyors caught up several years later.

After the Cheyennes began to return to the country following the creation of the reservation, Brewster began to worry about the safety of his cattle. He invited all the Birney Village Cheyennes to a big feast at the Quarter Circle U. While the feast featured horse racing and hand games, the center piece was an exhibition of long distance shooting by George Brewster. After watching him hit several pie plates at 300 yards, the Cheyennes were advised that Mr. Brewster wanted to be a friend of the Cheyennes but he expected them not to hunt his cattle. The Cheyennes got the point.

Figure 30. Brewster Ranch (Quarter Circle U). Photo Courtesy of Montana Historical Society

Willie rode up to the cookhouse where he was met by the foreman. When Willie explained he was buying cattle and produced his letter of introduction from Granville Stuart, he was immediately escorted inside for a cup of coffee and one of the cowboys dispatched to find Brewster.

George Brewster came bustling through the door a few minutes later. Introductions were made, credentials presented, and Willie's cattle buying mission made clear. In spite of his obvious Cheyenne appearance, Willie was met with hospitality and good will. In a private meeting Willie showed Brewster his badge and explained his additional law enforcement duties which were met with high enthusiasm. Brewster pledged support for the project and asked what he could do to help. Willie replied with instructions for information transfer, the use of the password, and need for a guide/fighter for Stuart's operations. Brewster said that if that became necessary, he would assume those duties himself. When asked about possible outlaw hangouts, he said that there was an old outlaw cabin in Pete's Canyon across the river from the FL Ranch, but he doubted that it was active now. He also said he would have ten head of cattle ready for Willie's inspection in a couple of days. The whole conversation took less than an hour and Willie was once more on his way.

Figure 31. Birney, MT circa 1892. Photo Courtesy of Montana Historical Society

A few minutes later he crossed Hanging Woman Creek and entered the soon-to-be town of Birney. Prior to about 1892, Birney was more of a name for a community rather than a town. A post office was established as early as 1882 in a ranch on the west side of Tongue River with Arthur M. Birney as the first postmaster. The post office location bounced around from that ranch to the Three Circle ranch with Ed Brown as the postmaster, on to the Ed McGee dugout, and from there to the Jack Hope house several miles south of Hanging Woman. It wasn't until the early 1890's that a formal post office and store was built on the current town site by Willie's former neighbor, Nannie Alderson.

Willie proceeded down river to the Three Circle Ranch, owned and operated by "Captain" Joseph T. Brown. The original Three Circle Ranch was established by his brother Ed Brown in 1884 and Captain Brown followed with a thousand head of cattle in 1886. The ranch expanded rapidly following Joe T. Brown's arrival. Strangely, Ed Brown disappeared from history shortly after the arrival of Captain Brown.

After a series of increasingly important jobs, Brown married another Mississippian, Mary Humprheys in 1883. In 1886 Joseph Brown established a partnership with John Weyth of Philadelphia on a herd in Oklahoma and drove the cattle north to his brother's ranch on Tongue River to stock the Three Circle Ranch.

Captain Brown was not a Confederate war captain as many assumed. He was a very young enlisted man during that war. Following the civil war Brown returned to school and attained a law degree from Virginia Military Institute which made him eligible for an officer's commission. He later joined the Rough Riders with Teddy Roosevelt and quickly rose to the rank of Captain.

Following the winter of 1886/87 many area ranchers were in desperate financial shape. Brown used his access to capital to buy many of the failing ranches and their remaining cattle. While he had to borrow heavily, the purchases proved to be fortuitous as the cattle market quickly recovered. By the year 1890 the Brown Cattle Company was on the march, owning thousands of cattle.

Early afternoon found Willie Rowland at the Three Circle. Using his usual procedure he presented his letter from Granville Stuart to Joseph Brown and announced the intent to buy cattle for the Cheyennes. He was warmly received and extended the southern hospitality for which the Browns became famous. Although unknown to Willie, Captain Brown was negotiating the purchase of the SH and was very interested in preserving peaceful and harmonious relations with the Cheyennes given the potential long common border between them. However, what Willis did not know was that Joe Brown was also actively promoting the dissolution of the Cheyenne Reservation. Brown quickly assented to a purchase of ten head and assured Willie that he would gladly help with the MSG feeding program. Since Willie had already recruited George Brewster for Stuart's operations, he did not disclose that part of his mission. He did however show Brown his badge and informed him of his undercover law enforcement activities. Brown immediately agreed to participate in information gathering on outlaw or Indian activities in the area. Although urged to spend the night, Willie elected to stay for supper and then proceed to Birney Village to spend the night and begin his Ghost Dance investigation.

Well before dark Long Forehead (AKA Willis Rowland) rode up to Tall Bull's teepee and met his old friend who asked him to share his lodge that night. Long Forehead immediately agreed. They talked late into the night about the Swift Foxes, the Ghost Dance Religion, the Ferguson Incident, cattle butchering, white outlaws, and the new census. Long Forehead learned much from his conversation with Tall Bull. One thing he learned was that his old Cheyenne Scout friend, Howling Wolf had accepted the Ghost Dance Religion and was an active priest. Howling Wolf was one of the Cheyennes that had been with Long Forehead when he counted the two coups against the hostile Sioux ten years earlier. Another interesting piece of information was that several white men on good horses had been seen near Crazy Head springs in the Rabbit Town District but no one seemed to know what they are doing there. Long Forehead told Tall Bull that he was going to find out more about the Ghost Dancers by going through their ceremonies and asked if Tall Bull would join him. Tall Bull agreed.

Chapter 19. Long Forehead Goes Ghost Dancing

The next morning Long Forehead sought out Howling Wolf. He found him carrying a bundle of fresh cut willow saplings with the leaves removed. The saplings were about twelve feet long and very limber. Bringing the bundle to the edge of the dance circle Howling Wolf informed Long Forehead that he was assembling the material to build a sweat lodge. The actual construction of the lodge must be done by or under the close supervision of a medicine man and was a solemn occasion. However, merely bringing the necessary components of the lodge to a central point did not require a strict protocol.

"How you been, old man?" Long Forehead asked jokingly.

"Pretty good, Long Forehead." Howling Wolf replied. "I haven't seen you in a long time. You working for the white man now?"

"Sort of. You were here the other night when I brought the cattle in. I am working with Agent Upshaw to get more cattle to feed the People. Am I working for the whites or the Cheyennes when I bring cattle in for you to eat?"

"I guess both," Howling Wolf grinned. "But, since I got the head of that cancer eyed cow, I wish you would do a little more for me."

"You must have pissed off the Swift Foxes," laughed Long Forehead. "They were the ones that passed out the meat. Maybe you should talk to them better. Looks like you are building a sweat lodge. Need any help?"

"Sure, be good to see you sweat before you even get into the lodge," Howling Wolf teased.

"I'm just trying help out a very much older friend in the last years of his life," Long Forehead teased back.

"Since you are only half Cheyenne, I will have to show you how to do everything." Howling Wolf shot back. "Like I had to show you how to count coup, many years ago."

"Hey, Whimpering Wolf. As I recall, I counted first coup both times and you were a slow second." Willie rejoined.

"I just hung back to let a little boy have a chance," Howling Wolf laughed. "Now he grows up and thinks he knows everything."

"I hear you are a big time priest in the new religion that the whites call Ghost Dancing. What is that all about?" Willie inquired.

"Are you asking because you want to know or because Agent Upshaw wants to know?" questioned Howling Wolf suspiciously.

"I want to know for myself." Willie said seriously. "I've heard some things and I've got questions. What happens to half breeds like me if the all the old Indians return and the white men are buried ten feet down? Am I a white man or an Indian? If I marry a Cheyenne girl and have kids, are they white or Indian if they are a quarter white?"

Howling Wolf thought a minute before answering. "Those questions are too hard for me. You better talk to Porcupine. He and Grasshopper went to see Wovoka last year and spent about three moons with him. Porcupine knows a lot more than me. Let's get the buffalo robes, rocks, wood, and young sage brush gathered, and then we will go ask him."

By 1890 Porcupine was probably the most important spiritual leader in the Northern Cheyenne Tribe at that time. His father was a Sioux and his mother a Cheyenne, but he was raised as a Sioux. However, when he married a Cheyenne woman he became a permanent member of the Cheyenne Tribe. He was

Figure 32. Porcupine. Photo Courtesy of Smithsonian Institute

not only an important medicine man but had been a noted warrior in his younger days. He and another Cheyenne named Red Wolf were responsible for the first known train derailment by Indians. This happened to a Union Pacific freight train in 1867 near the present town of North Platte, Nebraska. Porcupine was also with Little Wolf and Dull Knife when they broke out of the Darlington Agency in 1878. He was captured with Dull Knife at Fort Robinson, was one of the Cheyennes sent back to Kansas and tried for murder and rape, released for lack of evidence, and returned to Tongue River shortly thereafter. He concentrated on medicine man activities and became a one of the most respected priests of the Cheyenne Tribe. In 1889 three Cheyennes, Porcupine, Grasshopper, and a young helper named Ridge Walker travelled to the Paiute Reservation and spent the winter with Wovoka. There they learned the tenants of the religion from "the Christ" himself before returning to the Cheyenne Reservation.

The Ghost Dance Religion as explained by Wovoka was a strange combination of Native American Religion and Christianity. Each tribe had its own Creation Myth, taboos, laws, and ceremonies. The attraction of the Ghost Dance was that it could be an addition to whatever religion a particular tribe was using rather than a replacement for it. At its core the Wovoka teachings were Christian-like in that it was a call for all Indians to live a good and virtuous life, baptism by sprinkling water on the heads of converts, and treatment of others as you would like to be treated. Central to the faith was a Great Spirit who had found the white man to be impure and adopted the Indian as his favored race. If Indians were pious and added the Wovoka dances and ceremonies to their existing religion, then at some time in the near future there would be a miracle in which the buffalo would return, Indians and their ancestors would repopulate the earth, the white race would disappear, and the Indians would live happily ever after. It is important to note that at no time did Wovoka advocate a war with the whites. The Great Spirit would destroy the white race for their misdeeds, not the Indians.

While Wovoka's teaching was inherently peaceful, it was subject to different interpretations by the Ghost Dance priests as it was presented to the various tribes. Each tribe adopted portions of the Wovoka principles according to their own circumstances and cultures. For example, the idea that wearing

Ghost Dance shirts would keep the pious wearer in tune with the Great Spirit, was perverted by the Sioux to mean that the Ghost Shirts would turn bullets fired by the white man. While some Cheyenne Ghost Dancing may have been influenced by Short Bull, a Sioux priest who visited the Cheyenne reservation, history seems to record that Porcupine remained true to the peaceful intentions of Wovoka and never advocated violence.

Figure 33. Cheyenne Sweat Lodge, No Cover. Photo Courtesy of Montana Historical Society

Following the assembly of sweat lodge material, Long Forehead and Howling Wolf went to Grasshopper's teepee where Porcupine was staying during his visit to the Suhtai part of the Cheyenne tribe. Calling a greeting as they approached the lodge, they were met by Grasshopper who invited them inside. There he was introduced to Porcupine who greeted them with a wide smile. Long Forehead turned to Grasshopper and made him a present of a can of coffee which he immediately gave to his wife with instruction to make coffee for the men. Talk centered on the new sweat lodge, preparations for a Ghost Dance, the feeding program, the census, and the

Ferguson Incident. Long Forehead reported to Grasshopper and Porcupine that their white neighbors were concerned that Ghost Dance activities could mean Cheyenne young men would begin raiding on them as had happened on ranches close to the Sioux Reservations. Grasshopper and Porcupine strongly insisted that Wovoka's teaching encouraged peace and that any renegade activities by young Cheyenne men were not the result of Ghost Dancing.

Then Long Forehead addressed Porcupine directly, "I am interested in this Wovoka's teachings but I would like to know more about it. Howling Wolf tells me one must live a life of honesty, work, and peace to participate in the miracle of Indian renewal. I am half white, and if I have children they will be at least one quarter white. When the miracle comes and Indians inherit the earth, what becomes of me and my children? Are we Indians or white? There are good white men and bad Indian mcn. Will good white men be killed by the Great Spirit and bad Indian mcn allowed to thrive? How does this work?"

Porcupine was quiet for a long time. When he spoke it was with great deliberation. "Long Forehead has asked good questions. It was to answer questions like these that Grasshopper and I traveled to see Wovoka and hear his teachings. I will tell you what we learned. Everybody wants to be part of the miracle which says that the Indian will rise above the greedy white race, the buffalo will return, all our ancestors will be restored to us and we will all live in an Indian Heaven. That is mostly true. But it is not exactly right. The big miracle depends on each man or woman living an upright and honest life before he or she can enter into Indian Heaven. If you please the Great Spirit whether you are all white, all Indian, part white or black and part Indian, then you will be accepted into heaven. For most Indians of whatever tribe, we can describe Indian heaven as life before the white man. But heaven will be different for each man when gets there. A white man may not see the same heaven as a breed or an Indian. But for him it will be heaven."

Willie (Long Forehead) nodded. "That makes me feel much better about the religion. But is virtuous living and honesty enough to get to Indian Heaven or do you have to Ghost Dance?"

Porcupine smiled. "You might get there on your own, but most people need the help of medicine men or priests to insure they make it. The Dance provides a way to teach the people about the religion, makes them one people, causes them to look out for each other, helps people to do good, and punishes people who do bad."

"How are the ceremonies of Wovoka different from the Cheyenne ceremonies?" Long Forehead asked.

"We keep all the old ceremonies because that is what makes us Cheyenne." Porcupine said strongly. "The Wovoka teachings just help give us hope to get through these bad times. A people must have hope."

"What if Wovoka's visions don't come true? Doesn't that just destroy hope?" Long Forehead pressed.

"Perhaps, but we had hope for a while," suggested Porcupine. "The sweat baths, prayers, and dancing keep people occupied so they don't get into trouble. It's a lot better than white man whiskey. Besides, maybe they work and we get to Indian Heaven."

"Can I go through these ceremonies?" Long Forehead asked solemnly.

Porcupine and Grasshopper smiled broadly. "Of course, we want everyone to hear the message of Wovoka."

"Good," replied Long Forehead. "Tall Bull is also interested in hearing about it. Can he come too?"

"Sure, we want everyone to come," Porcupine grinned.

Grasshopper and Porcupine had already arranged a sweat lodge ceremony and dance for the initiation and instruction of new recruits. Long Forehead (AKA Willie Rowland) was added to the list of new members.

The sweat lodge material collected by Long Forehead and Howling Wolf was prepared for the ceremonies by Porcupine and Grasshopper. Porcupine supervised the lodge construction with the help of Grasshopper and Howling Wolf. A sweat lodge about five feet high and eight feet in diameter was built using willow saplings covered by buffalo robes with its entrance facing due east. Lava rocks about the size of a fist were placed near the entrance of the lodge together with forked sticks to be used for passing the hot stones into the entrance. A buffalo skull was set on a small mound about eight feet away facing the lodge entrance. No one was permitted to pass between the buffalo skull and the lodge entrance. In the exact center of the lodge a depression was dug to receive the hot stones. Near the outside of the lodge entrance a fire pit was built and stones arranged in preparation for heating. A small teepee of dry wood constructed over the stones was prepared for lighting. A large bag full of fresh young sage brush leaves and certain grasses was emptied all over the interior lodge floor and carefully spread. Finally, a small container of water was placed outside near the entrance. All of these preparations were done to a strict protocol set according to Cheyenne tradition.

Porcupine lit the fire outside the sweat lodge and carefully tended the fire until it was burning hot. Then pieces of ash branches were added to increase the heat content. Porcupine used this time to instruct Long Forehead and Tall Bull in their quest to understand the sweat lodge in the Cheyenne Way. Both had been through a sweat lodge ceremony before but not with a well-informed Cheyenne Priest like Porcupine.

Porcupine explained that the Great Medicine had used the sun to infuse energy into all things on the earth. However, all things grew old and died. Since man lived a long time compared with most other living things on the earth, it was necessary for his life to be renewed periodically which could be accomplished by releasing the sun's energy from burning the wood. The energy from the wood was then transferred to the stones through the burning process. When the stones were reaching their hottest point they would be passed inside the lodge by the forked sticks and arranged in the depression in the center of the lodge. Then songs requesting renewal would be sung followed by sprinkling of water on the hot stones. The energy from the stones would then be released as steam which would be inhaled by the worshipers to provide new energy to the body and the old worn out energy would be driven out as sweat. This process had to follow a strict order of songs, smoking pipes, and offerings to the buffalo skull in order for body and spirits to be renewed.

Porcupine entered the lodge first followed by another initiate, then Long Forehead and Tall Bull, followed by Grasshopper. Howling Wolf remained outside to tend the fire. The ceremony began with Porcupine filling a medicine pipe with tobacco and lighting it with a flaming branch brought by Howling Wolf. Porcupine then stuck the pipe out of the lodge opening and with a prayer and offered the smoke to the Cheyenne cardinal directions, east, west, up, and down and with a couple of puffs directed to the Buffalo Skull. Each member of the lodge took four puffs on the pipe and passed it to the next man who also took four puffs until the pipe had returned to Porcupine who then deposited the ashes on a piece of prepared bare ground next to the hot stones. This was repeated four times until the ash deposit was completed which signified the renewal of the earth that had been removed of vegetation. Then Howling Wolf picked up the container of water next to the sweat lodge and passed it in to Grasshopper. Grasshopper made three unsuccessful attempts to draw water into a dipper in the container, succeeding on the fourth attempt. He then sprinkled a small amount of water on the hot stones four times as Porcupine sang four songs. Each song had four verses and four refrains. The entire process was repeated four times and timed so that the rocks would no longer produce steam following the final sprinkle. The teachers and students then exited the lodge careful not to get between the energy being transferred back and forth between the cooling stones and the Buffalo Skull. This concluded the ceremony and unlike the stories, the participants did not jump into a river following the ceremonies.

Long Forehead was impressed with the devotion and professionalism with which the ceremony had been performed. No peyote had been present at this ceremony although Porcupine told him that he had tried the drug but found it a poor substitute for pure devotion. He said it seemed to help some people see their dead relatives and visions of Indian heaven. Forehead did feel refreshed and renewed after his sweat bath. He also felt a closer relationship with his fellow Cheyennes and a relief that at least so far he had seen no evidence of any violence or anti-white teachings. However, the "Ghost Dance" would be held later that evening and he was suspending judgment until that ceremony was completed.

Porcupine, Grasshopper, Howling Wolf, Tall Bull, and Long Forehead then continued the preparations for the dance that evening. The "dance circle" was prepared in the same area that where the hand game had been held on his last Birney visit. The leafy "arbors" had been reinforced with fresh branches with new leaves. Large amounts of wood were brought to the edge of dance circle and a young cotton wood tree about six inches in diameter was cut and placed in a hole in the center of the circle. It was stripped of its branches except for some at the very top. Porcupine carefully laid out the correct positions for four fires at the cardinal directions about five yards outside the dance circle. Long dry poles were arranged like teepees at the designated fire points. Porcupine explained that the fires had to be placed exactly on the east/west and the north/south lines that bisected the dance circle but far enough away that disoriented dancers could not fall into the fires. The young cottonwood tree represented the new life the faithful would see when they reached "Indian heaven". Porcupine said that new recruits would be "welcomed" into the new religion by approaching the Messiah's representative, bowing their heads, and receiving the Messiah's blessing by the priest sprinkling water upon his head prior to beginning the dance.

In the late afternoon people began to arrive for the night's activity. They brought with them food and drink and began visiting and socializing while individually preparing for the dance by painting their faces, bodies, and dressing in "Ghost Shirts." Long Forehead was introduced to two "strong" Ghost Dancers, Left Hand and Little Woman who were also "priests". Little Woman was particularly known for her visions during trances and composition of songs. She had been drawn into the religion after losing a baby and four year old son to early deaths. During her trances she said she had seen her two dead children, played with them, and spoke to her dead grandmother and grandfather. While Long Forehead had his doubts, the woman and her husband seemed sincere in their beliefs.

The dance began with two old man "heralds" going through the crowd and asking people to assemble at the dance circle. Once the dancers were assembled, Porcupine welcomed them to the ceremony, introduced his fellow priests, and offered a prayer to the Great Medicine or "Spirit'. That was followed by a request that all potential new initiates come to the center of the dance circle to receive instruction. Long Forehead and his friend Tall Bull came forward to receive the initiation. Porcupine advised the initiates that nothing in the teachings of Wovoka changed anything that Sweet Medicine (the First Cheyenne medicine man) had taught. All Wovoka's teachings were additive to Sweet Medicine's laws about how Cheyennes were to treat each other. Porcupine went on to explain to the initiates that

Sweet Medicine had predicted the coming of the white man and had warned them against white man ways. However, the white man had come and they were too numerous for the Cheyenne to defeat by warfare. Therefore, Cheyennes needed to make the best of a bad situation.

Wovoka taught that he had seen a vision in which the future of all Indian people was bright. A time was coming in which the earth would tremble and shake, a great whirlwind would come, and all good Indians would be taken to a new place. In the new place the buffalo would be numerous, summer would last all year, and the Indians would live a life peace and plenty. White men and bad Indians would be left behind and the dust from the whirlwind would bury them forever. To be a "good" Indian required the individual must be peaceful, hardworking, not steal or kill anyone and "treat other people as you would like to be treated." To Long Forehead this sounded a lot like Christian teachings which he could willingly accept. Porcupine concluded this portion of the ceremony by asking the initiates if they could accept these principles. When they stated their acceptance Porcupine sprinkled water on their heads (baptism) and welcomed them into the arms of Wovoka.

The dance started with everyone in the dance circle holding hands and moving clockwise, the same way the sun moved through the sky. Drummers in the center of the circle and priests began a series of songs with the dancers moving in time with the drums. Porcupine led the first song which he had composed:

"My children, my children.

Here is the river of turtles. Here is the river of Turtles.

Where the various living things. Where the various living things.

Are painted different colors. Are painted different colors.

Our Father says so. Our Father says so.

I waded into the yellow river. I waded into the yellow river.

This was the Turtle River into which I waded.

This was the Turtle River into which I waded.

I see the mountain. I see the mountain.

It is circling around. It is circling around.

My father. My father.

I come to him. I come to him.

The Crow. The Crow.

I cry like it. I cry like it.

Caw, I say. Caw, I say.

The bad spirit. The bad spirit.

We have put him aside. We have put him aside.

The Good Spirit. The Good Spirit.

He is our Father. He is our Father.

He has blest us. He has blest us.'

The significance of Porcupine's song was that in the beginning of the Cheyenne Tribe it was at Minnesota's Turtle River (probably St. Croix River). Then they wandered west in search of renewal. Then they saw the sacred mountain Noaha'vose (Bear Butte, S.D.) where Sweet Medicine gave them their laws, Sacred Arrows, and the Cheyennes were renewed. They wandered again. They needed renewal. The Crow (messenger) brought them to Wovoka where they would be renewed again.

With his help they would reach Indian Heaven. That would be their final renewal.

The dance became intense. The circle would move rapidly to the left then lurch back to the right. People sang their individual songs. Dust rose from the dance circle. The priests began to look for people who were close to exhaustion and subject to losing consciousness. To those people the priests "presented the feather" where they spun an eagle feather in front of their eyes to induce hypnosis. When the dancer was in a trancelike state and lost consciousness, a buffalo robe was thrown over them until they awoke and reported their vision. The dance lasted until about midnight for three nights and on the fourth night it went on until dawn when the Morning Star was seen.

Long Forehead and Tall Bull never lost consciousness or saw a vision. Perhaps because they were young and strong, or did not believe strongly enough, they were never able to surrender their consciousness to the dance. However, neither saw anything especially dangerous to the dancers or the tribe from the activities. It looked to Willie Rowland like the Ghost Dancers didn't differ substantially from the Shakers, Snake Handlers, or other religious offshoots of white society. He resolved to report to Upshaw and the military that he saw nothing for them to be concerned about from these Ghost Dancers.

Chapter 20. The Clean Up Begins

Willie and Tall Bull left Cheyenne Birney the morning following the Ghost Dance. They rode to George Brewster's Quarter Circle U Ranch, and picked up eight head of dry cows, and started down the river toward the Three Circle. Crossing to the west side of Tongue River before reaching Hanging Woman Creek, they passed the old Alderson/Zook homestead where Walt and Nannie Alderson had moved after the Cheyennes had burned their house in 1884. They were accompanied by Shorty Caddell, one of the cowboys from the Quarter Circle U who had to pick up three horses at the Three Circle and return them home. Arriving at the Three Circle they were met by "Old Man" Brown at the corral. While he was showing Willie and Tall Bull the eight head of cull cows he was willing to sell, he turned to Shorty Caddell and asked:

"Shorty, on your ride over here from the Quarter Circle U, did you see any Three Circle bulls?"

Shorty, who was no fan of the Browns, replied, "Nope Mr. Brown, I never seen any of your bulls today. But I heard one of them up on Zook Crick."

"Well Shorty," Old Man Brown asked, "If you didn't see him how did you know it was a Three Circle bull?"

"Why Mr. Brown, he was a-calling: You'all! You'all! Ain't nobody else around here talks like that except Browns."

Willie suppressed a laugh and Tall Bull didn't speak enough English to get the joke. He quickly said, "Those cows look good enough to me. What do you need for them?"

Mr. Brown smiled and replied. "How about $50.00 and I'll throw in some southern fried chicken? I might even have enough for Shorty."

"It's a deal, Mr. Brown." Willie said as he handed to money to Brown.

"Come to the cook house and we will make you and your friend a good sack lunch." Brown stated. "Shorty, do you want to stay for lunch or do you want a sack, too?"

"Uh, I guess I'll just take a sack lunch," replied Shorty in a slightly embarrassed tone. "I better get on the road with them horses."

Willie made a quick trip to the cookhouse where he picked up a freshly fried chicken, some potato salad and two pieces of cherry pie. In high spirits they started the sixteen head of cows toward the reservation. Tall Bull smacked his lips as he took a bite of the cherry pie. "Heapie good. Heapie good." He said in English.

Late in the afternoon, Willie and Tall Bull made it back to Birncy Village. Willie dropped six cows with Tall Bull and proceeded on to Rabbit Town with the other ten. He arrived there just at dark and turned them over to Little Hawk and his Elkhorn Scrapers before crossing the river to the Mission.

At the Mission he was received by Father van der Velden who gave him a letter from Agent Upshaw. Upshaw's letter said:

"Dear Willie,

Please return to Lame Deer as soon as you can.

Col. Swaine is upset about the Ghost Dance activity and received orders from Washington to investigate the Cheyenne Ghost Dance.

I got a letter from CPT Howes stating that he has 26 head of cattle he wanted to sell right away.

We received the Montana Stock Growers money from Stuart. I bought 10 head from Gaffney and 15 from Lynch. Your brother is taking 10 to Busby and Two Moons turned over the Lame Deer bunch to the Crazy Dogs.

I have your $20.00.

I hope to see you soon.

Your obedient servant",

R.L. Upshaw.

Willie folded up the letter and made an executive decision. He would spend the night at the Mission and then ride immediately to the Circle Bar. It sounded like Captain Howes had some very important information for the Stuart operation.

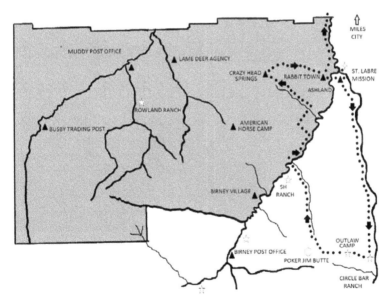

Figure 34. Willis Rowland's Travels on the Trail of "Big Nose" George Parrott

Daylight found Willie on the trail to the Circle Bar. He rode into the ranch right about breakfast and was immediately taken to Captain Howes who hustled him into his study.

"Willie, two guys rode into the outlaw camp on Cow Creek two nights ago. They were driving about 30 head of horses. Charlie Thex watched them come in and thinks he saw one of them on a wanted poster some time ago, but didn't remember who he is. He sneaked up to the cabin and listened to them. He didn't hear all the conversation, but heard something about Crazy Head Springs on the Reservation and Sim Robert's place on the Rosebud. I don't know if they are still there but Charlie got a good look at the horses and there are a lot of fresh brands on that bunch. What do you think?"

"I think I need to talk to Charlie as soon as possible. They probably won't be here much longer. Usually two or three days are as long as they will stay put in one place before they move. How can I reach Charlie?" Willie asked.

"I'll send Ed over to get him. He will probably be here in less than an hour. You may as well stay for breakfast. By the time you eat he will probably be here." Captain Howes finished.

The meeting adjourned to the breakfast table where the subjects turned to the Ferguson Incident and the Ghost Dance Craze.

"So what happened to Ferguson?" Mrs. Howes asked.

Willie described the search which ended just off the Cheyenne Reservation with the discovery of Ferguson's horse, a butchered cow carcass, and finally the body in the bottom of the ravine. He noted that Ferguson had been shot twice and that in addition to the cow there were seven horses also missing. He also described how the suspected killers were identified and sent to Miles City for trial.

Levi Howes asked about the Ghost Dance Craze having been very impressed with his exposure a couple weeks earlier. Here Willie could be more reassuring. He explained that he had just gone through the Ghost Dance ritual at the request of the Agent and found it non-threatening to whites. However, he repeated that what he had seen was true of the Cheyennes and probably the Arapaho tribes, but might not be true for the Sioux who were inclined to be more warlike.

Upon completion of breakfast Willie returned to the corral to await the arrival of Charlie Thex. Captain Howes and Willie continued their conversation.

"How many really fast horses do you have here on the ranch?" Willie asked.

"What are you thinking?" Captain Howes rejoined.

"If I had to get a quick message to Miles City, How many fast horses could you provide to carry the message? Willie asked.

"Probably three," replied Howes. "But we might be able to borrow some of Sir Sidney Pagent's race horses. He lives pretty close. I can ask Grant Dunning. He is Pagent's foreman and head trainer. Pagent races horses all the time in Miles City."

"That would be great!" Willie exclaimed enthusiastically.

Their conversation was interrupted by Charlie Thex and Ed McGee's return to the corral. Because of Ed McGee's increased involvement, Willie decided to include him in the narrow circle of disclosure. Willie showed Ed his Custer County badge and explained his undercover status as a deputy sheriff. He did not however disclose Stuart's activities. Willie asked Charlie what he had seen and heard.

Figure 35. Sir Sydney Pagent. Photo Courtesy of the Montana Historical Society

Charlie began. "Since you were last here I spent some time watching that cabin on Cow Crick. There are three guys up there that are more or less permanent. They are a shiftless bunch who don't do a hell of a lot of work. Supposedly they are wolvers but the only traps they have are hanging on the wall outside of the cabin. The corral they have built is different than any one I have ever seen. It is in a bunch of cedar trees and built for concealment. Anyway three nights ago two guys brought in a bunch of horses. I counted 28. The permanent guys take the horses out to graze during the day. They day herd them away from the trails and bring them in at night. Night before last I slipped up next to the cabin and listened to their talk. The new guys were complaining that they hadn't had any fun in three months. They said something about picking up more horses at Crazy Head Springs and moving the whole bunch to a safe spot on the Rosebud for a few days. Then they thought they could spend a couple of days in Miles City raising hell and peddling a few horses."

"What did these new guys look like?" Willie asked.

"One guy is kind of thin, has a mustache and a big nose that really stands out. He is a big mouth who talks loud. The other one is kind of average but dark and quiet. I couldn't stay too long because one of them came outside to take a leak and I had to get out of there." Charlie concluded.

"How much longer do you think they will be there?" probed Willie.

"Hell, they may be gone already." Charlie replied.

Captain Howes thinking out loud, "I guess the first thing to do is to see if they are still there. If they move we know they will be probably be going to Crazy Head Springs which means they will have to cross the trail to Poker Jim Butte and the East Fork of Hanging Woman. Twenty eight horses make a lot of tracks."

Ed McGee chimed in. "Charlie and I could gallop up there and take a look. Those guys know who we are so if we run into them it shouldn't raise any suspicion. We could go up there and back in two hours."

Willie thought for a minute. "I think I'll go with you. If they are still there, maybe I can put the field glasses on them and identify somebody. If they are gone I can follow the tracks and maybe catch up to them on the reservation. If they are hiding horses at Crazy Head Springs, the odds are that one or both of them will show up at one of the Ashland bars to buy whiskey to pay off the Cheyennes who are helping them. In either case we have a good chance of finding out who they are."

Charlie spoke up. "If they are gone do you want me to go on the trail with you?"

"That would be great," Willie said thankfully. "I would rather have Sheriff Irvine and Marshall Beidler arrest them down in Miles City where they have plenty of help than get in a fight on the trail. On the other hand, if it did turn into a fight before they got there, I'd rather not be by myself."

With that Charlie Thex, Ed McGee and Willie hit the trail to Cow Creek. About an hour later they arrived at the junction of the trail to the cabin and the Poker Jim trail. Sure enough, fresh tracks of a large horse herd moving in the direction of Poker Jim Butte were noted. The three stopped for a conference.

"What do you think?" Willie directed the question to Charlie.

"Why don't you stay here and Ed and I will ride down to the cabin. We will say we were scattering bulls and ask if they have seen any. I'll know right away if it's just the three permanent guys or if the new guys are still there. They could be day herding the horses up towards Poker Jim, but I think they are probably on the move. If it was me I would take the horses down the divide between Otter Creek and Tongue River to O'Dell Creek and go down O'Dell Creek to Tongue River. Then I would cross the river to the Reservation and go down the west side of Tongue River to Logging Creek and up Logging Creek to Crazy Head Springs. You avoid the commonly traveled roads and don't get tangled up in a lot of rough country."

"I think that is a good plan," replied Willie. "I'll ride with you close enough to help if you have trouble, but not up to the cabin."

The three turned onto the cabin trail and rode about a hundred yards before Charlie raised his hand and signaled Willie to move off the trail and stop. Ed and Charlie proceeded on to the cabin. He heard Charlie hail the house and heard a conversation take place but could not distinguish the words. About fifteen minutes later he spotted Ed riding up the trail toward him. As he passed he motioned Willie to fall in behind him. They continued back to the fork in the trail, took the Poker Jim fork and rode about another half mile before they were joined by Charlie.

"They ain't seen any Circle Bar bulls," Charlie said dryly. "There is only one of them at the cabin. The other two must be helping them with the horses, probably acting as guides and outriders. Near as I can tell they left this morning and are probably three or four hours ahead of us. They can move damn near as fast as we can so we probably can't catch up to them today."

"O.K. Let's do this. Ed, you go back to the Circle Bar and brief Captain Howes. Then go to Pagent's ranch and see if you can borrow one of Pagent's racehorses, a long distance one, and take it to the Mission. Charlie and I will follow these horses and make sure they are going to Crazy Head Springs. If they camp there maybe I can get the glasses on them. If they dropped the horses there for Cheyennes to take care of and rode on into Ashland for a drink and to pick up some firewater for their Cheyenne help like I expect, we will see them in Ashland. Once I can get them identified, I'll get on the race horse and ride like hell for Miles City and have Irvine get ready. How does that sound?"

"Sounds good to me," Charlie replied and Ed nodded. "That way I can help with the identification and you have a fresh horse at the Mission."

Ed left to do his part while Willie and Charlie followed the wide obvious trail of twenty eight horses and their herders. They made good time and it looked like they were gaining on the herd because the outlaws were letting the horses do some grazing. By midafternoon the tracks were significantly fresher as they approached Tongue River. The trail crossed the river and turned north as expected. However, the trial unexpectedly turned west up an unnamed drainage immediately west of the mouth of King Creek. Willie surmised the outlaws wanted to avoid the increased Cheyenne population on the river as it neared Rabbit Town and Ashland. The trail up the drainage turned north about three miles west of Tongue River and after another three miles dropped on over to Logging Creek. From there it was about another six miles west to Crazy Head Springs. Willie noted that from Crazy Head Springs it was a straight shot north down the Rosebud/Tongue River divide to Green Leaf Creek and the Lower Rosebud.

The tracks up Logging Creek were really fresh and horse manure indicated that the herd was less than an hour ahead of Charlie and Willie. When they hit the top of the divide the shadows were getting long. Willie figured that there was maybe an hour of daylight left. When they were within a mile of the Springs, Willie pulled off the trail into a patch of timber.

"Have you ever been to Crazy Head Springs?" Willie asked Charlie.

"Nope," said Charlie. "When we were hunting buffalo through here before the Reservation was set, we stayed mostly on the cricks. I never thought there was water up here on top."

"Crazy Head Spring is not just one spring, it's a series of springs and there are ponds for about half or three quarters of a mile down this creek. It's a gentle fall but the water runs off to the Rosebud side. I think from here we better stay out of the open and pretty close to the timber. I would expect to find a couple of teepees down there for the Cheyenne herders. Do you think those guys would spend the night with the Cheyennes?" Willie finished.

"I wouldn't," offered Charlie.

"They won't either," reasoned Willie. "As near as we can tell they are all white men. I doubt any of them speak Cheyenne, but maybe they can use sign language. I'd bet my bottom dollar there is a breed down there that is the go between. He gets the whiskey from the outlaws and pays off the herders. Those guys will either camp separately or go on to Ashland."

Charlie and Willie rode in the shadows of the timber for another half mile when they spotted a lodge and makeshift corral. There was a large herd of horses scattered down the creek. A fire with a coffee pot was burning in front of the lodge and four white men and two Indians were sitting on logs talking. Willie got his field glasses out and zeroed in on the white faces. As he turned the knob the faces came into sharp relief. Willie immediately recognized the skinny man with the big nose and mustache as "Big Nose" George Parrott, a member of the Wild Bunch responsible for the murder of two deputy sheriffs with a reward of $2,000 on his head. Also on the log was Bill Carey another member of the Parrott gang which had killed the deputies with an additional $1,000 on his head. The other two white men Willie didn't know. He then turned his attention to the two Indians. One was a muscular young brave about twenty five years old and the other was a light skinned man who was surely a mixed blood. Most of the talking was done between Parrott and the light skinned Indian. Just as the whites arose and emptied their coffee cups a third Cheyenne came in from the horse herd. He was small and young. Willie recognized him immediately as Young Mule, the messenger that had Bob Ferguson's post office key. Turning back to the muscular young Cheyenne, he studied him intently. The man was classic Cheyenne with chiseled features, braids, a buckskin shirt, leggings, moccasins, and not one stitch of white man clothing. He exuded an attitude of arrogance, distrust, and distain for the white men at the fire. The light skinned Indian was about thirty five years old, dressed mostly in white man clothes, slovenly, slack jawed, with the red face and watery eyes of an alcoholic.

After carefully examining all of the players very closely Willie signaled Charlie to move back quietly. Both of them moved back to their horses hidden in the timber about two hundred yards east of their observation point.

Willie mounted his horse, pointed northeast, and after another mile, Charlie broke the silence. "Well, did you get anything good from that look?"

Figure 36. "Big Nose" George Parrott.
Courtesy of the Carbon County WY
Archives

Willie turned with a grin, "Damn right. The big nosed gent with the loud mouth and black mustache is "Big Nose George Parrott" who I am sure you have heard of. His partner is Bill Carey one of the old Parrott Gang but they are both now working with the Wild Bunch. The horses are probably destined for Landuskey, MT and then north to Canada. I think you heard their plan right. They will stay here about two days before they go on to Sim Robert's ranch on the Rosebud."

"Why do think they won't go on in the morning," Charlie asked.

"It's already damn near 10:00 at night. They have been in the saddle for seventeen or eighteen hours. I doubt that they will go to Ashland tonight because it is about dark now and Ashland is another three hours from here. That would put them into there at 01:00 in the morning and nothing would be open. They don't like to work real hard, but I doubt they will stay in the Cheyenne Camp. I bet they will bed down a couple of miles from the

Cheyennes and come on into Ashland tomorrow. They all will be at Olga's tomorrow at lunch and the Club Buffett the rest of the afternoon. I reckon they will stay in Ashland tomorrow night and bring the Cheyenne's whiskey to them the following morning."

Charlie shrugged wearily in his saddle, "Where are we going?"

"About three miles down this divide we can drop down on Stebbin's Crick next to the trail between Ashland and Lame Deer. I know where there is a little spring that we can camp at and water the horses. It's off the main trail and even if those guys get up early and get ahead of us, we won't be seen."

"Sounds good to me, I'm tired and hungry," grumbled Charlie.

Forty five minutes later they reached the spring, unsaddled and hobbled their horses, and spread their yellow slickers on the ground. It was a warm June night, with a quarter moon, and a slight breeze. Willie dove into his saddle bags and got out a box of crackers, a large chunk of cheese, and two cans of his precious peaches. Charlie's attitude brightened right up as Willie handed him a can of peaches and half the crackers and cheese. With a little food and fresh water from the spring, they lay down on their yellow slickers, pulled the saddle blankets over their shoulders and were soon fast asleep.

The following morning Willie and Charlie were on the trail to Ashland. It was almost a race to Olga's for breakfast. After breakfast they split up with Charlie on the lookout for the expected outlaw arrival, while Willie went to the Mission to see if Ed McGee had secured the race horse from Pagent's ranch. When Willie arrived at the Mission he met with Deacon Yoakim, who took him out to the Mission's barn and corrals and showed him the sleek athletic racehorse which Ed McGee had left there the day before.

"Ed said that the horse's name is Black Diamond. He is a young horse that Grant Dunning is training for Pagent. He told Ed the horse has lots of "go" but remember he is young so hold him back so he doesn't hurt himself. Yoakim advised.

Willie said to the Deacon. "I might need him to make a quick trip to Miles City within the next 24 hours. Please keep him up close and undercover and if anybody asks, tell them that Grant is leaving him here for a potential buyer."

Deacon Yoakim agreed to those requests.

Upon returning to Ashland, he met Charlie at the mercantile store across the street from the Ashland Bar. Charlie reported that Bill Carey and the two Cow Creek outlaws had just ridden into town were having an early lunch at Olga's Eatery. Willie was surprised that Parrott was not with them, and wondered if his absence meant an earlier departure than he had anticipated. They took a seat on one of the benches and waited for the outlaws to finish lunch. Their patience was rewarded when about fifteen minutes later the three emerged from Olga's and made their way to the Ashland Bar. A short time later Carey exited the bar carrying four bottles of whiskey which he deposited in his saddle bags, mounted his horse and rode toward Tongue River.

Willie said to Charlie, "You follow Carey and see if he takes the road to Lame Deer or north to Miles City. Once you know, meet me at the Mission. I'm going to go talk to Olga to see if she overheard anything. Then I'll go over to the Ashland Bar and see if those guys are still there. They won't recognize me like they would you. O.K.?"

"Sounds good to me," Charlie replied as he tightened the cinch on his horse.

Willie crossed the street to Olga's. Taking a seat at the counter, he ordered a cup of coffee and looked around the place which was nearly empty at that moment.

Olga asked, "Why you back already, Willie? You back for more pie?"

"I never turn down pie," Willie answered. "Do you know those three guys who were in earlier?"

"Two those guys come in once in while. Never seen the third guy before," Olga replied.

Willie palmed his deputy's badge and put his finger to his lips. "Did they say where they were going?"

Olga's eyes got big, "The smaller dark one say he would see other two at Chinnicks in Miles City next week. You are lawman now?"

Willie nodded, "Anything else?"

"Nope, something about getting' paid." Olga replied doubtfully. "What is Chinnicks?"

"Saloon," answered Willie. "I got to go now. Remember, don't talk about badge."

Willie crossed the street and secured his horse. Then he turned his horse and trotted quickly toward the Mission. A few minutes later he arrived at the Mission Barn and changed his saddle to Black Diamond. The question of which direction Bill Carey had gone was answered when Charlie Thex came loping through the Mission gate.

"I think he's headed back to Crazy Head Springs," reported Charlie. "I followed him to the top of the hill on the road to Lame Deer. He was well past the Miles City road turnoff."

"Good," Willie replied. "Olga said she overheard them mention Chinnick's place in Miles City. I'm going to ride like hell to tell Irvine to keep an eye on Chinnick's Saloon. Thanks a lot for the help!"

"What about the boys from Cow Creek?" asked Charlie?

"I wouldn't worry too much about them. Right now they are still in the Ashland Bar, probably headed home. When Stuart gets here we can take care of them. Right now the big fish are on their way to Miles City. Give Ed and Captain Howes my best and especially thank Grant Dunning for the loan of the horse. I'm sure I can get to Miles ahead of them." With that Willie turned and loped toward the Tongue River Crossing.

The big strong thoroughbred made excellent time on the way to Miles City. Willie thought he had been on some good horses in his day but he had never seen a horse like this one. He would lope for a mile or two and then trot for about the same distance before returning to a lope. The horse just never seemed to tire, always wanting to go. Willie loped into Miles City at about 8:30 in the evening and went straight to the Red House.

Deputy Johnson went to find Sheriff Irvine while Willie took care of the horse which had carried him so successfully from Ashland. Johnson and Irvine came back to Red House a few minutes later.

"That's quite a horse," Irvine exclaimed. "Where did you get him?"

"Borrowed him from Pagent. I got news and had to get here quick." Willie explained.

"Well, come on in. Do you think the horse will be O.K.?" Irvine asked in a concerned tone.

"He's been great and I have been cooling him out while I was waiting for you. I think he will be alright," answered Willie as he tied the horse to the hitching rail.

The three men went into the Red House and gathered in Irvine's office. "What have you got?" inquired Irvine.

"Big Nose" George Parrott and Bill Carey are on their way to Miles City. They should be here tomorrow morning, if I have it figured right. Word is that they are going to Chinnick's Saloon and also have a few horses to peddle. They plan to spend a couple days here before going to Junction City and on up to Landuskey." Willie reported.

"How did you get that information?" asked an astonished Irvine.

Willie disclosed that Charlie Thex had heard the men discussing their plans at the outlaw cabin on Cow Creek. Then Willie explained how they had followed the four men to Crazy Head Springs on the Reservation, then watched as Carey and the other two came into Ashland to buy whiskey and then Carey returned toward Crazy Head Springs. He also reported that they intended to go to Sim Roberts' ranch on the Rosebud and park the horses. They would then take a few horses on to Miles City to sell and pay for a "spree".

"Better get "X over here," Irvine told Johnson. "He's at the MacQueen House. We need to figure out a plan to make an arrest. It's not going to be easy. Those two will shoot at the drop of a hat and we don't want any of us or civilians getting killed. I already arrested him once last year so he will be on the lookout for me and "X".

While Deputy Johnson went to find Marshall "X" Beidler, Willie took the big horse down to the County Barn, gave him a rub down and a generous helping of oats. He then returned to the Red House to find "X" and Sheriff Irvine in deep conversation.

"Parrott and Carey will bring those horses to John Chinnick's corrals in back of the saloon. We better have somebody watching it so we know when they get here." Beidler was saying.

"Then I'm sure Parrott will want to visit Chinnick's wife. He had a pretty good thing going with her the last time he was here. Chinnick doesn't pimp out his wife to everybody but he will to Parrott. Just a matter of money and Parrott probably has plenty." Irvine added.

"Are you going to need me to be in on the arrest?" Willie asked.

"Not unless you want to. We already know what Parrott and Carey look like so you don't need to identify them. It might be better for you to stay undercover." Irvine suggested.

"That's alright with me. I'm no gunfighter. Besides I need to get over and see Col. Swain about a reservation problem first thing in the morning. I'm going to the MacQueen House, get some supper and rent a room if you are done with me." Willie declared.

"See you tomorrow sometime. Good work! We'll take it from here." Irvine replied.

Willie went to the MacQueen House registered for a room, washed up, went down for a late supper and went to bed.

The next morning after breakfast, Willie made the short ride to Ft. Keogh. He entered the Post Headquarters and asked the Adjutant if he could get an appointment with Col. Swaine. The Adjutant ducked into Col. Swaine's office and quickly emerged to escort Willie in to see the Colonel.

Col. Swaine rose quickly from his chair with hand extended while the Adjutant beat a hasty retreat and closed the door.

"How have you been, Willie?" Col. Swaine asked as he pumped Willie's hand. "What are you doing back in Miles City?"

Col. Swaine motioned for Willie to take a seat.

"I got a note from Upshaw that you needed to see me about these Ghost Dancers," replied Willie.

"Yes, I'm getting intelligence reports from all over the west about what the War Department is calling the Ghost Dance Craze. They haven't seen anything like it. From the Paiutes, Sioux, Arapaho, Comanche, Kiowa, Southern Cheyenne and even Apache tribes, they are all Ghost Dancing. Tribes that otherwise are enemies are all doing the same thing. The Sioux are getting especially worked up and their Agent has requested military support. Given the close relationship between the Sioux and the Northern Cheyennes, they are asking me to assess the danger from the Cheyennes in our area. Some of the local civilians are also becoming upset," finished Swaine in a highly concerned tone.

"So what do you want to know?" Willie asked with a knowing grin.

"What the hell is going on?" The Colonel boomed. "What do you know? I need answers!"

"O.K., OK. I just might happen to have some since I just went through the Ghost Dance initiation three days ago," answered Willie.

Colonel Swaine was suddenly quiet. "What have you found out Willis?" he inquired intently.

Willie began his report. "I went to the Birney Village as part of the Stock Growers Cheyenne feeding scheme and delivered some cattle to them. I was staying with an old friend, Sergeant Tall Bull who used to be in the Cheyenne Scouts. They were preparing for a dance under the supervision of Porcupine, a respected medicine man. I had heard that he was a Ghost Dance priest, so I asked Tall Bull what he thought about it. He thought it was a bunch of crap but otherwise didn't know much about it. Then he told me that another old Cheyenne Scout, Howling Wolf was a priest in the Ghost Dance. So, if I wanted to know something, ask Howling Wolf. Howling Wolf and I fought some hostile Sioux about ten years ago when we both were in the Scouts. Anyway, I helped him build a sweat lodge in preparation for the dance and I started asking him questions that he couldn't answer so he introduced me to Porcupine. Porcupine told me all about the Ghost Dance, how he and Grasshopper had traveled all the way to Nevada to meet Wovoka, the Paiute Messiah. They stayed there for about three months learning the dances and the songs of the religion. When they returned they asked and received permission of the Council of 44 Chiefs to talk about what they had learned to the Cheyenne people. I asked if I could go through the ceremonies and he agreed, so I did."

"Do you think they are a threat to whites?" asked Swaine.

Willie replied cautiously. "Not at this time. Everything I saw was entirely peaceful. In fact, the religion is a curious mixture of Christian and old Indian religions. The central idea is that Indians are the favorite people of the Great Spirit. If the people are peaceful, live good lives, wear the right clothes, sing the right songs, and dance the right dances, a great whirlwind will bury the white race and take all the good Indians to Indian heaven where they will join their dead relatives and live happily ever after."

"Then why did you just say they are no threat at this time?" demanded Swaine.

"Because of the Sioux influence. I have no doubt that Grasshopper and Porcupine are peaceful and they have the most Cheyenne influence. However, there is a Sioux Ghost Dance priest named Short Bull who has visited some of his relatives in the Rabbit Town area near Ashland. In his version of the Ghost Dance, the right clothes include "Ghost Shirts" which will turn away white man bullets. Porcupine's Ghost Shirts claim no such power. My question is: If the religion is totally peaceful, why would they need Ghost Shirts to turn bullets?" Willis concluded.

"I see," said Col. Swaine thoughtfully. "I need to send a report on this to the War Department. Do you think Porcupine would testify as to how he heard about this Messiah, where he travelled, what he learned about the religion, and what he is preaching to the Cheyennes?"

"I think so," replied Willie. "I found him to be completely honest. All the songs and dances were innocent enough. If the Cheyennes followed Porcupine's teaching they would stay away from whiskey and be a peaceful group. My concern is that the Sioux try and speed up the arrival of Indian Heaven. There are young men here and on the Sioux Reservations who would like to go back to war if the Ghost Shirts really can turn white man bullets. I have heard some names of Sioux who are advocating that." Willie declared.

"What are their names?" Col. Swaine asked while picking up a pen.

"This is just rumor. But I heard that Kicking Bear, Short Bull, and Big Foot are pretty strong on their Ghost Dance idea. They may even have old Sitting Bull convinced that the Ghost Dance can bury the white man," finished Willie.

"Great work, Willie." Col Swaine said as he stood up. "You have found out more in two days than the rest of the Army has in the last few months. If you can get Porcupine to talk, I'll send a message to Major Carroll at Lame Deer to record his testimony.

Maybe if we can separate the real Ghost Dance religion from the adulterated ones, we can arrest the troublemakers and save Indians and Whites from a big outbreak."

"I'm confident he will testify if I do the interpreting," Willie responded. "I found him to be completely open about Wovoka's teachings. If the whites knew how peaceful he really is they would be cheering him."

"Well, I doubt that," Colonel Swaine said disgustedly. "The Yellowstone Journal lobbies every day for the elimination of all the reservations and the land opened to white settlement. It is a constant battle. When do you think you can get back to Lame Deer?"

"Probably not before day after tomorrow," replied Willie. "I have some business going with Sheriff Irvine and I have an expensive horse to return to Otter Creek. It may take a while to locate Porcupine, he moves around a lot."

"Then I think we are finished here. I'll get a Cheyenne Scout off to Upshaw and Major Carroll with instructions to locate Porcupine and prepare for taking testimony. When you get there maybe we can button this up." Col. Swaine finished as the two men moved to the door.

Willie left the Fort and made his way back to Miles City. He stopped by the Red House to touch base with Sheriff Irvine before deciding what to do next. The Sheriff was in his office.

"Hi Sheriff," greeted Willie. "Anything new happen overnight?"

"Good to see you this morning, Willie." Sherriff Irvine replied. "It looks like Parrott and Carey got in last night. I had a man watching Chinnick's corral last night. He said two riders with eight loose horses showed up last night after it got dark. They went to Chinnick's shack and had a conversation with him and then moved on to the saloon. We have to confirm that it really is

Parrott and Carey. I sent an old "working girl" named Beavertooth over there to find out what is going on. She is friends with Chinnick's wife but she works for me as an informer sometimes. When she gets back to me we will develop a plan to take them down."

"I'm just trying to decide what to do next," explained Willie. "I need to get back to the Reservation on a project for Upshaw and Swaine. I also thought that on the way back up the Rosebud I would try and poke around Sim Robert's place and see if I can find out where Parrott's big bunch of horses are stashed. But, I didn't think it would be too healthy to do that if Parrott and Carey were still there."

"You better be careful up there by yourself. Sim Roberts has killed at least three men that I know of. He is no slouch with a gun so keep your observations long range and ride a fast horse." Sheriff Irvine advised.

"He can't catch me if I'm on the Pagent horse. I'll be careful. Send me a message through Upshaw and let me know how the arrest turns out." Willie said as he turned to go.

Later that afternoon Sheriff Irvine and "X" Biedler met in front of the Bella Union Theater.

"Well, Parrott and Carey are definitely here," said "X". They are sitting out on the porch of Chinnick's Saloon as pretty as you please. I just don't see how we can get close enough to make an arrest without starting a major gunfight in the middle of town."

"I got an idea "X". See that guy across the street. That's Lem Wilson. He is a packer from Ft. Keogh and a pretty tough guy. I think he was in that Beecher Island fight and just got here this morning with a load of coal for Fort Keogh. Let's go talk to him."

They crossed the street and met Lem Wilson who was about as unlikely looking tough guy as one would ever see. He was dressed in a pair of bib overalls covered in coal dust, a pair of high topped farmer shoes, a disreputable hat, and looked for all the world like a dim witted farm hand.

Sheriff Irvine started the conversation. "Hey Lem. How would you like to make $100 for five minutes work?"

Lem Wilson's eyes narrowed. "What do you have in mind Sheriff?"

"There are two guys down there on Chinnick's front porch that have "Wanted" posters out on them. Both of those guys know "X" and I, so we can't get close enough to make an arrest without a fight. If you put a couple of holsters inside of your bib overalls, I'll bet you can walk right by them. Then "X" and I will come down the street and while their eyes are on us, you can get the drop on them. What do you think?" Irvine asked.

"You got pictures of them?" Lem inquired.

"Right here," replied "X" pulling the "Wanted" posters from his vest.

Lem studied the pictures for a minute. "I guess I could do that. If it something goes wrong and I can't get behind them, I guess I could just get a drink and walk back out."

"Good man," Sheriff Irvine said enthusiastically. "Give us fifteen minutes to get into position and then start your walk."

Sheriff positioned Deputy Johnson with a shotgun behind Chinnick's Saloon overlooking the corrals, while he and "X" went back to the Bella Union. Lem went to his wagon and secured his two pistols which he tucked inside his bib overalls. When the group was ready Sheriff Irvine gave a signal and Lem started his walk.

As Lem got to Chinnick's Saloon, he was challenged by Parrott, "Where in the hell are you going in such a hurry?"

"To get a drink and wash the coal dust out of my mouth," replied Lem as he brushed by Parrott.

Immediately following Lem's entry into the saloon, Irvine and Beidler armed with shotguns moved down the wooden sidewalk towards Chinnick's Saloon. When they got within a block, they crossed the street in full view of Parrott and Carey. Since Lem didn't come out right away, they turned toward the Saloon. Both Parrott and Carey tensed up as they saw the lawmen approach. As Parrott began to reach for his rifle, the command behind them rang out.

"Hands up, boys!" Followed by two clicks from Wilson's drawn pistols.

Both men's hands shot up immediately and they were disarmed by Irvine while "X" joined Lem Wilson in covering the two with a double barreled shotgun. They were taken directly to the blacksmith shop where permanent shackles were attached to their hands and feet and escorted to the Red House where the shackles were further joined to the bars of the jail.

"You will never hold me Irvine!" Parrott taunted. "I'll get off just like last time."

"I don't think so, George. You killed two popular deputies, and Carbon County, Wyoming wants you pretty bad. You may not even make it to trial." Irvine replied with remarkable foresight.

Once the prisoners were secured Irvine hurried to the telegraph office and sent a message to Sheriff Rankin in Rawlins, Wyoming announcing the capture of the two outlaws. Rankin and an additional deputy immediately proceeded to Miles City by train. Because most trains ran east to west and not north to south, this required a trip east to Omaha on the Union Pacific and then west again to Miles City on the Northern Pacific.

About two weeks after the capture, Sheriff Rankin arrived and with a large number of guards the two outlaws were taken to the train and sent east. In Omaha Parrott was taken to the Union Pacific Headquarters where he was photographed and questioned about his train robbing activities. Carey was sent on to Rawlins under the care of the deputy. When the train stopped for fuel in the town of Carbon, Wyoming fifteen armed men boarded the train and removed Carey from the train and promptly hanged him from the nearest telegraph pole.

Given the treatment of Carey, Sheriff Rankin was prepared when he and Parrott reached the town of Carbon. This time twelve armed and masked men boarded the train and demanded Parrott. Sheriff Rankin resisted but was disarmed. The vigilantes cut Parrot loose by destroying his train seat and took him to the overhead beam of a nearby corral and demanded that he confess and reveal all the members of his band. At this point Parrott's bravado faded and he made a full confession. He was then restored to Sheriff Rankin and allowed to proceed on to Rawlins. (It has always been an open question as to whether or not Sheriff Rankin was a willing participant in the forced confession.) At any rate he was allowed to take Parrott on to Rawlins for a legal hanging. He pleaded guilty and Judge William Peck ordered that Parrott be hung by the neck until dead.

This was not the end of "Big Nose" George Parrott. His execution was stayed from September to March, during which time he supposedly converted to Christianity. He got possession of a small knife which he used to file off the rivets of his shackles. Then he attempted to escape by striking the jailer in the face with the removed irons. The jailer's wife heard the noise and grabbed a pistol and covered Parrott until her husband regained control of Parrott. He was returned to his cell but later on that night a party of vigilantes entered the jail and hanged him from a telegraph pole. Notably, as news of the hanging spread, several known outlaws left the Rawlins vicinity for parts unknown.

A grisly post script to the Parrott affair was the disposition of the body. Because no one claimed the body, Doctor John Osborne, a local physician, asked to examine the body for scientific purposes, specifically an examination of the outlaw's brain. His skull cap was removed and the brain compared to other brains the doctor had examined at medical school. He found no significant differences. However, that was not the end of the Doctor's interest in Parrott. He had a large portion of the skin on Parrott's chest and thighs removed and sent to be tanned. From the tanned skin he had a pair of shoes and a medical bag made from the human leather. The skull cap served as a door stop for his young female assistant, Dr. Lillian Heath. The skull cap, a piece of the tanned skin, and leg irons now are on display at the Union Pacific Railroad Museum in Omaha, Nebraska. The bottom part of the skull and shoes he was wearing when hanged are in the Carbon County Museum. His death mask and shoes made from his skin are displayed in the Rawlins National Bank. Dr. Osborne went on to become the Governor of the State of Wyoming.

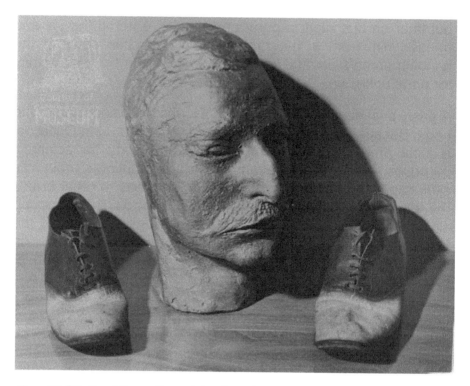

Figure 37: "Big Nose" George Parrott's Death Mask & the Shoes Made from his Skin. Picture Courtesy of the Carbon County, WY Archives.

Chapter 21. The Cattle Slaughter Site

Leaving Miles City, Willie headed cross country to Rosebud Creek, and then turned south paralleling the creek. Sheriff Irvine had pointed out on the big map in the Red House the approximate location of the Sim Buford Roberts place. Willie did not intend to spend much time there because he had to return the Pagent horse to the Mission but wanted to have the horse in case he had to outrun Roberts or another outlaw. Reaching the vicinity of the Roberts Ranch he left the trail and turned east up into the hills that bordered the creek. Riding to the highest hill in the area, Willie rode up the hill before stopping just short of the crest. He dismounted, tied his horse to a cedar tree and walked the remaining few yards to the top of the hill. Making sure he did not silhouette himself at the top of the hill, he unlimbered his field glasses and began a careful examination of the surrounding area.

The survey of the area revealed a modest house, barn, and set of corrals located on the edge of Rosebud Creek. A few scattered cattle ranged up and down the draws on the west side of the creek. Looking off the south side of the hill and into a deep wide dry creek that emptied into Rosebud Creek, Willie noted a fence across the mouth of a brushy draw which seemed to be bounded by sandstone cliffs. The presence of a few cottonwood and ash trees indicated that a spring or other water source was present in the draw. Since none of the other draws were fenced, Willie's suspicions were immediately aroused. It appeared to be a box canyon well off the normally traveled path with water and a modest amount of pasture, a perfect hiding place for stolen horses.

Continuing his survey, Willie noted that while there were cattle grazing throughout the area, it did not look like the ranch was fully stocked. A wagon track proceeded east up the dry creek toward the high divide which separated the Rosebud and Tongue River Valleys. He decided to try and get a look at the draw and then follow the wagon tracks to find out where they went. Taking one last look around and seeing no human activity, Willie untied his horse and rode to the bottom of the dry creek and up the hill that bordered the suspect draw on the east. He rode to the top of the box canyon cliff and peered over the edge. Below grazed about 30 horses which strongly resembled the ones he had seen at Crazy Head Springs. A small deserted campsite lay on the west side of the draw between two cottonwood trees. Willie had seen enough and beat a hasty retreat to his horse.

Moving at a high trot Willie returned to the wide dry creek bed and skirting the edge of the hills, he proceeded east until he reached the top of the divide between Rosebud and Tongue River. Observing that the wagon tracks turned south at the top of the divide, he continued to follow them as they moved toward the reservation. The wagon tracks wound around tree covered buttes with sandstone outcrops until coming to a wide buffalo trail which followed Greenleaf Creek east toward Tongue River. Topping over the divide the buffalo trail caught the beginning of Lay Creek and followed that drainage to the Miles City road which ran parallel to Tongue River. At the Miles City road the tracks turned toward Ashland.

By this time Willie had become very familiar with the wagon which had made the most recent tracks from the Roberts ranch. He was very surprised when the wagon tracks suddenly turned off the Miles City road and headed west up Reservation Creek. Willie figured he was barely on the Cheyenne Reservation. About two miles up Reservation Creek, Black Diamond snorted and Willie caught the scent of rotten meat. Pulling off the trail into the timber he slowly urged the horse forward. Picking his way carefully up the draw, Willie came to place where he looked out on a small park with a tiny stream running into Reservation Creek from the north. In the park was a big cottonwood tree with a large limb perpendicular to the ground. From the limb a pulley system was rigged to pull carcasses up to the limb. A series of hooks nailed to the limb provided an area for hanging several carcasses while they were skinned and allowed to cool out. It was clearly a cattle slaughtering site.

As Willie reviewed the scene he saw no heads, feet, hides, or gut piles which would account for the smell. He also did not see the magpies or turkey buzzards which should have been present. Circling the site to the south, he again cut the wagon tracks west of the park going further up Reservation Creek. As he proceeded up creek the smell increased and Willie observed what appeared to be blood trails between the wagon tracks. About a mile from the slaughter site further up the creek, the wagon tracks turned sharply to the north away from the creek. Climbing out of the Reservation Creek bottom, the wagon tracks paralleled a deep draw which entered the creek from the north. About three hundred yards out of the creek bottom he reached a highly timbered bench where the tracks again turned west to the edge of the sandstone rimed draw. There, a flat sandstone rock protruded out over an abyss below. On the rock was a log designed to stop a wagon when the tail gate was over the edge.

As Willie approached the edge the smell became overpowering and Black Diamond refused to go further. Backing away from the rock, Willie dismounted and tied his horse to a dead pine tree and went on by foot. When he looked over the edge, a flock of magpies flew up and two coyotes bolted away. The bottom, nearly thirty feet down, was littered with cow heads, feet, and gut piles.

Willie returned to his horse, mounted, and retraced his trail back to the Reservation Creek bottom. He sensed that he had missed something. He knew the cattle had been killed and butchered at the park. Their carcasses had been raised up on the pulley system where they had been gutted, heads, and feet cut off and all of the unusable parts allowed to spill into the wagon box. From there, the wagon took the offal to the disposal site about a mile and a half away where it was shoveled off into the draw. The cattle would then be skinned, the brands cut out, and the meat allowed to cool out for a day until it was taken to Ashland. Water from the stream had been used to wash the carcasses. But how had the cattle been accumulated before slaughter? There should be a corral or a pen near the park to hold them until slaughter. Willie decided the pen must be in the side draw where the stream originated and he missed it when he circled the park to the south.

Following the wagon tracks east back to the slaughter site, Willie again dismounted and tied his horse before checking out the side draw. He removed the rifle from his saddle scabbard and quietly moved toward the draw. He walked up the hill on the west side of the draw until he could look over and into the draw. What he saw amazed him. Inside the narrow opening to the draw was about a two acre sand stone bowl which made a natural corral. A stream of water cascaded down a small waterfall at north end of the bowl and trickled through the bottom of the draw which was closed off by a crude gate. While there were no cattle in the corral, the bottom of the bowl was churned up with cattle tracks.

Willie had seen enough. A picture of the whole operation was now clear. Groups of cattle numbering about ten at a time were driven from off the reservation to this remote site on the reservation. Ten head of cattle from a big outfit would not be missed until the fall roundup if at all. Since the roundups did not go on the reservation, there was little chance of discovery of the kill site by whites. Because the reservation was not yet fenced even the occasional Cheyenne who discovered the site may have thought that the kill site was off the reservation. The cattle were driven into the natural corral where they were shot and the carcasses dragged to the cottonwood tree where they were butchered. The carcasses were hung for a day and then delivered to the lumber operation's butchers in Ashland to fill Sim Roberts' meat contract. Sometimes the carcasses were

Robert's own cattle, but more often they were stolen from a variety of herds throughout the area. Hides, minus the brands, were shipped out of the area and sold at bargain prices to unethical hide buyers.

Willie returned to his horse and loped down the Reservation Creek trail to the Miles City Road. Less than an hour later he trotted into the St. Labre Mission barn and unsaddled Black Diamond. He was very sorry to lose the use of such a beautiful animal. It was late in the day so he elected to stay at the Mission for the evening and catch up on any Ashland/Rabbit Town news he may have missed. Deacon George Yoakim and Father van der Velden welcomed him to supper and a bed for the night which Willie gratefully accepted.

At supper Willie asked Deacon George, "Can you get a message to Grant Dunning that Pagent's horse is here and ready to be picked up?"

"Yes, of course." Deacon George replied. "He and Anna will probably come for church tomorrow since it is Sunday. He can take the horse back with him."

"Great. Tell him "thank you very much". I don't know if we did any good yet but it was sure worth the effort. Have you heard any news out of Rabbit Town?" Willie inquired.

"Your two cattle deliveries were very welcome. Everyone I talked to says they got some of the meat. The Elks did a good job of distribution. On the negative side there is more Ghost Dance excitement," Father van der Velden reported.

"Is Porcupine running the Ghost Dance over here, or is it someone else?" Willie asked pointedly.

"I think it is somebody else," said Deacon Yoakim, who spoke passable Cheyenne. "I heard that Porcupine was holding a big dance at Busby. Almost all the Cheyennes from all over the reservation are going over there after they pick up their rations next week."

"I have to get him to testify for an Army inquiry as soon as possible. Maybe I can catch him tomorrow or the next day. His version of Ghost Dancing is not dangerous but I hear some of the Sioux versions are not good. Keep an ear out for a guy named Short Bull from Pine Ridge and let me know if he shows up over here." Willie concluded. "I probably won't see you in the morning. I'm leaving for Lame Deer before daylight. Thanks again for your hospitality."

Chapter 22. Porcupine's Testimony

The next morning Willie saddled up and headed to Lame Deer. He briefly considered waiting for Olga's Eatery to open, but decided to press on and see if Agent Upshaw had any news. He also was looking forward to spending some time with Bear Woman who was probably feeling neglected because he had been on the road so much. The ride to Lame Deer took about three hours and Willie arrived at Agency Headquarters well after sunrise. Because it was Sunday and the Headquarters was closed he had to go to Upshaw's house to find the Agent.

"Oh, Willie. Am I ever glad to see you!" exclaimed Upshaw. "Go on over to the office, I'll be there in a minute."

Willie walked over to the office and was quickly joined by Upshaw who unlocked the door and invited him into his office.

"What have you been doing for the last few days?" demanded Upshaw. "We have big problems over here with this Ghost Dance stuff. The military is all upset."

"I know all about that," Willie replied. "I spent two hours with Col. Swaine the day before yesterday talking about Ghost Dance activities. As a matter of fact, Major Carroll should have received a message yesterday or maybe today to interview Porcupine. I talked to Porcupine at length and even went through a sweat lodge ceremony and a Ghost Dance initiation with him as the leading Ghost Dance priest at Birney Village. I didn't like to do it because I felt like a spy, but it was the only way I could get accurate information. The man and the message are not dangerous to white people, if whites don't overreact to the singing and dancing."

"That is really good to hear!" Upshaw gasped in obvious relief. "Major Carroll has been telling me that the Army is really concerned about the dancing. He says reservations all over the west are doing it. The Sioux Agents are really scared and have asked the military for help."

"I have heard the Sioux Ghost Dance priests are changing the message to suit some of the knot heads and crazies over there. They hear what they want to hear. Porcupine's message is a message of peace. As long as our people listen to him we will be fine. If the Sioux message starts to get going over here maybe we could have trouble. I don't think we have that problem yet." Willie opined.

"That's a real relief. I was afraid this reservation was going to come apart between Ghost Dancing and the Ferguson incident." Upshaw said as he mopped his brow. "What else have you been doing?"

"Moving like hell. Besides the Ghost Dance stuff, I bought cattle from Brewster and Brown and distributed them to Birney Village and Rabbit Town. Then I got your message about Captain Howes, which said he had important information for Stuart. I went up there and met Charlie Thex who had been keeping an eye on the outlaw cabin on Cow Creek. Two guys and about thirty horses came in one night about a week ago. Charlie slipped up and listened to their talk. He found out they were going to Crazy Head Springs here on the reservation and then on to Sim Buford Roberts ranch on the Rosebud. Also said they thought they might spend a couple of days having some fun in Miles City. Charlie thought the horses were stolen so Captain Howes sent that message for me. Charlie and Ed McGhee accompanied me to the cabin and they went in to see if the horses were still there but they had flown the coop with two of the local outlaws. Charlie and I decided to follow them to Crazy Head Springs since we figured they were only about three hours ahead of us. Ed went back and borrowed a racehorse from Syd Pagent and left it at the Mission for me in case we got an identification on the two guys. We got to Crazy Head Springs about dark and I was able to identify the two as "Big

Nose" George Parrott and Bill Carey, both wanted men with reward posters out on them. There were also three Cheyennes there. One looked to be a breed, another I didn't recognize, but the third was Young Mule, the kid I found with Ferguson's post office key. The breed did all the talking to the white men. Charlie and I beat it out of there and spent the night between Lame Deer and Ashland. The next morning we galloped to Ashland figuring they would come in to get whiskey for their Cheyenne help. The two local guys plus Bill Carey showed up and had breakfast and then went to the Ashland Bar. Bill Carey came right back out with four jugs of whiskey and rode back toward Lame Deer while the two local guys stayed. Charlie followed Carey as far as the hill past the Miles City road and then fogged on back to the Mission to meet me. I saddled up the racehorse and hit the trail for Miles City to notify Irvine to be on the lookout for Parrott and Carey. He saw them ride in the next morning so he and "X" Beidler were trying to figure out a plan to arrest him. They said they didn't need me so I went to see Col. Swaine and gave him the information on the Ghost Dance stuff. Yesterday I rode back to the Mission to return Pagent's horse, by way of Sim Robert's Ranch. I managed to locate Parrott's horses in a box canyon on Roberts' place and then followed some wagon tracks to the Reservation. There I found a cattle slaughter site where I suspect Roberts kills his stolen cattle before taking them to the saw mills in Ashland. I spent the last night at the Mission and came on here. Other than that I ain't done a damn thing!" Willie concluded somewhat out of breath.

"My God!" Upshaw exclaimed. "You have been busy. Have you eaten today?"

"Nope," Willie replied laconically.

"Come on over to the house, the wife will fix you something to eat." Upshaw suggested. "Then I think we should go over and see Major Carroll and set up the Porcupine interview and see if he has any Cheyenne Scout dispatches for us."

Later that morning Agent Upshaw and Willie rode the ¾ mile to Camp Merritt (sometimes referred to as Camp Crook) and entered the modest building that served as Camp Headquarters. Since it was Sunday, the Officer of the Day, Lt. S.C. Robertson was on duty. When apprised of the seriousness of the matter, he sent an orderly to bring Major Carroll to the Headquarters. A few minutes later Major Carroll entered the building and greeted Agent Upshaw and Willie. Inviting them over to a table which served as a conference room, Major Carroll opened the conversation.

"What brings you gentlemen to Camp Merritt on a Sunday morning?"

Agent Upshaw took the lead. "Have you received any dispatches from Fort Keogh for me yesterday or today?"

Major Carroll turned to Lt. Robertson. "Did any posts come in late yesterday or last night?"

"Yes, but they weren't marked "Urgent", the lieutenant replied. "Sergeant Jones, bring me the dispatch case, please."

Sergeant Jones brought the case to the table. Lt. Robertson removed the contents and handed two envelopes to Upshaw and one to Major Carroll. Upshaw's envelopes were from Col. Swaine to Upshaw and the other was from Sheriff Irvine to Upshaw. Major Carroll's envelope was from Col. Swaine. As the two men reviewed their respective letters, Major Carroll muttered sarcastically, "Damn it. This should have been marked "Urgent" and brought to my attention. So much for Army efficiency."

Upshaw opened the envelope from Sheriff Irvine first. It read: "Tell Deputy Rowland that Parrott and Carey were captured today without incident and are in jail. Thanks for the good work. Sheriff Irvine." Upshaw handed the letter to Willie who scanned the missive and handed it back to Upshaw with a grin. He couldn't help but see dollar signs as his share of $3000 in reward money danced in his head. The other letter to Upshaw was a copy of Major Carroll's instructions from Col. Swaine to conduct a thorough interview of the Cheyenne medicine man Porcupine on the subject of the Ghost Dance Religion. Upon completion the results were to be forwarded the through the Department of the Missouri to the Adjutant General of the Army.

Major Carroll looked at Upshaw and said. "I assume that your copy of Col. Swaine's letter is the same as mine. It looks like we better find Porcupine and see if he will give us a statement. Is there any reason to believe he will do that?"

Willis spoke up. "Yes, I believe he will if approached correctly. At the direction of Agent Upshaw I met with the man about a week ago. We discussed the Ghost Dance Religion at some length and I asked if he would initiate me into the Ghost Dance Religion by teaching me the songs and the dances. He was completely open to doing that in spite of the fact that he knew I worked for Agent Upshaw. I found his version of the Ghost Dance Religion to be entirely peaceful and worthy of support by the Agency. If you allow me to approach him in an open and respectful manner and invite him to meet with us voluntarily, I think you can expect a full and complete account of his trip. How he met Wovoka, the Paiute Messiah, the basics of the Ghost Dance religion, some of the songs and dances which will lead Indians from all over the west to what I will call "Indian Heaven". Now having said all that, I have heard that there is a Sioux version of the Ghost Dance Religion which is not so peaceful. It teaches that the "Ghost Shirts" which in Porcupine's version turn away evil, instead turn away the bullets of the white man. Why would you need to turn away bullets, if your intentions are entirely peaceful? If the Sioux version got going on this reservation, there are a lot of young men who could be tempted to get in trouble. If there is Ghost Dancing on this reservation, we want it to be Porcupine's Ghost Dance and not the Sioux Ghost Dance."

Major Carroll and Agent Upshaw were astounded at Willie's revelations. Major Carroll was the first to speak. "My God, Willis. Did you really go through the whole initiation ceremonies?"

"Yes, I did. And the Cheyenne part of me is not proud of it. I feel like a traitor to my mother's people. However, the white side of me says it was the right thing to do to find out the truth so I could preserve the peace between the two sides. And the truth is that Porcupine is a wise old man trying to preserve the best of the old Cheyenne ways while living in a white man world. Let him tell the truth as he sees it. He is an honest man." Willis concluded.

"Agent Upshaw, what are your views on this situation?" asked Major Carroll.

"I think we are lucky to have a man like Willis Rowland to stand between the Red Tribe and the White Tribe while talking truth to both sides. Let him go and find Porcupine and invite him to talk to the Great Father through the Army. If Porcupine agrees, the Army is educated about the nature of the Ghost Dance threat, be it real or imagined. The War Department and the Indian Department can make better decisions with accurate information and this looks to me like the best opportunity to get that information." Upshaw finished strongly.

"I completely agree," replied Carroll. "Let's figure out how to make it work the best for Porcupine and the Army. Willie, where and how do you think would be the best place for Porcupine to give his testimony?"

"I would think it best to be at the Agency but not in the offices or here at the Army Camp. Probably in a tent outside the office under a shade tree would make him most comfortable. He will want to have the other two Cheyennes who traveled with him there to help him remember. Cheyennes always want what they say in council to be completely accurate. When you swear him in I will ask him what sacred object he wants to use. It will probably be a buffalo skull but don't be offended if it is not the Bible. When he gives his testimony, I will ask him to talk slowly and deliberately. Some Cheyenne words do not translate directly into English. You should have someone with good writing skills who can sort out the testimony. We will have to go over the same ground two or three times to get the full truth. You may want two people to transcribe the testimony so the transcripts can be compared. We can't rush Porcupine or show impatience. It may take a couple of days." Willie finished.

Major Carroll nodded to Willie, "I think that is good advice."

Then turning to the Officer of the Day, Major Carroll spoke in a commanding tone, "Lt. Robertson, you will be the primary transcriptionist. I've read your reports and you write clearly and concisely. Get one of your fellow lieutenants to check your transcript for content. Remember, this is going to the highest levels of the War Department. When the testimony is over and the transcript complete, I want Agent Upshaw and Willis Rowland to review the entire transcript for accuracy before we take it to Col. Swaine for his review. We must make sure as much as possible to present facts only, not opinions or conclusions."

"Willis, you are authorized to go find Porcupine and invite him to come to the Agency to give a Statement to the Army of his knowledge of the Ghost Dance Religion. We will set up as you suggested. If there is anything else we can do to make Porcupine and his companions more comfortable, please tell us. I want to make this event a learning occasion for everyone.

Willis, you go with our thanks." Major Carroll stood up signifying the meeting was over. He shook hands with Agent Upshaw and Willie and escorted them to the door.

Following the Camp Merritt meeting, Agent Upshaw and Willie parted company, Upshaw returning to his home and Willie hit the road to Muddy Creek. Willie was tired, really tired and it was all catching up to him. He needed a day to sleep, eat, and sleep again. While one part of him wanted to go see Bear Woman, the rest of him said go home, get some sleep, and then go see her when he felt better. The rest of him won.

After napping most of the afternoon and a good night's sleep, Willie felt much better. He had a long conversation with Daddy Rowland about Porcupine and the Ghost Dance Craze. Bill Rowland agreed with Willie that the big risk was the Sioux influence seeping onto the Cheyenne Reservation through the active movement of people visiting relatives. And the best defense against that influence was to encourage Porcupine's vision of how the Ghost Dance Religion and the Cheyenne traditional beliefs could combine to produce a positive result for the whole tribe. No other living Cheyenne knew more about the old Cheyenne ceremonies and religion than Porcupine. They both concluded that support of Porcupine by the Council of Forty Four Chiefs and the Army/Agency leadership was the best policy. The threats to peace on the Reservation came from radical Sioux ideas and a paranoid fear in the neighboring white population of Ghost Dancing whipped up by interests supporting elimination of the Tongue River Reservation.

Willie took time out from his Porcupine duties to examine the Mormon horse and his bad foot. During Willie's travels, Bill Rowland had arranged for the Agency blacksmith to come to the Rowland Ranch and put a corrective horseshoe on the foot. The horse had filled out from good feed and little exercise and now showed only a slight limp from his injury. Both Bill and Willie were impressed with what an exceptional animal he really was. Completely gentle, but powerfully built and athletic, the horse showed an intelligence and eagerness to please that warmed the heart of a horseman. The two men agreed that in about another week he would be well enough to ride, and both looked forward to that event.

In the afternoon Willie made the short ride from Muddy Creek to the Busby Trading Post which was the center of commercial and social life in the area. There he asked the patrons if anyone had seen or heard of Porcupine's location. He was told that Porcupine was at his lodge on Rosebud Creek two miles south of Busby. Willie quickly covered the two miles and approached Porcupine's large teepee situated on a small knoll next to the creek. He found Porcupine outside his lodge working on his medicines in preparation for the big dance later in the month.

"Hello, Father." Willie called out as he approached the lodge.

Porcupine scrambled to his feet with a big smile on his face. "Hello Long Forehead. How are you? Come sit with me and we can talk of great things."

Long Forehead dismounted and tied his horse to a sage brush. Removing a full bag of coffee beans from his saddlebags, he approached Porcupine with hand extended. As the two men clasped hands, Long Forehead said, "Here is a small gift for your lodge, may we all live in peace."

Porcupine accepted the bag from Long Forehead, turned and called his wife to come from the teepee. Giving her the bag he directed her to prepare some coffee. The he seated himself and gestured for Long Forehead to do the same.

"What brings my friend Long Forehead to my lodge today?" Porcupine asked.

Long Forehead started slowly and carefully. "The white people are very afraid of the Ghost Dance. They don't understand all the singing and dancing and fear that the Cheyenne mean to make war upon them."

"But, Wavoka and his message is a message of peace," protested Porcupine.

"I know. But our white people do not know Wavoka's message like you and I do. While I was gone Agent Upshaw asked for more white soldiers to live at the Agency in case there was trouble. I have told the soldier chiefs that the Cheyenne Ghost Dance does not mean war and that they have nothing to fear from the Cheyenne. They have asked that you come to Lame Deer Agency and tell them of your visit with Wavoka, his teachings, and what you told the Council of Forty Four when you came back. Will you do that?" Willie finished.

Porcupine looked concerned and confused. "Why do they think that Wavoka wants war?"

"There has been some trouble with the Sioux Ghost Dance. They are teaching that the Ghost Dance shirts can turn white man bullets, which doesn't sound peaceful to the soldier chiefs. Some young men have caused trouble there." Long Forehead replied.

"But, that is not the teaching that I heard from Wavoka. That is not what I have been telling the Cheyennes," complained Porcupine.

"That is why you must tell the white soldier chiefs the truth about what you learned from Wavoka. They will take the truth all the way to the Great Father in Washington. Some bad white men are trying to get the Great Father to move the Cheyennes over to live with the Crows so they can take this land for their cattle. You can help the soldier chiefs and the Great Father know the truth." Long Forehead entreated.

"I will talk to the soldier chiefs," Porcupine declared. "But Long Forehead must the one who tells the soldier chiefs in their tongue what I say in Cheyenne. You know what I have said in the Councils, we have smoked together in the Medicine Lodge, you have danced in the Ghost Dance, and I trust you to make white people to understand the truth."

"Do you want to bring Grasshopper and Ridge Walker with you to see the soldier chiefs?" Long Forehead asked.

"Yes, I want them to tell that I remember everything right. When do you want me to come and is there anything else I should bring?" asked Porcupine.

"How about three days from today?" Long Forehead suggested. "I can send a messenger to Birney Village for Grasshopper and Ridge Runner. The Soldier Chiefs want you to swear to tell the truth on a sacred Cheyenne object. Do you want to bring the sacred buffalo skull we used in the Medicine Lodge Ceremony?"

"That would be good. I need time to finish preparing for a big dance just after ration day. I will be at Lame Deer in the morning three days from today." Porcupine declared.

"The Soldier Chiefs thank you very much for your help. We all want to keep the peace. Your talk may keep Cheyennes and white people from fighting when there is no need to fight." Long Forehead said forcefully.

With his meeting with Porcupine concluded, Long Forehead proceeded back toward Lame Deer. He stopped briefly to visit Sy Young and bought a bag of coffee beans and a side of bacon for Elk River, father of Bear Woman and a new skinning knife for her brother. Under Cheyenne custom the girl's brother selected her husband after conferring with the family, so Long Forehead wanted to keep all her family happy until he was ready to proceed to marriage. He delivered the gifts to her father and brother who received them with great appreciation. They talked at length about upcoming ration day, the new reservation census, the Ferguson killing, and Porcupine's Ghost Dance.

Elk River was a very traditional Cheyenne who had a reputation in his youth as a superior catcher of wild horses. He was a supreme judge of horseflesh and Long Forehead wanted him to look at the Mormon horse to get his opinion of the animal. Elk River invited Long Forehead to supper after which he said goodnight and left the lodge. Sometime later Bear Woman left the lodge for a walk and Long Forehead threw a blanket over her head and the two of them lay under the stars and they talked for a long time.

Figure 38. Elk River & Wife. Photo Courtesy of the Montana Historical Society

Blanket courtship was a tradition which began with the Sioux. It came into Cheyenne favor after the old war days when the young men could no longer count coups. In the old days a man who had coups to his credit could walk right up to a girl and her mother could say nothing. After peace broke out there was almost no way a couple could get together since mothers watched their daughters very carefully. There developed a tradition in which a boy would hide at night near the girl's house or teepee and if she came out to get water or wood, the boy would throw a blanket over her head and they could get to know each other. If the girl was late coming back the mother would come out and sometimes run the boy off. After a while the families would agree to a wedding with the appropriate gifts of horses or trade goods.

The next morning Willie slept late after his long night with Bear Woman. He was now sure that as soon as the Porcupine Affair was concluded he would begin the arrangements necessary to make Bear Woman his wife. However, he still had chores necessary to complete the Porcupine Testimony. First he rode to Lame Deer and informed Agent Upshaw and Major Carroll that Porcupine would testify two days hence. He suggested that plenty of food and drink be available to the party and that some kind of gifts be presented to Porcupine and his fellow Cheyennes on conclusion of the Statement. Then he made the ride to Birney Village to inform Grasshopper and Ridge Walker that they were expected at the Agency in the morning of the day after next to assist Porcupine in his testimony. Both agreed to make the trip the next day and be available first thing the following morning.

Following the notice to Grasshopper and Ridge Walker, Willie turned his horse back onto the road to Lame Deer. It was very late in the afternoon when he reached the top of the Lame Deer/Birney divide and he was hot and thirsty. Remembering the cool water at American Horse's camp, he resolved to stop by his old family friend's lodge and water his horse and himself.

As he approached the camp he noticed in the distance and moving away from him was another rider on a big sorrel horse. The rider was a young Cheyenne man but he was too far away to see any features. What drew Willie's attention was the similarity between the man's horse and Red Mormon, the lame horse in Willie's barn. He also noted that the man's direction of travel was toward Crazy Head Springs. When he reached American Horse's camp, Willie observed that the cabin was almost complete. He watered his horse in the cold water pond, dismounted and drank himself before remounting and hailing the cabin. He was greeted by four friendly dogs but no one else seemed to be at home. Disappointed with the failure to talk with American Horse, Willie picked up the pace and managed to make Lame Deer just at dark. He stopped at the house of his older brother James Rowland and invited himself to spend the night with his family.

The next day (June 13th) was spent in preparation for Porcupine's testimony. A large Army tent was pitched outside the Agency Headquarters. The tent sides were rolled up to allow the air to flow freely and keep the heat down. A long table was placed at one end of the tent with four chairs behind the table for Major Carroll, Agent Upshaw, and two transcriptionists. In front of the table were two chairs, one for Porcupine and the other for Long Forehead/Willis Rowland, the Cheyenne to English interpreter. A tiny table was placed in front of the two chairs to hold the buffalo skull and a bible, which represented the two sacred objects of both "tribes". The remainder of the tent held a few benches to seat Porcupine's fellow travelers, Grasshopper and Ridge Walker, and other Cheyenne chiefs who wished to attend. The setting was designed to make the witnesses comfortable while establishing a dignified, formal, and yet practical setting for the taking of testimony.

June 14, 1890 dawned with blue skies and a few high cirrus clouds. Lieutenant S.C. Robertson was making final

Figure 39. Porcupine, Cheyenne Ghost Dance Priest. Courtesy of the Montana Historical Society

preparations for his task of transcribing Porcupine's testimony. He faced a daunting task. The Statement would go to the highest levels of the War Department and inform U.S. Army policy toward Ghost Dancers in tribes all over the western United States. He had the difficult task of rendering raw testimony in a difficult language as told through an interpreter into a cogent and understandable statement. In so doing he had to navigate the biases held by settler's "the only good Indian is a dead one" mindset, the Cheyenne desperate struggle to retain their cultural identify in the face of defeat, and a second guessing of Army policy by the eastern press.

The intellectual eastern establishment based in Boston and New York being a long way from the on-the-ground realities, often failed to appreciate the magnitude of the culture clash between the "noble red man" and the "manifest destiny" element of the white settler. In addition, the culture of Washington politics was heavily influenced by trading of favors, government contracts, and outright graft and corruption. But Lt. Robertson and his Army superiors had to make life and death decisions for Indians and settlers as they tried to keep the peace between the two. In the end Lt. Robertson decided to simply stick to the facts in a totally dispassionate manner and let the chips fall where they may. In so doing he upheld the best traditions of the U.S. Army.

Porcupine, Grasshopper, and Ridge Walker met Long Forehead at the Agency Headquarters Building later that morning. He showed the Cheyennes the tent, explained the seating arrangements and asked Porcupine to place his Sacred Buffalo Skull on the small table next to the Holy Bible. The Cheyennes were served coffee and Long Forehead introduced the three to Major Carroll, Agent Upshaw, and Lieutenants S.C. Robertson and Pitcher, the two transcriptionists. The group proceeded to the tent where the proceedings began.

Major Carroll opened this hearing by stating:

"The purpose of this hearing is to receive information on behalf of the U.S. Army regarding the Ghost Dance Religion, its founder, and the precepts of the religion. Today we will hear testimony from Porcupine, Grasshopper, and Ridge Walker, three Cheyenne Indians who traveled to Nevada to meet and study under the Paiute holy man Wavoka, the founder of the Ghost Dance Religion. I will now swear in the witnesses. Normally we would use the Holy Bible, but since our three witnesses are not Christians but Cheyenne Indians, we will use their holy object, a Sacred Buffalo Skull. Willis Rowland whose Indian name is Long Forehead, our Cheyenne to English interpreter, will swear on both sacred objects, the Holy Bible and the Sacred Buffalo Skull to insure that the testimony given by the Cheyennes is true and complete in both languages. Do the witnesses have anything to say before they swear?"

Long Forehead repeated Major Carroll's statement in Cheyenne, and asked the three if they had any questions. Porcupine answered, "I will do most of the talking for the three of us. Grasshopper and Ridge Walker will listen very closely and correct me if they hear me say something they do not think is true. Do the people making the marks on paper have to swear that what they put down on paper is true also?"

Willis Rowland turned to Major Carroll. "Porcupine wants to know if the transcribers have to swear that what they write down is the truth."

Figure 40. Ridge Walker, Porcupine's Ghost Dance Witness. Photo Courtesy of the Montana Historical Society

Major Carroll smiled. "We will have them go first so our witnesses can see how it is done."

At this point the two lieutenants transcribing the testimony came around the table, faced Major Carroll, placed their hands on the Bible and swore that they would record the testimony exactly as given. Porcupine smiled and placed his hand on the Sacred Buffalo Skull, swore that he would tell the truth, and finally Willis Rowland/Long Forehead swore in English with his hand on the Bible and again in Cheyenne with his hand on the Sacred Buffalo Skull, that his translations would be as true as he could make them. Porcupine began his Statement. Within the first minute, Willis Rowland/Long Forehead called a halt to the testimony.

Facing Major Carroll, Willis Rowland explained that there was no Cheyenne word for Messiah in the Cheyenne language. The man they had gone to visit they called "the Christ" because Ghost Dance Religion was a mixture of Christianity and the old Indian religion. The term "the Christ" did not necessarily mean

Jesus Christ, only a Christ like figure for Indians. It was the best way they knew how to describe him. Major Carroll told the transcriptionists to record "the Christ" rather than the Messiah because that was closer to Porcupine's real testimony. The following statement was recorded by Lt. S.C Robertson over the course of the remainder of the day:

STATEMENT
OF THE CHEYENNE "PORCUPINE" OF MEETING
WITH THE NEW "CHRIST"

"In November last (1889) I left the reservation with two other Cheyennes. I went through Fort Washakie and took the Union Pacific railroad at Rawlins. We got on early in the morning about breakfast, rode all day on the railroad, and about dark reached Fort Bridger. I stayed there two days, and then took a passenger train, and the next morning got to Fort Hall. I found some lodges of Snakes and Bannocks there. The chief of the Bannocks took me to his camp nearby. The Bannocks told me they were glad to see a Cheyenne and that we ought to make a treaty with the Bannocks. The chief told me he had been to Washington and had seen the President, and that we all ought to be friends with the whites and live at peace with them and with each other. We talked these matters over for ten days. The agent at Fort Hall then sent for me and some of the Bannocks and Shoshones, and asked me where I was going.

I told him I was just traveling to meet other Indians and see other countries; that my people were at peace with the whites, and I thought that I could travel anywhere I wished. He asked me why I did not have a pass. I said because my agent would not give me one. He said he was glad to see me anyhow, and that the whites and Indians were all friends. Then he asked me where I wanted a pass to. I told him that I wanted to go further, and that some Bannocks and Shoshones wanted to go along. He gave us passes- five of them- to the chiefs of the three parties. We took the railroad to a little town nearby, and then took a narrow-gauge road. We went on this, riding all night at a very fast rate of speed, and came to a town on a big lake (Ogden or Salt Lake

City). We stayed there one day, taking the cars (trains) at night, rode all night, and the next morning about 9 o'clock saw a settlement of Indians. We traveled south on a narrow-gauge road. We got off at this Indian town. The Indians here were different from any Indians I ever saw. The women and men were dressed in white people's clothes, the women having their hair banged. These Indians had their faces painted white with black spots. We stayed with these people all day.

We took the same road at night and kept on. We traveled all night, and about day-light we saw a lot of houses, so we got off, and there is where we saw Indians living in huts of grass (tule?). We stopped here and got something to eat. There were whites living nearby. We got on the cars again at night, and during the night we got off among some Indians, who were fish-eaters (Paiute). We stayed among the Fish-eaters till morning, and then got into a wagon with the son of the chief of the Fish-eaters, and we arrived about noon at an agency on a big river. There was also a big lake near the agency. (Pyramid and Walker lakes, western Nevada?)

They told us they had heard from the Shoshone agency that the people in this country were all bad people, but that they were good people there. All the Indians from the Bannock agency down to where I finally stopped danced this dance (referring to the late religious dances at the Cheyenne agency), the whites often dancing it themselves. (It will be recollected that he traveled constantly through Mormon country) I knew nothing about this dance before going. I happen to run across it, that is all. I will tell you about it. (Here all the Indians removed their hats in token that the talk to follow was to be on a religious subject.) I want you all to listen to this, so there will be no mistake. There is no harm in what I say to anyone. I heard this where I met my friends in Nevada. It is a wonder you people never heard this before. In the dance we had there (Nevada) the whites and Indians danced together. I met there a great many kinds of people, but they all seem to know about this religion. The people there all seemed to be good. I never saw any drinking or fighting or bad conduct among them. They treated me well on the cars, without pay. They gave me food without charge, and I found that this was a habit among them toward their neighbors. I thought it strange that the people there should have been so good, so different from those here.

What I am going to say is the truth. The two men sitting near me were with me, and will bear witness that I speak the truth. I and my people have been living in ignorance until I went and found the truth. All the whites and Indians are brothers, I was told there. I never knew this before. The Fish-eaters near Pyramid Lake told me that Christ had appeared on earth again. They said Christ knew he was coming; that eleven of his children were also coming from a far land. It appeared that Christ had sent for me to go there, and that was why unconsciously I took my journey. It had been foreordained. Christ had summoned myself and others from all heathen tribes, from two to three or four from each of fifteen or sixteen different tribes. There were more different languages than I ever heard before, and I did not understand any of them. They told me when I arrived that my great father was there also, but did not know who he was.

The people assembled called a council, and the chief's son went to see the Great Father (messiah), who sent word to us to remain fourteen days in that camp and that he would come to see us. He sent me a small package of something white to eat that I did not know the name of. There were a great many people in the council, and this white food was divided among them. The food was a big white nut. Then I went to the agency at Walker Lake and they told us Christ would be there in two days. At the end of two days, on the third morning, hundreds of people gathered at this place. They cleared off a place near the agency in the form of a circus ring and we all gathered there. This space was perfectly cleared of grass, etc. We waited there till late in the evening anxious to see Christ.

Just before sundown I saw a great many people, mostly Indians, coming dressed in white men's clothes. The Christ was with them. They all formed in this ring around it. They put up sheets all around the circle, as they had no tents. Just after dark some of the Indians told me that Christ had arrived. I looked around to find him, and finally saw him sitting on one side of the ring. They all started toward him to see him. They made a big fire to throw light on him. I never looked around, but went forward, and when I saw him I bent my head I had always thought the Great Father was a white man, but this man looked like an Indian. He sat there a long time and nobody went up to speak to him. He sat with his head bowed all the time.

After a while he rose and said he was very glad to see his children. "I have sent for you and am very glad to see you. I will teach you, too, how to dance a dance, and I want you to dance it. Get ready for your dance and then, when the dance is over, I will talk to you". He was dressed in a white coat with stripes. The rest of his dress was a white man's except that he had on a pair of moccasins. Then he commenced our dance, everybody joining in, the Christ singing while we danced. We danced till late in the night, when he told us we had danced enough. The next morning, after breakfast was over, we went into the circle and spread canvas over it on the ground, the Christ standing in the midst of us. He told us he was going away that day, but would be back the next morning and talk to us.

In the night when I first saw him I thought he was an Indian, but the next day when I could see him better he looked different. He was not so dark as an Indian, nor so light as a white man. He had no beard or whiskers, but very heavy eyebrows. He was a good looking man. We were crowded up very close. We had been told that nobody was to talk, and even if we whispered the Christ would know it. I had heard that Christ had been crucified, and I looked to see, and I saw a scar on his wrist and one on his face, and he seemed to be the man. I could not see his feet. He would talk to us all day.

That evening we all assembled again to see him depart. When we were assembled, he began to sing, and he commenced to tremble all over, violently for a while, and then sat down. We danced all night, the Christ lying down beside us apparently dead. The next morning when we went to eat breakfast, the

Christ was with us. After breakfast four heralds went around and called out that the Christ was back with us and wanted to talk to us. The circle was prepared again. The people assembled, and Christ came among us and sat down. He said he wanted to talk to us again and for us to listen. He said: "I am the man who made everything you see around you. I am not lying to you, my children. I made this earth and everything on it. I have been to heaven and seen your dead friends and have seen my own father and mother. In the beginning, after God made the earth, they sent me back to teach the people, and when I came back on earth the people were afraid of me and treated me badly. This is what they did to me (showing his scars). I did not try to defend myself. I found my children were bad, so I went back to heaven and left them. I told them that in so many hundred years I would come back to see my children. At the end of this time I was sent back to try to teach them.

My father told me that the earth was getting old and worn out, and the people getting bad, and that I was to renew everything as it used to be, and make it better". He told us that all of our dead were to be resurrected; that they were all to come back to earth, and that as the earth was too small for them and us, he would do away with heaven, and make the earth itself large enough to contain us all; that we must tell all the people we meet about these things. He spoke to us about fighting, and said that was bad, and we must keep from it; that the earth was to be all good hereafter, and we must all be friends with one another. He said that in the fall of the year the youth of all good people would be renewed, so that nobody would be more than 40 years old, and that if they behaved themselves well after this the youth of everyone would be renewed in the spring. He said if we were all good he would send people among us who could heal all our wounds and sickness by mere touch, and that we would live forever. He told us not to quarrel, or fight, nor strike each other, nor shoot one another; that the whites and the Indians were to be all one people. He said if any man disobeyed what he ordered, his tribe would be wiped from the face of the earth; that we must believe everything he said, and that we must not doubt him, or say he lied; that if we did, he would know it; that he would know our thoughts and actions, in no matter what part of the world we might be. When I heard this from the Christ, and came back home to tell my people, I thought they would listen. Where I went to there were lots of white people, but I never had one of them say an unkind word to me. I thought all of your people knew all of this I have told you of, but it seems you do not.

Ever since the Christ I speak of talked to me I have thought what he said was good. I see nothing bad in it. When I got back, I knew my people were bad, and had heard nothing of all this, so I got them together and told them of it and warned them to listen to it for their own good. I talked to them for four nights and five days. I told them just what I have told you here today. I told them what I said were the words of God Almighty, who was looking down on them. I wish some of you had been up to our camp to have heard my words to the Cheyennes. The only bad thing that there has been in it at all was this: I had just told my people that the Christ would visit the sins of any Indian upon the whole tribe, when the recent trouble (killing of Ferguson) occurred. If any one of you think that I am not telling the truth, you can go and see this man (Wovoka) I speak of for yourselves. I will go with you, and I would like one or two of my people who doubt me to go with me.

The Christ talked to us all in our respective tongues. You can see this man in your sleep anytime you want after you have seen him and shaken hands with him once. Through him you can go to heaven and see your friends. Since my return I have seen him often in my sleep. At the time the soldiers went up the Rosebud I was lying in my lodge asleep, when this man appeared and told me that the Indians had gotten into trouble, and I was frightened. The next night he appeared to me and told me that everything would come out all right."

S.C Robertson
1 Lieut. 1st Cavalry
Camp Crook, Mont.
June15, 1890

241

Upon completion of the testimony, Major Carroll thanked the witnesses, observers, and staff who had made the inquiry possible. He said that Lieutenants Robertson and Pitcher would write out the complete statement and that the next day the hearing would reconvene. At that time the statement would be read aloud in both Cheyenne and English to insure that both White and Red tribes agreed that the testimony they had given was accurate and truthfully recorded. He invited the witnesses and chiefs that had observed the hearing to an evening feast. Thus ended the first day.

June 15th, 1890 saw the hearing reconvene the following morning. The Statement as prepared the previous evening was first read in English and then again in Cheyenne. Then Major Carroll ordered that each paragraph be read in both languages and that agreement be secured for each paragraph. The inevitable differences between what Porcupine had intended and what the transcribers had recorded were systemically ironed out. Long Forehead/Willis Rowland was sorely tested as he helped resolve the nuanced meanings imposed by both languages. It took until late afternoon for differences to be resolved. Then the final record was again read aloud in both languages and Porcupine, Major Carroll, Agent Upshaw, and Willis Rowland/Long Forehead agreed that the document was complete. Major Carroll asked Agent Upshaw to say a few words and present some gifts to Porcupine and his two companions. Agent Upshaw again thanked all present for their cooperation and made a gift to Porcupine in the amount of fifteen silver dollars to be divided among the three witnesses as he saw fit. Porcupine immediately gave five dollars each to Grasshopper and Ridge Walker, and kept five dollars for himself. With one last round of handshaking the meeting broke up and the parties went their separate ways. Lt. Robertson was instructed to personally deliver the Statement to Colonel Swaine, brief the colonel on the process, and answer the questions he would have before the Statement was forwarded to the Department of the Missouri and on to the War Department. Under typical Army protocol each commander in the direct chain of command between Colonel Swaine and the Secretary of War was expected to read the Statement and comment as to how the Statement would inform the actions of their individual commands. The Statement of Porcupine made a substantial impact on how the military approached the Ghost Dance Craze. Of the fifteen or sixteen western tribes which had significant Ghost Dance Activity, only on the Sioux Reservation was military action required.

Chapter 23. Stuart's Stranglers

With the conclusion of the Statement of Porcupine, things returned to some semblance of normal on the Cheyenne Reservation. Since the infusion of the extra beef from the Montana Stock Growers Association, most of the Cheyennes were no longer on starvation rations. Scattered Ghost Dancing continued but was largely ignored by the Army and the Agency. The "Statement" was circulated to the western press to varying degrees of approval or disapproval. The Daily Yellowstone Journal continued its drumbeat of criticism against the Army and Indians in general. Nothing less than the entire removal all Indians from the State of Montana would satisfy their readership.

One continuing thorn in the side of the Army, Agency, and civil authorities was the disposition of the Cheyenne Scouts implicated in the Ferguson murder. Powder on the Face, Little Eyes, Black Medicine, and White Buffalo were indicted in Miles City for the Ferguson affair, but no direct evidence could be found to try them. White Buffalo and Black Medicine were dropped from the case because they were found to be at Fort Keogh during suspected time period of the murder. Most neutral observers thought that the two young Cheyennes knew a lot more than they were telling, but did not participate in the actual murder. The prime suspect of the four was either Powder on the Face who was in possession of one of Ferguson's pistols, or Little Eyes' possession of a key chain thought to be Ferguson's. Both admitted knowing where the body had been buried, but denied that they were involved in the killing. By July 1, 1890 the first two had been released and the other two were let go about a month later for lack of evidence. The Daily Yellowstone Journal raged at this perceived travesty of justice.

While Willie was tied up with Reservation issues, Granville Stuart and his Stranglers had been finalizing the big outlaw clean up. The Selection Committee had completed their tasks with "X" Beidler providing a list of potential targets, Sheriff Irvine marshalling the evidence against each target and its most probable location, and Judge Strevell passed judgement on each. A list of targets was generated for Granville Stuart's Operations Committee. The list contained a list of names and the maximum punishment which could be administered. The punishments ranged from warning, whipping, or banishment, to death, depending on the severity of the target's crimes and the strength of evidence against them. In all, about 75 men, most of which had "Wanted" posters on them, were marked for the most severe punishment. However, many more were served with the lesser sentences.

Late in June the Operations Committee began their work on the Lower Musselshell and Upper Missouri Rivers. The first target was a trading post at the confluence of the Musselshell and Missouri Rivers occupied by two well-known outlaws named Billy Downs and California Ed. The Committee found 26 stolen horses in their corral together with a stack of freshly salted cattle hides with the brand of the Fergus Stock Co clearly present. California Ed and Billy Downs were invited to accompany the Operations Committee to a nearby grove of trees where they were summarily hanged.

On June 25th two men named Joe Vardner and Narciss Lavardure stole seven saddle horses from the ranch of J.A. Wells while the horse herder was across the river looking for stray stock. A neighbor named William Thompson ran into the pair on the trail, recognized the horses, and commanded the two to stop. When Lavardure turned and fired a shot at Thompson a running fight ensued in which Thompson shot and killed Vardner. He then captured Lavardure and took him back to the Wells Ranch stable where he was placed under guard. Word of this activity was brought to the attention of the Operations Committee which overpowered the guard on the early morning of June 27th and promptly hanged Lavardure from a nearby gate post.

Then on July 3rd, a supposed wolver named Sam McKenzie who was known to steal horses in Montana and sell them in Canada was found in possession of two stolen horses in a brushy canyon about two miles below Fort Maginnis. He was taken by the Committee to a handy cottonwood tree and promptly strung up. Soldiers from the Fort found his body gently swaying in the wind the following day.

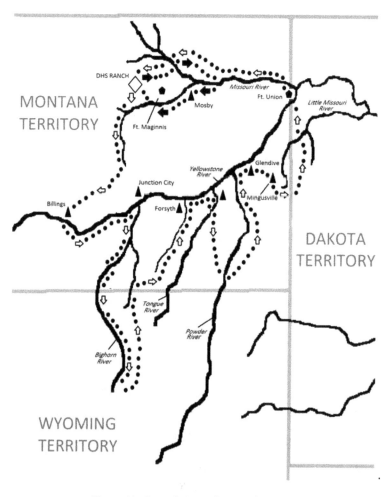

Figure 41. Stuart's Stranglers On the March

The full Committee with Granville Stuart in the lead proceeded down the Missouri River to the next target. This action is best described from a passage in Granville Stuart's journal:

"Fifteen miles below the mouth of the Musselshell, at an old abandoned wood yard, lived old man James, his two sons, and a nephew. Here also was the favorite haunt of Jack Stringer. There was a log cabin and a stable with a large corral built of logs, connecting the two buildings., One hundred yards from the cabin in a wooded bottom was a tent constructed of poles and covered with three wagon sheets. At the cabin were old man James, his two sons, Frank Hanson and Bill Williams. Occupying the tent were Jack Stringer, Paddy Rose, Swift Bill, Dixie Burr, Orvil Edwards, and Silas Nickerson.

On the morning of July 8, the vigilantes[39] arrived at Bates Point. The men were divided into three parties. Three guarded the tent, five surrounded the cabin and one was left behind with the saddle horses. They then waited for daylight. Old man James was the first to appear. He was ordered to open the corral and drive out the horses. This he did but refused to surrender, backed into the cabin and fired a shot from his rifle through a small port hole at the side of the door. This was followed by a volley from the port holes all around the cabin and in an instant the whole party was in action.

Two of the vigilantes crawled up and set fire to the haystack and the cabin. The men inside stationed themselves at port holes and kept up the fight until they were all killed or burned up. The cabin burned to the ground. The tent was near the river bank and almost surrounded by thick brush and it was easier to escape from it than to get out of the cabin. Stringer Jack crawled under the tent and reached a dense clump of willows from which he made his last stand. Dixie Burr had his arm shattered with a rifle ball but jumped into an old dry well and remained until dark. Paddy Rose ran out of the tent, passed back of the men engaged at the cabin and concealed himself in a small washout and after dark made his escape. Nickerson, Edwards, and Swift Bill reached the river bank and crawling along through the brush and under the bank, succeeded in passing above the men at the cabin and hid in some brush and drift wood. Orvil Edwards and Silas Nickerson were the only ones that escaped without wounds. After the fight at the cabin the men went down the river and spent the day looking for the men who had escaped but failed to find them. There were one hundred and sixty-five stolen horses recovered at Bates Point and one hundred and nineteen at other places."

With the execution of the outlaws on the Musselshell and Upper Missouri Rivers, the Committee turned its attention to the Yellowstone River and the associated drainages. A special locomotive was secured from the Northern Pacific at Billings, Montana to which was attached a passenger car and two stock cars. The Committee boarded the cars and proceeded down river, stopping at the mouth of each major tributary that emptied into the Yellowstone River. There they were met by a local guide who directed them to the location of certain outlaw hideouts or residences. The activities of the Committee on most of these drainages has not been recorded but can be inferred.

Figure 42. Montana Manhunters –L to R- Billy Smith (stock detective), Jack Hawkins (ex-Texas Ranger), Tom Irvine (Sheriff of Custer Co.), Louis King (saloon keeper) and "Eph" Davis (frontiersman). Photo Courtesy of the Montana Historical Society

On the Big Horn River there was no recorded vigilante activity on the Cheyenne and Crow Reservations which comprise most of its length. However, two unidentified men were found hanging from a boxelder tree on Pass Creek near Dayton, WY and shortly thereafter it was noted that a number of suspicious characters were seen leaving the Dayton/Sheridan area in the direction of Buffalo, WY.

The Sim Buford Robert's Ranch on the Rosebud was visited one evening where he was taken from his barn to a nearby cottonwood tree, shown a hangman's noose and warned to stop his association with the Wild Bunch and his cattle butchering activities. Only the fact that he had a wife and four young children saved him from the fate he deserved. He took the warning seriously and mostly halted his illegal activities.

Significantly, of the twenty eight head of horses discovered in Robert's box canyon, most had Utah brands except for seven which had the brand of Bob Ferguson.

No known Committee work was done on Tongue River. The Committee had scheduled a trip up Otter Creek to the Cow Creek hideout but the three outlaws who had been occupying the cabin "flew the coop" back to the Nebraska area from whence they came. Charlie Thex reported their departure when the train stopped at Miles City. However, they did made a short move down river where a known rustler, horse thief, and common thug named "Bronco Charlie" was located and summarily hanged. Shortly thereafter, and in the same area but ten miles upriver from Miles City, "Half Breed Jack" and "Turkey Williams" met a similar fate.

As the Committee moved on to the Powder River Country, word of their work proceeded them and there was significant outlaw movement toward the Hole-in-the Wall country. The strategy employed was to try and cut off the fleeing outlaws before they could get across the Wyoming line. The Committee moved up Tongue River to Pumpkin Creek and followed that watercourse to its head on the old Texas Northern Cattle Trail before crossing the divide to the head of Mizpah Creek. Ed Cole was rumored to be the Powder River guide much like Charlie Thex on Otter Creek. There the Committee divided their force and one group proceeded down Mizpah Creek, while the other group moved on to Powder River. Somewhere in this area "Humpy Jack" was shot to death in his cabin.

The two groups joined at the mouth of the Powder River where they boarded the train and went on to the Little Missouri River. Spencer Biddle was the main contact in this area. The town of Stoneville (now Alzada) was a favorite outlaw hangout of the Axelby Gang which had gained quite a reputation for horse stealing, rustling, and general bad manners. However, in February, five months before the Stranglers made their appearance, the gang tried to rescue Jesse Pruden from the clutches of Deputy Marshall Joseph Ryan who had agreed to transport Pruden from Miles City, MT to Deadwood, SD. Fearing that such a rescue might occur, a posse of three men each from Deadwood and Spearfish rushed to meet Marshall Ryan. All four parties met at Stoneville in the middle of a snow storm where the Battle of Stoneville took place. The results were that Deputy Jack O'Hara was killed, a cowboy spectator named William Cunningham was killed and another cowboy was wounded. On the outlaw side Henry Tuttle was shot in the elbow and captured, George Axelby was shot in the thigh but escaped as did "Billy-the-Kid" McCarthy, and Alex Grady. Outlaw Hank Campbell was wounded in the head but escaped to a cabin five miles downriver where he was tracked down and killed by the posse. Tuttle was hung by Spearfish Vigilantes.

The Stoneville battle didn't signal the end of the Axelby Gang. While they laid low for a while, they resumed their activities on the Little Missouri in time for the arrival of the Committee. However, upon hearing of the hanging of "Splayfoot Harnett" in late July, George Axelby and McCarty lit out for New Mexico where they faded from history. Another sometimes Axelby and "Doc" Middleton gang member named Kid Wade was hung near Bassett, Nebraska but that may not have been the work of the Committee.

Moving on toward the Montana/North Dakota line the Committee attacked suddenly and with good effect. At Mingusville (Wibaux) they hung four outlaws before moving on to Boxelder Creek and the Little Missouri in North Dakota where approximately 13 rustlers were shot or hung. Moving on to Medora and a little north back into Montana, Stuart's Stranglers made their way back to the DHS Ranch. By the end of August their work was largely complete. An estimated 63 men were either shot or hung.

Chapter 24. Political Turmoil

Shortly following the Porcupine Statement, Agent Upshaw received word that his contract as Agent would not be renewed effective July 26, 1890. He had been expecting the news so it was not a shock to him, but it was to the Agency staff and Cheyenne Nation. Agent Upshaw was a lifelong Democrat and in the late nineteenth century the "spoils system" was still in effect. Republican Ben Harrison was elected in 1888 and so with his ascent to office in 1889, most of the Indian Agents could expect replacement. He had actually lasted a year longer than he expected. In addition to the fact that his political party was on the "outs", the Yellowstone Journal and the local white establishment had kept up a constant drumbeat of criticism against him. His biggest "crime" was that he was an honest and effective advocate for the Cheyenne Tribe and their Reservation. Local ranchers including Joe Brown, engaged in a letter writing campaign against Upshaw, calling him an "Indian lover" and complained bitterly of the cattle killings they had endured. While some reports of the cattle killings were true, many of the ranchers exaggerated the scope of their losses in hopes of government compensation or the elimination of the Cheyenne Reservation.

To some degree, loss of Army support in the person of Major Henry Carroll played an additional role in Agent Upshaw's demise. Generally the Army and the Indian Department worked closely in the administration of Indian affairs. Most of the early Indian Agents had been Army officers and in fact Agent Upshaw was a former Army officer although a Confederate. However, the graft present within the Interior Department ran counter to the ethics of most Army officers and they were on the lookout for what they regarded as poor administration or evidence of wrongdoing. While Upshaw was scrupulously honest, he had made some poor decisions which put him in conflict with the tribal power structure. He discharged John Two

Moons as the head of the Indian Police thereby incurring the wrath of Chief Two Moons. Also he refused to discipline the Agency Trader who the Cheyennes felt was overcharging them for items purchased at the Lame Deer Trading Post. In addition, the Cheyennes wanted the cow hides from the ration beef to make clothing and repair lodges, but Upshaw sold the hides to replenish the Agency general funds. In the short term, Upshaw opposed the transfer of additional Cheyennes from Pine Ridge and Darlington to the Tongue River Agency because he couldn't feed all the people he had. These complaints were all communicated to Major Carroll via the Cheyenne Scouts.

Major Carroll in turn wrote several reports critical of Agent Upshaw's administration as being somewhat lax in dealing with the Cheyennes and insensitive to their needs. He also accused the Indian Department of being deficient in their provision of rations to the Cheyennes. Of course that was true, but that was certainly not the fault of Agent Upshaw who had moved heaven and earth to get the beef ration increased. Now besieged by Indian Agency bureaucrats, complaining ranchers, obstinate Cheyennes, unfriendly newspaper reporters, and a critical military, Upshaw was ready to be replaced. Nonetheless, he resolved to make his departure as professional as possible. To do so he requested that Special Agent James A. Cooper be immediately transferred to the Agency so the transition could begin. At the same time he also requested that his release date be changed from July 26th to July 1st so he could take some of the leave he had accrued after his extended service. Special Agent Cooper officially took charge of the Agency on July 8th, 1890.

The arrival of a new agent created a wealth of problems for Willis Rowland. While his contract as full time agency interpreter was still intact, he wasn't sure that the new agent would approve of his ongoing projects. Agent Cooper's appointment was temporary, because he was only expected to be agent for a period of one or two months pending the permanent assignment of John Tully. There was only a week's overlap between the Upshaw/Cooper terms, so there was a lot to accomplish. Agent Cooper was briefed on the Montana Stock Grower's Feeding Plan, the Custer County Deputy Sheriff connection, the Cheyenne Scout's activities, the Ghost Dance (including Porcupine's Statement), the Cheyenne Census, the garrison at Camp Crook (Camp Merritt), and the possible deposit of stolen horses on the Reservation by white horse thieves. Agent Cooper stated that his intention was not to make any changes to Agent Upshaw's policies. He was happy to leave things as they were until the arrival of the permanent agent. Agent Upshaw and Major Carroll both suggested that Agent Cooper take the advice of Willis Rowland in his decision making requiring communication with Cheyenne leadership.

The period from mid-June to mid-August was a reasonably quiet period on the Reservation with only one serious incident. That incident involved another Cheyenne interpreter named Jules Seminole and the family of an old Cheyenne named Big Deafy. Earlier in the year Seminole and John Two Moons (a relative of Chief Two Moons), the Captain of the Indian Police, had a disagreement which resulted in John Two Moons' resignation. The disagreement involved Seminole's interpretation of a report given to Agent Upshaw by John Two Moons in which Seminole questioned his truthfulness. When John Two Moons found out he demanded that Upshaw fire Seminole which he declined to do. Two Moons was supported in his position by the rest of the Cheyenne Police including Bill Rowland, Jr.

On ration day in mid-July, the Cheyenne Police were shooting beef cattle at the Muddy Corrals when a bullet fired by Jules Seminole glanced off the horn of a cow and killed an old Cheyenne named Big Deafy. While most witnesses thought it was an accident, the relatives of the old man thought it was on purpose and took off after Seminole who lit out for the Agency. The Cheyenne Police did not intervene because they didn't like

Seminole's treatment of Two Moons. He made it to the Agent's office where he was hidden in the basement until he could be moved to Camp Merritt after dark. Major Carroll gave him an escort to Crow Agency where he spent the remainder of his life. He was eventually joined by his wife and children.

Other than the Big Deafy incident the only other major Reservation news was the release of Little Eyes and Powder-on-the-Face, the suspected killers of Bob Ferguson. They were released for lack of evidence and made their way back to the Reservation in the last week of July 1890. A review of records by Captain Casey revealed that Little Eyes, Black Medicine, and White Buffalo had been at Fort Keogh the entire time, leaving Powder on the Face as the only one without an alibi but no affirmative evidence that he was involved in the shooting. Upon hearing of Powder-on-the-Face's return, Long Forehead traveled to Busby to talk to him. He was reluctant to talk so he was conducted to Porcupine's teepee and in the presence of White Bull and Porcupine, Long Forehead questioned Powder-on-the-Face.

"Powder-on-the-Face do you know who these two men are?" pointing to White Bull and Porcupine.

Powder-on-the-Face nodded, "White Bull is a great Cheyenne warrior and an "Old Man Chief". Porcupine is a very important medicine man."

Long Forehead continued. "White Bull and Porcupine are both medicine men with contacts to the spirit world. They will know if you do not tell the truth. They are here because the death of the white man Ferguson has caused big trouble for the whole Cheyenne Tribe. The white men in Miles City want to take this Reservation away from the Cheyennes and make the Cheyennes go to live with our enemies the Crows. If you do not tell us how you knew where the dead white man was buried, the whole Cheyenne People could be destroyed. Is this not true – Porcupine and White Bull?" Both of the men nodded.

Powder-on-the-Face trembled slightly. "Will I be taken back to jail and be hanged?"

Again Long Forehead pressed on. "No you have been released by the white man sheriff. You are in Cheyenne country now. We will not send you back to the white man jail. But you must tell us if you killed the white man and how you knew where he was buried."

"I did not kill that white man." Powder-on-the-Face said strongly. "I saw the people who did but I do not know their names. It happened when I was out hunting for some meat for my mother and grandmother. I had ridden a long way into what the whites call the "Little Wolf Mountains" looking for deer or maybe an antelope. It was a long way off the reservation because there is no game here. I was on my way back when I saw two men driving some horses back toward the reservation. One of the men was a Cheyenne and the other a breed. I rode up to them and asked if they had seen any deer that I could feed to my family. The breed grinned at me and said, "Why don't you just kill a slow elk?" I didn't understand and said I hadn't seen any elk. They both laughed and told me to come with them and they would show me the elk. After we had gone a little way we saw a white man cow and the Cheyenne killed it. He said, "There is your slow elk." And then they rode on with their horses. The cow was dead and I needed the meat so I was gutting out the cow when I heard four more shots – bang, bang, bang, and then one more shot. I jumped on my horse and went to the top of the hill and looked over. The Cheyenne and the breed were standing over a dead horse with a white man's saddle. There was dead white man a little way off. I watched as they loaded up the dead man on one of the horses and took him down to the washout. After a little while they came back and brushed out tracks with a piece of sagebrush and rode on with their loose horses. After they were out of sight I rode down to the dead horse where I found a pistol and a circle of arrowheads (key ring) which I kept. Then I went back to the cow and loaded up some of the meat and went back to Busby. The next day I went back and got the rest of the meat but I didn't go back to the dead horse. That is all I know about it."

"What did the Cheyenne and the breed look like?" Long Forehead asked sharply.

"The Cheyenne was a good looking man. He was dressed all in the old Cheyenne way, no white man clothes. The breed had on a white man hat, white man shirt with Cheyenne leggings." Powder-on-the Face replied. "The breed was not a good looking man."

"Anything else you remember about the two men?" Long Forehead demanded.

"The Cheyenne was riding a big sorrel horse. He was a really good looking horse." The young man offered.

Long Forehead turned to White Bull and Porcupine, "Do you have any questions for this man?"

White Bull cleared his throat. "Who did you tell about this thing?"

"When Little Eyes came back from Ft. Keogh, he asked me if I wanted to join the Cheyenne Scouts. I told him about what I had seen. He said come join the Scouts because no one will think that you had anything to do with it if you are in the Scouts. So I joined and gave him the "circle of arrowheads". When the search started to get close to the place, Little Eyes told Black Medicine and White Buffalo and we tried to keep Big Red Nose (Captain Casey) from going that direction." Powder-on-the-Face concluded.

Porcupine joined the conversation. "I think this man has spoken truthfully. He did not kill the white man or even the white man's cow, but he has put the whole tribe in danger by not telling our chiefs what happened."

White Bull added. "Powder-on-the-Face, you cannot stay here. If the white men find out that you did not tell them what you saw, they will say that the Cheyenne Tribe is helping hide his killers. Do you have any relatives anywhere else?"

"I have a sister married to a Sioux over at Pine Ridge," Powder-on-the-Face offered. "I guess I could go and stay with her a while."

"Do so!" ordered White Bull. "You are a danger to all Cheyennes if you stay. We cannot have that. Maybe someday you can come back, but not for a long time."

With White Bull's decision the meeting concluded. Long Forehead was satisfied. The boy really had not done that much wrong. He had not shot Ferguson or even the cow. If anything he was guilty of being "an accessory after the fact" but that was a concept totally foreign to the Cheyennes. Banishment for the boy was sufficient punishment. Long Forehead was convinced by his description that the breed and the Cheyenne on the sorrel horse were the same two men that he had observed with the outlaws at Crazy Head Springs. He was getting closer to the truth.

John Tully, the new Cheyenne Indian Agent was officially appointed as Agent effective August 16, replacing Special Agent James A. Cooper. However, Agent Cooper was directed to continue his day-to-day management of Cheyenne affairs until the arrival of Tully later in the fall. Tully had a significant advantage over Agent Upshaw because he was on very good political terms with Secretary of Interior Noble and Commissioner of Indian Affairs, Thomas J. Morgan. In fact,

Secretary Noble asked that Tully remain in Washington pending receipt of important reports from Inspector Robert Gardner who was traveling the State of Montana on his annual audit of reservations and the Cheyenne Commission which was appointed on August 19, 1890. The Cheyenne Commission with members Major General Nelson A. Miles as Chairman, Bradley Smalley and John Zerfass as General Members, were tasked with the mission to make recommendations on the following issues: the unification of the Northern Cheyenne Tribe on the Tongue River Reservation, size and location of the Reservation, the resolution of Cheyenne property rights on other reservations in the event of unification, and removal of white settlers from the west side of Tongue River and the Cheyennes from the east side. Inspector Morgan was to bring back reports specifically related to the management of the Tongue River Agency, ration adequacy, and Cheyenne complaints.

In Washington, Agent Tully was carefully reviewing the confusing terms of a series of treaties involving Cheyennes dating back to the Fort Laramie Treaty of 1851. The Cheyennes had split into the Northern and Southern Tribes about 1825 but still maintained family ties between the two even after the Tongue River Agency was established in 1884. The Southern Cheyennes and Arapaho Tribes were given a Reservation in Oklahoma by the Treaty of 1868 while the Northern Arapaho and Cheyenne were given an undivided interest in the Great Sioux Reservation which included most of the tributaries of the Yellowstone River east of the Big Horn River including the Black Hills and Big Horn Mountains. But this arrangement was modified by the Treaty of 1876 where by much of the Great Sioux Reservation was ceded back to the U.S. Government and opened to white settlement. Since the Northern Cheyenne and Arapaho Tribes were relatively small and their bands scattered, their wishes were largely overlooked and they were lumped together with more populous tribes. The Northern

Arapaho and Shoshoni (former enemies) were placed together on the Wind River Reservation in Wyoming while the Northern Cheyennes were scattered between the Sioux at Pine Ridge Agency in South Dakota, the Arapaho at Fort Washakie, Wyoming, the Southern Cheyenne Darlington Agency in Oklahoma, and a few at Fort Keogh, Montana. Then in 1884 under pressure from General Miles after the fighting return of Little Wolf and Dull Knife, President Benjamin Harrison established the Tongue River Agency by Executive Order for the Northern Cheyenne Tribe.

What Tully found was that the Northern Cheyenne Tribe was enmeshed in a bureaucratic morass which prevented reunification, deprived the Tongue River Agency of the resources it deserved, and enhanced the opportunity for political mischief in Reservation administration. Upon close examination of Agent Upshaw's annual reports and correspondence, he gained a healthy respect for his predecessor's problems and efforts. From Upshaw's correspondence with Gen. Miles he knew the likely content of the Commission's report. He informed Secretary Noble of his findings and suggested that they use the anticipated report from the Cheyenne Commission to straighten out some of the bureaucratic mess that enveloped the Agency. Noble agreed they began laying the political groundwork necessary for a Congressional fix to the situation.

The political situation in Washington was polarized between a great concern for the noble red man by idealistic reformers centered in New York and Boston and the more pragmatic and materialistic populists of the Midwest and West. Both camps were negative for the betterment of the Cheyenne people. The populists as represented by the Western delegates to Congress wanted most of the Reservations reduced to their absolute minimum size and their land distributed to white settlers as soon as possible. Most had little to no regard for treaty obligations or the fate of the Indian populations. On the other side the idealistic reformers were convinced that road to Indian salvation lay in giving each family their own 160 acres of land which they could farm and become yeoman Jeffersonian farmers within a generation. Both supported the elimination of native religion and language and the promotion of Christianity on the Reservations under the "doctrine of assimilation". Also the day of the "spoils system" was coming to its welcome end as the scandalous conduct of corrupt politicians and bureaucrats was laid bare by the enterprising newspapers of the day. The time was ripe for action.

Noble and Tully began by informing some of the more ardent reformers of the plight of the Northern Cheyenne people. They recounted their proud history, desire for peace in the face of white provocation, and extreme poverty brought on by failure to observe sacred United States treaty obligations. By carefully leaking some of Upshaw's more inflammatory reports of starvation and poor treatment, they raised the political cost of opposing positive actions. The two also exposed reformers to some of the more extreme views of the western press like the Yellowstone Journal which opined that "the only good Indian is a dead Indian". When the Cheyenne Commission report seemed to validate some of the reformist's views, the stage was set to move Noble's budget recommendation which sailed through the Congressional Committee process and survived to be included in the final budget signed by the president. For the first time the Cheyennes were on the verge making their reservation secure and prepared for progress in a largely white man's world.

The political situation on the Reservation took more time than Willis Rowland would have liked and pulled him away from his cattle buying duties especially on the Rabbit Town and Birney Village side of the Reservation. Education of Agent Cooper was almost a full time job. He knew the objectives and policies of the Indian Department, but next to nothing about Cheyenne culture and politics. Fortunately, acting as Long Forehead, he had convinced Agent Cooper and Major Carroll to allow the annual Sun Dance Ceremony to occur without interruption. This was counter to Washington policy to suppress Indian ceremonies and break old Indian customs to enhance the process of assimilation. Rowland thought that the policy was unnecessarily harsh and counterproductive especially at this time. If the Sun Dance Ceremony was prohibited it would strengthen the Sioux version of the Ghost Dance rather than Porcupine's more moderate and peaceful ceremony. Besides, he was convinced that ceremonies would continue underground where the Agency could not influence their more unproductive elements. Completion of the Cheyenne census which drove the ration process was much more important in promoting peace and progress than halting innocent ceremonies. At least in the short term he was successful in moderating the more egregious Indian Department policies.

Chapter 25. The Noose Tightens

On September 2nd Willis Rowland received the September cash from the Montana Stock Growers and began a new cattle buying trip to the eastern districts of the Reservation. Due to the turmoil with the Agency Administration he had not been able to buy cattle for the Birney and Rosebud Districts since early July. Therefore those districts had been shorted and he planned to buy double their normal amount as a makeup.

He traveled first to the Quarter Circle U and Three Circle Ranches where he put in orders for seven head from each for delivery in three days. Stopping briefly at Birney Village, he told Tall Bull that the Foxes would have cattle to distribute in three days. He then rode on to Ashland where he spent the night at St. Labre Mission with Father van der Velden and Deacon Yoakim. During the evening meal he brought the churchmen up to date about the Ghost Dance, his fast ride to Miles City, Porcupine's Statement, some of the Vigilance Committee's public activities, and the administrative turmoil on the reservation.

Conversation turned to local issues, Willie asked, "What has been going on around here?"

"The Cheyennes are happier since they started getting the extra meat." Deacon Yoakim stated. "The women are all excited about the cow hides they get to use. I am beginning to see some kids with new moccasins and lodges being repaired. The cows you brought are being put to good use. But they are wondering when the next bunch will be delivered."

"What about Sioux visitors?" Willie inquired. "Is there any word of Sioux Ghost Dance medicine men?"

"Last week I heard of a man named Short Bull who came over to talk to some of the other Sioux people about four months ago. He gave a talk to some of the young men until Little Chief told him to go away. He was talking up the new Ghost Dance Religion," finished Yoakim.

"Do you think anybody listened to him? Did he hold any ceremonies?" Willie asked anxiously.

"I don't think so. He was trying to get one going but Little Chief ran him off." Yoakim replied.

"Good," said Willie. "How about Ashland? Anything happening here?"

Father van der Velden jumped into the conversation. "Some of the sawmill crews are a little upset. Their beef contractor has stopped delivering carcasses to the mills. They are now trying to buy beef locally and Ron is doing a booming business. The sawmill bosses are complaining that their costs have gone up."

Willie smiled to himself and thought, "It looks like Stuart's Stranglers put Sim Buford Roberts out of business." However, he did not impart that bit of information to the two churchmen. He said good night and retired to his bed. He was tired from a long day.

The next morning as Willie rode to Olga's for breakfast, he considered how to plan the remainder of his trip. He resolved to talk to Ron at Ron's Butcher Shop to find out from whom and what kind of beef he was buying from the local ranchers. It was still doubtful that the kind of beef he would buy for the Cheyennes would be impacted. He decided that he would ask Captain Howes first if he could supply the beef for Rabbit Town If not, then he would go to the Bug Ranch and ask Tom Bryan if he could supply their needs. Tom Bryan was a former president of the Montana Stock Growers Association and current Chairman of the Roundup Committee.

Olga's was so busy that Willie had to wait for a seat. When she finally got to him, he asked, "How's business, Olga?"

"Crazy," she replied. "Can't talk now! Too many sawmill men."

Willie laughed and ordered breakfast which he gulped down to open a seat for the next man. Next he went on to Ron's Butcher Shop, where he found Ron busy skinning a freshly killed beef.

"Hi Ron," he greeted. "I thought you only killed on Wednesday's, what up?"

"I got a contract to supply the sawmill kitchens with beef carcasses. The old contractor couldn't deliver and lost the contract. Now I kill two days a week." Ron grinned.

"Where are you getting your cattle and what are you buying?" Willie asked intently.

"I am buying steers, one to three years old, from local ranchers that I know own the beef. It costs the saw mills a little more but they get along with their neighbors a lot better," Ron declared.

"I wonder how that happened," Willie drawled knowingly.

Ron gave Willie a sharp look. "You got any idea what happened to the old contractor?"

"Not me, I'm just a little old cattle buyer from the reservation. "Do you think it will affect the price of the cattle that I buy?" asked Willie in a concerned tone that changed the subject.

"I doubt it. The price of steers is up a couple of dollars a head. The price of old cows and killer bulls won't go up much. I can't buy them because the quality is low and it takes too much labor to mess with them. Your squaws work pretty cheap." Ron observed.

"That my idea too," Willie agreed. " Well, I better get on my way. I got cattle to buy. See you later, Ron."

A couple of hours later, Willie rode into the Circle Bar where he found Ed McGee shoeing a horse. Seeing Willie, he put the hoof down and extended his hand with a huge grin. "Hi Willie, long time no see."

Willie pumped Ed's hand. "What's happening on Otter Creek?"

Ed quickly looked around and seeing no one else near replied, "The guys up on Cow Creek pulled out three days after the word came down that Parrott and Carey were arrested in Miles City. A few days later Charlie Thex went down to meet the Committee train and tell them not to bother to come on up Otter Creek. While he was there Irvine asked him to show the Committee where Sim Robert's place was and give them any assistance he could. Charlie led the Committee to the Roberts place. Because he had a wife and four little kids the maximum sentence for Roberts was a rope beating." Charlie said the Committee caught him out behind his barn and took him into custody. He was told that Parrott and Carey had given his name as a place where stolen stock was stored. The Committee then showed him a hangman's rope and asked if he wanted his wife to be a widow and his children orphans. Roberts was a tough guy but when faced with death asked what he could do to keep that from happening. The Committee told him to tell what he knew about the stolen horses. He told them about the box canyon on his place, the horses that had been stashed on the Reservation, and that Parrott and Carey were supposed to pick up Turkey Williams, Half Breed Jack, and Bronco Charlie to move the horses on north. He also gave their locations. Since he had been cooperative, he was ordered to accompany the Committee to where the horses were hidden. There the stolen horses were recovered and Roberts was given a stern warning that if he did not cease his association with the Wild Bunch and stop his butchering activities, the Committee would return and finish the job. He vigorously agreed to abide by the Committee's instructions which included not leaving his ranch for three days. Among the horses found were seven which were packing the brand of Bob Ferguson. The rest had "worked over" Utah brands." Ed finished breathlessly.

Willie was intensely interested in the information concerning the Ferguson horses because it confirmed his suspicion that the two Cheyennes which Powder-on-the-Face had seen with Ferguson's body, were the same ones he had seen at Crazy Head Springs. They had traded the Ferguson horses to the white outlaws for money, whiskey, food, or other horses. The killers of Ferguson were a full blood Cheyenne riding a sorrel horse, and a breed with a drinking problem. A third Cheyenne, Young Mule, was probably helping the other two as a horse herder but was not directly involved in the killing.

Ed took Willie up to the main house for Captain Howe's approval to sell more cattle to the Cheyenne feeding program. Ed and the Captain agreed that they didn't have anything close that would work but Charlie Thex had some he would like to sell. He had asked Captain Howes to let Willie know the next time he came around. Given Thex's service to Montana Stock Growers, Willie quickly assented to purchase of up to 20 head of Charlie's stock. He told Ed that if Charlie would bring them to the Circle Bar, he would pick them up and pay for them in three days.

Having made arrangements for the cattle buy on the Eastern Reservation, Willie resolved to return to Rabbit Town, inform the Elks to prepare for the receipt of more cattle, and make inquiries about a young Cheyenne riding a sorrel horse who never wore white man clothes. There couldn't be more than a few men who would match that description. Big "reservation hats" were much in fashion so anyone who didn't wear one would be an oddity.

Leaving the Circle Bar, Willie rode back to Ashland, had lunch at Olga's Eatery and crossed the river to seek out Little Hawk, head of the Elkhorn Scraper Warrior Society. He found Little Hawk at his lodge where he was invited to sit and drink coffee.

"Long Forehead, welcome to my lodge. It has been too long since we have seen you. My people all ask when you will bring more cows." Little Hawk declared.

Long Forehead replied. "That is my reason for coming. I will be bringing a double ration of cows to Rabbit Town in two more days. Will the Elks be ready for them?"

"Good, Good." Said Little Hawk. "Our people are getting hungry again. We will be ready."

"Do you know a young Cheyenne man who never wears white man clothes and rides a big sorrel horse?" questioned Long Forehead.

"Why do you ask, Long Forehead?" Little Hawk asked in reply, immediately on guard.

"The soldier chiefs heard that such a man has travelled to the Pine Ridge Agency in the past few months to learn the Sioux Ghost Dance Religion. They are afraid that he will bring the Sioux Religion back to the Cheyennes. As you know their religion is different from the Ghost Dance that Porcupine brought back from Wavoka. The Council of 44 Chiefs approved Porcupine's way, but not the Sioux way taught by Short Bull. The soldiers asked me to find out if there is such a man, and if so – his name," Long Forehead finished.

"I think someone is mistaken," replied Little Hawk. "The man you describe is Head Chief, one of my warriors in the Elk Horn Scrapers. The Sioux medicine man Short Bull was here four or five moons ago to visit his relatives. He brought word of the Sioux Ghost Dance with the idea that Ghost Shirts would turn white man's bullets. Head Chief and a few other young men were interested but Little Chief said that Porcupine's way was the only way that ceremony should be taught to the Cheyennes. Little Chief told Short Bull to go back to Pine Ridge and quit causing trouble."

"What kind of a man is this Head Chief? Is he a troublemaker?" pressed Long Forehead.

Little Hawk was silent for a long time. "Head Chief does not know who he should be. He was too young to be a warrior when Morning Star (Dull Knife) and Little Wolf came back from the Darlington Agency but he was there when it happened. His father taunts him about having no coups to his credit. He wants to be a good Cheyenne in the old way. When the Elks got permission to go off the Reservation and hunt deer, he was my best hunter. I think he may go off the reservation to hunt deer and bring the meat back to old folks and widows with kids like single warriors did in the old days. He has not been to Pine Ridge. This I know because he has not left Rabbit Town for more than two or three days at a time. I don't know if he has taken to the Sioux Religion, but he did talk to Short Bull."

Long Forehead felt sorry for Little Hawk. He did not want to talk badly about one of his Elk warriors but he felt compelled to give a truthful answer. "Who are his friends? Do you think he has been involved in any cattle killing off the Reservation?"

"Long Forehead, last winter people were starving here. What is a Cheyenne man to do and still call himself a man when little children are crying for food? Did I forbid my Elks to go out and find food for the People? I did not! Did Head Chief go kill a few cows that belonged to white men? I don't know that he did, but some Elks may have. I didn't ask any questions. Head Chief does not have many friends other than Young Mule who follows him like a dog. He studies the old Cheyenne ceremonies, dresses all in the old way, does not drink whiskey, and hates the white man ways." Little Hawk concluded.

"How long ago did he get the sorrel horse?" Long Forehead asked.

Little Hawk tried hard to remember. "It must have been about five or six moons ago. He didn't have the horse last winter."

"Is there anyone else you have seen him with? Long Forehead held his breath waiting for an answer.

"No, I don't think so," Little Hawk said honestly.

Long Forehead thought that Little Hawk had told him the truth. Like many Cheyennes he was caught between loyalty to his warrior society and tribe in the short term, even when that loyalty might be harmful in the long run. He did not want to implicate Head Chief in any illegal activities but appreciated the fact that those same activities saved many vulnerable Cheyennes from starvation in the previous winter.

"Little Hawk, I have one last question. Do you know where Cheyennes are getting whiskey here in Rabbit Town? You know what whiskey is doing to the Tribe." He commented.

Little Hawk, with fire in his eyes answered. "It's the damn breeds! I don't mean you, Long Forehead, but some of the other mixed bloods. They don't care what happens to the People, they are only out for themselves. They use the Cheyenne weakness for the whiskey to make money from them."

"Do you have any names? Long Forehead asked cautiously.

"Just go sit in the bar and you will meet them pretty quick," Little Hawk shot back. "They all like the whiskey."

With that last remark, the interview was over so Long Forehead thanked his host and went on his way. He was elated that he finally had a name for at least one of Ferguson's killers. Willie thought about what Little Hawk had said about sitting in an

Ashland bar to find out who was selling whiskey to the Cheyennes. He had a day to kill before he had to return to Birney and pick up the fourteen head of cattle he had contracted from Brewster and Brown. Willie didn't want to spend the day drinking whiskey but that didn't mean he couldn't spend some time in a bar. Since it was late afternoon, he decided he could go to the Club Buffet and the Ashland Bar, nurse a beer and see what developed. He crossed the river to the Mission and made arrangements to spend another two nights there.

He went to the Club Buffett first, bellied up to the bar and ordered a beer. The place was relatively well appointed with a mirror behind the bar, pool table, and a poker table in one corner. The bartender looked him up and down and said, "We don't serve Indians in here."

Willie looked back at him and replied, "I'm not an Indian, I am half white and a cattle buyer for the Cheyenne Reservation. Is that good enough?"

The bartender thought for a second, "I guess so. Sorry if I pissed you off, but so many breeds are begging my white customers for drinks that I have about run them all off."

"That's O.K., we all know what a pain in the ass a drunk can be. How many breeds are making trouble for you?" Willie asked.

"Oh, there are five or six regulars and another two or three that show up on payday." The bartender answered.

"Are there any that buy whiskey in quantity?" Willie inquired.

"Not lately," said the bartender. "There used to be a funny little guy that came in a few months ago that would walk out with three or four bottles. At first he always paid in gold or silver coin but the last time he came in it was to try and trade me a beaded headstall for a drink. I passed and ran him out of here. He spends most of his days at the Ashland Bar now."

"Do you know his name by any chance?" Willie asked. "The new Indian Agent is trying to find out where the liquor is coming from that makes it on to the reservation."

"Well, let's see. I think it was Ferris or something like that. Ira Ferris. He probably is not in the best of shape, he coughs all the time." The bartender offered.

Willie finished his beer. "Thanks a lot for the information." He left a silver dollar on the bar and moved to the Ashland Bar.

Entering the Ashland Bar, Willie was taken with the difference in the two bars. Where the Club Buffett was well appointed, the Ashland bar was just a dive. The bar was made of rough planks, there were no bar stools, just small benches big enough for two people, and the smell of stale beer and sawdust permeated the place. There looked to be three semi-permanent residents, two of them breeds, all had the watery eyes and flushed faces of chronic alcoholics. One of the breeds detached himself from the group and sat down on the same bench Willie.

"Buy me a drink?" he asked hopefully.

Willie knew that among alcoholics there existed a kind of fraternity. They knew each other, where they lived, health status, what they liked to drink, and would help each other out in times of trouble. They would also sell their souls for the next drink. So he said, "Sure why not? What's your name?"

A big smile came over the dissipated face. "My name is Henry Miller. What's yours?"

"Willie Rowland" came the answer.

"Are you from the Muddy Creek Rowlands?" asked Henry Miller.

"Yep. What about you?" Willie asked.

"Well, I was born down in Oklahoma on the Southern Cheyenne Reservation. My mother was a Cheyenne married to a white man named Charlie Miller. He was a buffalo hunter. He left when I was a little kid. My mother had relatives in Montana so after the Reservation was started, she came up here. She got remarried to a Cheyenne named Yellow Eyes on Tongue River."

"How come you speak English so good?" Willie inquired.

Henry responded, "I learned some English from my dad before he left. Then when I was ten I got taken away from my mother and sent to a missionary school in Pennsylvania. They wouldn't let us speak anything but English so I picked it back up pretty quick. I was only there three years when they sent me back to the Darlington Agency to Indian School. They still taught everything in English. I went on to the sixth grade. I hung around the Darlington Agency until I was about sixteen when I got a job on a white man farm. I stayed there two years and then got a job with a trail herd as a cook's helper. Followed the trail herd Montana and learned how to cook. I went up and down the trail a couple of times. The last time I went down to Oklahoma, I found out my mother had moved to this reservation so I looked her up."

Henry had already finished his drink and was drumming his fingers on the plank bar top. Willie glanced toward the bartender and signaled to give Henry another drink. "Do many other breeds come in here?" he asked.

Henry looked around and said, "There are about a half a dozen of us I guess. That guy over there is Bud Barr, he lives on Tongue River too."

Willie probed. "Do you know a breed named Ira Ferris?"

"You mean Ira Harris," corrected Henry. "He died about a week ago, coughed himself to death. I think white people call it consumption (tuberculosis). He had money for a while but his job ran out."

"What did he do?" Willie asked.

"He had some kind of horse trading or horse herding business for some white men on the reservation at Crazy Head Springs. It paid real well for a while. We drank a lot of whiskey together but that cough finally got him."

Willis had heard enough. He laid two dollars on the bar and bought the bar a round of drinks and left the bar. He had found out who had killed Bob Ferguson and one of the killers was already dead. The other was Head Chief and Willie knew he could probably be found on ration day in Lame Deer. He would look for the big sorrel horse with the other young people at the horse races. With Head Chief and Young Mule's faces firmly placed in his memory, he headed back to the Mission.

Chapter 26. The Death of Hugh Boyle

About the time of Bob Ferguson's death, a young man named Hugh Boyle arrived in the Lame Deer vicinity. His mother had sent him out from Illinois to Montana to visit his aunt, Ellen Lynch Gaffney, and an uncle, Patrick Lynch. Both the Gaffneys and the Lynches had taken up homesteads in the vicinity of the confluence of Lame Deer and Rosebud Creeks, a couple of miles north of Lame Deer. The reason for his visit was to get him away from Illinois to Montana's high dry climate. Hugh Boyle's sister was dying from tuberculosis and his mother wanted to get the young eighteen year old out of the house to avoid infecting him. He lived at the Gaffney house and worked over the summer on both homesteads and was by all accounts a good upstanding young man.

The Gaffney's and the Lynches were Irish immigrants. They had come to the country at the behest of a cousin who made his fortune in the Butte, Montana copper mines and needed help to run a cattle ranch in the Rosebud area. They both took up homesteads and eventually had their own ranches and raised families near the reservation. In fact the Lynch children grew up playing with Cheyenne children and spoke good Cheyenne. Alice Lynch (Mal Wissa – Yellow Haired Girl) was adopted into the Cheyenne Tribe and helped the Cheyennes sell horses to the British during the Boer War. Because of the close relationship of the Lynch and Cheyenne children, the Gaffneys and Lynches were much more sympathetic to the Cheyenne plight than other nearby white settlers.

One of the duties of Hugh Boyle was to go find the milk cows and bring them back to the barn for the evening so they could be available for morning milking. On the evening of September

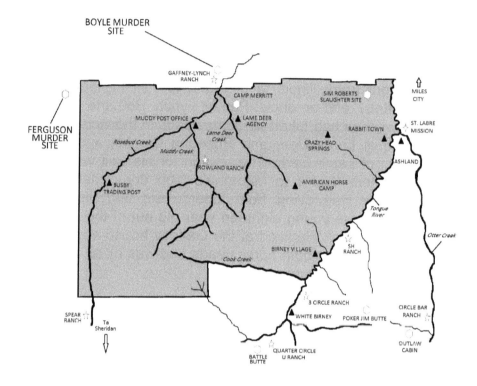

Figure 43. Bob Ferguson & Hugh Boyle Murder Sites.

6th, 1890 he went out to find the cows and did not return. Once darkness arrived Ellen Gaffney became very concerned and sent Hugh Gaffney and Patrick Lynch to look for him. His horse was found grazing the next morning with blood on the saddle. They immediately suspected foul play and contacted the Army at nearby Camp Merritt and the Indian Police at the Agency to begin a search. Late the next day the searchers found the butchered remains of a dead milk cow and the boy's bloody cap a short distance away.

Two days before the Hugh Boyle killing, Willis Rowland had picked up the Brewster and Brown cattle and dropped them off at the Birney Village before riding on to the Circle Bar where he spent the night. The next morning he met with Charlie Thex, bought 20 head from him and moved them on to Rabbit Town for Little Hawk's Elks to slaughter. He hoped to see Head Chief and convince Little Chief and Little Hawk to have the Elks bring Head Chief to the Agency to answer for the Ferguson killing. However, when the cattle were delivered, both Head Chief and Young Mule were nowhere to be found so he didn't raise the issue. Riding on to the Agency, Willie made his report to Acting Agent Cooper on the cattle buying trip. He did not discuss his suspicions with Cooper about Head Chief because he wanted to talk to his father, Porcupine, White Bull, and Two Moons about what he had found. Head Chief's charitable distributions of meat to needy widows and old people would engender widespread sympathy and many Cheyennes would rise to his defense. Willie wanted time to convince the Old Man Chiefs and the heads of the military societies that the Ferguson killing proved that Head Chief's activities were reckless and dangerous to the Tribe. However, Willie's good intentions were rapidly overcome by events.

The morning of Sep 7, 1890 dawned with heavily clouded skies and a late rising Willis Rowland. He had been looking forward to taking his long first ride on Red Mormon since his father had pronounced him fully recovered. He ate a good breakfast, discussed the Head Chief situation with Daddy Rowland and decided to ride Red Mormon to Busby to talk to White Bull and Porcupine. After saddling Red Mormon he trotted and loped down to the Muddy Post Office/Trading Post.

Sy Young rushed out to meet Willie as soon as he rode up. "Willie, Willie, have you heard the news about Gaffney's nephew Hugh Boyle?" Sy asked breathlessly.

"No Sy, what happened?" responded Willie.

"I heard he went out to wrangle the milk cows last night and didn't come back. Pat Lynch found his old white horse grazing and there was blood all over the saddle. The Army has called out a search party." Sy reported. "Cheyenne riders have been galloping through here all morning."

"Oh, shit!" Willie exclaimed. "I guess I better get my ass to the Agency. Cooper will be plumb goofy."

Red Mormon was put through his paces in the next hour as Willie made the ride to Lame Deer in record time. Instead of stopping at the Agency he went straight to Major Carroll's Headquarters. Having been associated with the military early in his career, he knew that all reports come to the Battalion Headquarters where they are evaluated and action taken. That is the place where rumors are discredited, facts established, patrols sent out to collect specific data, and the best overall picture of the true situation can be found. He galloped into up to the Headquarters and asked to speak to Major Carroll. He was directed to the Operations Center which manned by a lieutenant, a sergeant, and a clerk. Also present was a large map of the Reservation and a conference table at which Major Carroll and Captain Casey of the Cheyenne Scouts were deep in conversation. Upon notification that Willis Rowland wished to see him, Major Carroll immediately waved Willie over to join the conversation.

"Hi Willie, take a seat. I am really glad to see you here. What do you know?"

"Not much at this point. Sy Young told me that Gaffney's nephew is missing and that Pat Lynch had found his horse with a bloody saddle. That is about all." Willie said.

"Well, there is more. Your brother Bill and some of the Cheyenne Police tracked the boy's horse back to where he was probably killed. They found the remains of a butchered milk cow and his red cap under some bushes with brain tissue in it. It looks like he came up upon some Cheyennes butchering the cow and was killed. The body is missing and Captain Casey's

Cheyenne Scouts and the Cheyenne Police are trying to find it. Your brothers Bill, Zack, and James are with them. Colonel Swaine has ordered an additional two troops from Fort Custer's 1st Calvary and a Fort Keogh company of mounted infantry to reinforce us here at Camp Merritt. The Cheyennes are in a state of high excitement and white women and children are fleeing to Miles City." Major Carroll reported.

"Did my brother Bill say what the tracks said about the number of people in the kill party?" Willie asked.

"The police reported that the according to the tracks there were two riders and a pack horse not including Boyle's horse. It looked like the killers unloaded the meat and put the body on the pack horse. The Cheyenne Police tried to follow the tracks but lost them in the hills because it stormed last night." Carroll concluded. "What do you think we should do now?"

Willie thought and then answered carefully. "Don't bring any soldiers further on the Reservation than Camp Merritt. You might want to send a troop of cavalry to calm the whites in the Ashland area but don't come on the reservation. That would just fan the flames. By tonight this news will be all over the Reservation. Call a meeting of the Old Man Chiefs. I will help set that up. Maybe we should have the meeting here at the Headquarters after all the reinforcements have arrived. Tell them the white people are very angry and they are talking about attacking the Reservation. You should be very firm with these Chiefs. Tell them that the body must be found and the killers given up to the Army. Show them the extra Army troops and tell them you don't want to bring them on to the Reservation to search for the killers because it may mean war. You will try and control the white settlers but cannot guarantee Cheyenne safety. Make them understand this is a Cheyenne problem and you are holding the Chiefs responsible to solve this problem."

"Do they know who the killers are?" asked Captain Casey.

"They probably don't know right now but they will in a couple of days." Willie answered.

Major Carroll mused out loud. "I think that is a good plan. If I send a troop to Ashland, is it to protect the whites or the Cheyennes or both? Probably both. We must try and keep the two sides separate. Let's try and get the Chiefs over here day after tomorrow. Try and put the fear of god in them. Let's make it 14:00 hours (02:00 P.M.)."

With facts and a plan firmly in mind Willie returned to the Agency and reported to the Agency where Special Agent Cooper was pacing the floor. Seeing Willie he immediately ordered him into Agent's office and demanded to know the latest news and what Willie thought should be done. Willie patiently explained to the shaken Agent the facts as he knew them, his conversation with Major Carroll, and the prospective meeting with the Chiefs. Somewhat relieved, Cooper told Willie that he was going to ask Major Carroll to post guards around his house and the Agency office. Willie suggested that he rethink that idea, noting that it would further convince the Cheyennes that the Army intended to attack them. If Cooper was concerned for his safety, he should spend most of his time at Camp Merritt. Meantime Willie would do his best to talk to all the principal chiefs and military societies and try and identify the killers.

The first chief that Willie talked to was Two Moons because he was already in Lame Deer. He listened carefully to what Long Forehead told him was going on at Camp Merritt. Two Moons was especially glad to hear that the soldiers would not be proceeding beyond Camp Merritt. He agreed to contact the head of the Crazy Dog military society and make sure they had control of the young men around Lame Deer and Muddy. He also told Long Forehead he would send a rider to Busby to ask

White Bull and Porcupine to come to the Chief's meeting and to ask that the Crazy Dogs also police the young men at Busby. Following his meeting with Two Moons, Long Forehead mounted Red Mormon and hit the road to Ashland. He wanted to talk to Little Chief and Little Hawk about Head Chief and specifically ask if he had been in Rabbit Town when Hugh Boyle was killed. Given the similarity to the Ferguson murder, Head Chief and Young Mule were his prime suspects.

By the time Willie galloped into Rabbit Town it was nearly dark. He rode straight to Little Chief's teepee and called out a greeting and asked to enter the lodge because he had important news. Little Chief waved him into the lodge and asked the nature of the news. Long Forehead told him a white man had been killed by two Cheyennes and they probably belonged to his village. One of the men belonged to the Elks society so he wanted to talk to Little Hawk also. Little Chief called one of his children and told him to tell Little Hawk to come to the lodge. A few minutes later Little Hawk appeared.

Long Forehead addressed the two. "Have you heard of the killing of a white man outside of Lame Deer?"

Both nodded. "We heard about it this afternoon. Why do you think it is somebody from this village?" Little Chief asked angrily. "It was probably somebody from Lame Deer."

"Have Head Chief and Young Mule been in the village in the last two days?" Long Forehead asked pointedly.

"Why do you think it was them?" demanded Little Hawk.

Long Forehead gave the two chiefs the full story of what he had learned about the murder of Robert Ferguson by two men matching the description of Head Chief and Ira Harris. He reported what Powder-on-the-Face had told White Bull and Porcupine about a Cheyenne man who dressed only in old time Cheyenne clothes and a breed in mostly white man clothes driving seven horses, killing the cow, and later hearing shots and watching them move a white man's body. A big sorrel horse was ridden by the Cheyenne. Then Long Forehead described how he had followed five white outlaws to Crazy Head Springs and seeing a breed, Young Mule, and a man who was dressed in the old Cheyenne way at a camp near the Springs. Finally he told them how he had identified the breed as Ira Harris who sold whiskey to Cheyennes and herded some horses for white men at Crazy Head Springs. He ended with the fact that the white men had taken the horses to the Rosebud where seven of them were identified as horses belonging to the murdered Robert Ferguson.

Then he looked at Little Hawk and said, "You told me that the man I described sounded like Head Chief. Now we have a similar killing by two men out butchering white man beef. Is it Head Chief and Young Mule? I don't know but I want to know where they have been the last two days. Do you know for sure they were in this village?"

Little Hawk shook his head. "Head Chief's father lives in the village but Head Chief has his own lodge at Crazy Head Springs. Young Mule is an orphan and he is with Head Chief all the time. He used to go to the school at the Mission and still doesn't wear braids because they cut his hair. Most of the time he stays at Head Chief's lodge. I haven't seen either one for a few days but I haven't been to Crazy Head Springs."

"Who else could have seen him?" Long Forehead asked.

"He spends a lot of time over at American Horse's place. He is pretty interested in Goa, American Horse's daughter. If anyone has seen him it probably would be her." Little Hawk offered.

Long Forehead addressed his next question directly to Little Chief. "Will you give up these two boys to the Army if they come into your camp?"

Little Chief shook his head. "Not right away. Head Chief helped feed many people in this village. If he admits that he did kill these two white people then I will do whatever the Council of 44 decides. But if he says that he didn't do it, then I will not turn him over to the Army to be hung. My people won't stand for it."

"The white settlers are already making plans to search for the killers, even if they have to come on the Reservation. Will you try and fight them? You will lose. There are too many of them. The Army will try and keep the white settlers off the Reservation but don't count on them killing white people. Remember that they are white too." Long Forehead said strongly.

Little Chief was angry. He knew Long Forehead was right but he was a hard and obstinate man caught between loyalty to his village and the reality that the Cheyennes had already been defeated. Further conflict might result in loss of their beloved Tongue River Reservation and more bloodshed by an already vanquished people. No easy option was available to him but he nonetheless was not going to admit that – at least right away. Finally, he turned to Long Forehead and said:

"You are right in some of the things you say. A Chief must look out for all his people for many tomorrows. But I don't yet know if Head Chief and Young Mule are guilty of this thing. If they are guilty then somehow they must be punished. We will go into council and the chiefs will decide. That is the Cheyenne way."

Long Forehead knew that he had pushed Little Chief as far as he could go – for this night anyway. He decided to go to the Mission, spend the night, and ride to American Horse's camp in the morning. Hopefully, he could get some hard evidence to inform the Chiefs before they went into council. He said his goodbyes to Little Chief and Little Hawk before mounting Red Mormon and crossing the river to the Mission. After a brief supper and short visit with Deacon Yoakim, he went to bed and slept soundly.

The next morning Willie Rowland rose early, saddled Red Mormon, and made the short ride to Olga's Eatery. There he knew he would get a good meal which could last him all day and there was no place better to test white public opinion than the most popular restaurant in the white community closest to the Reservation. As Willie sat and nursed his coffee, the murder of Hugh Boyle was on everyone's lips. One man was loudly reading The Yellowstone Journal to an attentive audience, following which their opinions freely expressed that "all them murdering Injun bastards should be killed or run plumb outta the country." Another man reported that Captain Howes was raising a big force of heavily armed cowboys from surrounding outfits to protect Otter Creek and accompany women and children to Miles City. In Ashland, the sawmill companies had placed log breastworks around their mills and had stockpiled food, water, and ammunition in anticipation of a Cheyenne outbreak. Willie left the Eatery with a full stomach and a high level of concern as he started his ride to the camp of American Horse.

Upon leaving Olga's, Willie began the ride up Tongue River. He had to go to Birney Village to tell Grasshopper to come to Lame Deer for the Old Man Chief meeting and still visit American Horse on the way back to Lame Deer. If he did not have so much on his mind he would have enjoyed the ride. Late summer and early fall days were beautiful along the Tongue River. The cottonwood trees were beginning to turn from green to yellow and the ash showed the bright red/orange color that

Figure 44. Fort Howes Defenders. Charlie Thex - Top Row Far Right. Photo Courtesy of Neil Thex

would be universal in another two weeks. Early cool weather had reduced the mosquito population from their mid-summer clouds into a bearable occasional insect. Red Mormon was joy to ride with an easy gait, be it a high trot, lope, or full gallop. Moving at a high trot with and occasional lope, it only took about an hour and a half to travel the fifteen miles to Birney Village.

Willis Rowland changed into Long Forehead as he trotted into the Birney Village and rode up to Grasshopper's lodge. He found the old chief outside talking to Tall Bull when he pulled Red Mormon to a halt and dismounted. The old man welcomed Long Forehead with a toothy grin and Tall Bull also called a greeting. The three sat down on a couple of cottonwood logs to talk.

"I guess by this time you have both heard about the white man killed at Lame Deer." Long Forehead stated in a questioning tone.

Tall Bull answered first. "We heard that somebody was killed, but how do they know it was a Cheyenne that killed him?"

"How do they even know he was killed if they haven't found a body?" asked Grasshopper.

Long Forehead responded with the whole story all over again including the brains in the red cap, blood on the saddle, the butchered cow and the tracks. He also told them what he had seen at Camp Merritt, the additional soldiers that had been sent to stop violence, and the reaction of the white settlers to the killing. White women and children were moving to Miles City under guard and the settlers were organizing armed cowboys for a Cheyenne attack.

"Major Carroll from Camp Merritt has called for an emergency Council of the Old Man Chiefs for tomorrow. He is demanding that the Cheyenne Tribe find out who did this killing, help the Army find the body, and give up the killers to the Army for punishment. The Army wants the Tribe do these things so he does not have to bring soldiers on to the Reservation where there could be more trouble. He is also sending some soldiers to Ashland to keep white settlers from coming on to the Reservation. I would suggest that you take your women and children to a safe and defensible place. Put out scouts to watch the roads for groups of white cowboys. If any whites come making trouble, try and avoid a fight and send a messenger to the Agency and the Army will send some troops to protect you. Keep control of your young men!" Long Forehead strongly advised.

"Who do you think did the killing?" asked Tall Bull.

"I have good information that it is two Cheyennes from Rabbit Town. One of them always wears old time Cheyenne clothes and rides a big sorrel horse that looks a lot like this one." Long Forehead pointed to Red Mormon. "Have your Swift Fox warriors keep a close watch out for this man. The other man is just a kid, maybe thirteen or fourteen. You have seen him. He was the one that brought you the message from me when I brought cattle from Rabbit Town the first time. Now I must ride quickly back to Lame Deer. The Agent would like Tall Bull to come also. He would like to have all the leaders of the Warrior Societies present so everyone understands what must be done."

The two leaders gave their assent to attend the meeting and then began organizing the village for movement to a more defensible location on Tie Creek.

Figure 45: American Horse at his lodge. Photo courtesy of the Montana Historical Society

Long Forehead continued his ride to the American Horse Camp on the Birney/Lame Deer divide. He reached American Horse's Lodge in the early afternoon. American Horse was in his new cabin and there were a number of other Cheyenne men gathered there excitedly talking about the events. Because he didn't want to announce his business in front of the excited crowd, he quietly asked American Horse to join him while he watered his horse. As Long Forehead led his horse to the pond, American Horse quickly appeared with questioning eyes. "My friend, I may bring trouble to your lodge,"

Long Forehead began. "Do you know a man named Head Chief who visits your daughter?"

"Of course, Long Forehead. Why do you ask?" a concerned American Horse asked.

"Because I think he may have been the one who killed the white man Robert Ferguson, and maybe the Boyle kid too," replied Long Forehead. "When was the last time you or Goa saw him?"

American Horse was shocked. "Why do you think it was Head Chief?"

Long Forehead recounted the reasons he thought that Head Chief was involved in the killing of Ferguson, his involvement with the white outlaws, and his association with Ira Harris. Then Long Forehead talked of the similarities of the two killings, Head Chief and Young Mule were absent from Rabbit Town during the crime, and the Cheyenne Police had reported that the Boyle killers were two men, one of which was small, and finally the horse that Head Chief rode.

He asked American Horse, "Did you ever see Head Chief's horse?"

When American Horse nodded, Long Forehead asked, "Does he look like this horse? He pointed to Red Mormon.

American Horse's head snapped around and he stared at Red Mormon. He circled the horse examining him closely. "He has the same coloring, same head, and same good looks. He could be a brother to Head Chief's horse." He concluded.

"This is the Mormon horse with the bad foot that came to our place back four or five moons ago. I think he was stolen by white men from the Mormons on the other side of the Big Horns or as far away as Salt Lake City. At about that same time you told me that a bunch of shod horse passed your camp moving toward Crazy Head Springs. That is where I saw Young Mule and a Cheyenne which fits Head Chief's description herding horses for the outlaws. Little Hawk said Head Chief wasn't riding his red horse until this spring. I think Head Chief's pay from the outlaws was this horse instead of whisky or money." Long Forehead finished.

American Horse hung his head. "Poor Goa, she loves that man," he said sadly. "I never liked him very much. He was too wild and kind of strange. He should have been born in an earlier time. What should we do now?"

"First we have to find the white boy's body so he can be properly buried by his own people. The Old Man Chiefs are meeting tomorrow to discuss what to do about this killing. Major Carroll will tell them that the killers must be turned over to the Army to be taken to Miles City and turned over to the Sheriff. There will be a judgment by the white men as to what should be done with them. They will probably hang. Tell Goa I am sorry to bring this news, but only giving them up will save the Tribe from big trouble from the Army or the white settlers." Long Forehead squeezed American Horse's shoulder in sympathy.

"I will talk to Goa and find out what she knows. Maybe she can get Head Chief to tell me where the boy's body is. If I can find out something, I will come to the Chief's meeting and tell them what I found out." American Horse turned and dejectedly walked to his cabin.

Willie mounted Red Mormon and trotted off to Lame Deer.

Later in the evening American Horse called his daughter Goa to his side and asked her to take a walk with him. They walked to a small grove of trees near the cabin where American Horse motioned Goa to sit on a dead tree and he took a spot on a nearby rock.

Figure 46. American Horse's Daughters. Photo Courtesy of the Montana Historical Society

"Daughter, I have some hard questions for you and you must tell me the truth. When was the last time you saw Head Chief?"

Goa stared at her father and her eyes filled with tears. "I saw him day before yesterday at midmorning. I brought him some fry bread to eat and told him I was sorry there was no meat." She started to cry softly.

"What did he say?" American Horse asked gently.

He said, "That's all right, I'll get you something better." Goa cried harder. "You don't think he had anything to do with the white boy in Lame Deer, do you?" she asked hopefully.

"It doesn't look good for him. Long Forehead came by this afternoon and told me a lot of reasons why the Army thinks the killers are Head Chief and Young Mule. The Boyle boy rode up on two Cheyennes butchering a milk cow and was shot. Long Forehead said that he also thinks that Head Chief killed the Ferguson man over by Busby. Another Cheyenne saw the killer and described a Cheyenne dressed in old time clothes riding a big sorrel horse. You know how Head Chief is. He should have been born fifty years ago."

"But Father, he has fed widows and orphans all over this Reservation all last winter." Goa exclaimed.

"Daughter, the days when Cheyenne's could go out and kill white men is long gone. We are living in a new time and must find new ways. Head Chief has been reckless and put the whole tribe in danger. Do you know where he is?" American Horse demanded.

"No, not unless he is at Crazy Head Springs. But he will probably come and talk to me pretty soon. I hope so!" she said.

"Goa, if you see Head Chief, tell him I must talk to him. The Chiefs are meeting tomorrow to discuss this with the Army. They may send all the military societies out to find him and they could kill him. If he has done this, he must tell me where to find the body of the white boy and then turn himself in. If not, there could be war between the Cheyenne and the whites. The Cheyennes could not win that war. I must talk to him before the Chiefs meet!" American Horse implored his daughter.

"If I see him, I will tell him." Goa said as she fled to the cabin with her eyes streaming.

Well after dark she heard the sound of an owl give three hoots in quick succession. Recognizing Head Chief's signal, Goa rose from her buffalo robe bed, quietly slipped outside, and ran to the grove of trees where she had talked to her father. Head Chief threw a blanket over her and pulled her onto the soft pine needles.

"Where have you been? I have been so worried." She said breathlessly.

"I have some meat for you. I told you I would get you something better than fry bread." Head Chief replied softly.

Goa pushed Head Chief away and asked angrily. "And did you have to kill a white man to get it?"

"That was a mistake, he called us dogs!" Head Chief uttered heatedly.

"So it was you and Young Mule!" Goa exclaimed. "Are you crazy? Everyone is looking for whom ever killed that that white man. People were visiting my father all day talking about the killing. The whites are sending their women and children to the big white villages and organizing war parties. They may attack the reservation. The Army has called for more soldiers to be sent to the Agency and the Chiefs are meeting tomorrow to decide what to do. How could you do this to me?" Goa broke out sobbing.

Head Chief tried to hold her close and calm her down. Again she pushed him away. "You will be killed! If not hung like a dog by the white man soldiers, then hunted down by the Cheyenne military societies. The Chiefs can't let the whole tribe die because you lost your temper!" Goa was crying uncontrollably.

Head Chief was not happy. All the pleasant plans for the evening he had envisioned had gone like smoke in a high wind.

"Can't you and I just go away somewhere where there are no white men or Cheyenne fathers?" he asked plaintively.

"No, the Crazy Dogs and Swift Foxes would track us down in less than a day. Even your Elkhorn Scrapers would be against us if the Old Man Chiefs told them to bring you in," she said strongly.

"What should we do?" complained Head Chief.

"You better talk to my father, first thing in the morning. Tell him the truth, including where you put the dead white man. He will talk to the Chiefs and they will decide." Goa finished.

Head Chief thought long and hard. Finally he told Goa, "Tell American Horse I will be at this place at sunrise. He can do what he wants with me."

With that Goa hugged Head Chief and ran for the cabin, sobbing the whole way.

American Horse woke to the sound of Goa's sobs an asked her, "What is the matter?"

She sobbed, "Head Chief will meet you in the trees at sunrise. He said you can do what you want with him."

American Horse spent a restless night turning over in his mind how he should handle Head Chief in the morning. He could not bring him into the Agency and turn him over to the Cheyenne Police or the Army before the Chief's council. Perhaps the troubles could be resolved in the old Cheyenne Way, where the family of the victim could be compensated by gifts of horses or buffalo robes. That would be the Cheyenne way, but he doubted that the Army and the white family would agree. Anyway, the Chiefs must decide.

The next morning, just before sunrise, American Horse walked to the grove of trees near the cabin. There a dejected and unhappy Head Chief greeted him in low tones.

"I am glad you have come to see me, Head Chief. You have caused everyone great trouble, but your presence here shows me that you are a man, not a child. Did you kill the white boy at Gaffneys?"

"Yes Father," he replied softly.

"Tell me what happened!" commanded American Horse.

Head Chief sighed, "I came to see Goa three days ago. She brought me some fry bread and told me your family had no more meat. I said I would go hunting and get something better then fry bread. Young Mule and I went off the reservation to the west and hunted for deer. There were no deer. Too many hungry Cheyennes had been hunting in those hills. We hunted down the draws to the west all day until we came to Lame Deer Creek. It was starting to get dark when we saw a cow and I shot it. We were almost finished dressing it out when a white man on a white horse came up and yelled something at us. I only talk Cheyenne so I asked Young Mule what he was saying. Young Mule speaks some White Man talk. He said to me, "The white man says he sees that a Cheyenne dog has snapped up one of our cows!" That made me mad and I pulled my gun up and he turned to run. I fired a shot which knocked him off his horse but he was still alive so I shot him in the head. It was a foolish thing to do. We unloaded the meat from the pack horse and loaded up the white man's body and rode a long way into the hills. It started to rain. We were crossing a shale slide when the body fell off the packhorse. It was dark and wet. I told Young Mule, "Let's bury him here and push shale over him." So we did. He had a white piece of cloth in his pocket (handkerchief) that I put over his face so it wouldn't get dirty. Then we rode back to Lame Deer and spent the night.

"Did you also kill the white man over by Busby?" American Horse probed.

"How did you know about that?" an astonished Head Chief asked. "He shot at me and Ira Harris. We both shot back."

"What were you doing when he shot at you?" American Horse asked.

"We were driving seven stray horses back on to the Reservation." Head Chief responded.

"From what I was told by Long Forehead, they were the white man Ferguson's horses. He shot at you because you were stealing his horses. Is that not true?"

Head Chief shrugged his shoulders, "I didn't know whose horses they were. They weren't Cheyenne horses so I thought they either belonged to white men or the Crows. I knew where I could trade them for other horses so I took them in the old way."

"Did you take anything from the white man's body?" demanded American Horse.

"I took his rifle," Head Chief replied. "Ira Harris took his money. When Ira took his money there was a small shiny thing in his clothes. I gave it to Young Mule.

American Horse threw up his hands. "Head Chief, can't you see what you have done! You put all Cheyennes in danger. We can't fight all the white men. They are too many."

"I was just trying to help my people in the old way," insisted Head Chief. "So what do you want me to do now?"

"Go to Crazy Head Springs and stay there until I get back. Now I have to go to the Chief's meeting and tell them what I have learned. By then the Chiefs will have made a decision about what to do with you. When I come back you will show me where the body of the white man is. Then I will lead a party to bring the body to the white people and his family. Don't shoot any more people!"

With that American Horse turned on his heel and strode back to his cabin shaking his head to prepare for the ride to Lame Deer. Head Chief mounted his red horse and rode toward Crazy Head Springs. Goa, who had been watching the two men through the cabin's only window, started crying again.

Willis Rowland was at Camp Merritt when American Horse rode up to the Headquarters and asked for Long Forehead. Willis came out and met his old friend who was clearly upset. American Horse said, "Long Forehead, my heart is sad on this day. I have seen and talked to Head Chief this morning. He is the man who killed the white boy and also the white man rancher Ferguson just as you suspected. He said he will show me where the body is buried. Before you tell the Army, I must give a report to the Chiefs so they will have full information."

White Bull, Grasshopper, Two Moons, and Little Chief, the Old Man Chiefs, met in Two Moons teepee before hearing what Major Carroll had to say. Also in attendance were Little Hawk of the Elkhorn Scrapers, Tall Bull from the Swift Foxes, Brave Wolf of the Crazy Dog Society, American Horse, and Long Forehead. American Horse and Long Forehead were present only to give information after which they would leave the meeting so the Chiefs and the Military Societies could conduct their deliberations and make the necessary decisions.

Long Forehead addressed the assembled Chiefs. He described how he had come to believe that Head Chief, Ira Harris, and Young Mule had helped white outlaws hide horses on the Reservation. Then when Ferguson was killed how he had ridden with the Cheyenne Scouts and with his brother Bill had found the Ferguson body by listening to conversation of four Cheyenne Scouts who knew where it was buried. He noted that he had seen Young Mule bet Ferguson's post office key at a hand game. Then when Powder-on-the-Face came back from the Miles City jail, how he had interviewed him with White Bull and Porcupine to find out how the four Scouts knew about the body, identified the two killers as a breed, and a Cheyenne man who wore no white man clothes and rode a good sorrel horse. They were driving seven head of horses. Finally, he reported what he had learned from Little Hawk and Henry Miller about Head Chief and Ira Harris. He finished by describing the recovery of the Ferguson horses and his conversation with American Horse.

Then American Horse told the Council about his conversation with Head Chief. He described how Head Chief and Young Mule had gone hunting, killed a cow, and were caught by Hugh Boyle while loading the meat. When discovered they heard the white man say something to them in English which Young Mule interpreted to Head Chief as "He calls us dogs." At that, Head Chief lost his temper and killed the white youth. They unloaded the meat and took the white man's body a long way off and buried it in a shale slide. American Horse said that Head Chief was willing to show him where the body was buried. He also said that he confronted Head Chief about the Ferguson murder. Head Chief admitted that he and Ira Harris killed Ferguson in self-defense while stealing the man's horses. He had "borrowed" the good red horse from the outlaw herd and later traded some of the Ferguson horses to the outlaws for the red horse. In defense of Head Chief, he reported that the man had fed many starving Cheyenne families the previous winter but most of the food was white man beef. He said he hoped Head Chief would not face death but thought that the man was reckless and a danger to the Tribe. At the conclusion of his report Long Forehead and American Horse left the Chiefs to their deliberations.

Later that afternoon with the Chiefs assembled, Major Carroll addressed them. "You men know the Cheyennes which have done this bad thing. Already the white settlers are forming big groups and want to search the Reservation for his body. They have sent their women and children to Miles City and Sheridan and armed themselves. If they enter the Reservation there will be war and many Cheyennes and white settlers will be killed. Go back to your people and find out who did this and where we can find the body. Turn them over to the Army so they can be punished. Otherwise there will be war." The Chiefs offered to make restitution in the Cheyenne way by making a gift of a number of horses to the Gaffney and Lynch families. Major Carroll turned this proposal down out of hand.

The Chiefs called the military societies together and told them what Major Carroll had said. The Chiefs had decided that they must turn the boys over to the Army after Head Chief had shown American Horse where the body was buried. In the meantime the Cheyennes began to prepare defensive positions near the major villages in the event the settlers attacked. A hill near Tie Creek was prepared near Birney Village and Cheyennes in Rabbit Town moved to the hills. A camp of warriors preparing for war was discovered by white ranch hand building a fence near the Mission who spread fear throughout the white community further inflaming the situation.

The next day American Horse rode to Crazy Head Springs and met Head Chief. From there he led American Horse about ten miles back into the hills from Lame Deer Creek to a shale slide area where he pointed out where the boy was buried. They then rode back to Lame Deer where American Horse told Head Chief that the Old Man Chief's had decided that he must be turned over to the Army for punishment by the white man law.

Head Chief drew himself up to his full height, looked American Horse in the eye and said, "I will not go to the white man's jail to be hung like a dog. Tell the white men that I will play with their soldiers on ration day. If my punishment is to be death, I will die in battle like a Cheyenne warrior should!" He then rode off toward Rabbit Town.

Chapter 27. Suicide by Soldier

American Horse rode to the Agency Headquarters to see if Long Forehead was there. Percy Cox, the Chief Clerk told him to check at Camp Merritt because the Scouts and Cheyenne Police were still searching for Hugh Boyle's body. In a few minutes he was at the Battalion Headquarters where he found Long Forehead. They went outside to talk.

"Long Forehead, I have talked to Head Chief. He showed me where the body was buried. Do you want to try and go get it tonight or wait until morning?

"How far is it? Long Forehead asked.

"Probably the same distance as from here to my camp," American Horse reported. "But there are lots high hills and steep draws. He is buried in a shale slide."

"I will go talk to Major Carroll. The searchers have been out all day so I will ask him to wait until morning. It would be good if we had you and maybe Two Moons or Brave Wolf to represent the Tribe and bring back the body. It would show the Army and other white people that the Tribe was being cooperative." Long Forehead suggested. "And where is Head Chief?"

"Head Chief has said he will not be hung like a dog. He wants to die the death of a Cheyenne warrior like a real man. He will "play with the soldiers" on ration day and they can have his body in exchange for the white boy. I think he has chosen the right path." American Horse said sadly. "For now he must purify himself and prepare for death."

"Maybe," Long Forehead agreed. "My big concern is whether or not the Military Societies can keep the excited young men from joining him."

"I think they can," American Horse sighed. "Most of the Tribe knows the Cheyennes can't fight the Army anymore. I will go tell Two Moons what has happened. He will want the whole Council of 44 to approve this. I will see you here in the morning and guide you to the body." American Horse mounted his horse and turned toward Lame Deer.

Willis Rowland hurried back into the Headquarters and knocked on Major Carroll's door where he was talking to the Captain Casey. Major Carroll waved him in and motioned for him to take a seat.

"You look like you have news," stated Major Carroll expectantly.

"Head Chief has confessed to American Horse that he killed the Boyle kid and also Bob Ferguson. Today he took American Horse to the place where he is buried. Tomorrow, American Horse and another of the Chiefs will lead a recovery party to the body. Who do you want to accompany the party?"

"Why not get him tonight?" demanded Carroll.

"It is a long ride through rough country. The body is buried in a shale rock slide and it would be really hard to find at night. Besides, the Chiefs will want to show that the Tribe is being cooperative so you can tell the white people the Cheyennes don't want war." Willie explained.

"What about Head Chief?" pressed Major Carroll.

"He wants to die in battle in the old Cheyenne way. Head Chief says that he will play with your soldiers on ration day, Friday the 13th." Willie grinned sardonically at the unwelcome coincidence of the unlucky date.

"What does that mean, exactly?" questioned the Major sharply.

"It means that he wants to commit suicide by attacking your soldiers and have you shoot him so he can die in battle as a Cheyenne warrior, "replied Willie.

"And why should I accommodate him?" Major Carroll asked sarcastically.

"Because he has declared war on you. If you don't stop him he will kill every white person at the Agency. Besides, it is the shortest route to justice. The Tribe doesn't have to back him up because it is his choice. The whites get the justice they want, death of Hugh Boyle's murderer. It is an honorable solution for everyone and it is over quickly so things can get back to normal."

"So you think I should agree to this?" the astonished officer asked.

"I think so. Head Chief is popular with many people on the Reservation because he had the courage and recklessness to kill a lot of white settler's cattle last winter to feed widows and orphans who were starving. They don't want to see him hang. The Chiefs are between "the dog and a wagon wheel" with this situation. One way or the other they are going to get pissed on. If they support Head Chief, they put the whole tribe at risk of a major war with the whites. If they give Head Chief up to the Army to hang, the tribe feels humiliated and the Chiefs lose the respect of their People. If Head Chief is killed fighting the Army, it is an honorable death in the eyes of his people. The Chiefs can add him to the long list of celebrated Cheyenne warriors in song and legend. But he is not running around killing settlers and their cows so the Tribe survives. I say let Head Chief die in the old warrior way. The white public is satisfied and the Cheyennes are satisfied. Even Head Chief is satisfied. An eye for an eye, justice is done." Willie got down off his soap box.

Major Carroll shook his head and declared, "I'll have to think about this!"

Captain Casey broke into the conversation. "The question we need an answer to now is who will go on the recovery mission tomorrow? I would suggest myself and some of the Cheyenne Scouts, Willie, members of the Cheyenne Police, and who ever shows up with American Horse. That way it is mostly a Cheyenne affair, but the Agent and the Army is represented. What do you think, sir?"

"I accept your recommendation, Captain Casey. You will command the recovery party." Major Carroll ordered. "The recovery party will leave at 09:00 hours from this Headquarters tomorrow morning."

With that decision the parties retired to their respective quarters. Willie again imposed on his brother James for the night.

The next morning the recovery party was assembled under the command of Captain Casey. In addition to the players discussed the previous evening, Brave Wolf, an older Chief and head of the Crazy Dog Society, joined the group as Two Moon's representative. An extra horse with a packsaddle and roll of tarp completed the party.

The recovery was relatively straightforward. American Horse led the party about ten miles through the hills and ravines to the red shale hillside he had been shown by Head Chief. They found a disturbed area in the slide which contained the body of Hugh Boyle. It was solemnly wrapped in the tarp, loaded on the packhorse, and the party made the sad ride back to the Lame Deer. The Gaffney and Lynch families were notified and the body returned to them. Father van der Velden from St. Labre Mission was asked to come from Ashland to perform the funeral services and the body was quickly buried at the Gaffney

Ranch. At his mother's request the remains were subsequently removed to Illinois and buried next to his sister.

Following the funeral there remained three days before ration day. Head Chief was guarded by his military society, the Elkhorn Scrapers, where he was joined by Young Mule who was not yet a member of a society. Although Head Chief had been the principal party responsible for both white murders, Young Mule chose to join Head Chief in what was later termed by Lieutenant S.C. Robertson as "The Rush to Death." Young Mule said, "When you are dead, I will have nothing. I will die too."

Having made the decision to sacrifice their bodies to save the tribe from further responsibility for their actions, Head Chief and Young Mule were treated by the tribe as cultural heroes. Head Chief visited his grandfather and was given the old man's headdress, a beautiful full length war bonnet to wear for the charge. To his father who had been so dismissive of Head Chief's lack of military experience, Head Chief said, "I have killed three white men, father. When I am gone, sing me a victory song and recognize me as a man." The two warriors were given a series of dances and feasts to celebrate their lives in advance of their impending deaths.

On the day before their fight, veteran warriors from the old battles instructed the two in preparations for their fight with the Army. They each selected a special animal which would help them in their fight. Head Chief selected a red tailed hawk which had been his grandfather's symbol for his battles with the white soldiers and Crows. His grandfather helped prepare Head Chief to receive the headdress he had given him. He was told to face the sunrise and sing a special song, lifting the war bonnet toward the sky three times before he put it on the fourth time. All the old men also sang songs while touching him all over his body instructing him how to fight the enemy. His grandfather suggested that he should always approach an enemy from his right side because most men were right handed, and it forced the enemy soldier to move his weapons across his body, putting him at a disadvantage. The boy's horses were painted on their shoulders and hindquarters with their sacred animal symbols. Animal faces were positioned to the front so they would not falter. Also included in the instruction were not to let their horses graze too long, lest their full stomachs slow their charge.

Head Chief reveled in the repetition of the old Cheyenne traditions for battle preparation. He told everyone that his sacred goal was to ride his red horse through the White Soldier's line before his death. Each ceremony further cemented his resolve to complete his mission.

At the Agency and Camp Merritt preparations were also in progress. Target practice from horse and foot was held every day up to ration day. Major Carroll had selected Lieutenants Robertson and Pitcher from the First Calvary to lead their respective troops to receive the expected charge by the two Cheyennes. Captain Casey and his Cheyenne Scouts were specifically excluded from participation in the event for reasons of both security and politics.

Willis Rowland was very busy shuttling back and forth between the Agency, Camp Merritt, and Old Man Chiefs. Virtually every Cheyenne on the Reservation was in Lame Deer by the day before ration day. Close contact between the Elks military society and the Agency was necessary to insure control of the timing of the boys' attack. The Agency wanted all the rations to be distributed well before the attack so people drawing rations would not be caught in the crossfire between the Army and the two warriors.

The night of September 12 was spent by the two young men among friends telling stories of good times in their young lives and feasting in the high hills east of Lame Deer. Head Chief disclosed to his friends that he had killed three white men and counted first coup all three times. He then described each killing in detail so his friends could tell his story around future camp fires.

The first was a white cowboy near the present town of Stacy, Montana in 1884 when he was hunting with Whirlwind, Little Eagle, Red Man, Sam Crow, and Spotted Hawk. Sam Crow said he wanted to eat some raw liver so Head Chief killed the next cow they saw. He said to Sam Crow, "There is your fresh liver." While they were dressing out the cow, Spotted Hawk noticed that their horses were all looking at something on a far ridge. Then they saw a flash and heard a shot. Everyone but Head Chief made a run for their horses. He dropped to one knee and fired a shot at a cowboy about 300 yards away. He hit the cowboy's horse which started bucking and then fell, pitching the cowboy out in front of his horse losing his rifle. Head Chief grabbed his horse and galloped to the cowboy and hit him with his quirt, knocking him down and counting first coup. Whirlwind and Red Man followed, counting second and third coups following which Head Chief shot the cowboy in the back of his neck and killed him. The body of the cowboy, his horse, saddle and tack were taken to a nearby sink hole and dumped into it and covered with tumbleweeds.

The second white man was Bob Ferguson who was shot by Head Chief and Ira Harris while stealing his horses. Again Head Chief said he counted first coup and Ira Harris counted second coup. They buried Ferguson in a dry wash just off the Cheyenne Reservation and traded his horses to white outlaws for his red sorrel horse and some whiskey for Ira Harris.

The third was Hugh Boyle, whose death was described to American Horse. According to old Cheyenne customs, all three murders were legitimate acts of war against a white enemy. However, Head Chief was the only Cheyenne still at war. The rest had surrendered and made peace over a decade before.

About midnight Head Chief left the group and met Goa to say goodbye. The goodbye lasted until morning when Head Chief rejoined the group and they began the final ceremonies before their death ride.

The fateful September day of Friday, the 13th dawned clear and cool. Ration distribution started early. The cattle had been slaughtered the previous day and the carcasses were brought to the butchering site where they were cut up and prepared for dispersal. The rations were totally distributed by about 02:00 P.M. in the afternoon.

Figure 47. Brave Wolf. Courtesy of the Smithsonian Institute

While the play had been choreographed with precision, none of the audience knew precisely what would happen. Unlike previous ration days, there were no young people racing horses, children playing hoop games, squaws playing "got none", or the men telling stories. Over a thousand Cheyennes were dressed in their finest regalia, Chiefs in their war bonnets, squaws in their best blankets, and most impressive and dangerous of all, young men dressed for war with cartridge belts and rifles in full evidence. Middle aged and older men of the military societies were circulating in and out of knots young men directing them to stay quiet and let the drama play out.

At about 03:00 P.M the sound of "Boots and Saddles" was played at Camp Merritt and echoed up the Valley of the Lame Deer to be heard by a thousand waiting Cheyennes. Lieutenants Robertson and Pitcher assembled their mounted troops and began the movement toward the Agency buildings. Arriving at the Agency Headquarters Lt. Robertson detached a squad to reinforce the Cheyenne Police and turned onto the trail toward Ashland. Here he was met by Long Forehead and old Chief Brave Wolf both dressed in Cheyenne war regalia. Brave Wolf directed them to ride up the road to the east. As they rode he explained that Head Chief and Young Mule would ride down the hills from the north and try and ride through the Army firing line along the road. Willis Rowland/Long Forehead carefully translated everything that Brave Wolf said so there would be no misunderstandings. When Lt. Robertson asked Brave Wolf if the two Cheyenne warriors were really going to attack two troops of

Figure 48. LT S.C. Robertson
Fredrick Remington Rendition. Public Domain

cavalry, Brave Wolf confidently replied that they will come and they will come shooting. At the eastern edge of the natural amphitheater Brave Wolf stopped the troop and explained that the two warriors would charge the soldiers between this point and the agency buildings. Again Long Forehead carefully explained the arrangement.

At this point 1st Lt. Robertson waved Lt. Pitcher to his side. He directed that Pitcher deploy his troops along the road at ten yard intervals facing the hill to the north. Every other soldier would remain mounted and the dismounted man's primary weapon would be a rifle. This allowed the dismounted soldiers to engage with accuracy at long range without the distraction of a plunging horse. Should the warriors get close, the mounted soldiers could use their side arms. Robertson then positioned the remainder of his troop in a similar manner between the end of Pitcher's line and the Agency buildings. While this was the appropriate disposition for the expected attack, it made Robertson's skin crawl when he realized that only two warriors were attacking from his front, but there were a thousand excited Cheyennes to his rear. He was about to ride down the entire line and tell the mounted soldiers to watch their back when a great shout went up from the crowd – the suicide warriors had been sighted. The curtain had opened and the drama was on.

Head Chief and Young Mule first made a bravery run at long range. They came down the hills toward the soldiers in all their finery and upon reaching the flat ground about 600 yards away, they fired their weapons as they galloped parallel to the soldier line. Thirty rifles returned fire with small effect. A thousand Cheyennes cheered. Then the two galloped to the top of the high hill to the soldier's front and fired from that point. Highlighted against the sky the two Cheyenne champions brought forth collective memories of Left Hand, Roman Nose, and Lame White Man, all storied Cheyennes who had died in battle. Again the soldiers returned fire.

Head Chief then urged his sorrel horse straight down the hill toward the soldiers of Lt. Pitcher, his eyes blazing, singing his death song, and firing from the hip. As he approached the road at a dead run, all rifles and pistols were trained upon him and the fire was deadly accurate. He lurched backward and then with a last gallant effort he fired once more as he breached the line. About ten yards beyond the line he toppled from his horse dead with two bullets in his brain and seven in his body. When Head Chief breached the line a great shout went up from the watching Cheyennes as Head Chief's dream was realized. He had died a warrior's death with courage in front of the entire tribe. Lt. Pitcher rode up got off his horse and checked to make sure Head Chief was dead and then remounted his soldiers and rode toward the Agency to support Lt. Robertson.

Meantime, Young Mule was not so lucky. As he had reached the top of the hill his horse had been badly wounded by soldier's bullets. There would be no grand charge for him. He tried to lead the horse down the hill following Head Chief's lead but was forced to abandon the animal. He turned toward the Agency buildings running down the hill in a zigzag pattern firing his rifle. Robertson's soldiers plus the Cheyenne police returned fire and Young Mule was hit but took cover in a small ravine. Occasional fire was detected coming from his position and again the fire was returned. Some of Robertson's soldiers flanked the position, and crawled through the brush behind him only to discover that he was already dead in the autumn leaves. The fire that had been coming from his position was from a burning cartridge belt.

Crying and lamentations for the young suicide men swept through the crowd. There was an emotional point where the young men surged forward with hands on their weapons but were quickly restrained by older members of their military societies. The Cheyenne Chiefs had kept their word and no further violence would result.

Willis Rowland counseled Lt. Robertson to take his soldiers back to Camp Merritt and leave the field to the Cheyennes to bury their new heroes. As he rode back to Camp Merritt, a greatly relieved Lt. Robertson related his concern to Willie about the Cheyenne crowd immediately to the rear of his troops during the incident. Long Forehead replied with a laugh, "Me too, why do you think I came dressed as a Cheyenne, white man!" Robertson did a double take not knowing if he was joking or not. Willis grinned and whipped his horse forward.

Willis/Long Forehead returned to the Agency buildings and accompanied a party composed of Agent Cooper, Chief Two Moons, a doctor, Major Carroll, and an artist named Walter Shirlaw to view the bodies and verify that justice was indeed done. After the viewing, Agent Cooper assured Chief Two Moons that as far as he was concerned the incident was finished and the Cheyennes had met their obligations.

The drama was over. As Lieutenant Robertson put it in a subsequent account in Harper's Weekly: "The tragedy was over and the Indian debt of blood for blood was discharged." The account by Robertson was accompanied a sketch made by artist Walter Shirlaw who witnessed the event. The name of the sketch "A Rush to Death" became the title of the Harper's article (and also serves as the lower half of the cover for this book).

The bodies of the two warriors were taken to American Horse's Camp where they were put on display in a teepee with the sides rolled up so the People could see them. Almost the entire tribe filed by their bodies to pay their respects. Head Chief's war bonnet was placed at the lodge entrance and a feather shot from the bonnet was placed on a piece of flagstone and held there by a smaller stone. They were later buried on Squaw Hill above Lame Deer.

The following day Goa's mother talked to her daughter. "Goa, did you lay with Head Chief before he was killed?"

With a tear in her eye Goa replied. "Yes Mother, I did. I loved the man."

Goa's mother handed her two big lumps of hardened pine sap. "Chew these for the next two days. If you do there will probably be no baby. Otherwise you could have a baby with no father."

Goa threw the lumps away. With her eyes streaming tears she cried, "I hope I do have his baby! At least that way I will still have some part of him!"

Goa's mother shook her head sadly and slowly walked away.

The death of Head Chief and Young Mule marked the end of an extraordinary era in the history of the American West. It was the last time that U.S. Army troops would face Cheyenne warriors on the field of battle. Three months later, a less wise and more poorly led Sioux Tribe, Indian Agency, and U.S. Army met at Wounded Knee in the last gasp of Plains Indian opposition to the United States. The result of that sad encounter resulted in the deaths of 31 U.S. Soldiers and about 300 Sioux, of which about 220 were women and children.

Over the next two years, a violent range war between large and small cattlemen broke out in Johnson County, Wyoming. Taking their cue from Granville Stuart's operations on the Missouri and Yellowstone Rivers, the Wyoming Stock Growers Association tried to carry out a similar operation in April 1892. Unlike Stuart's operation, the WYSA lost the moral high ground when they targeted small cattlemen and homesteaders with families in addition to the outlaws in the Hole-in-the-Wall. The murder of John A. Tisdale, riding home in a wagon with a load of Christmas presents for his young family outraged the county. Furthermore the operations were not tightly controlled as individual large ranchers and their crews settled scores with people who were not known to be "worst of the worst" outlaws. It should be noted that of all the deaths in the Johnson County War, none of the famous Wild Bunch outlaws which inhabited the Hole-in-the-Wall valley were killed in Johnson County. When the WYSA raised a force of 50 heavily armed men and attempted to ride through Johnson County, Wyoming with intentions of killing 75 rustlers and rustler sympathizers including Sheriff Red Angus, the "invasion" was met by over 300 angry small cattlemen and townspeople. Only the intervention of the U.S. Army from Fort McKinney prevented a massacre of the "invasion force." The wisdom of Granville Stuart's advice to the Montana Stock Growers Association was proven true – in America votes rule, and in a relatively short time the large cattle syndicates and cattle barons were gone from the public lands.

Figure 49. "The Challenge", by Walter Shirlaw, shows the First Calvary awaiting the Head Chief/Young Mule charge

Figure 50. "Sweeping the Plain Like a Whirlwind", by Walter Shirlaw, depicts the rush by Cheyenne warriors and women to recover the bodies of Head Chief and Young Mule

Chapter 28. Duty Done

Willis Rowland was tired, a really deep tired. The strain of the past six months had taken a great emotional toll. He had accomplished much. The Cheyenne census had been largely completed. John Tully, the newly appointed Cheyenne Agent arrived at the end of September with a better political relationship in Washington and the prospect of increased ration funding. White opposition to the Reservation's existence continued but had been substantially muted with the dramatic death of the two Cheyennes. Stuart's Stranglers had completed their work and the level of organized horse theft and rustling in Montana decreased dramatically. Cheyenne butchering of neighboring settler's cattle continued but at much lower levels. The Cheyenne leadership, Agency, and military at Camp Merritt had increased confidence in each other in their day to day transactions. Best of all the Cheyenne People's temperature had cooled from the white hot level over the summer. People were now more concerned with preparing for the approaching winter.

Willis Rowland took a fresh look at his own life. Over the past few months his bank account had been padded substantially by his dual salaries as a Custer County deputy sheriff and chief Agency interpreter. His 25% share of the reward money for the capture of Big Nose George Parrott and Bill Carey totaling $750.00 had been received. A note from Granville Stuart invited him to come to the DHS Ranch and pick up the twenty cows and the bull that he had been promised. With his economic prospects much improved, the prospect of marriage to Bear Woman was much on his mind. She had been patient as he had wrestled with the weighty issues of the day but in her quiet way let Long Forehead know that their time had come.

In accordance with the Cheyenne tradition, Willie's brother James talked to Bear Woman's brother about the marriage. This had already been expected and approved within the Elk

River family but the arrangement had to be worked out. James proposed a gift of two horses and three new Hudson Bay blankets in exchange for the families' consent. Her brother came back with a suggestion of four horses and six blankets. They settled for three horses and five blankets.

James with typical older brother empathy told Willie, "I got you a great deal, Bear Woman for just one horse and five blankets. She was cheap enough you can trade her for another woman if she doesn't work out."

"Which horse?" asked Willie.

"Oh, just some sorrel horse, Elk River didn't say exactly. It doesn't matter," retorted James.

"You traded away Red Mormon, my best horse ever?" grumbled an exasperated Willie.

"Well, don't you think Bear Woman is worth the horse?" replied an innocent sounding James.

"Jimmy, you are bullshitting me!" declared Willie.

James broke out laughing, "What's the matter, little brother?" Can't take a joke? The deal is done for three horses and five blankets. None of the horses has to be Red Mormon."

"You asshole," commented a relieved but smiling Willie. "I will get you back for this."

Willis and Bear Woman were married and moved into a new lodge on Rosebud Creek. He resigned from his position as an undercover deputy sheriff of Custer County but retained his role as a full-time interpreter at the Agency. A couple of weeks after the wedding, he and Bear Woman rode to Granville Stuart's ranch and picked up his twenty cows and a bull and drove them back to the Rosebud. On the way through Miles City, he stopped at the Land Office and filed for a homestead on the

Rosebud. He and his brothers started building a new cabin and the couple settled in for the upcoming Montana winter. Life was good.

The End

Figure 51. Willis Rowland & Family Post 1900. Picture from "A Cheyenne Album". Photo by Thomas B. Marquis, text by Margot Liberty.

Epilogue

Any reader of this novel with some knowledge of Southeast Montana history including the Cheyenne Reservation can rightly ask the questions, "How much of this is true? Where did the author take "poetic license" and "How will I know?" To really answer those questions you will have to take a deep dive into the historical record of Southeastern Montana and the Cheyenne Reservation. As I said in the Prologue, the purpose of this book was not to write a comprehensive history of Custer County and the Cheyenne Reservation but to tell a good story. I considered footnotes to indicate the references to many of the incidents, but because it is a novel, decided against them because they would detract from the story.

Almost all conversations in this novel are imagined. There are a few cases where there are reports of what specific people said, but those are not reliable. John Stands in Timber quotes Head Chief on a number of occasions but there were no tape recorders in those days and he was only six years old at the time. While we may not know the exact words used, the meaning and intent of the words have come down through time as oral history.

Some events are clearly out of the historical timeline and have been added to improve the story. To wit:

There is no evidence of a "conspiracy" between Colonel Peter Swaine, Granville Stuart, Judge Strevell, Bill Rowland, Agent R.L. Upshaw, Sheriff Tom Irvine and Marshal "X" Biedler to form the Stuart's Stranglers, but all were active participants in the major events of the period. If there were elements of such a conspiracy they occurred in 1884 and not 1890. Certainly Stuart's Stranglers were active during that time and did have access to U.S. Army telegraph operators. They must have had tacit if not overt help from the two lawmen. Their use of a

Northern Pacific locomotive, passenger car, and stock cars is true.

"Big Nose" George Parrott and Bill Carey were captured in July of 1880 by Sheriff Tom Irvine, not 1890. The details of the capture are true to the historical record, but Willis Rowland did not provide the information which led to that arrest. However, Tom Irvine was a prominent sheriff of Custer County throughout the 1880's and served in that capacity during much of the decade.

Granville Stuart served as the President of the Montana Stock Growers in 1885, not 1890. He was part of the Executive Committee in 1884 which led the Montana Stock Grower Vigilance Committee's "Stuart's Stranglers" in the elimination of an estimated 63 rustlers. The details, though sparse, generally adhere to the historical record.

There is no record of Charlie Thex leading the Stranglers to visit Sim Buford Roberts' ranch on the Rosebud or Charlie Thex being a "Stranglers" guide during their activity in 1884. However, there was a close relationship with Captain Howes of the Circle Bar. Captain Howes was an early and active member of the Montana Stock Growers Association during the 1884 "Clean Up". The other information concerning Charlie Thex is generally true. A "rustler" cabin was located on Cow Creek and the flour barrel incident is included in "Levi" Howes' memoirs.

There was no Montana Stock Growers Feeding Program. Perhaps had there been such a program, the two people killed in butchering incidents may not have occurred. This program was a device to explain the problem of cattle butchering and provide the opportunity tell a short history of a number of pioneer ranches in the vicinity of the reservation.

Sim Buford Roberts was a small time rancher on the lower Rosebud. He had been involved in several shootings in and around Bozeman and Big Timber and was suspected of horse stealing. When it became too hot for him in that area he moved to the Rosebud, got married and started a family. He was respected for being a good cowhand and hard worker with a sense of humor. However, rumors persisted that he was involved in illegal activities, especially cattle butchering. There was a story reported that a man named John Murphy of the 79 Ranch put coins in the briskets of some of his best yearling cattle. The idea was that if someone stole the cattle and worked over the brands that Murphy could prove the cattle were his by means of the coin hidden in their briskets. Sometime later Murphy received an envelope full of coins with the advice that he "should be more careful with his money." Roberts was widely suspected as the author of the note. He was often accused but never convicted of his butchering activities.

Willis Rowland did not play a central role in solving the mystery of Robert Ferguson's death or the killing of Hugh Boyle. However, John Stands in Timber records that Head Chief had killed two more white people besides Hugh Boyle. One of those could easily been Robert Ferguson since the other Cheyennes were cleared. Willis was an important player in the investigation surrounding both incidents. One note about the death of Bob Ferguson: the spelling of his name in the historical records are variously recorded as Fergersen, Fergunsen, Fergerson, and Fergunson. I believe Ferguson is correct since that is the name the family uses today. Zack, James, Willis, and Bill Rowland were all involved in the search for Hugh Boyle and most were present when the suicide boys made their charge. There is one report (probably not true) that it was a shot from Bill Rowland Jr. which killed Young Mule.

The Head Chief/Young Mule incident is true and I believe it to be accurately portrayed. Just east of Dull Knife College lies the Lame Deer Cemetery were the bones of the two boys were reburied from the top of Squaw Hill. Following his charge, Cheyenne women placed rocks in the horse tracks down the hill to remember the event. Today those rocks have been painted white to depict the route Head Chief took on his charge down the hill. Ironically, it ends in the cemetery. The site has been nominated as a "National Historic Site" and is shown on the back cover of this book as it appears at the time of its publication.

The eyewitness sketch by Walter Shirlaw entitled "A Rush to Death", was drawn on site shortly after the incident and is shown on the lower front cover of this book. He was employed by the Indian Department to assist in the Cheyenne census and purely by chance was present when the event occurred. He also made three additional sketches related to the incident: "The Challenge", "Nearing the End", and "Sweeping the Plain like a Whirlwind". The original sketch was published in the Oct. 1890 issue of Harper's Weekly and the others published in a Nov. 1893 Century Magazine article entitled Artist's Adventures: "The Rush to Death".

The Ashland described in the book is not located where it was in 1890, it is the Ashland of today. The original Ashland was down river from the St. Labre Mission. Likewise there was no Olga's Eatery or Ron's Butcher Shop either then or now. But Olga is typical of the Scandinavians who settled up Tongue River at the time and the meat cooling operations of the day are accurately recorded. Most railroad tie production was over by 1890 but the description of how they were handled was completely true a few years earlier.

The breeds, Ira Harris, Bud Bar and Henry Miller, are total fabrications and bear no resemblance to any real people. A student of history will note that a white man named George Harris, who was married to a Cheyenne woman, ran a saloon on Trabling Road in Buffalo, Wyoming in the early 1880s, and moved to the Cheyenne Reservation when individual Cheyennes were permitted to take land allotments. However there is no evidence that they brought their former whiskey selling business to the Reservation. Subsequent Harris generations have been prominent leaders on the Reservation.

Most of the remainder of the book is largely historically accurate. Willis Rowland was an interpreter at the Tongue River Agency during the period discussed. His father was William Rowland, interpreter for Gen. Nelson A. Miles, and the references to Willis Rowland's Cheyenne Scout exploits are true. Willis did live on Muddy Creek with his father until he was about 27 and then married. His first wife was not Bear Woman but she was his last one. His investigation of Porcupine and the Ghost Dance Craze are largely accurate. The "Statement of Porcupine" was interpreted by Willis Rowland and transcribed by Lieutenant S.C. Robertson. This is the same Lieutenant Robertson who commanded the two cavalry troops who killed Head Chief and Young Mule. He wrote an account of the incident for Harper's Weekly entitled "A Rush to Death" published in October 1890.

The references to the U.S. Army's role are generally true. There may be some details which are not correct. The names, dates, and actions of the soldiers I believe to be historically accurate.

Willis Rowland was a force on the reservation for many years. He was the "go to" interpreter for George Bird Grinnell and James Mooney's anthropological studies of Cheyenne Culture in the early 1890's. Much of what we know today is the result of his skill in imparting the nuances of both English and Cheyenne languages. He was chosen by the Cheyenne Tribe to represent them on two delegations to Washington for treaty and reservation issues. Both Marquis and John Stands in Timber quote him liberally in their books. Finally, Willis Rowland served as the Chairman of the Northern Cheyenne Tribal Council for a substantial period of time. Although largely overlooked by history he was a mighty contributor to our current knowledge of Cheyenne history and culture.

I reiterate what I said in the Prologue. The superior leadership of the "White Tribe" and the "Cheyenne Tribe" during this turbulent period is to be celebrated for not allowing a Wounded Knee or Johnson County War to take place. Special recognition should be accorded to the intrepid interpreters who made the communication "Between Two Tribes" possible.

Thank you for your interest in this book.

CPSIA information can be obtained
at www.ICGtesting.com
Printed in the USA
FSHW010325250419
57517FS